Matilda's SECRET

ALSO BY CORINA BOMANN

The Inheritance Series

The Inheritance of Lion Hall

Other Books

Butterfly Island
The Moonlit Garden
Storm Rose

Matilda's SECRET

Book 2 in The Inheritance Series

CORINA BOMANN
TRANSLATED BY MICHAEL MEIGS

AMAZON **CROSSING**

Text copyright © 2018 by Ullstein Buchverlage GmbH, Berlin
Translation copyright © 2022 by Michael Meigs

Previously published as *Mathildas Geheimnis* by Ullstein Buchverlage GmbH in Germany in 2018. Translated from German by Michael Meigs. First published in English by Amazon Crossing in 2022.

Published by Amazon Crossing, Seattle

www.apub.com

Amazon, the Amazon logo, and Amazon Crossing are trademarks of Amazon.com, Inc., or its affiliates.

ISBN-13: 9781542016827
ISBN-10: 1542016827

Cover design by Shasti O'Leary Soudant

Printed in the United States of America

Matilda's
SECRET

PART I

1931

1

I felt drowsy. I'd placed a notebook before me on the desk, and I really did want to write something, but my arms were far too heavy. I couldn't summon the strength to pick up my pen. The classroom windows were open, but the air was thick enough to cut with a knife, even though it was only June. Summer had come early in 1931.

I really wanted to be in a Stockholm city park instead of Miss Nyström's class at the young ladies' school. I could have lounged in the shade and let my thoughts wander, instead of putting up with my classmates' annoyed looks as they listened to her drone on about home economics.

But my parents had insisted I get a good education. My father had escorted me here, saying, *"In these times, you cannot count on finding a man to take care of you."* Mother had given him an odd look, but she'd added that beauty wasn't enough to guarantee a woman's happiness.

I didn't want my lack of focus to negate all their efforts. And especially not now, only days after Mother's funeral.

Death stole away Susanna Wallin in the middle of the night. I'd been surprised to wake and find our home so silent. She was always the first up, diligently going to the kitchen to light the stove and prepare breakfast—even after my father disappeared. But that morning was different. I went into her room to wake her and saw her eyes fixed upon the ceiling. At first I expected her to turn and look at me, but when I touched her, I found her rigid and cold.

Something inside me shattered. I ran in a panic to fetch a doctor, but he only confirmed the horrible truth. My memory is a blank after that. I guess I somehow managed to inform the neighbors and our priest.

Days later I was still huddling in my bed, crying my eyes out and clutching the cigarette lighter that had belonged to my father. The heft of it consoled me somehow, even though I knew scarcely anything about him.

Papa had always seemed a bit distant. Mama was often lost in dreams she never spoke of. Together they'd taken good care of me. Neither ever raised a hand to me. But sometimes they seemed like puppets, marionettes placed in my life only to keep me company.

One day Papa didn't come home. My mother waited two days before filing a missing person report. The police looked everywhere for Sigurd Wallin but in vain. One officer heard that someone had seen him on a bridge near Old Town Stockholm. Another officer confirmed that sighting, and someone found his cigarette lighter at the base of the bridge. I'd always admired it. Gilded and etched with an intricate floral pattern, that lighter was the only souvenir I had of him.

The authorities soon concluded he'd drowned himself. The search was extended along the shoreline, but the Baltic is deep, and strong currents drag floating objects far out to sea.

A judge declared him deceased a year after his disappearance. The delicate little lighter didn't interest my mother, so she gave it to me. Her mourning was silent and dignified. She gathered his clothing and possessions and disposed of them, as if they represented something that was over and done with.

I was devastated, but I clung to the consolation that I still had my mother.

Now she was gone too.

In the days after her death, I felt like a ghost of myself. Numb with grief, I was reduced to pure suffering and almost completely unaware of my surroundings. After a long while I began to emerge from my paralysis, but every day was a terrible trial. I burst into sobs at the most inappropriate moments. I hid myself away as much as I could. I would glide like a specter through our yellow house on a steep section of Brännkyrka Street. My childhood friend Paul was my only comfort. He visited regularly to make sure I was all right.

The time at school was even worse than the empty hours at home.

School had offered me a warm, sympathetic refuge when my father disappeared. Everyone was distressed by my plight. They all pitied me and my mother.

Now I was truly alone. My paternal grandparents had passed away long before, and my mother had never said a word about her own parents. When I asked, she told me they didn't exist.

Daga was the only girl who really spoke to me anymore. The rest of them huddled together and whispered about the pathetic orphan. I was deeply hurt.

A sharp knock on the classroom door startled me out of my unhappy musings. Miss Nyström opened it to an unexpected visitor. Principal Persson whispered a few words, then turned and peered over my classmates' heads to scrutinize me.

"Matilda Wallin," he said, "would you please come with me?"

Whispers spread through the room. I heard a malicious titter or two.

My heart began to pound. They were assuming that, since I had no parents, I was about to be expelled.

I tried to brace myself as I followed the tall, portly man in the bow tie and perpetually rumpled jacket. The odors of cologne and pomade trailed behind him like a banner.

Mr. Persson summoned students to his office only to deliver bad news or when they'd done something really bad. We entered. The office was quite large—and entirely brown. Brown bookshelves were filled with brown leather-bound books. The carpet was beige with brown stripes. No other colors broke the monotony.

A tall woman in an elegant dark-blue dress was seated there, waiting for us. Her blonde hair was gathered in a bun at the nape of her neck. A couple of strands on either side had worked their way loose, framing her regular features.

"If I may make the introductions," the principal said and nodded to the unknown woman. "Countess, this is Matilda Wallin. Matilda—Countess Agneta Lejongård."

A countess? I gave her a confused look. In the fairy tales my mother had often told me, countesses wore diadems and sparkling silver dresses. This one didn't even have a hat.

She smiled. "I am delighted to meet you," she said and offered me her hand.

I didn't know what to do. Curtsey? She was a countess! I dipped a bit as her hand met mine, wondering all the while what a countess wanted from the daughter of a bookkeeper.

"I suggest we all have a seat," the principal said.

The countess addressed me directly. "I am very sorry that you lost your mother. And so soon after the loss of your father."

How did she know? Was she from social services? An orphanage?

I must have looked bewildered, for she seemed to read my thoughts. "That is why I am here."

"Because of my father?"

She shook her head. "For your sake."

I appealed mutely to the principal, but Mr. Persson didn't respond. He looked like someone watching a thrilling drama.

"You are still a minor," the countess continued. "Therefore, you require a guardian."

A wave of panic washed through me. She *was* from social services! "I can do very well by myself," I replied. "I did the housekeeping whenever Mother was ill. And my schoolwork as well—" I stopped short, remembering that my tuition would have to be paid. My father had put aside money for it, but because I wasn't yet an adult, I had no access to the account.

The countess glanced at Persson and then back at me. "Do you like going to school here?"

"Yes," I answered and caught myself pulling nervously at my sleeve.

"Principal Persson tells me that you are a good student."

"She has some shortcomings as far as handicrafts are concerned, and she could do better in science. But her math is outstanding. And so are her studies in Swedish and in English."

"You study English?" the countess asked.

I nodded. "Yes, gracious lady."

"Well, that could prove useful someday. As could skills in writing and calculation."

Why was some lady from social services asking about my school record?

"What's this about?" I asked before Persson and the countess could delve further. "Why are you here? Do you want to send me to an orphanage?"

The woman's eyebrows shot up. "No, I do not," she answered calmly. "I am here to inform you that I am to be named as your guardian."

My jaw dropped. This unknown woman, a countess to boot, was going to take charge of my life?

"I know it seems rather sudden," she added, "but I did not want you to be surprised to learn it when your mother's will is read."

I gaped at her in confusion. "How's that?"

"I beg your pardon?"

"Why you, exactly? What possible reason is there for a countess to become my guardian?"

"Matilda!" hissed the principal, but the countess simply shook her head.

"The question is entirely in order." She took a deep breath. "Your mother made the arrangement."

"My mother? What do you have to do with my mother?"

"We knew one another. We had been acquainted for a long time. Shortly after your mother passed away, her lawyer sent me a document." She took an envelope from her purse and handed it to me.

I unfolded it and immediately recognized the flourishes of my mother's *B*'s and *R*'s. The letter was dated February 19 of the previous year. Had she had a premonition something was wrong? Did she already know she had a weak heart? If so, she'd hidden it well.

I was transfixed by one line:

> *In the event of my death, I wish for Countess Agneta Lejongård to assume the guardianship of my daughter, Matilda.*

"Why would she write that?" I asked. "Mother never mentioned a countess."

Suddenly I wondered if this so-called countess was up to no good. Was she scheming to sell me into bondage? Or was that only a thing in cheap romance novels?

"Matilda!" the principal snapped. "You should be grateful. This is a gift!"

"Oh, it is no gift," the countess replied. "Rather, it is my duty to take care of you. Life at Lion Hall will be good, and perhaps it can become something of a home for you."

Her words chilled me like a spray of icy rainwater. I would have to leave Stockholm. But what would become of Paul and me? And my plans to go to business college? Paul and I had dreamed of establishing a company. He would produce fine furniture, and I would take care of the bookkeeping, since I was a lot better at numbers.

But now that dream was in pieces. I would be obliged to rot away on her estate, hauling cartloads of manure and stacking hay. Forget about the jumping jazz clubs I'd secretly dreamed of visiting; I was to be torn away from everything I knew.

"And what if I don't want to go?" I cried angrily. Tears filled my eyes.

"Matilda!" Principal Persson was so incensed he practically came out of his seat. "You have no choice!"

The countess studied me. "If your mother had not passed away," she asked with an unexpectedly gentle tone, "what would you have done after finishing school here?"

"Does that matter?" I sobbed.

"It does to me. I do not know you, Matilda. I have no idea what you want. And believe me, I know what it is to have one's desires frustrated."

I stared at her.

The principal snorted, obviously considering me an impudent, ungrateful wretch. But this was my life we were talking about!

I hadn't shared my aspirations with anyone except Paul. Most of the girls in my class dreamed of finding a good husband to provide for them. Their only aim in secondary school was to become clever house-wives. If I'd told them my plans, they'd have shunned me even more.

"I want to go to business college and run a big company someday," I heard myself declare. "Whatever happens, I want to have my own income, my own house, and maybe even an automobile."

Agneta Lejongård looked me in the eye and nodded thoughtfully. "Those are laudable goals. I see no reason you should not be able to achieve them."

"But I'm an orphan with no money for school! And if I go live on a farm . . ."

"Well, Lion Hall is not exactly Iceland," the countess said with a smile. "Kristianstad is quite close. And it has a business college."

I almost protested that Paul wasn't in Kristianstad. But I didn't want her to know about him.

"But there is no need to decide all of that immediately," the countess continued. "I apologize. I did not intend to cause you distress. On the contrary, my aim is to help you realize your dreams."

I nodded. What other choice did I have? Principal Persson was right. My mother had picked this woman to be my guardian. I could not refuse.

"Here is the invitation to the lawyer's office for tomorrow morning. I will accompany you to the reading of your mother's will." The countess handed me the letter, got up, and turned to the principal. "She will be excused from class for the day, I presume?"

"Of course, gracious lady," Persson said, bounding to his feet.

"Good. Then we will see one another again tomorrow." The countess took her leave.

I found myself standing in the corridor, wishing I'd asked where she was staying in Stockholm.

Lost in thought, I ran my fingers across the envelope. Tears burned my eyes. More than anything, I yearned to flee the school and hole up at home. But the bell rang, and within seconds the hall was full of students.

Daga came running. "Matilda, what is it?" she asked in alarm when she saw my flushed cheeks.

I pushed the letter into my skirt pocket and rapidly wiped the tears from my cheeks. "Nothing, I . . . I'm just a bit confused." But I couldn't fool Daga.

"Did you get bad news?" When I didn't answer immediately, she gasped. "They didn't expel you, did they?"

I shook my head. "No. I—I met my new guardian."

"Some old biddy from an orphanage?"

"No. A countess."

Daga's mouth dropped open. "A countess? What's a countess got to do with you?"

I sought words for an answer, but saw the other girls heading in our direction. I didn't want them to know I'd been crying. They were probably already inventing all sorts of stories.

"Let's find somewhere we won't be disturbed," I murmured and led her out to the low wall at the southern end of the schoolyard.

2

I was terribly agitated that night. My arms and legs prickled as if ants were swarming over them. I couldn't settle down, despite the silence of our house.

The events of the day seemed so unreal. A countess turns up out of nowhere to take charge of a poor orphan child? It was something out of a fairy tale.

A rattle at the windowpane made me jump. At first I thought it was just one of the many random sounds the house made, especially after dark. Then I got up and went to look. I saw a familiar figure standing under the streetlamp.

I opened the window. Paul Ringström had just gathered more pebbles to throw, but he stopped short when he saw me.

"What are you doing showing up here so late?" I called, sounding more annoyed than I really was.

"A little bird told me something, and I wanted to know if it was true."

It wasn't hard to guess who that bird was.

I visited Daga's house regularly, but I'd met her brother only a couple of months earlier. After that he seemed to cross my path more and more often, purely by chance, of course. The courteous, attentive young man let me know he liked me. He gazed at me affectionately. He was clever, and I had the feeling he would protect me. It was easy to imagine a promising future with him. He was really handsome too. He had broad shoulders and powerful arms from building furniture in his father's workshop. When we strolled through the park together, I noticed the other girls' glances, and was pleased he ignored them.

We weren't a real couple—my mother wouldn't have permitted that—but from time to time he'd turn up unannounced below my window and toss a pebble or two. We had long conversations whenever we could.

Mother was gone now, but I wasn't ready to invite him in. Besides, the neighbor women had sharp eyes and loved gossip.

"Hold on, I'll be right out!" I called.

Paul nodded, clearly a bit disappointed. I knew he wanted to be alone with me at last, but I was afraid of giving in to something both of us would regret. I quickly slipped into my dress and threw Mother's thick wool shawl about my shoulders.

"Why don't we go inside, the way other people do?" he asked as I emerged.

"You know why," I said. "I'm not going to do anything my mother wouldn't have approved of."

"I understand that. But wouldn't your mother want you to have a faithful boyfriend?"

"Of course, someday. But she insisted that seventeen was too young for that."

I looked at him. The streetlamp lent his skin a rosy shimmer, but failed to reveal the glorious green of his eyes. In that light they were the muddy brown of a rainy day. Still, the artificial light accentuated the sharp jut of his chin, his broad forehead, and those marvelous arched eyebrows.

"I just wanted to come in, that's all." He sighed. "But maybe our friendship is fated to end."

I stared at him, taken aback. "What do you mean?"

"Daga told me that your new guardian is a countess from somewhere near Kristianstad?"

"Yes," I said and felt the word weigh upon my heart like a stone.

"That means you're leaving."

"Yes, but—" I hesitated. "It's not like I want to."

Paul sniffed and put his hands on his hips. "You should have told her you want to stay."

"I tried, but I was completely overwhelmed. The principal took me to his office, and there she was. She told me she owned this estate and asked me about my plans for the future."

"And am I still part of those plans?"

"You know you are, but I couldn't tell her that, could I?"

I stepped toward him and raised my hands, intending to place them on his chest, but stopped when I saw his body stiffen.

"You're going to leave," he said and gently pushed a strand of hair out of my face. "Unless you find a way to keep her from becoming your guardian."

I bowed my head. If only I were older and could do what I wanted! Four years! Why hadn't I been granted those four years with my mother? It seemed terribly unjust.

"My mother chose her," I said. "But even if I have to leave Stockholm, we mustn't lose contact . . . After all, it's only for four years."

"Four years!" Paul's eyes widened in alarm. "That's practically forever, don't you see? I'll be twenty-three by then!"

"What do you mean?" I asked. "We'll still be young."

"But—" Paul stopped short. "What if I want to marry you?"

I looked deep into his eyes. "You know I won't be allowed to marry without my guardian's consent."

"Exactly!" he replied.

I shook my head. "Don't you think it'll be worth waiting?" I felt a sudden surge of anger and had trouble keeping my voice down so the neighbors wouldn't hear. "I'm not disappearing off the face of the earth, Paul. And anyway, why are we talking about marriage already? Neither of us is legally an adult yet. How would your family react if you tell them you want to get married? And besides, what about your apprenticeship? Shouldn't you finish and get your certificate? Remember our dream!"

Paul had a five-year plan for establishing a workshop. He wanted to have his own business, even bigger and more successful than his father's. And someday, maybe—*Paul Ringström and Son, Furniture Manufacturers since 1936.*

But five years might be long enough for him to forget me entirely. Paul stared at his feet. "I—I don't want to lose you."

"And you won't!" I said, but felt myself beginning to tremble. "I'm moving to the south, to Skåne province, for four years, no more. Then I'll come back. I'll be an eager, full-fledged businesswoman, and I'll stand at your side."

This time I placed my hands on his arms. Paul gathered me in and pressed me to his chest as if to keep me from the cold.

I was keenly aware my words sounded bolder than I was feeling. Four years was an eternity. So much could happen.

"Skåne must have lots of young men who'll want to court you."

"Not a single one like you!" I responded. "And what about all the attractive young women here in Stockholm?"

"I don't want anyone else," he said and kissed my hands. He gave me an embarrassed grin. "Are you sure we can't go inside?"

My pulse accelerated. I knew I might rue my hesitation later, but I just couldn't.

"Not tonight," I told him. "But that doesn't mean we can't get together in private some other time."

He frowned. "In Skåne? Maybe if I take time off to visit you?"

15

"Why not? Maybe I'll visit you too. And then we can meet right here."

"But what if the countess sells this house? She's your guardian. She can do what she likes."

His comment flooded me with even more anxiety. "I'll find a way."

I leaned forward and gave him a little peck on the cheek. Paul threw his arms around me, pulled me close, and kissed my lips. He'd never done that before. His lips were hungry and demanding, and he was so close. I felt a yearning low in my abdomen and almost changed my mind. But then I broke away.

"I'll write you. Every month."

"That's not often enough," he responded, a quaver in his voice.

"Every week?"

He smiled. "Better." He stuck his hands into his trouser pockets and stared at his feet again. "If you change your mind, let me know right away, okay? I'm willing to wait, but I want to be sure you still want me."

"I want you!" I blurted and fought against my fear that so little in this world was sure. As a young girl, I'd assumed my parents would live forever. Now I'd lost them both. "Nothing will change that, you hear? And as soon as I'm free, really independent, we'll marry, and nothing will ever stand in our way again."

Paul nodded and again pressed me to his heart. I desperately wanted him to kiss me again, but after a moment he let go.

"Take care and be well, Matilda! We'll write!" he said with an unhappy smile. He disappeared into the darkness.

"Take care!" I called after him and raised my hand in a helpless little wave, but he didn't turn back to see it.

Suddenly I felt fearfully alone. Had I made a mistake? What would have happened if I'd brought him into the house? But I couldn't; someone might tell the countess that I allowed men into the house, and regardless of what my mother had requested, the woman was probably perfectly capable of dumping me into an orphanage.

No, I'd made the right decision. The day would come for Paul and me. And then no one in the world would be able to separate us.

The next day we met at the lawyer's office. He was an elderly man with gray sideburns, a style so old-fashioned that even aged men rarely wore them that way. "Please take a seat, ladies," he said and settled behind the desk.

He officially informed me that Agneta Lejongård would be my guardian from that day on. I was grateful to the countess for one thing at least: it would have been considerably more unpleasant to have the arrangement sprung upon me there in the office. Even so, I wished my life could have remained the same, with both my mother and my father still alive. I wished I had siblings or grandparents. Now there was only me, and the person providing me shelter was a total stranger. She'd promised to help fulfill my dreams, but what if she didn't keep her word?

I glanced at the countess. We'd exchanged only a few words outside the building. Now it looked as if her eyes were fixed on some somber vision I couldn't perceive.

"Today, the second of June of 1931, I read aloud the last will and testament of Susanna Wallin, maiden name Korven," the attorney intoned, sitting up straight. "*It is my will that my only daughter, Matilda, should receive all of my possessions, namely: the house, my jewelry, and my savings of approximately five hundred crowns.*' Signed: '*Susanna Wallin, maiden name Korven.*'"

And that was that. No personal message—nothing at all. I knew nothing about wills, but I'd thought my mother would have at least included a few words to console me.

"Do you accept the bequest?" the lawyer inquired. His words came to me as if from some great distance. I knew I was supposed to reply, but my tongue wouldn't move. My mind was obsessed by a single thought: *Why had my mother's farewell been so impersonal?*

"Matilda?" The countess's voice intruded into my thoughts. I flinched when her hand brushed my arm. "An immediate response is not required, if you do not feel ready." Our eyes met, and she withdrew her hand.

"I'm ready," I responded, almost resentfully, and I turned to the lawyer. "I accept the bequest."

He nodded, then turned to Agneta Lejongård. "Do you accept the responsibility of serving as legal guardian?"

"Yes," she answered. "I do."

"Very well. Countess Lejongård, you will manage the funds of your ward until she reaches the age of majority. I will prepare the corresponding documents and have them delivered to you." The lawyer gathered the papers and rose. "My best wishes to you," he said and shook first the countess's hand and then mine.

I knew it was time for us to leave, but I felt helpless and too drained take a step.

Countess Lejongård took my elbow. "Come, Matilda. I am sure a cup of tea will do you good."

A warm summer rain was pouring down as we left the building. It lent the air a pungent smell of greenery. We lingered under the awning.

Thank goodness I'd been excused from school. I couldn't have endured hours of class.

"Do you really mean it?" I asked, looking up at the dark clouds. The raindrops were so huge that one could follow their individual trajectories through the air.

"To what are you referring?"

"What you said yesterday. That I can go to business college."

"I cannot imagine anything that would stand in your way." Agneta Lejongård paused for an instant, then added, "I know you feel apprehensive. Only a few months ago your future seemed predictable, and now . . . Do you know, many years ago I had to confront and adapt to a similar situation? I was on my way to becoming a painter. I dreamed of astonishing Paris and other cosmopolitan cities across the world. But life rarely takes one's desires into account. It proceeds as it will, with unpredictable twists and turns. In my case, the deaths of my father and my brother."

She gave me a rueful look. "I was presented with the choice of allowing my family home to fall into ruins or assuming responsibility for the estate. I chose responsibility. And now, eighteen years later, I can confidently say I made the correct choice. I have a husband, I have children, and Lion Hall is my home."

She paused again. A soft smile spread across her face. "Lion Hall is very beautiful. There are deep woods and broad meadows. And horses. That may not sound particularly enticing to a young woman from the city, but I assure you it is enchanting. Once there, you may eventually find you don't want to leave."

I didn't believe her, but I didn't have the energy to protest just then. I asked a question instead. "Why were you so quiet? I mean, back there, inside?"

"What might I have had to say?" the countess responded, her eyes still meeting mine.

"I don't know. Nothing, I guess. But still, I had the impression you were thinking of something else. Something unpleasant."

The countess contemplated me. She appeared tired and sorrowful, and I really did want to know why.

"I was remembering all the times I have had to attend readings of wills. Days like this one change people's lives, whether they wish it or not. One can accept an inheritance or refuse it, but in either case one's life is changed."

"You mean your life has been changed because of me."

"Yes," she replied. "And yours because of me. The two of us, who previously did not know one another, have now been permanently bound together by your mother. It is up to us to make the best of the situation. That is the truth of it; do you agree?"

I nodded. "Where did you know my mother?" I asked, for that was the great enigma. What could possibly have motivated Mother to place me in Agneta Lejongård's care?

"Oh, that was a long time ago," the countess said. "I will tell you the story one day, but for now we should see to it that you settle comfortably into your new situation. The changes ahead will keep you occupied for quite some time."

I wondered what, exactly, the countess wasn't ready to tell me. Had she and my mother been classmates? Or something else?

We stood silent under the awning for several minutes, watching the people hurrying by and doing their best to protect themselves from the rain with folded newspapers or umbrellas. The clouds soon lifted, and sunshine glistened once again on the wet pavement.

"Shall we go?"

"Where to?"

"To your house. You heard the lawyer: it belongs to you now."

"Yes, but not really until I'm of age."

"I assume that does not prevent us from going there?"

The countess set out. I wished I could have remained under the law offices' awning, but finally I roused myself, caught up with her, and walked alongside.

To my great astonishment, when we arrived at my parents' house, we were met by the fragrance of lemons and a woman I'd never seen before. She wore a light-gray dress and had her hair neatly done up in a bun. Slim and quite attractive, she seemed to be in her mid- or late twenties.

"This is Anna Grün. She will be living here as your governess and will help keep house until you move to Lion Hall."

The woman gave me her hand with a friendly smile. "So happy to make your acquaintance, Matilda."

I heard a slight accent. What part of Sweden was she from?

I pressed her hand a bit uncertainly. "You mean, I don't have to go to the estate yet?"

Agneta Lejongård shook her head. "You will stay in Stockholm another four weeks, until the end of the school term. Your life at Lion Hall will begin after that, and I will see that you obtain the instruction necessary to qualify you for whatever professional goal you may set for yourself. But now we should give ourselves the pleasure of a lemonade and get to know one another. What do you think?"

I nodded. This was all too much, but perhaps things would become clearer.

The three of us chatted all afternoon, although my mother was never the subject of conversation. The countess had clearly already given the governess detailed instructions for me. Anna Grün did her very best to win my confidence, and she really was very nice, but I couldn't help thinking she was a sort of watchdog.

Eventually, the countess departed with a promise to write. I'd never shared the house with a stranger before. Even solitude had been better. Now I had to stay aware of my actions, my facial expressions, and my words. I was no longer an independent young woman but a ward subject to the instructions of my governess and Countess Lejongård.

I lay in bed staring up at the ceiling, my eyes wide. Of course, Miss Grün would do me no harm, but I was still reluctant to close my eyes with a stranger in the house. *Sleep and death make people equally vulnerable,* my father used to say. That notion had so disturbed me as a child that often I found it hard to go to sleep.

What I really wanted was to get up, go into the living room, and play one of my wobbly old shellac records on the gramophone, so I could lose myself in music that would keep me awake. But I didn't want to disturb my governess.

The thought that the young woman could look around, touch, and pick up my mother's things made me uneasy. Why had the countess brought her here? I'd gotten through the past weeks perfectly well, so what was another month, just to finish up the school year?

I opened the drawer of my bedside table. It took a moment, but then my fingertips found the cool metal of my father's lighter. I wrapped my hand around it, reassured by its touch.

I lay back in the pillows and recalled images from my childhood, when everything was in order and I knew nothing about suffering. I saw myself strolling with my parents through one of the city parks. My mother wore a wonderful pink dress with a matching bonnet. My father was clad in a dapper summer suit. I could almost feel the warmth of those carefree days—not an outer warmth, but the sort that radiates from within. I was so happy back then. At the age of six or seven I'd been tiny and clumsy, but I was convinced even so that one day I would resemble my mother. I'd wear a beautiful dress and a lovely hat, and I'd have a handsome man at my side.

My thoughts turned idly to the future. This time I envisioned myself as the beautiful woman in pink and Paul as the man with me. Perhaps all wasn't yet lost. Paul had promised to wait, and so had I. We would write. Once I finished business studies, the countess would probably allow me to marry.

That's exactly what I'd tell Paul when I saw him. We would marry even before I became of age. There was nothing in the law to prevent it, for in that case the woman became the responsibility of her husband. He'd have nothing against that, surely. And neither would I.

"One more month," I whispered to the lighter in my hand. And then my eyes fell shut.

3

I held tight to the handle of my suitcase and looked down the railway platform. I noticed a poster advertising mouthwash. It must have been hanging there for quite a while, for it was terribly faded, and not just at the edges. A smiling woman dancer sporting an old-fashioned top hat held up a bottle with a label that promised *brilliant breath!* The station air was warm and heavy, and crickets chirped noisily from the far side of the embankment.

The train that brought me to Kristianstad had departed a good ten minutes earlier, but I hadn't been able to summon the courage to exit the station. I felt as if I were about to pass through a checkpoint into a hostile foreign land.

I regretted that my governess had taken her leave at the Stockholm train station. She was going back to Germany in a couple of days. Miss Grün was kind, but had indeed been very strict and made sure I obeyed a list of rules the countess had written out for us. Still, I'd managed to see Paul a couple of times, and I'd opened my heart to him. We'd met briefly one last time before my departure, when I visited the Ringströms with the excuse of saying goodbye to Daga.

The northbound train was announced. I made my way down the stairs and lugged my case to the station exit. The few travelers coming the other way ignored me.

To my great surprise there was no driver with pilot's goggles and brimmed cap waiting for me outside by the somewhat old-fashioned automobile. Agneta Lejongård herself leaned casually against the vehicle's hood. Her hair was tightly gathered and covered by a thin mauve scarf. Her clothes were elegant—a suit of the same color, and a jacket fastened with silver-colored buttons.

She was clearly startled by the sight of me. She stepped away from the car and came over.

"Hello, Matilda," she said. "Did you have a good trip?"

"Yes, thank you," I replied and accepted her soft, manicured hand. Her grip was as strong as a man's. I couldn't find anything to say.

The countess inspected me carefully and finally spoke. "I was beginning to wonder if you might have missed the train."

"I—I needed a few moments," was my awkward excuse.

The countess nodded. "That I can understand. After all, you found yourself obliged to leave behind everything familiar. But I promise Lion Hall will be to your liking." That said, she took my case, heaved it onto the back seat, and opened the passenger door. "Climb in! We are fortunate. The weather is pleasant enough that we will have no need of the car top for our drive today."

I got in and realized no driver would be accompanying us. My expression must have betrayed my surprise, for as Agneta was settling herself behind the steering wheel, she asked, "Is something on your mind?"

"No, it's just that I thought—"

"—that I would not be the driver?" Agneta threw her head back and laughed. "I have been driving for the past four years. I enjoy it, especially because the roads here are calm and I can get the vehicle up to a respectable speed."

"What about your husband?"

"He drives as well." The countess glanced at me expectantly. "Would you like to learn? I can teach you, if you like."

The *No!* remained stuck in my throat, but she read it on my face.

"Did you think perhaps that women are not capable of such a thing?" She smiled, turned the key in the ignition, and brought the engine rumbling and shaking to life. The automobile promptly set off down the street.

We left Kristianstad on a broad country road. The only other motorized vehicle we saw was a milk truck. We overtook a horse-drawn wagon with the driver soundly asleep on his seat. I half expected Agneta to honk to wake him up. Plenty of Stockholmers would have enjoyed scaring the old man. But she simply drove around him.

I leaned back and closed my eyes as we roared through a stretch of forest. The tension of the trip gradually drained away, and a sluggish feeling settled over me. The breeze caressed my face. For a moment I even managed to put aside my fears about the future, the unknown Lion Hall estate, and the long years ahead. Perhaps things here wouldn't be so bad after all. I would miss the city and Paul and Daga terribly, but there must be a post office. Once I had done my time in the country, I would return with many tales to tell.

There was still the question of the relationship between my mother and the countess. I'd puzzled constantly over that. Miss Grün apparently knew nothing about it.

The automobile came to a stop, and I opened my eyes. Were we there already?

Before us was an imposing gate that opened to a long, tree-lined boulevard. A tall, splendidly shining white manor stood in the distance.

Amazed, I turned to the countess. "Why did we stop?"

"I wanted to give you a moment to appreciate the manor from this vantage point," the countess explained. "I know from experience that it is rare for someone to take it in fully at first sight."

"So that's Lion Hall?"

"Yes, the house. And the front gardens. The fields we passed through are part of the estate, as are the horse barns and the pastures. If you like, we can make a little excursion to the village later. I consider it important for you to understand where everything is and to know where to find whatever you need."

I turned to gaze at the house. It was far in the distance, but even so it looked massive and imposing. Foreign to my eyes, as well, but more than that: it was isolated. As a city girl, I was used to having neighbors. Houses and buildings in Stockholm usually pressed up against one another, which gave the streets a crowded, friendly aspect. Here the manor house stood alone, and the various outbuildings seemed to humble themselves before its presence.

We took the long approach, entered the circular drive, and halted before the front steps. The motor fell silent, and I heard nothing but the twittering of birds.

A young woman dressed in black with a white apron appeared at the door. She curtsied. "Shall I help you with the suitcase, gracious lady?"

The countess shook her head. "Thank you, Silja, but I think Miss Matilda can manage her own valise."

The young woman curtsied again. "As you wish, gracious lady."

"Oh, Silja, would you please tell Mrs. Bloomquist to prepare a little refreshment for our newest family member?" She turned to me. "I assume you are hungry?"

I felt I should decline, but the mention of food made me aware of the hollow feeling in my stomach.

"Yes, I am, in fact."

"Good! You heard her, Silja. Mrs. Bloomquist certainly must have some of her delicious pastries. And perhaps she might come up with something extra to offer the young lady."

The maid curtsied and disappeared. We climbed the steps and passed through the front door. I stopped, awed, in the hallway. My governess had told me the house was impressive, but I'd imagined something far plainer. Elaborate chandeliers cast dazzling light, the marble floor gleamed, and the colors of the carpets were intense. I gaped, feeling like a tiny girl visiting a candy shop for the first time.

The countess waved her hand in invitation. "This will be your home from now on. Do not be intimidated by all the art and gold. My ancestors loved all that nonsense, and in our social circles there is a certain expectation of ostentation. But when it comes down to it, it is only a house. And I do hope you will soon consider it your home."

I had no idea what to say. Could this place of pomp and display ever seem like home? I doubted it. I was here because I had no other choice; I had to obey my guardian.

I stopped to look at portraits hung on either side of the staircase. A man and a woman stared down at me, each alone within an elaborate frame. The woman wore a cream-colored dress, and her hair fell in gently undulating waves. She was extremely beautiful, but her pale skin and blue eyes had a chilly look. The man was robust, with broad shoulders; although tall, he stooped slightly. He had dark hair and brown eyes, and a faint smile played across his lips. Like the woman, he seemed about the same age as Agneta Lejongård now.

"My father and mother," the countess told me. "I painted these portraits after my mother passed away. My father had been dead for many years by then."

"You painted those?" I asked, amazed. Of course, I remembered she'd mentioned her dream of becoming a painter, but I'd never imagined this kind of talent. "Why didn't you put them in the same picture?"

She gave me an odd look. "I had my reasons. But now we should see to your room." She turned and went up the stairs.

A young man came barreling toward us down the hallway lined with ancient paintings and small shaded lamps.

"Ingmar!" the countess exclaimed. "You should be downstairs!"

The boy, about my age, stopped to stare at me. He seemed not to have heard a word.

"Ingmar?"

"Sorry, Mother," he replied and shook his head as if to drive away a bothersome thought. "I forgot something."

"Now that you are here, Matilda, I can introduce you to my son Ingmar. Ingmar, this is Matilda."

"The girl you have been talking about for weeks," he said, and bowed briefly. "I am very pleased to meet you, Matilda."

I should really have offered him my hand and replied that the pleasure was entirely mine, but all I could manage was a nod.

"Do you know where Magnus is?" the countess asked.

"Where do you think?" Ingmar replied. "Probably sitting with elves under a tree, making up some kind of story."

"You know I do not appreciate it when you speak of your brother in that tone."

"He knows what I think. And if he does not care, it should not bother you."

The countess shook her head. I couldn't hide a grin. He gave me a satisfied smirk, for that's exactly what he'd been angling for.

"When you see Magnus, tell him I wish to present our new resident."

"Sure will. Unless he has already fallen down his rabbit hole and is being pursued by the Queen of Hearts."

"*Alice in Wonderland*!" I exclaimed.

The boy nodded and vanished before his mother could rebuke him again.

"I fear you will simply have to get used to Ingmar's manners," the countess said. "He has a saucy comeback to everything. You should not pay too much heed if he tries to tease you."

I was tempted to tell her I enjoyed his impudent manner, but I bit my tongue.

We continued along the hall and stopped at a doorway.

"This was my room when I was a girl," she said. "Of course, we have refurbished it since then. You need not worry about running into any lingering ghosts." She opened the door and stepped back.

The sweet odors of soap and flowers streamed out. My mother had often smelled like that, especially in the morning when she'd washed with a new bar of soap. I hesitated, for the familiar fragrances bothered me. I had a momentary, irrational hope my mother would be waiting for me within.

But of course no one was there. The room had a splendid canopy bed with pink curtains and a fluffy pink comforter. A tidy little vanity sat across from it, and a large white-painted wardrobe stood against the wall. The pink of the bed was reprised in the colors of the carpet. The drapes, gathered with satin ties, were a sprightly green. Evidently the countess took pleasure in delicate colors.

This chamber could have been the bedroom of a tiny princess. My room in Stockholm was sober and stark in comparison. The furniture pieces here were elaborately carved. How old might they be?

"I hope it pleases you," the countess said.

I nodded.

"Good. Then make yourself comfortable and do not hesitate to tell me of any desire you may have." She went to the door and looked back.

"Thanks," I croaked. The room was splendid. I could hardly believe it was mine, but I still yearned for my humble home in Stockholm. "Countess, I—"

"Call me Agneta," she corrected me. "Just Agneta. What is on your mind?"

"You told the servant I'm a new member of the family . . ."

"And you are exactly that!" she responded. "You are my ward. I will treat you like any other member of my family. I do hope you did not think you were brought here to live in the ashes like Cinderella!"

"No, I—" I couldn't help smiling at that image. This was too much; it seemed unreal. Was I really going to be happy? Could I trust this apparent tranquility?

"Welcome to Lion Hall!" Agneta Lejongård said with a smile and left the room.

I stood there alone, in a room that seemed too vast and too strange to be mine.

4

By that afternoon I'd managed to locate my things. Miss Grün had dispatched a steamer chest with most of my possessions the day before my departure. She had even been kind enough to pack both of my favorite gramophone records. I didn't know if I'd be able to play them, but it was comforting to have them with me.

Following afternoon coffee in a splendid salon, Agneta had accompanied me on a brief tour of the kitchen, the horse barns, and the garden pavilion. I had the eerie feeling I was wandering around in a painting.

The kitchen looked as if it had been taken directly from an ancient copper engraving, although the ovens were smaller and not as heavy as in olden days, and the house wasn't equipped with old-fashioned copper pots and pans. Mrs. Bloomquist, the cook, was very busy, but Agneta said she insisted on overseeing service at mealtimes as well. Svea, her assistant, wasn't entirely pleased with that, but she didn't object, for she revered the elderly cook.

In earlier days there had been a housekeeper and even a sort of butler, but Miss Rosendahl had married and moved with her husband to Kristianstad, and Mr. Bruns had retired. Now the housemaids were supervised by the countess's personal maid, and the count had his own valet, a silent, almost invisible man in his forties; according to Svea, he was only to be seen at mealtimes.

The horse barns were more modern than the kitchen, and one of the buildings was noticeably newer than the rest. The horses were all out in the paddocks, so I saw them only from a distance.

Surely one could spend many hours reading in the delicate pavilion at the rear of the gardens. I imagined myself sitting there and sipping tea. Windup gramophones had fallen out of fashion now that electricity offered a source of uninterrupted power, but how lovely it would be to have one so I could listen to my records in the garden.

Back in my room, I picked up a book, but I was too distracted to follow the narrative. Images of blooming flowers of every imaginable color, of horses, and of the woods came between me and the printed page. I remembered predicting to Daga that Lion Hall would be grim and gray, but in fact it had more colors than a rainbow.

A knock at the door made me look up.

"Come in?" I said tentatively, expecting the countess. But it wasn't Agneta.

The slim woman who stepped into my room wore her hair in an intricate braid gathered in an elaborate bun behind her. The apron over her dark dress was impeccably starched.

"Good day!" she said. "I'm Lena, the mistress's personal maid. The gracious lady has asked me to assist you as well."

"Um, thanks, but that's not necessary," I replied. "I can manage by myself."

The maid smiled merrily. "I'm sure you can. But there are a couple of things I need to tend to. And for evening events, you will need someone to assist with your clothing and your hair."

"My hair? In the evening?"

"We often receive guests for the evening meal. You'll need to be appropriately dressed. In the old days the dowager countess was extremely strict, but in these modern times we're a bit more relaxed. Still, you should put your best foot forward when you greet our visitors."

Visitors? I felt a wave of panic. The last thing I wanted was to respond to inquiries from people I'd never met. "But I'm just the countess's ward. It's not as if I were the daughter of the family."

"The countess gave me strict instructions," Lena said. "Your status as her ward means you are just as much a part of the Lion Hall family as her sons are."

Except that the countess's sons didn't have to endure having their hair pinned up. I had a sudden thought: What was Magnus like? I hadn't met him yet. And Ingmar seemed to have disappeared after our encounter. There must be places in the house and on the estate the countess hadn't shown me, retreats to which one could withdraw and vanish for a couple of hours.

"Are they expecting visitors today?" I asked.

"No, but today's your first day at the manor. The countess is celebrating it with a lovely dinner."

"And that's why you've come to put my hair up." I took a deep breath. I was relieved there would be no outsiders, but a formal dinner with the countess's family sounded stiff and awkward.

I'd often wondered what it would be like to have siblings. Now I had two . . . but what were they to me? Stepbrothers? Was that the right term? In any case, I was glad not to be the only young person in this imposing mansion.

When Lena had finished my hair, the face in the mirror was that of a beautiful stranger. I looked older and more mature. What would the girls in my class have said? And what about Paul?

I felt a deep pang. Paul would have found me enchanting.

"You are a marvel of beauty," Lena pronounced. "Your mother would have been proud. She always liked hair arrangements like this so much—" She suddenly fell silent, apparently dismayed, as if she'd made a huge mistake.

"What did you say about my mother?" I asked, amazed.

"Nothing," Lena replied. "I must be going now."

"Wait!" I called, stopping her in her tracks. I went to her and put a hand on her arm. "How did you meet her?"

Lena seemed to squirm. "I can't tell you that."

"Lena," I begged. "Did you know my mother?"

Lena shook her head. "I really cannot say." She pulled away and practically fled the room. I gazed after her in disbelief. What wasn't she telling me?

I stared after her for a while and then turned to regard myself in the mirror. The figure there was still that of a stranger. I patted the elaborate hairdo tentatively, afraid of spoiling it. So, my mother had liked this kind of arrangement? She'd never worn her hair like this at home. And she'd never done my hair like this. Suddenly I was bursting with questions. And there was only one person who could answer them.

I descended the stairs somewhat timidly. I still found it impossible to comprehend the riches on display in the foyer.

Once downstairs, I looked at the portraits of Agneta's parents. I recalled her reaction to my question about why she hadn't painted them on the same canvas. What was that about? I'd heard that all ancient manor houses had their own stories and ghosts. What secrets were hidden here?

"Ah, Matilda, there you are!" The countess approached with a smile. Her hair was in a lovely bun that seemed almost casual at first glance, but had clearly been done by a cunning hand.

She put her arm around me. "Come with me into the dining room!"

I stiffened. "Um . . . Agneta, may I have a word alone with you?" I couldn't spend all evening wondering how Lena knew my mother.

"Of course!" She pulled me along, but I resisted.

"Best not in the dining room."

Agneta raised an eyebrow. "As you wish. Follow me!"

She turned and took me to the salon. The rays of the evening sun falling through the tall windows gave the room an almost magical glow.

"Now, then, what is on your mind?" Agneta asked gently and waved toward the chairs placed in the middle of the room.

We sat, and it took me a while to find the words. "While Lena was putting up my hair, she let it slip that Mother liked to wear her hair like this. How did she know that?"

Agneta's face froze just as Lena's had. An eternity seemed to pass before she responded. I remembered how lost in thought she'd seemed during our visit to the lawyer's office. She took a deep breath, as if realizing this discussion was unavoidable.

"Your mother was in service here at Lion Hall."

I stared at her, not understanding. "You mean she was a housemaid?"

I couldn't imagine such a thing. Yes, Mother had a special talent for housekeeping, but I'd always assumed that was because she—unlike me—had enjoyed putting things in order. I was amazed she'd never mentioned her work here. I'd never imagined there was anything hidden in her past. Was there something she'd found painful and wanted to forget?

"Yes, she was a servant here at the manor. And an extremely capable one."

"Then why didn't she ever tell me?" If I'd known, I wouldn't have been so surprised when the countess appeared out of nowhere.

"That I do not know. She must have had her reasons."

"Did she have unpleasant memories?"

Agneta regarded me, almost tormented. "I hope she did not. In any case, we stayed in contact after she left. If she had disliked me, would she have confided her only daughter to my care?"

I stared into space for a time. Why wouldn't Mother have told me of her time here? While servants were less common these days, their employment was entirely respectable.

35

"I apologize; I should have told you immediately," Agneta went on. "Then perhaps it would have been less of a shock."

I nodded, wondering if she'd have said anything at all if her maid hadn't mentioned Mother.

"Please don't punish Lena!" I exclaimed.

"Why would I punish her?" the countess asked. "After all, I did say that I would tell you. I simply wanted to give you some time to become familiar with Lion Hall, before—" She stopped and reflected. For a moment she seemed about to add something, but then she shook her head slightly.

"Before what?" I insisted.

She just smiled. "You will learn everything in due time. Get used to us and then we will see." She got to her feet. "For now, I hope you have a robust appetite. Mrs. Bloomquist has made a very special effort to impress you today."

A man in a dark suit, Ingmar, and a second boy were waiting in the dining room. This must be Magnus—he was the spitting image of his brother. The man, I assumed, was the count. He was tall, his blond hair and reddish beard tinged with gray.

"Aha, we have the two of you at last!" he exclaimed. He stepped forward, embraced Agneta, and kissed her. "I apologize for not coming directly to you. I just returned, and one of the maids said you were in the salon with our new family member. I took advantage of that to change as quickly as I could."

"Quite all right," Agneta replied. Her eyes were full of adoration, an expression I'd never seen on my own mother's face. Mother and Father had been unfailingly friendly and polite to one another but never openly affectionate. "May I introduce Matilda Wallin? Matilda, this is my husband, Count Lennard Ekberg."

He gave me his hand. "Welcome, Matilda. I have heard so much about you."

I almost blurted out my first reaction—*But I've never heard of you*—but fortunately I managed to limit myself to a demure smile. I was still confused after the brief conversation with Agneta.

"Very pleased to meet you, Count Ekberg," I answered at last, then I looked at the two boys. They were astonishingly alike. The only difference was in the way they were dressed.

I recognized Ingmar from his shirt and trousers, so the other had to be Magnus. He seemed a bit calmer than his brother. In response to a gesture from the countess, both rose and came to me.

"Matilda, you have already met Ingmar," she said. "This is Magnus. We cannot hide the fact that they are twins."

Magnus took his time extending his hand.

"Our new sister!" Ingmar told Magnus with a mischievous smile.

Magnus's expression didn't change. He was not amused.

"She is my ward," Agneta corrected Ingmar. "But in any case, you two must never make the mistake of treating her as anything less than a full member of our family."

"Yes, Mother," the twins chorused.

"Good. Now we can turn our attention to dinner."

Agneta guided me to the seat on her husband's right. The two boys settled to his left, across from me. They didn't look at me. No one said anything.

Meals in Stockholm had been like that. Father would arrive home, greet Mother briefly, then go to the dinner table. Often the two didn't exchange a word. Was that the custom here? Dinners with Paul and Daga's family were full of chatter. I knew, because I'd sometimes been invited there.

No sooner had we taken our seats than two serving girls appeared with the first course. Both were quite young; one was blonde, the other brunette. I watched the girl with darker hair. Had my mother served dishes this way? Had she worn a uniform like theirs? And those sturdy low shoes so she could be on her feet all day long?

I so lost myself in contemplating the serving girls that I didn't follow what was happening at the table. My pulse fluttered as I wondered how this scene must have been when my mother was employed here.

"Matilda?"

The sound of my name jolted me out of my reverie, and I became aware that there was, indeed, dinner table conversation among the Lejongårds. "Excuse me," I said and looked abashed at the countess. "I was lost in thought."

"I asked if you liked the soup."

I looked down at a bowl of cream-colored liquid.

"The chanterelle mushrooms were gathered in our forest," she explained. "Before Mrs. Bloomquist retires, she absolutely must reveal the recipe to me. She has always stood guard over it like Cerberus."

Everyone was watching me. My stomach growled quietly, but somehow I'd lost my appetite. I did my best, picking up the silver spoon decorated with the family crest and politely trying the soup. The complex flavors of mushrooms and spices exploded in my mouth.

"It's delicious!" I said, and I meant it. I'd never had a better mushroom soup, even though my mother had been a superb cook.

"Matilda probably is not used to fresh chanterelles," Ingmar commented with a smile. "You cannot just wander around and pick them in Stockholm."

"The weekly market has mushrooms," I replied. For some reason I felt the need to defend myself. "Everything is available in the city. The main difference is that we don't have to hunt them in the woods ourselves."

I turned back to the soup, but I had an uneasy feeling. It had tasted wonderful before, but now it seemed unpleasantly sticky. I consumed every drop anyway as a way to avoid saying anything.

The next course didn't change the mood very much. The count and countess did their best to carry the conversation, but everyone seemed to feel awkward. I was like some alien they couldn't entirely comprehend.

I longed for Stockholm. I'd gotten used to Miss Grün, and we'd had several lengthy conversations. That's how I'd learned she was Jewish and came from Germany. Each Friday evening she lit candles in her room and prayed quietly. That fascinated me.

"Matilda?" the countess asked. "Are you not well?"

I started. "Me? Yes—I mean, no. Everything is fine." Failing to follow the conversation was impolite, but how could I focus when my unruly mind preferred to take refuge in the past? My heart pounded.

"Perhaps you two should take Matilda on a stroll," Lennard told his sons.

I immediately sensed their reluctance. I wasn't interested either, but Ingmar declared, "Gladly! I can show her the old cabin or the horse paddock. If she does not mind coming along, dressed as she is."

"I can change!" I replied. I didn't want to look clueless in front of them, a city girl afraid of getting dirty.

"It seems to me that will not be necessary," Agneta said. "Stay away from the cabin, however. The place is not safe." She glanced at her husband.

He raised his wineglass. "And take the paved path to the paddock."

"Yes, Father," Ingmar said.

I said nothing as the meal progressed.

A few minutes later, Magnus spoke up. "What, exactly, happened to your parents?"

I looked up, astonished. Hadn't his mother told him? "They died."

"Magnus!" the countess scolded.

He put on an innocent expression. "What? It interests me. How did they die?"

My throat closed up. I gave him a long, paralyzed stare, then managed to say, "My mother's heart failed. And my father—drowned."

"Drowned? How?"

"He fell in the water." Hot indignation welled up in me. I had the distinct impression Magnus knew the details already and just wanted to torment me.

"What a terrible death. He could not swim?"

"Evidently not."

"Can you?"

"Magnus!" the countess again reprimanded her son.

"I was just asking!" he protested.

"I can swim perfectly well. We had lessons in school, in physical education class. Our teacher believed that, as Swedish citizens and inhabitants of the capital, we needed to be able to swim. The city is surrounded by water, after all."

"Your teacher sounds quite progressive," Agneta commented. "I am very much in favor of providing young ladies with a comprehensive education."

"He was. He said that, since we'd been a seafaring nation, any Swedish man or woman who didn't know how to swim was a national disgrace."

Agneta gave her husband a meaningful look.

After dinner, I went outside with Ingmar and Magnus. The evening air was still warm, almost oppressive, a bit dusty and heavy with the odors of drying hay and straw. Everything around the outbuildings was still. There was no sign of servants or employees.

We walked in silence for a while. I felt ill at ease between the two boys and didn't know what to say.

Paul and I had often discussed his apprenticeship and future plans. I'd told him of my own dreams too, and they'd flourished and melded with his. I could imagine myself in smart business attire managing the office while furniture was constructed in the workshop and turned over to busy deliverymen. I couldn't share any of that with the twins. They were only a year and a half younger than me, but I saw them as a pair of sheltered young scamps.

What's more, I was disturbed by Magnus's questions over dinner. Why had he wanted to know if I could swim? Was he planning to push me into a ditch somewhere? I silently thanked our physical education teacher. My memories of those classes weren't particularly agreeable, for I'd thought I was going to drown more than once. But afterward I no longer had the slightest fear of water.

I'd lied to them about Father, who was a fine swimmer. He stayed in the water for hours when we went to the shore on summer days. He hadn't simply fallen into the water and drowned. He'd taken his own life.

Ingmar finally broke the silence. "What is Stockholm like?"

"What do you think?" I replied. Had he never visited the capital? "The streets smell of smoke, and they're filled with automobiles. Some places are really hectic and noisy, especially around the train station. Stockholm has lots of parks, and the most impressive building is the royal palace. There are houses of all sizes."

"How about the people?"

"They look no different from the people here. Poor people and rich ones, workers and businessmen, women and men." I looked at him. "Haven't you ever been? I'm sure your parents have contacts in the capital. They probably get invited by the king!"

"In fact, the royal family come here as our guests," Magnus spoke up. "Just a couple of weeks ago, Crown Princess Louise was here with her stepchildren. She visits every year, so you must remember to mind your manners. Or, better, just make yourself scarce."

I stared at him. "You're telling me I have no manners?"

"Not the sort one should use with a future queen."

"I've seen the king lots of times in Stockholm," I defended myself. "I saw him in the funeral procession for the queen."

Mother and I had stood on the sidewalk when Victoria was conveyed through the streets of the capital to her last resting place. My mother was unusually silent and withdrawn that day. I'd thought nothing of it at the time, but now, knowing she'd lived at Lion Hall . . . perhaps Mother had actually met the queen?

"You saw him from the crowd! That does not count! We were invited to the funeral!" Magnus gave me an indignant look. "You will never be a Lejongård, do you hear? You are nothing but a servant's daughter our mother agreed to shelter! You should vanish as quickly as you can. You will *never* be one of us!" He turned on his heel and stamped away toward the manor.

I was completely taken aback. I turned to Ingmar, wondering why Magnus was so hostile and how he knew my mother had been a servant. Perhaps he'd been eavesdropping when Agneta and I were in the salon? Or had everybody known—except me?

Ingmar looked baffled. He took off after his brother. "Magnus, wait!"

I stood rooted to the ground. What had I done to the boy? Why did he want to get rid of me as soon as possible? I watched them disappear into the dusk. Only then did I walk back toward the residence. My heart was thundering.

Back in my room I discovered a tiny posy of roses on my pillow. The bed had been opened, and a glass pitcher of milky liquid stood on the bedside table. The scent of lemons hung in the air. I took no real pleasure in these things. Magnus's harsh words echoed in my mind. Of course I would never become a Lejongård, that much was obvious, but why would he ever suppose I'd want to? I'd never said anything of the kind. His mother was my guardian, so she was the one to decide where I was to live. She'd freely accepted my mother's request. If that didn't suit Magnus, if he didn't want me here, he could complain to her!

I wished I'd said exactly that. But that's how it always went: I always came up with the most apt, cutting response when it was too late. I dropped onto my bed and reached for the posy. Tied to it I found a little bag containing a delicate chocolate-dipped cookie. Did people here get one of these every evening? Surely not! But the thoughtful gesture brought a smile to my face. Magnus didn't like me, but maybe I could get used to Lion Hall anyway.

Several times that night I woke up abruptly, only to realize that the moonlight was flooding through the window into a spacious room unknown to me. I had the irrational fear the walls would close in and crush me. I wrestled with my covers and pulled them over my head, only to fling them away moments later because they were so terribly warm.

I got up finally, went to a window, and opened it. Mosquitoes might swarm in, but I needed the fresh air. The deep silence unnerved me. Stockholm was always alive with sounds—screeching cats, howling dogs, drunken men humming to themselves as they staggered down the street, and the sound of an automobile or horse-drawn cart from time to time. Here the silence was absolute. I became more and more agitated, as I always did when I was overtired and couldn't sleep. Why hadn't Mother ever told me anything? Had I known my mother at all? What was her life like when she lived here?

I couldn't remember her ever mentioning this place or even how she and Father had met. Daga had loved reciting the romantic tale of her parents' first encounter, and I'd had no such story to offer in return. When I asked Mother, she cut me off with the tart reply that it wasn't a tale fit for a child's ears.

Perhaps if I took a walk, I could tire myself enough to sleep. I wrapped myself in my morning robe, shuffled into my slippers, and stole to the bedroom door. There was no light in the corridor. The silence was oppressive. For a moment I was assailed by misgivings and thought about turning back to my room, but dark, brooding thoughts awaited me there. Outside I could brave any ghosts haunting the house. I really wished I could light a candle, but I wanted to avoid attracting attention, and I especially didn't want to answer any questions.

Fortunately, brilliant moonlight poured through the tall windows and lit my way. My ears were full of the chirping of crickets. I'd never heard them this clearly in Stockholm. In the downstairs hall I made my way past the old paintings. How often had my mother hurried through here? I imagined her carrying a tray to the salon to serve coffee. I felt a deep longing to speak to her and ask all these questions.

Her death was the reason I was here.

I hesitated beneath the great chandelier in the foyer. I could go anywhere I pleased. For example, I might go into the salon and take a look at the tropical plants and empty birdcages. But I felt drawn elsewhere.

I turned, took the narrow corridor that led to the servants' stairs, and descended to the cellar. Who in the world had come up with the notion of locating kitchens in the basement? Was it a demonstration of the difference between "upstairs" and "belowstairs"?

The odor of fresh-scrubbed pots and damp wood filled my nostrils. Moon rays filtered through small windows set high up on the wall. I went past the oven that still radiated mild heat and took a seat at the long kitchen table. Which would have been my mother's place? What stories had she told here, and what jokes had made her laugh?

Footsteps! I jumped up. A handheld lamp bobbed into sight.

"Miss Matilda, what are you looking for?" It was Lena, the maid who had arranged my hair. She wore a nightgown like mine and a brown crocheted wrap around her shoulders.

"I can't sleep," I told her, "so I thought I'd take a walk around the house."

"Milk with honey is the best thing for insomnia. I'd be happy to prepare some."

I waved away her offer. "No, but thank you very much."

Lena came closer and put her lamp on the table. "Do you want to talk? About anything?"

I stared at her. My head and heart were full of questions, but could I ask them without getting her into trouble? Surely it would be wiser to leave, but suddenly I had no control of my own mouth. "My mother . . . did you know her really well?"

The maid's expression went rigid. "Have you discussed this with the gracious lady?"

I nodded. "She told me that Mother worked here as a servant. And that she was a good one."

There was a shift in Lena's expression that I couldn't decipher. It was almost as if she didn't share her mistress's opinion. But then she said, "Very well, let's sit down. But just for a moment. You really should go back to bed." We settled at the long kitchen table with its faint odor of lemon and scrubbing powder. How long had it stood here? How many servants had gathered around it? Lena folded her hands and placed them on the tabletop. "What would you like to know?"

"What was my mother like when she was here? She never mentioned it." I stared at a glimmer of light reflecting off the floorboards. It still seemed so strange to me that my mother had hurried across this same floor.

"Well, your mother had very good reasons not to speak of it. I didn't work with her long enough to know her really well." Lena paused, appearing to search diligently through the nooks and crannies of her memory.

Then she spoke again. "I don't really have a lot to tell you, but I do remember how she received me the day I arrived. Susanna had been employed here for several years by then. She took me under her wing and showed me everything. She was a happy person, very friendly. But we had no idea that a terrible catastrophe was about to strike."

"What kind of catastrophe?"

"A fire broke out in one of the horse barns, and the gracious master and his son died. The gracious mistress took over management of the estate, and I was given the responsibility of tending to her. Susanna stood by me and helped. Over time, we almost became friends."

"And why did my mother leave?"

Lena met my gaze, an odd expression on her face. "Well, the fact is, she became pregnant and wanted to marry. When a maidservant married, she had to give up her position."

"As simple as that?"

"That was the rule in establishments like this. The gracious lady has taken a more indulgent view since then, but how on earth are we to meet an eligible man? The men visiting here are above our station, and village men prefer wives with proper dowries. In many ways your mother was really lucky."

Perhaps, but still, why hadn't she ever told me of her time here? Or how she'd met Father, if there was so little possibility a man invited here would notice her? Father had never said anything about working in the countryside. Had she encountered him on a trip to the city?

The questions burned in my mind, but I couldn't gather the energy to ask them. I felt terribly heavy and wanted to go back to bed.

Lena noticed. "It's best for you to go back upstairs and try to get a little sleep. I know it's difficult. I went through a similar time when my mother died."

"Thank you, Lena," I said and got up.

"Don't think about it so much, Miss Matilda. You're in a good place and in good hands. Surely you'll find your happiness." Lena also rose. Why had she come to the kitchen? I'd forgotten to ask.

Back in my room I stood at the window for a time. Mother had wanted me to be here, even though she'd never told me about Lion Hall. I was confused, but perhaps it was all for the best. Maybe I would get used to this place. After all, it was only for four years; then I'd be able to decide for myself.

5

Birdsong filled my ears as I sat at the desk and stared at the blank sheet of paper before me. I'd promised Daga and Paul I'd write as soon as I arrived, but the days had flown by. Soon Daga would start her job sewing for Mrs. Vagström. And Paul . . . all I could think was: four years! Four years, and I would hardly ever see my Stockholm friends.

A knock interrupted my thoughts.

"Yes?"

Ingmar appeared in the doorway. He wore a riding outfit and boots, and he was carrying a riding crop.

"Mother thinks it would be good for you to learn to ride," he said, looking around the room as if he'd never been there before. "We are on an estate, after all, and it takes a long time to walk anywhere."

I gave him a skeptical look. He'd done nothing so far to gain my confidence. I didn't like the way he looked at me, and I was just as happy not to run into him.

"I'm supposed to learn to ride? Was this really your mother's idea, or are the two of you planning to make me look ridiculous?" I narrowed my eyes, for I'd had to put up with such tricks at school. I had no desire for the twins to make a laughingstock of me in front of the stable boys.

"Why are you so suspicious?" Ingmar asked with a broad grin that made me distrust him that much more. "It is for your own good. And it would not hurt a city girl to have a horse shake up her bones a little bit."

"Oh, really?" I snapped. "I can hardly resist it when you put it that way!"

"Oh come on—unless you really are a scaredy-cat!"

I decided not to let him intimidate me. Perhaps the twins would take this as proof of my courage and leave me alone afterward.

"All right, I will."

"Really?" Ingmar sounded surprised.

"Yes, really. And I'd better not fall off and break my neck. Then you'll be in big trouble!"

Ingmar gave me a huge grin. "I promise to be careful. Besides, you would have to be awfully clumsy to fall off one of our horses, city kid!" He turned away.

"Shouldn't I change my clothes?" I asked, glancing down at my light summer dress.

"If you like," he called from the hall. "You will find me at the barn." He disappeared.

I closed the door and thought for a moment. I shrugged, opened the wardrobe, and took out my only pair of trousers. Nothing prevented a woman from choosing her attire, at least. Once I was twenty-one and independent, I could even cut my hair short if I wished.

My mother had always disapproved of "girls dressing like young men." But now appropriate attire was necessary. I didn't want to ride on one of those funny-looking sidesaddles.

Ingmar was indeed waiting for me at the horse barn. Two horses stood beside him, already saddled. Was he expecting me to spring up and ride off after him? My belly clenched in panic.

"Well, look at you! You came after all!" He surveyed me. I felt my cheeks start to flush. "Maybe you should get yourself some proper riding breeches. You might have trouble staying in the saddle in those. They look more suited to a wild night in a jazz club."

"As if you knew anything about nightclubs!" I shot back. These country people thought themselves so high and mighty that they taunted people from the city.

"Hey, we are not living on the dark side of the moon," he responded. "I know perfectly well what goes on in those clubs. In any case, none of them are places for a young lady to go unescorted."

"They're no more appropriate for a kid like you!"

"I did not claim they were!" He smiled and reached for the reins. "Ready to go?"

"I've never been on a horse before!"

Ingmar laughed aloud. "Do you actually think we want to send you out on your own? Nobody is going to just ride off. The first thing to do is to lead the horse around, then allow it to follow you. That way it gets used to you and you will be able to guide it."

Of course. I felt foolish. But I was still a little frightened of the massive animal. Maybe it would be better out in the meadow.

"All right, pay attention. No time to waste!" Ingmar pressed the lead into my hand. The horse didn't react, but I tensed up.

"Berta is a very calm mare. She will never nip you or throw you. Everyone here on the estate learns how to ride with Berta."

I looked at the horse chewing on its bit. "What do I do?"

"Just get started," Ingmar responded. "Like this." He took a step forward, and his horse followed.

I looked a bit skeptically at the animal, then also took a step. The mare followed as if that was exactly what she'd been waiting for. "It's working!" I cried.

"What did you expect? That she would stand there like a donkey? Now we guide them to the circle."

We moved away from the stall and walked toward the enclosed area of the paddock I'd seen a few days earlier. A man was waiting for us there.

"This is Olaf Blom, our riding instructor. He will teach you how to get into the saddle."

"An instructor?"

Ingmar didn't reply, just waved to the instructor. Blom was trim and muscular. I was sure he could control any restless animal.

"Happy to meet you, Miss Matilda. Ingmar told me you're from a city."

"From Stockholm," I answered uneasily.

"People don't see many riders there anymore, do they?" Blom's smile was friendly, and he addressed me with a warmth I hadn't often experienced.

"No, people there prefer automobiles," I answered.

"In the country, however, one frequently needs to travel on horse-back. The gracious lady was hoping you would learn to ride." So Ingmar hadn't been lying. "Are we ready?"

The instructor went to the horse, put his hands on the saddle horn, placed his left leg in the stirrup, straightened it to lever himself up, and swung his right leg across the horse's back. He made it look smooth and easy—nothing at all to fear. I suspected I wouldn't be nearly as graceful. My stomach clenched.

I looked toward Ingmar. He was watching closely, and he'd probably be quick to inform his brother if I hesitated or made a mistake.

Blom dismounted. "Would you like to try?"

I nodded, terrified. I stepped toward the horse, and it swung its head to look at me. I jumped back and heard Ingmar laugh.

"No reason to be scared, city kid. Old Berta is not going to eat you!"

I gave him an angry look, which just added to his amusement.

"Don't worry," the instructor said, his voice soothing. "It's important not to feel frightened. Horses sense their riders' emotions. If the animal thinks there's danger, it might shy away. Breathe deeply and steadily to calm your nerves. The horse isn't your enemy."

No, I thought, *my adversary is the young man behind me.* But I did as Mr. Blom asked. I slowly reached out to the horse. She shied away a step, then stood quiet. I grasped the saddle horn with both hands and realized I was holding my breath.

I let it out and took another deep breath, felt the leather under my palms, caught the scent of the horse's hide, and lifted a foot to the stirrup.

"Left foot, not right!" Ingmar called and ended the brief moment I thought I was doing it correctly. I pulled back, and so did the horse, and before I could free my right foot from the stirrup, I was lying facedown on the ground.

The riding master came to me instantly, freed my foot, and helped me up. I spat out sand and tears surged into my eyes.

"Are you hurt?" Blom asked. I shook my head.

"That happens to every beginner," he said, helping me up. "But only once."

I brushed the dirt from my clothes and raised my chin high. I was holding Ingmar responsible. Now he'd have a story to tell his brother! Furious, I wiped the dust and tears from my face and turned my back to him. I wasn't going to give him the chance to gloat. I grasped the saddle horn again, put my left foot in the stirrup this time, and swung up. An instant later I found myself in the saddle, surprised by my own daring. The horse seemed equally impressed, for she didn't budge. I breathed deep and looked around.

Mr. Blom stood there watching, hands on his hips, evidently surprised. A grin broke across his face. "Well done! Not everyone who suffers such a tumble is willing to get back up immediately."

"I refuse to give up," I declared and glared at Ingmar. "I'm not going to be stopped by one little mistake. I've been through worse."

Ingmar, still smiling, nodded his appreciation.

"All right, then, let's see if we can get you back down," Blom said. "And then we'll try it with the lead."

We practiced mounting and dismounting, and I began feeling somewhat more confident. My movements weren't as elegant as the instructor's, but I gradually overcame my apprehension. When I was more or less at ease in the saddle, he began leading the mare on a long leather leash. I had almost nothing to do, other than to hold on tight and heed Blom's instructions to sway in time with Berta's movements. I was intimidated by the beast's power but also fascinated. And I admired Berta's calm as she paced around and around and out through the gate.

When I finally dismounted, my legs were trembling, and for a moment I thought the ground beneath my feet was giving way. I clung to the fence and took deep breaths, not from nervousness this time but instead to control my exhilaration. What an experience! Ingmar would probably laugh himself silly, but I felt fully aware of my own body for the very first time.

He came over with a smile on his face. "So, then—not so bad, was it?"

"No, it wasn't." I returned his smile, and for a moment I forgot I'd been annoyed with him.

"You were really impressive when you went right back at Berta, mad as hell, and swung yourself up into the saddle. I thought city girls were weaklings."

I grimaced. "How many city girls do you even know?"

"A few from Kristianstad," he replied. "We see them all the time at the young ladies' school next door. Not one of them has your determination."

"See? You don't really know me."

"True! But we can change that, right?" He winked. "How about coming on a jaunt?"

"Where to?"

"I thought I would take a ride through the fields."

"You saw I'm not ready to ride."

"No need for you to be the rider. I will take you with me."

I had immediate doubts. Ingmar wanted me to ride behind him? "Why? So you can dump me somewhere?"

Ingmar's expression darkened. "You should not always assume the worst! The fact that my brother cannot stand you does not mean that I share his sentiments."

"Can't stand me, huh? Is that what he told you? What a surprise!"

"My brother cannot stand most new faces. Do not let it bother you." We stood looking at one another for a moment. "Well? Are you coming? The sun will be up for a while longer, but you know Mother wants us spic-and-span for dinner by eight o'clock."

"Fine, but you're going to be in real trouble if anything bad happens. It wouldn't be the first time I beat up a man."

Ingmar laughed again. "I must ask you to tell me all about that first time." He took me by the hand and drew me with him.

He climbed up into the saddle, and before I could ask where to go, he'd already pulled me up. I landed on the horse's back, just behind the saddle, and though I was afraid I'd slide off, he cried, "Hold on tight!" and set the horse in motion. His mount seemed much stronger than the even-tempered Berta and certainly was less placid.

I clutched Ingmar's waist as he urged the horse onward and cantered across the pasture. At first I was sure I was going to fall, but then I felt the wind in my hair and against my skin as Ingmar urged his mount into a gallop. A quiver of excitement spread through me and became joyous exultation.

We rode past a herd of horses grazing under wide-spreading shade trees and then along a field where a farmhand was harvesting wheat with two mowing machines, each drawn by a team of ten horses. The air was full of dust and the smell of new-mown grain. Ingmar stopped the horse so we could watch.

"We have tractors that can pull the threshing machines, but in some places—for example, here along the edge of the field—the horses do a better job," he told me. "My father converted the harvest at Ekberg to a completely mechanical operation. They can reap the fields there much more quickly."

"Those machines must be terribly expensive," I speculated, for I'd never before seen such huge contraptions in a field.

"Oh yes! We import the tractors from America, and our newest hay baler is German. They cost a fortune, but they are efficient in fields like these, so you recoup the investment quickly." There was pride in his voice. "Ordinary farmers cannot afford threshing machines, so often we harvest their fields for them. For a very small charge, of course. But I am certain the prices of these machines will drop. Then all the larger farms will be able to afford them."

We watched the harvesting for a while and listened to farmhands shouting to one another. Then we rode on, along a country road that wound through bushes and meadows. Some of the scattered trees were split and splintered as if struck by lightning.

At last we reached the edge of the forest. The land there was wilder, with tall grass and dead scrub. Just inside the woods stood a cabin with a roof completely overgrown with moss. The shutters were closed; the walls were dark and weather-beaten.

"What's that?" I asked Ingmar.

"That cabin is our property," he told me. "You should get down."

"What?"

"From the horse."

"You want to stop here?" I shuddered, and the fine hairs along my arm rose in apprehension.

"Yes. I want to show you something."

"I don't know if I want to see it," I said hesitantly. "Besides, I don't know how to get off."

"Just jump!" Ingmar snorted. "No reason to worry, nothing will happen to you here. This is the old cabin of our former estate manager. Nobody has lived there for a long, long time, and I enjoy the peace and quiet."

He swung one leg over the horse's neck and slid off. Ingmar reached up to me. "Jump! I will catch you."

The horse shifted its weight uneasily from one leg to the other. Before it could get the idea of running away, I let myself slide backward. Ingmar grabbed me. I was surprised at how strong he was.

"There, you see? Easy!" He put me down. "Not the most elegant maneuver, but you will learn. After all, nobody expects a city girl to know how to ride bareback."

"Can you ride bareback?" I asked and freed myself. His proximity and embrace might have been more agreeable if he weren't always teasing me.

"Of course! I tried it as soon as I felt ready. But it is not for everyone; Magnus cannot do it either. He is the real scaredy-cat." He grinned and offered me his hand. "So what do you say? Are you coming?"

I looked at the cabin. It still seemed threatening. But Ingmar had just called his brother a scaredy-cat, and I didn't want to be labeled the same way. I went first, without taking his hand. "All right, then, let's take a look at your house of horrors." Out of the corner of my eye I saw his delighted grin.

He hitched the horse to a twisted old apple tree, caught up, and led me through the bushes. The narrow footpath wasn't obvious from where we'd left the horse, but Ingmar probably could have trod it in his sleep. Thistles and twigs scraped my legs. The building looked even more intimidating close up.

"Just a minute," Ingmar said. He went up the steps, took a key from his pocket, unlocked the door, and pushed it open.

"It's black as the pit in there," I objected.

Ingmar give me a look and reached just inside the door. The interior immediately flooded with light. The front room was furnished with an old table, a chair, and a sideboard. "It looks abandoned, but we had electricity installed. It's a sort of retreat for Magnus and me."

"Where did you get the key?"

"From the keyboard in the kitchen. Mother has no reason to hide it."

"And why did she warn us against coming here?"

"Because she did not want you to break your neck riding across difficult terrain. And the cabin is not exactly one of her favorite places."

"She seems to have no use for it," I replied. My curiosity was piqued, but I didn't want him to see that.

"Right, and managing the estate takes up practically all of her time. Father helps, but he also has to deal with his own properties. Aunt Lisbeth lives on the Ekberg estate, of course, and tends to day-to-day business, but Father is constantly having to travel back and forth between Lion Hall and Ekberg. It's a long way."

"Doesn't that get to be a terrible chore?"

Ingmar laughed. "Yes, of course. Mother is always complaining about it. She would like nothing better than for him to be here all the time. Frankly, it is embarrassing, the way those two carry on like newlyweds."

I was glad I hadn't had to witness that. The count and countess had been very affectionate when I was in the room, but they'd been entirely correct.

"Anyhow, the cabin is a great place for peace and quiet. Magnus often comes here to read and get away from me. Just imagine: I get on his nerves! His very own twin!"

I was tempted to comment that his brother struck me as weird, but I held that back.

"Do you want to go inside or not? Maybe you too need a place where you can be alone sometimes."

"Magnus would certainly object."

"Oh, Magnus objects to everything. He has a lot of trouble getting used to any change. But the rule here is that the cabin belongs to whoever has the key. After all, you can lock the door from the inside too." He beckoned to me and disappeared inside. I steeled myself and followed.

The interior was astonishingly clean. The front room was a combined living room and kitchen, and through a doorway to the adjacent room, I saw the shape of a bed. A proper residence! I'd never have suspected such a thing, given its shabby exterior. "It looks really comfortable."

"It is. You hear nothing out here except a bird or two. And the woods owls at night."

"You sneak out here at night?"

"Often! In summer, like now, it is really pleasant, and the air is cooler than in the manor house. In winter you can light the oven."

"Oh, then I'll come here all the time in winter," I joked.

The place was certainly tidy and comfortable, but I didn't like the fact that it was so isolated. I'd always been surrounded by people in the city. Out here if you ran into an ax murderer, they'd never find your body.

"Let's ride back," I said.

"So soon? I thought we'd sit down and talk."

"We can talk on the way back if you want. Besides, what would I have to say?"

"Oh, something about yourself. Your childhood. Your favorite color, even!"

"You're not really interested in that, are you? Anyway, you know how I grew up. In a house on a steep street, daughter of a bookkeeper and his wife—who, as I've just found out, was employed here as a servant once upon a time. I have nothing else to offer. Not even a family tree, like the one you certainly have."

Ingmar nodded. "That's true, we do. A family of warriors and feudal lords. Pretty boring."

"Lots of people would think differently."

"Sure, but they do not understand how meaningless all this splendor is. I often wonder what it would be like to live in an ordinary house. Without all those curlicues and silk carpets."

"You'd find your room pretty bare," I laughed. Why would someone who already had everything want a simple life? After all, he wasn't locked up here!

"Well, maybe I will try it one day. When I go to university, for example."

"You want to study?"

"I do. I have to. These days it is not enough just to inherit an estate. You have to know all about agriculture. Father's will makes me heir to the Ekberg estate, and Magnus will get Lion Hall. Magnus gets to study veterinary science or horse breeding, and I will become an expert on raising grain. It is just that simple."

"Sounds like this was decided a long time ago." I brushed my fingertips across the tabletop, which was rough to the touch. I tried to imagine Ingmar sitting here. What did he do? Read? Dream about his future?

"Yes, all that was probably decided right after we were born."

"And is it what you want?"

"It is. I can hardly imagine anything better than spending my days in the fields and the forests. But Magnus . . . well, he has no particular affinity for horses. I think they disgust him a bit, actually."

"Why? Because they're too tame?"

"No! Because they bite and sometimes they bolt. Magnus was thrown from a horse once when he was young. There was a huge to-do, and the doctor had to be called in because his head was badly injured. I was so scared for him I almost went crazy."

If I hadn't already met Magnus, I'd have expressed sympathy, but given the circumstances, I had nothing to say. "I guess he has no other choice, so he'll accept the estate."

"Correct: no alternative at all, even if Mother were to have another child. Magnus is the heir to Lion Hall, I inherit the Ekberg property. Thus was it decreed, practically chiseled in stone."

"In stone?"

"Oh, there must be a stone tablet somewhere." Ingmar laughed, but I had a notion the arrangements didn't please him quite as much as he was pretending. "Very well, we will go back if you want. I have to check on Magnus and make sure he doesn't get lost in his reading. Even though he would prefer just that."

I followed Ingmar outside.

"How about changing places?" he proposed. "You in the saddle and me behind?"

"I don't know how to guide the horse!"

"I will take the reins. This way I will not have to worry about you sliding off his rear."

I gave him a dubious look. "All right, I'll try. But if he runs off, it's your fault!"

"Shooting Star will not bolt. My mother adored his father, Evening Star, and with good reason. He was one of the best stallions in our stud."

"A horse named Shooting Star?"

"Yes—why not?"

I raised my eyebrows. I hadn't expected a name like that.

"You can get up in the saddle, right?"

I grabbed the saddle horn, put my foot in the stirrup, and mounted. A moment later Ingmar was seated behind with no help from me.

Having him so close unnerved me for a moment, but then he reached around for the reins, and we were off.

He took a different path across the fields, and for a moment I thought I was going to shake loose from the saddle. That was irrational, of course, because Ingmar had his arms securely around me. His embrace bothered me so much initially that I couldn't enjoy our return ride. But once we reached a level path, it was better. I tried my best to stay in rhythm with the horse and just about got the hang of it. I even forgot for a moment that Ingmar was behind me. I enjoyed the breeze in my face and hair and relaxed a bit for the first time in quite a while.

When we rode up to the barns, Magnus was standing outside. He was astonished to see me. Ingmar jumped down and held Shooting Star's reins as I dismounted.

"Where were you two?" Magnus wanted to know.

"I showed Matilda the old estate manager's cabin. You do not mind if she visits there from time to time, do you?"

Magnus gave me a surly look, turned his back, and walked away.

"Obviously, he does," I murmured. Ingmar stood there looking embarrassed. "Never mind, I won't go snooping," I declared and arranged my clothing. "Thanks for the excursion!"

"Glad you came," he replied, though he did seem dismayed.

His brother would probably lecture him, but I didn't care. I had no desire to push my way into their precious kingdom. I could hole up in my own room anytime I wanted.

6

I got up the next morning brimming with confidence. I'd had another restless night, but this time the reason was different. As friendly as Ingmar had been to me the previous day, I could scarcely expect him to invite me on another excursion across the fields right away. I was looking forward to the day I'd be able to ride a horse without help. Then I could explore the region and stay out of sourpuss Magnus's way. He'd brooded throughout dinner the previous evening as Ingmar and I chattered about lessons and our promenade. Whenever Agneta addressed Magnus, he replied with a single syllable.

I went to my bath, pleased to be able to wash away the sticky heat of the night. Afterward, I braided my damp hair to control its unruly curls. Paul liked it that way best of all. He said it made me look like an angel. The thought of him warmed my heart. That's why I decided to wear one of my most beautiful summer frocks to breakfast.

I opened the wardrobe and couldn't believe my eyes. My clothes were gone! The space held only a few clothes hangers, on one of which was draped something in black fabric. I was so shocked, I couldn't move. Where were all my things?

I hurried to my bureau and opened the underwear drawer. Fortunately, nothing there had been touched. But I couldn't possibly turn up to breakfast in my shift!

My pulse thundered, and I could hardly breathe. Could the servants have removed my clothes? But why? Or was this a stupid practical joke?

I turned around and focused on the wardrobe. The thing hanging there looked like a mourning dress. I reached out.

The garment was stiff and musty. I pulled it down and stepped back in horror. It was a housemaid's uniform!

I dropped it and felt as if someone had just slapped my face. My first instinct was to howl in despair, but tears wouldn't come.

I staggered back to my bed and sat on the edge, my eyes still fixed on the repulsive black thing on the floor of the wardrobe. Time seemed to stop.

The knot loosened at last, and I burst into tears. Rage flamed within me, far fiercer than the anger I'd felt when bullied in school. This wasn't an insult to me; it was an affront to my mother. I was sure the twins were behind it.

I collapsed sobbing on the bed, so distraught I didn't hear someone enter my room.

"Gracious miss?" called a delicate voice. "What is wrong?"

I opened my swollen lids and recognized Rika, the girl who took care of my room.

I sat up and again saw the wardrobe standing wide open, the crumpled black uniform inside. "My clothes have vanished!"

Rika followed my gaze. "Perhaps they're in the laundry? I'll go downstairs and look."

"Don't!" I cried. She stopped, stunned, and gave me a bewildered look. "Leave everything just as it is!"

I knew what I had to do.

"I could bring you something from the laundry—"

"Later!" I snapped and stormed into the bathroom.

"But . . ."

I wrapped my bathrobe around me and marched out of the room. If I got my hands on the culprits, I'd tear their hair out!

I raced downstairs. A maid carrying a coffee service through the hall pulled back in shock.

"Sorry!" I cried, but didn't stop.

Agneta and her sons were already at the table, but breakfast hadn't yet begun. Their cups were empty—too bad! I'd have been pleased to drench Ingmar and Magnus with coffee. "Good morning," I said and went straight to the boys. Ingmar's expression was astonished, but Magnus was having trouble suppressing a laugh. I loomed over him. "Where are my clothes?"

"How should I know?" Magnus asked. He avoided my eyes.

"You know perfectly well! And you also know how that servant's uniform got into my wardrobe!"

I felt a hand on my arm. "Matilda, please come with me!"

I was tempted to smack the grin off Magnus's face, but I obeyed. The countess led me to the salon.

"What has happened? Why are you not dressed?"

"My clothes disappeared!" I told her. "There's a moldy servant's uniform hanging in my wardrobe instead."

Agneta was at a loss. "But who can have done such a thing?"

"I'm sure it was Magnus." My heart hammered in my throat. "He can't stand me!"

"He has told me nothing of the sort."

I managed not to roll my eyes. Of course she wouldn't think her darling boy would do such a thing. I saw the whole plan now: Ingmar persuaded me to go riding, tempting me away from my room so Magnus could carry out his despicable plan. I hadn't looked in my wardrobe the day before, because the maid had already laid out my evening things.

"Is he obliged to notify you he hates me?"

"Now, now," Agneta said. "It cannot be as bad as that." She thought for a moment. "We will go to your room so I can see for myself."

"You don't believe me?" I cried.

"I do believe you, and I want to see it with my own eyes."

She encouraged me with a smile and went first. I followed. I could barely contain my indignation, but I said nothing. If the countess wanted to see what her son was capable of, I was more than glad to show her.

When I yanked my bedroom door open, the ancient uniform had been returned to the hanger in the open wardrobe. Agneta followed me into my room and carefully shut the door behind us. After a long moment, she sighed and settled on a chair.

"Matilda," she said gently. "I am very sorry this happened."

"Magnus overheard us," I said, feeling my rage ebbing and leaving me strangely numb. "He must have heard you say my mother was a servant."

"Not necessarily," Agneta replied. "Your mother . . . Many of the employees knew her. Perhaps he heard it from someone else."

A dark void descended upon me. Were there others here who wanted to humiliate me? Who knew what other vileness people were capable of?

"And he despises servants?" I exclaimed bitterly.

"Our household staff are important members of our household. No, I do not think that is it. It was probably intended as a stupid joke, that is all. If Magnus was responsible."

Could she doubt it?

"I will speak to him," the countess said at last. "No one has the right to attack or demean you. You are under my protection, and I will see that you are treated as a member of this family." She got up. "I will have Lena bring you something to wear. And, if you like, your breakfast."

I nodded. "Please."

Agneta gave me a wan smile and left the room.

I bowed my head and stared at my hands. I'd been here for just over a week. I'd known that Magnus didn't like me, but hadn't imagined he would try anything. Would Magnus snoop through my letters when I wasn't in my room? Should I lock my door from now on?

After eating breakfast, I did exactly that. Magnus wasn't going to have the opportunity to poke through my things.

Lena had brought me a lovely summer dress, probably belonging to the countess, and she'd assured me that all my things would be back in place no later than the following morning. They'd apparently been dumped in the laundry basket for used sheets and stained tablecloths. I was still furious, but Lena sought to console me.

"A servant's uniform is honorable attire. You have no idea how proud I was to be hired here." She'd been taken on at a very young age and had participated in all the ups and downs of the estate. Lena had worked at Lion Hall for eighteen years and hadn't regretted a moment. Her kindness and friendly assurances calmed me somewhat.

Even so, I was not looking forward to encountering either Magnus or Ingmar as I walked from the mansion to the barns.

"Matilda!" someone called behind me. My heartbeat accelerated, and so did my steps. More than anything, I wanted to run away from Lion Hall. "Matilda, just wait a minute!"

I didn't slow down, but Ingmar quickly caught up and blocked my way. "Just stop for a minute! I must speak to you!"

"Why?" I stepped around him.

"Because I had nothing to do with it, I swear!"

"You can swear all you want," I snapped and kept moving. "I don't believe a word you say! You distracted me by taking me out riding, so your brother could steal my things. I should have known!"

I hurried away, but it was no use. He was there again in a second and grabbed my arm.

"Let me go!" I snapped.

He did. "We should talk! Please!"

I pressed my lips into a tight line. What I really wanted was to tell him to go to hell. But his desperation looked real, so I gave him a chance. "Well?"

"I swear I had nothing to do with it. Mother asked me to take you riding. She will confirm that, if you want!"

I wasn't buying it.

"If my brother did it, I apologize. But you have to believe it was *not* my idea. I did not know he was planning anything."

Magnus and Ingmar were twins, and as far as I knew, twins were supposed to be closer than even married couples are. And Ingmar claimed he hadn't known? "Has he told you how much he hates my mother?"

"No. He has never said a word about your mother."

"No? Then why does he insult her by rubbing my nose in her past as a housemaid, using a dirty uniform to make it seem it was dishonorable?"

Ingmar raised his hands helplessly. "Lots of times I do not understand him. We are twins, but we are not the same person. I cannot read his thoughts. If I could, I would have stopped him, I promise you."

I wanted to believe him, but could I? Could I trust him?

"Neither of you has ever lost anything!" I cried. "You two silver-spoon babies see all this as funny, right? The poor orphan child was taken in by the rich countess and now you're stuck with her." Though Ingmar had apologized, I still wanted to grab him by the collar and give him a good shaking. "Stockholm was my home! I had to uproot myself to come here. As soon as I can legally make my own decisions, you'll be rid of me. For now, just leave me alone!"

I glared at him for a moment more, then turned away. I stamped away in the direction of the estate's main gate, my hands clenched into fists.

I wandered aimlessly for a long time. I didn't know where to go, but I was certain I didn't want to stay on this estate. I was scheduled for a riding lesson with Mr. Blom in the afternoon, and I refused to return to the manor until after that.

Finally, I walked to the village Agneta had briefly shown me. It was idyllic, practically a scene from a picture postcard. Some houses were painted red, others blue. Each had a lush front garden with flowers. I saw towering sunflowers, mallows, lupine, and roses. I hadn't really noticed the flowers before, but now I was fascinated by them, as well as by the prevailing calm. The village was so still I heard honeybees buzzing. The air was heavy with the scents of harvested wheat and drifting pollen.

A sudden move brought me out of my contemplation. A tabby cat had leaped up on a fence and was studying me. "Hello, kitty!" I called. "Hope I'm not bothering you!" The cat yawned and then sprang down. I stood spellbound. It came directly to me and rubbed against my leg. I hesitated, then bent down and patted it. The tabby pressed its head against my palm as if seeking a caress. It licked my fingers with its rough tongue and started purring.

"Susanna?" asked a voice behind me. I stiffened. I'd been so enchanted by the cat that I hadn't heard anyone approach.

I turned and saw an old man in the street. He seemed a little lost. His jacket was torn, and the knees of his trousers were worn through. He looked about seventy years old. His mustache was gray, with yellow stains; he was probably a heavy smoker. His eyes were an intense but watery blue. He tilted his head to one side, squinted, and peered at me.

"Excuse me," I said, "is this your cat?"

He didn't answer. His lips quivered, but he didn't say a word.

I found this terribly spooky. Why had he called me by my mother's name? Had he mistaken me for her? That was conceivable. After all, as a servant on the estate, she certainly must have visited the village.

"I'm sorry, but I'm not Susanna," I replied. The man stood rooted there. "I—"

I almost gave him my real name and mentioned Lion Hall, but something stopped me. I slowly backed away, and the cat scrambled to one side, surprised. I whirled about and fled. Was the confused old man going to follow me? I ran to the end of the street and looked back.

He hadn't budged. I took a deep breath and tried to calm myself. My heart was racing. I resembled my mother, but no one had ever mistaken me for her. And besides, I was seventeen, and she'd been gone from here almost twenty years. Surely he must realize Susanna would be older now.

At last I set off toward the estate.

The specter of that man haunted me all the way back. How pitiful he'd looked! Wasn't there anyone who could have mended his jacket? Was he so poor that he couldn't even afford a proper pair of trousers? Who was he, anyway?

My fear of him seemed more ridiculous with every step I took. Instead of panicking and running away, I should have told him my mother was named Susanna. Maybe I'd have learned something. Mother might have been concealing a whole host of secrets.

But I wasn't willing to turn back. My wristwatch, the last gift from my father, said 1:10 p.m. My riding lesson was in three hours. If Ingmar happened to turn up, I would simply ignore him.

I reached the gate of Lion Hall and continued to the manor. A couple of young stable hands were sitting in the shade under a tree, talking during the midday break. I greeted them, not knowing if they'd heard my angry words with Ingmar. Lena came rushing out as I climbed the front steps.

"Where were you? We've been looking for you everywhere!"

Why? I almost asked. But I said nothing. What had happened?

"Come. I'll take you to them."

"What is it?" I was suddenly seized with fear. What now? The thought of Paul fell upon me in a hot rush. Had something happened to him? Or to Daga? They were the only ones who knew where I was living now . . .

My heart hammered as I followed Lena to a small room next to the office. Agneta had told me that she was in the habit of receiving her business clients here, where the atmosphere was a bit more relaxed. Still life paintings and landscapes decorated the walls. Instead of intimidating bookshelves loaded with heavy ledgers, the room was furnished with comfortable upholstered armchairs and a bright carpet. The decoration was mostly in hues of blue.

I took one of the chairs until Lena left, and then I jumped up and began pacing. I knitted my ice-cold hands together as my thoughts ran in circles. Since Mother's death, I'd had constant premonitions of other undefined disasters.

After a while I heard a door shut in the other room. I returned to the armchair and folded my clammy hands in my lap. Why hadn't the countess come in? The seconds dragged. Was she trying to decide how to break some really bad news? Seconds later I heard the door open again.

"You wanted to speak to me, Mother?"

I went rigid at the sound of his voice. I wasn't sure I could tell Ingmar and Magnus apart by their appearance, but their voices were unmistakable. Ingmar tended to speak in a rush, while Magnus's pace was quite measured.

"Sit down," the countess told him in a chilly voice.

Magnus must have done so, for she went on, "You doubtless know why I called you here."

"I have an idea of it." Magnus's tone didn't betray any apprehension or shame. He was as calm as if his mother were simply inquiring about his homework. I was tempted to get up and peep through the keyhole.

Why had she called him in? And why was I stationed here on the other side of the door?

"To be entirely frank, I am not quite sure where I should begin," I heard the countess say. "I am asking myself if I was explicit enough when I announced that we would be receiving a new family member."

"She is not a family member," Magnus declared. "She is a house-maid's daughter."

"And I have accepted legal responsibility for her as my ward. You are a clever young man, Magnus. You know what a ward is, I think?"

He didn't reply, but his words had already jolted me. Why did they hurt my feelings so? A servant's duties imply no disgrace; they are no reason to feel shame. Many young women who begin as servants go on to work at a profession. My mother had married a bookkeeper, moved to Stockholm, and become an urban matron. We owned our house.

But Magnus's contempt and disdain offended me. The maid's uniform he'd hung in my wardrobe was an emblem of everything my mother had left behind when she quit the estate.

I felt a terrific urge to intrude and tell him and the countess exactly that. But it appeared I'd been placed in the adjacent room so I could overhear their meeting. I scarcely dared to breathe.

"Matilda has been formally given into my care. And it does not matter in the least who her mother was. There is nothing dishonorable about a career as a servant, nothing at all. And when a serving girl manages to build a life for herself, as Matilda's mother did, she deserves praise, not scorn."

I tried to imagine the expression on Magnus's face. It was probably a dark look, but he wouldn't dare to sneer at her the way he did at me.

"You are extremely privileged, a status you should never forget. Your life could have been quite different. You will inherit this estate, but that should never mislead you into looking down upon those who work here. These people are important to our family, and one day they will be important to you. I have no intention of putting this property into the hands of a man who does not understand that privileges entail responsibilities. Your obligation is to serve. We serve the king, and we also serve our people. We are their points of contact, their employers, and their examples. Never forget that; never harden your heart against those you make the mistake of seeing as less than yourself."

"But—"

Agneta cut off his objection, either with a look or a gesture. "There is no 'but,'" she said. "Now tell me what displeases you so about Matilda."

I held my breath. Here it came.

"She does not belong here. She is from the city."

"I once lived in the city myself. Furthermore, I have not heard her complain at any time. She asks for no special favors and has settled well into our home. Has she insulted or injured you in any way?"

"You mean other than by the mere fact that she is here?"

"Magnus!" His name echoed like a slap. "Either present me with rational arguments or hold your tongue! What do you have to say?"

"I simply cannot stand her. Sooner or later she is going to try to come between me and Ingmar. I see already that you like her more than me."

"That is absurd," Agneta responded. Her voice was calmer than before, but I suspected she was still struggling to control herself. "I treat her as I treat the two of you. I give preferential treatment to no one. You know that."

Magnus muttered something I couldn't make out. The countess must have heard, however, for she said, "Very well, Magnus, since it appears that rational discussion is useless, let me conclude with this. I expect you to refrain from making Matilda the butt of your derision, whether you like her or not. If you should prove guilty of anything similar in the future, I will send you away to boarding school. Without your brother."

"You cannot. You would not!"

"If I should learn that you put your hands on Matilda's personal property or humiliate her in any way, I will send you away to learn some manners. It has become evident that I am unable to instill them in you. Come what may, if you offend a second time, I will turn you over to sterner tutors. The choice is yours. Behave properly, and everything will remain as it is. Otherwise, I will make certain that my failures with you are remedied."

A silence followed. I took a deep breath and realized I was trembling. From school I knew that those sorts of threats were of little use when an antagonist was determined to hurt someone. The bully would just try a different tactic. That was exactly what I feared: sooner or later Magnus would avenge this scolding by taking action against me.

"Do you understand me?"

"Yes, Mother," Magnus said in an offended tone.

Both were silent.

"Very well. You may go."

I heard a chair scrape against the floorboards. A door opened and closed.

I collapsed back against my chair. My pounding heart almost choked me. I couldn't believe what I'd just heard. At the same time I wondered why the countess had set me up to hear the interrogation. To make sure I would believe her?

After a while the door opened. I shot to my feet.

"Calm yourself and sit down," the countess said. She shut the door behind her and took the chair across from me. "You were wondering why Lena brought you into this room, I expect?"

I nodded.

"I am not in the habit of reprimanding a family member in the presence of others," she began, folding her hands in her lap. "We handle things face-to-face. But in this case I wanted you to hear it. I wanted to make sure you do not feel unprotected. I meant exactly what I said to Magnus. You are part of our family, and he has no right to humiliate you."

"I do appreciate that," I croaked, wishing I felt reassured.

Agneta looked at me for a while, then she added, "I am sure that Magnus will get used to you eventually. He always has difficulty dealing with change."

She fell silent and seemed lost in thought. I wondered what Magnus had done in the past. Had he tormented some newly employed housemaid? Hidden her clothes? Scolded her? Maybe his fall from the horse had left scars deeper than the gash on his head.

"I am certain he will heed my words."

"Would you really send him away to school?"

"The truth is, it would almost break my heart," Agneta replied with a doleful little smile. "But my heart also breaks to see you plagued unjustly. I will make sure it does not happen again. Agreed?"

I nodded, but I couldn't escape the impression that Magnus would merely bide his time and find another way to get at me. After all, I couldn't hide from him for four years, unless I withdrew to live a hermit's life in that horrible cabin in the woods.

Agneta took my hand. Her fingers were warm, while mine seemed like slivers of ice.

"You are welcome here with us, never forget that. I made a promise to your mother, and I will keep it. I regret that Magnus has taken an antipathy to you, but perhaps eventually he will change his mind."

"If I were to intrude between him and his brother—" I said unhappily.

"That is nonsense, an invented pretext! I know my son well. He often takes an arbitrary dislike to things without knowing why. He was that way even as an infant. Ingmar was always the more outgoing of the two. He takes everything with a grain of salt and a joke, and he does his best to engage with other people. That is why I gave him the assignment of accompanying you to your riding lesson."

I recalled the wind in my hair as we'd gone out to the cabin on horseback. If it hadn't been for Magnus, I'd probably be looking forward to the afternoon's lesson.

"Good. Then I will leave you in peace." Agneta rose. "Do not hesitate to tell me if Magnus does anything else to offend you."

I nodded, but I already knew that, the next time something happened, I'd take direct action against him. I couldn't rely on the countess to stand up for me for four years. I'd defended myself in school too, with blows when necessary. If Magnus bullied me again, he would pay for it.

"Thank you," I told her with a pained smile. "I really do appreciate your support."

"You will always have it." She returned to her office.

I let a few moments pass in silence before I stepped out. As I walked down the hall, I sensed a movement in the shadows. Had Magnus been eavesdropping? I clenched my fists and breathed deep.

Four years, I told myself. *I can get through them!*

7

The weather turned cool, making me sorely miss Stockholm. I often sat at the window and stared out across the garden with its graceful little pavilion far in the back. Did they ever hold parties there, like in novels?

I'd heard about a huge annual celebration at midsummer, a fall hunt, and a ceremony for Saint Lucia's Day in December. Christmas and birthdays were observed on a much smaller scale, which I found comforting. Perhaps I could invite Daga and Paul to my birthday in November.

One compensation for staying inside more was that I saw Magnus only at mealtimes. I tensed up every time, even though he usually acted as if I weren't there. He never spoke to me. Agneta's face darkened when he ignored me at the dinner table, but he didn't do anything else, so she said nothing.

My relationship with Ingmar wasn't the same as on the day we rode out together. He attended my riding lessons for a while, but when I steadfastly ignored him, he eventually gave up. I wanted to make sure Magnus had no reason to feel jealous, so I saw Ingmar only at meals as well.

Fortunately, I received a steady stream of letters from Daga and Paul. My girlfriend described her first days of work for the seamstress. Once her employer saw how nimble her fingers were, she regularly gave Daga small tasks and occasionally allowed her to take a couple of bolt ends home. Daga sewed pillowcases and table runners with them, and she used some of the larger pieces to make clothes for herself. She promised to make me a scarf as soon as she had the right material. I was happy to hear how enthusiastically she'd plunged into her work. To tell the truth, I was even a little envious. She would soon have a very clear idea of where life was taking her. Maybe she'd set up her own workshop; perhaps she'd even open a boutique. Her future seemed wide open.

As for me, I had business college to look forward to, but also long years of guardianship. Paul and I schemed about how best to endure our separation, but came up with nothing better than simply waiting it out. Paul admitted that he went by my house from time to time, almost as if looking for me there.

I know it's childish, he wrote. *But it makes me feel close to you. And besides, someone has to keep an eye on your property.*

His words infused me with agreeable warmth. My future was wide open too—in my dreams, at least.

I was due to start at Kristianstad Business College on an overcast day. Raindrops splattered against the dining room panes and ran down in long, blurry streaks.

At breakfast the maids delivered a tin lunch box to the table for each of us. Classes ran well into the afternoon, both in the business school and the boys' high school.

"Mind your manners and take advantage of your education," the countess advised us. "And watch out for yourselves!"

"Watch out for what?" Ingmar grumbled. "It is only school."

Agneta nodded, and before the boys could resist, she embraced them and kissed their cheeks. She turned and hugged me as well. "Good luck on your first day. I can hardly wait to hear how you like it."

My cheeks flushed. Somehow it seemed painful to be hugged in the presence of the boys, especially given that Magnus resented me so. But her gesture was so spontaneous and warm that tears filled my eyes— tears because I was moved, but tears of mourning as well. My mother should have been the one to send me to school that day. But at least there was someone who cared. At least I wasn't totally alone.

We set off fifteen minutes later. I'd have liked to sit beside the driver, but Magnus assumed that place himself. The chauffeur steered the vehicle expertly around the potholes and puddles that looked like shining lakes. I stared out the rain-blurred window at the distorted semblance of the passing landscape.

"Are you excited?" Ingmar asked as the car emerged from the woods.

I turned to him. "Of course."

"Well, I am not."

"I'm not surprised." I looked straight ahead, aware that Magnus was watching me through the rearview mirror. "You've been going to your school for a while now. I have no idea what to expect at mine."

"You never know how school will go after the summer holidays," Ingmar replied. "Maybe there will be new teachers or students. And each year the curriculum gets more challenging. Right, Magnus?"

"If you say so," his brother replied.

"Damn it, what is wrong with you?" Ingmar cried. "You two act like cranky old folks in a sanatorium! Stop being afraid of your own shadows!"

"What shadows?" I asked, astonished.

"You are still angry about that thing with Magnus. Good God, I had nothing to do with it!" He glared at his brother. "And you, Magnus, get ahold of yourself! Matilda is not going to steal the estate away from you. The two of you might as well just kiss and make up!"

I stared at Ingmar. I hadn't realized it was important to him for his brother and I to get along. I was tempted to declare it wasn't up to me. Magnus had plainly demonstrated that he was my adversary; how was I ever to reconcile with such a person? We continued the trip in stony silence.

We finally arrived in Kristianstad, where venerable old buildings lined the streets. A graceful church spire reached toward heaven. I knew it was Trinity Church, for Agneta had pointed it out when we were in town to buy school supplies. The streets were crowded, despite the bad weather. Younger children didn't seem bothered by the rain. They ran through the puddles, their books strapped together and bouncing against their backs. I'd expected to be deposited some distance from my school, but now I was glad the driver could drive right up to the front entrance.

"Have a good day, Ingmar," I said. He muttered something that I didn't catch. I climbed out and ran up the steps of the classically styled building. I sought shelter from the rain in the arched entrance and watched the automobile drive away.

Rain dripped from the gutters, and a veritable cascade gushed from the downspouts. The murmur of voices from the interior reminded me of the buzz of my school in Stockholm. I felt a familiar queasy feeling. There would be no Daga here to turn to if others treated me badly, but perhaps that wouldn't matter, because nobody knew me. They'd ask about my family, of course, but I could simply tell them I was the countess's ward. I was no longer defenseless.

Clutching my school bag under one arm, I followed a couple of girls running to the main door. The rain poured down, and water splashed underfoot. My hair was dripping wet. Once inside, I didn't know where to go. I hesitated in the corridor and looked around for some kind of printed notice or guidance.

A girl came up to me. "Hi, you're one of the new girls, aren't you?" she asked in a lively voice. She was tall and good-looking. Her black hair was neatly gathered into buns on either side of her head.

"Yes," I answered. "I'm supposed to be in Mrs. Eden's class."

"Terrific!" She clapped her hands. Her enthusiasm put me off a bit.

"My name is Birgitta." She offered me her hand. "I'm new this year too."

"Um, pleased to meet you," I responded. "I'm Matilda."

"Great! Come on, I'll introduce you to the others."

Clearly Birgitta had been assigned to gather up the lost souls. She accompanied me to a group of other girls. Most were blonde like me, but there were a couple of brunettes, a redhead, and two others with black hair. The redhead looked a bit wild, like some troll out of a fairy tale, but it was immediately obvious she was very shy.

"This is Matilda!" Birgitta announced.

The others didn't seem to share her enthusiasm. They gave me a quick glance and went back to their conversations.

Birgitta gave me a wry little smile. "I'm afraid we'll need some time to warm up to one another."

"Of course," I said. "This is the first time we've met. Everyone's nervous. Aren't you?"

Birgitta awkwardly folded her hands in front of her and shifted her weight from one foot to the other. "Of course. That's why I'm such a blabbermouth."

I smiled. "You'll see. The others will be chattering too, soon enough."

She nodded, suddenly appearing just as uncertain of herself as I felt. "Hope so." Birgitta looked around, a bit lost. "Where are you from? Kristianstad or one of the villages?"

"Neither," I said. "I'm from Stockholm."

Birgitta was impressed. "And what are you doing here? There are piles of schools in Stockholm. They even have universities!"

"My guardian sent me. But that's not a problem. Business school is exactly where I want to be."

"Guardian?" Birgitta echoed. "Did your parents die?"

"Yes, they did," I replied, hoping she wouldn't pry. I was saved by the school bell.

The hours flew by. There weren't a lot of lessons that day, since each teacher wanted to get to know us. We went around the room introducing ourselves.

The classrooms of incoming girls vibrated with excitement. Older students gave us knowing, dismissive looks. They were sure we wouldn't stay that enthusiastic once classwork began in earnest.

At the end of the school day, I hurried outside to find the driver. Ingmar was waiting at the entrance.

"What are you doing here?" I asked. "Where is your brother?"

"He did not want to come," Ingmar told me. "I told him there are lots of pretty girls, but they seem to interest him less than his books."

"Your brother doesn't like girls?"

"My brother does not like *people*. I am really the only person he tolerates."

"I believe that." I gave him an embarrassed look. "Maybe he feels too awkward to act like a normal human being."

Girls from my class were sauntering by and eyeing Ingmar. Okay, he was very handsome in his tailored jacket, but couldn't they see he was practically a child?

Ingmar winked at me. "Seems that I have admirers!"

"You should get away as fast as you can or you'll have to fend off proposals. Most of them are whiling away their time until they can find a husband."

"Too young for that!" he replied and flashed them a charming smile. "You know, some of your classmates look really jealous."

I rolled my eyes. Birgitta broke away from the pack and came up to us. "Hey, Matilda, you didn't tell us your brother was so handsome!" She batted her eyelashes at Ingmar.

"He's not my brother," I said. "This is Ingmar, my guardian's son."

"Delighted to meet you." Ingmar took her proffered hand and gallantly brushed his lips against the back of it.

She giggled and blushed. "The pleasure is entirely mine. Would you like to join us on Saturday for a walking tour of the city?"

"I fear I cannot. Duties on the estate, you know."

"You live on an estate?" Birgitta asked. She tilted her head and batted her eyelashes again.

"I told you that already," I commented, but as far as Birgitta was concerned, I might as well have been a will-o'-the-wisp.

"How exciting!" she gushed.

Ingmar grinned. Fortunately, the driver interrupted us by honking his horn, preventing Birgitta from deploying any more of her wiles.

I took Ingmar's arm. "Come on, time to go."

"See you again soon!" he called to Birgitta as he allowed himself to be hauled away.

"What on earth was all that?" I exclaimed once we were in the car.

"What was what?" Magnus asked.

"I had a conversation with Matilda's new friend," Ingmar explained with a grin. "Apparently the young lady was pleased."

"Oh, it pleased her all right!" I snapped.

"But not you?"

Magnus shrugged at all this and turned around.

"You can talk to anyone you like," I said, annoyed that now Birgitta would surely pester me with questions about Ingmar.

8

And just as I expected, Birgitta was waiting for me the next morning at the entrance. I recognized her from afar. Her black hair was loose, and she stood out in her light-pink dress. Had she taken special pains for Ingmar? She craned her neck as I climbed out of the automobile after giving Ingmar a warning look. He smiled innocently, then raised his hand and waved. I knew very well the wave wasn't aimed at me. Her eyes followed the vehicle until it disappeared around the corner.

"Good morning, Birgitta. What are you doing out here?" I asked artlessly as she looked down the street, entranced. "Were you waiting for me?"

"Oh yes," she said. "I thought—"

"—that you'd see Ingmar again?"

She turned red. "Well, yes."

"Put him out of your head! He has a twin brother who gets really possessive."

Birgitta's eyes widened. "Really?"

I nodded. "You have no idea what I've had to put up with."

"So sorry to hear that." The glint in her eye showed she didn't believe a word of it. "Maybe you can persuade him to do something with us, though. Without his brother."

"I can try," I said, doubting Ingmar would agree. He'd presented himself as a charmer, but he wouldn't abandon the estate to spend the day gallivanting around Kristianstad.

Birgitta's cheeks glowed. "Yes, please do."

I took her arm. "Come on, we should go inside." The school bell would soon sound, and perhaps the lessons would make her forget the notion.

But of course they didn't. Birgitta stuck beside me after school until the car pulled up.

"Remember your promise!" she admonished me before letting me go.

I nodded, called out, "See you tomorrow!" and got into the automobile.

"And how was your day?" Ingmar asked. "Looks like you made a new best friend."

"If only you knew!" I murmured. "But other than that, it wasn't too bad."

"What do they teach in business school anyhow?" Magnus asked. "How to tell apples from oranges?"

"Among other things." I pressed my school bag to my chest.

"Stop talking rot," Ingmar growled. "Their education is just as good as ours. They have a specialized curriculum."

Magnus grumbled something I didn't catch, but I didn't care. I never expected an agreeable word from him.

That afternoon it took me a while to bring myself to seek Ingmar out. I came face-to-face with Magnus in the hall.

"Well, well. Enjoying your afternoon off?" he sneered and stepped past. "Unlike those of us who take our education seriously?"

I spun around. "Hey! Can you please just cut it out?"

"Who, me?" he asked with a look of angelic innocence.

"You treat me like an idiot!" I said, crossing my arms across my chest. "I know my presence here bothers you and you think I'm worthless. But why are you always goading me? In four years, maybe even sooner, you'll be rid of me. So what exactly is your problem?"

Magnus smirked and walked away without a word. That brought me to a boil. I gritted my teeth and thought about running after him, grabbing his arm, swinging him around, and making him look at me. But I knew it'd probably be useless.

Furious, I stamped down the hall. My pulse was still elevated when I got to Ingmar's room. I paused, breathed deep, and knocked.

"Come in," Ingmar called. He was sitting at his desk, his back to the door. "When did you start knocking?"

"It's the proper thing to do," I said and looked around. I'd never been in here.

Ingmar's room was full of heavy furniture that I doubted he'd chosen for himself. The desk must have belonged to his grandfather. The same was true of the wardrobe and bed, which were surprisingly plain. Apparently they didn't install canopies over men's beds here.

Ingmar spun around. "Matilda! I thought you were Magnus."

"Okay. We don't look much like one another, but . . ." My attention was distracted by a model airplane on a little table by the window. It was only about half finished.

"You certainly look nothing alike!" he laughed. "And thank heaven for that, for otherwise we would be triplets. To what do I owe the honor of this visit?"

"I have a question for you," I said. "A fairly unusual one, but I promised a friend."

Ingmar's eyebrows went up. "Might the friend be that perky brunette who was waiting with you today?"

"Birgitta."

"I thought you did not want me to speak to her."

"I didn't say that," I replied. "I just wouldn't want you to give her any false hopes."

"Which I have not."

"Well, that's not what she thinks. She has charged me with asking you to meet her. In Kristianstad. For a lemonade."

Ingmar stared at me in dismay. "You are not playing Cupid now, are you?"

"Maybe so, but she can't exactly grab you out of the car and ask you herself. What do you say?"

"No!" His reply came like a pistol shot.

"Really? She's a nice girl."

"I do not know her at all."

"Her father owns a store."

"And would be happy for her to marry into a title. My mother would be ecstatic to have a shopkeeper's child as her daughter-in-law."

My eyebrows rose. "You really think Agneta wouldn't allow you to marry an ordinary girl from Kristianstad?"

"That is irrelevant. I have no intention of getting married anytime soon. I am not even of age yet!"

"I'm aware of that, and I'm just asking. Birgitta was hanging around me all day long. She is obviously quite taken with you."

"Such a sweet little thing!" Ingmar murmured sourly.

I couldn't hold back a grin, and he saw it.

"You are teasing me, it seems?"

"Not at all. Birgitta is on fire to spend time with you."

"What about what I want?"

"Hello? Am I asking you that or not?"

Ingmar sighed and then became serious. "Even if I wanted to, I could not just go out with some random girl. You know I have things to do here on the estate. Besides, the local press would be all over me the instant anyone noticed. Heir to Lion Hall Seen with Eligible Young Maiden! If my parents heard of it, they would jump out of their skins. I have my high school diploma and university studies ahead of me. I cannot afford to be distracted by women."

"Because she's not from your social class?"

"Did I say that?"

"Well, what should I tell her?"

"Tell her I am not interested. That is the simple truth."

"Then you shouldn't have kissed her hand! That was trifling with the girl's emotions."

Ingmar rolled his eyes. "Surely you have homework to do?"

"Lessons have only just begun, so we have no assignments yet."

I'd never before thought about what the aristocracy had to consider when they entered into relationships, but now I realized that, once he was ready, Ingmar was bound to marry the daughter of some cordially allied noble family. Someone from his own world. Birgitta wasn't from that world any more than I was.

"That's a beautiful airplane," I said, pointing toward the window. "I had no idea you were interested in model building."

"In flying, actually," Ingmar replied, immediately relaxing. "I would really like to take lessons, but my parents say it's too dangerous. They have this outdated concept of airplanes; they think they are the sort of soap boxes the Wright brothers used to fly."

"And you can't convince them otherwise?" I knew too little about airplanes to understand if they were really dangerous. But flying sounded fascinating.

"I will probably have to wait until I turn twenty-one, when they will not be able to forbid it. Until then I have to make do with models. And dreams."

I heard longing in his words. "I hadn't thought of that."

"Of what? That I would like to fly?"

I shook my head. "That even in your circles there are wishes you can't fulfill right away."

Ingmar sighed. "You have no idea how many restrictions we face. The property, the business, our parents . . . Sometimes I want to be just a normal boy. Like Pinocchio."

"But 'normal' people don't have it easy either," I pointed out. "If someone like me dreamed of flying, people would think I was crazy."

"So, there, you see, we are not so different after all!" He favored me with a sincere smile.

"I never said we were!"

"Even so, you should not assume life here is all roses. We have to make sacrifices too. Different ones, but we do have our constraints. And our dreams."

His candor moved me. "Do you mind if I stop by from time to time to see how your model is progressing?"

"Not at all. But the truth is that I have little time to work on it at the moment. What with school and all . . ."

"Probably not tomorrow or even next week. Just from time to time. And then maybe you can tell me more about flying. I'd really like to learn more about it."

Ingmar at first seemed to doubt me, but then he nodded. "All right, if you do not find it boring."

"Why would I? I find the idea thrilling. And surely someday women will learn to fly too, won't they?"

"To tell the truth, they already have. Elly Beinhorn and Amelia Earhart are famous pilots."

"Well, if that's so, maybe someday you'll take me up in an airplane."

"Or you will take me." We exchanged smiles. Ingmar seemed about to say something more, but just then Magnus came into the room and destroyed the mood.

"What is she doing here?" he grumbled.

"She had a question for me," Ingmar said. "And what do you want?"

Magnus glared at me.

"I'm going now," I said.

"We will discuss those other things later, right?"

At the door I turned and smiled. "Yes, we will!"

Naturally Birgitta was disappointed when I told her the next morning.

"Don't be sad," I told her. "I'm sure you'll find a fine young man."

"I'm not good enough. Is that it? I'm sure it is!"

"He doesn't know you at all." I sighed. How was I supposed to get her to understand the obligations and pressures on the Lejongårds?

"I'm not an aristocrat. That's why he doesn't want me."

"He didn't say that," I replied and put my hand on her shoulder. "Listen to me. The fact that he kissed your hand meant nothing at all. That's what people in his circles do. They consider it polite, and they have no notion what kind of expectations it can arouse in a girl."

Birgitta bore up bravely, but I could tell she was still disappointed.

"Anyhow," I added, "like I said, you wouldn't want his twin brother as your in-law."

Birgitta sighed. "I do so wish that someone would fall in love with me."

"That day will come," I told her. "Give yourself time, and the right one will turn up."

"What about you?" she asked after a moment. "Wouldn't you marry into the aristocracy if a count offered you his hand?"

"No!" The word burst out of me. "Not for all the riches in the world would I marry into the Lejongård family! I told you already, his brother—"

"But if it were another family? Some other aristocrat?"

I shook my head. "Not even then. I've already pledged my heart."

That made her eyes grow large, and I saw a sudden glint of envy. "And who's that?"

"A young man in Stockholm. He's the son of a cabinetmaker. We talked about marriage the last time we saw one another. That may sound a bit strange, considering he's not of age yet and I won't be permitted to marry without my guardian's consent."

Birgitta's eyes shone. "It sounds like a novel: the knight frees the poor girl from the toils of the estate!"

"Well, I wouldn't put it quite like that," I said, but Birgitta had already launched into her fantasy.

"When does he come of age?"

"In two years."

"And then he'll come and whisk you away to Stockholm?"

"I hope so."

She clutched my hand. "Oh, it'll be so romantic! Can I be your bridesmaid?"

"Well, we haven't given thought to any of the arrangements yet, but . . . yes, as far as I'm concerned."

Birgitta clapped her hands and squealed in excitement. "I can hardly wait! I always wanted to be a bridesmaid!"

I could hardly wait either, but more than anything I was looking forward to getting away from Magnus.

9

The autumn brought golden sunshine but also an occasional storm to thrash the branches of the trees in the park. On sunny days I enjoyed walking the last stretch back to Lion Hall, while in bad weather I was happy for the driver to bring me to the front door.

The lessons at business school were challenging, but I liked them. Some of my classmates, Birgitta included, probably didn't feel the same way, but I was enthusiastic about numbers and tables and fascinated by the way businesses interacted and depended upon one another. I studied conscientiously and did extra homework in the evening.

The season of the great autumn hunt arrived. People on the estate spoke of nothing else and said King Gustav would be there. His year of mourning had ended in April.

"It will do him good to exchange his precious little tennis racket for a gun," I heard one of the stable boys comment as I brought Berta back into her stall.

The burst of laughter attracted the attention of the stable master, who suddenly appeared behind them. "I'd hold my tongue if I were you," he said. "Otherwise I might think you don't have enough work to keep you busy." Lasse Broderson, who'd served for seventeen years as stable master, didn't tolerate disrespectful jocularity. Everyone knew the king had close relationships with men, but it was better not to mention it when Broderson was around, for he was sure to give you a tongue lashing.

I could hardly believe that the king was going to be there in person.

"And are you going to ride with the hunt?" Ingmar asked the afternoon before the great event. I'd made a little tour of the estate on Berta and was in the process of taking off her saddle.

"On the hunt? By no means! I have no desire to break my neck. And anyway, hunting is barbaric. I feel sorry for the animals."

"Well, in fact it is necessary, since the wolves and bears have mostly disappeared," Ingmar replied. "Wildlife has to be culled and managed. If not, the animals starve in the winter."

"You can go hunting as far as I'm concerned, but I'll stay at the manor. Your mother knows what she's doing, and she's already given me duties that will spare me from having to see animal corpses being dragged in."

"Let me suggest that your view may be a little extreme. Are you planning on becoming a vegetarian? After all, you usually have meat on your dinner plate, whether it comes from a hunt or from a butcher's."

"Hmm. Maybe I will become a vegetarian, then. One of my classmates is. Eating animals disgusts her."

"You cannot be serious!"

"You'll see soon enough."

Ingmar walked away, shaking his head. I grinned after him.

The first guests arrived that evening. Agneta wanted me to attend, so I slipped on a dress purchased especially for the occasion. In the past such garments had been made by seamstresses, but recently the countess had taken to purchasing her wardrobe in select boutiques. That was all for the good, since the old dresses I'd seen in her collection were simply horrifying. They looked so stiff and uncomfortable one could scarcely imagine a real person crammed into them. I wondered why Agneta was conserving those garments. Some had been worn by her mother at a young age. In fact, a fair number were from her grandmother. They were practically museum pieces.

My dress seemed almost too grown-up for me. It was taffeta, knee length, and generously decorated with lace. The blue sheen of the fabric made me look slightly pale but nicely matched my eyes. Lena had again done her magic with my hair, but even so, I wasn't entirely comfortable. Agneta hadn't told me how to behave toward the guests. Or the king. I'd never made a formal curtsey. Was that expected in modern times?

"You look lovely," Agneta commented as I presented myself to her. She adjusted my silk corsage. "Your mother would be very proud of you."

She had a habit of saying that, apparently unaware of how deeply it affected me. Her mention of Mother sent a pang through my heart.

"Thanks," I said and shook off the image of my mother in her coffin. "Is there anything I need to be particularly aware of when the king arrives?"

"No, just be friendly, and do not forget to make a little bend at the knees. Here in my house the royal family's protocol is entirely relaxed, so there is no need for a ceremonial curtsey. Fortunately! When I recall how long it took me to get the court curtsey right . . ." She paused, enjoying the memory. "My mother was quite exasperated with me. She declared that I would never get a husband unless I could impress people upon my debut at the palace."

"She was wrong, wasn't she?"

"Yes. Even though I wound up going the long way around. But looking back at it, I can say that I made the right decisions. And they had nothing to do with being a debutante or perfecting a full court curtsey."

She looked past my shoulder, noticing someone behind me.

I turned and saw Ingmar and Magnus. They were wearing dark suits that made them look quite grown-up. Only their ties were different. Ingmar's was red and Magnus's was blue and yellow.

"Look at this," Agneta said and straightened Ingmar's tie. "My son has turned into a Dane!"

"It is Bordeaux red, Mother," he replied. "I borrowed it from Father so people would not confuse the two of us. I yielded the Swedish colors to Magnus so he could receive the entire room."

I couldn't hide a smile.

"Very well. But you are not to prank people by changing your ties."

"Nothing to worry about, Mother," Magnus answered. "We are not children."

Count Lennard appeared in a dark tailcoat, and we took our places in the entry hall. Fortunately, I was not next to Magnus. He stood beside his mother and seemed lost in thought.

The first carriages arrived. Most of those who came through the great front entrance were business associates and acquaintances. The majority were already in evening dress, but some were in traveling clothes after long journeys. Agneta and Lennard greeted each one. Those who would be staying overnight were shown to their rooms by the maids. Many names flew by, but I retained very few. Within moments the manor was vibrant with movement and voices.

"So then, impressed?" Ingmar asked me.

"Not until I see the king," I replied, though in fact I really was overwhelmed by the people crowding the house.

"Oh, you will not have long to wait. The king is always on time."

More headlights cut through the darkness. The automobiles rolled to a stop, and the sharp odor of gasoline exhaust wafted through the front door. A couple of men in dark full-length coats mounted the steps. "The king's bodyguards," Ingmar whispered. Grim faces surveyed us and checked the foyer, and then the king appeared, impressive with his monocle and twirled mustache, thin as a flagpole.

He wore a simple loden coat, a fedora on his head like any ordinary traveler. But the reverence paid as he mounted the steps was evident. The staff gathered there stood at attention, and both Agneta and Count Lennard held themselves straighter than before.

"Your Majesty, it is a joy and a privilege to welcome you to Lion Hall," Agneta said.

The king took off his hat and gave her his hand. "The pleasure is entirely mine, Countess Lejongård."

Agneta curtsied and Count Lennard bowed.

"He would probably prefer to be on his tennis court," Ingmar muttered to me. "But the royal family is bound to us, just as we are to them. He would not decline our invitation unless he was gravely ill. And his health is legendary."

The count and countess drew the king's attention to us. The twins stepped forward and bowed.

"I am pleased to see you two again," Gustav responded. "You have become proper young men."

I pressed my lips together, noticing that Ingmar was clearly embarrassed by the king's compliment.

Magnus wasn't bothered at all. "Thank you, Your Majesty," he answered with a polite smile.

Agneta turned to me. "And this is my ward, Matilda Wallin. She came to live at Lion Hall three months ago."

The king inspected me, which made me so terribly uncomfortable I almost forgot to curtsey. Fortunately, Ingmar gave me a gentle nudge. I bobbed a bit awkwardly and gave the king my hand. He pressed it carefully.

"I am pleased to meet you, Matilda Wallin."

"The pleasure is entirely mine, Your Majesty."

Gustav smiled, then turned to Agneta. "You should see to her debut at court soon. My late wife is unfortunately no longer with us, but her faithful supporters will be arranging the ball in her honor."

"Well, we will see," Agneta responded pleasantly. "Matilda will be the one to decide. She has her own plans, and I do not know if they include a husband quite yet."

"She should not exclude the possibility. Having a beloved person in one's life gives one the fortitude to reach one's own goals."

"We will consider it, Your Majesty."

The king nodded and allowed Count Lennard to escort him to his suite. I knew that the entire upper floor of the east wing had been reserved for him. Agneta had checked the arrangements two, then three times, to make sure all was ready. Gustav V might not care for ostentation, but he very much liked order and cleanliness.

Close behind the king came another impressive individual. Agneta greeted him effusively. I'd never seen her like that before. There was something almost comic in her abnegation. "Welcome to my house, Mr. von Rosen," she said, humbling herself as she gave him her hand. Von Rosen had an egg-shaped head with a bristle of snow-white hair at the temples. He projected a certain disdainful air even while delivering words of thanks to the countess.

"I am extremely pleased that one of the best cross-country riders in the world will be participating in our hunt," Agneta said.

"Well, the king insisted I accompany him, and I must say I am pleased to see the estate again. I am curious about your latest crop of foals."

"You will have ample time to look them over." They exchanged another couple of courteous phrases, and then a servant escorted him to his quarters.

Agneta sank back into herself slightly once he was gone. "Clarence, Count von Rosen," she explained to me. "Crown equerry to the king and member of the International Olympic Committee. A very important man, particularly for our estate."

"Why is that?"

"He decides which horses to purchase. Our business prospers as long as we remain in his good graces. I should note that he is a fairly unpleasant individual. I have been dealing with him for fifteen years, but the relationship has always been chilly." She looked in the direction in which he'd disappeared. "But you did not hear me say that. You will be friendly to him at all times."

"Of course." Why would I want to have anything to do with her guest? Perhaps I would happen to see him at a meal. That would be more than enough for me, for Agneta was right. He seemed arrogant and conceited.

Additional guests arrived, and eventually the front door was closed.

"There, now that's done," Agneta exclaimed and clapped her hands in dismissal. "I have gone through it so many times, but each time I find myself agitated."

"As if you would ever make a mistake, Mother," Magnus said, shaking his head. "I have never seen you at a loss for words."

"*Never* is no promise of *forever*," she replied. "I think I will consult with Svea once more. Matilda, would you come with me?"

"Yes, of course," I said. Why did she want to go to the kitchen? As far as I knew, everything there had long been ready to go.

Once we were away from Ingmar and Magnus, she asked, "Coming back to our own concerns and the king's suggestion: Would you like to be presented at court?"

"I don't know . . ." At my old school in Stockholm, some of the older girls had said they'd soon be celebrating their own formal debuts. Any one of them would have been overjoyed to debut before the crown princess. "What is it like?"

"You would be thoroughly instructed ahead of time with lessons on etiquette and comportment, of course. And you would have to learn to dance. A court dignitary would assign you a dance partner from among the eligible young men who come out into society at the same time."

"It's like a dance school?" I asked.

"It is much more than that. You are presented to society and thereby become an eligible marriage partner for the sons of leading families."

"So it's really just a mating ritual?" I'd imagined more emphasis on entering adulthood and starting one's independent life.

Agneta couldn't hide her amusement. "Well, there is a fairly good chance of meeting a wealthy bachelor."

"And if I don't want a rich man? If I want someone to give my heart to?"

"Then . . . ," she said with a melancholy look, "that will not be so easy. It might take you quite a while. But in the long run, it could be worth more than gold."

"Did you have a debut like that?"

Agneta laughed, but obviously the memory wasn't a pleasant one. "Yes, I did. And I must confess that I did not find it amusing."

"Then I doubt I would like it at all." I looked her in the eye. "I intend to find a man for myself." I again considered telling her about Paul, but I didn't want to worry her.

"Fine, then. We can cross off the notion of a debut." She turned back.

"And what about the kitchen?" I asked with a little grin.

"Oh, everything there must be under control. Some things we women simply have to discuss in private. Surely you agree?"

I nodded and fell into step with her.

The banquet was held that evening. The actual ball would take place the next evening after the hunt. Even so, the great hall was decorated as elaborately as for a wedding. The servants had polished the mirrors to a high gleam and dusted the paintings and displays of stag antlers. The chandeliers were as brilliant as small suns.

Looking up at the mounted trophies, I wondered about the animals that would be hunted the next day. How big would they be? Given the elaborate antlers on display here, some of the deer and elk from previous hunts had been quite old.

I was rapt surveying the guests and hardly heard any of the conversations. The jewelry and expensive fabrics were fabulous. Birgitta would have swooned. The king made a quite sober impression, but he had no need of an expensive tiepin or dazzling cuff links to impress. Everyone was quick to fall silent and pay attention whenever he spoke.

"Majesty, what is your opinion of the developments in Germany?" asked one of the guests, the owner of a huge feed mill. It was the second time the topic had come up. "This so-called Harzberg Front against the chancellor—do you believe they will succeed?"

"The people will never repudiate Germany's Social Democrats," the monarch replied.

"And what about Hitler?"

The king picked up his wineglass and took a sip. "An upstart who will fail spectacularly when the German chancellor so wills it."

"But are these far-right forces not dangerous? The National Socialists have gathered a great deal of support, and, after all, in last year's election they placed second only to the Social Democratic Party." The man was red in the face and clearly worried.

"We hear that the German parties of the right are quite divided," the king replied. "I see no reason for panic. The people are suffering from the economic crisis, that is the essential point."

"Where do you get your information, Magnussen?" another guest asked the feed mill owner.

"My sister has acquaintances in Germany who are extremely concerned," the industrialist responded. "Their Jewish household employees are terribly worried. Hitler's party regularly speaks out against the Jews."

"And neglects the fact that many Jews served in the war. He cannot simply exile them. Many are honored veterans."

I thought of Miss Grün. She'd been looking forward to her return to Germany and her family. What must she think of all of this?

The men engaged in an increasingly heated discussion, although Agneta tried several times to steer the conversation elsewhere. The king appeared increasingly displeased, but Clarence von Rosen encouraged the back-and-forth. "Actually, we have little reason to care who rules in Germany. Sweden is neutral, and our principal concern is for our businesses to prosper."

"What do you know of business, von Rosen?" protested the man who had originally brought up the subject. "Your world is that of the royal court and equestrian sports."

"Do you really think equestrian sports are not a business? I fear you are quite mistaken. My view is that when the day comes, we must reconcile ourselves to what we cannot change."

"That is, we should do business with Hitler if he comes to power?" Agneta asked, doing her best to maintain her calm.

"Business has no opinions concerning politics. I would recommend that attitude to you, Countess, if you aspire to keep this marvelous estate functioning. I am perfectly aware you refused to sell horses to Germany during the last war. That attitude may have to change."

Agneta went pale.

Lennard spoke up. "In any event, we should wait to see how things develop. It is of no use to become agitated over uncertainties. We have the prospect of a promising hunt tomorrow."

These words cooled spirits a bit, but I could see that Agneta was still stricken.

After the meal I went back to my room. Von Rosen's words echoed in my mind. He seemed convinced that these National Socialists would come to power. I wondered what Agneta was feeling, and why she'd been so upset.

In any case, I hoped Miss Grün wouldn't have to leave her homeland.

10

The howls of excited hounds roused me from my bed early the next morning. I got up and went to the window. As always, the stable boys were already hard at work. They were leading horses into the courtyard, cinching saddle girths, and putting bridles in place.

Some guests with their own horses and grooms felt compelled to show them off as proof of their status and manliness. The king, in contrast, relied on our horses and firearms. I was glad I wasn't advanced enough as a rider to accompany them.

The company of hunters assembled in the courtyard after breakfast. I watched the hustle and bustle from the window niche in the foyer.

Von Rosen appeared, completely at ease and carrying on a lively conversation with another guest. The bodyguards, dressed in hunting attire, stuck close to the king. I assumed they'd be riding alongside. There was a lot to describe to Birgitta when I next saw her. I was surprised by the number of spouses participating. I'd supposed they'd be chatting cozily in the salon as their husbands raced through the forest firing in every direction.

"There was a time when I thought occasions such as hunts and balls terribly old-fashioned," Agneta commented as she came down to the entry hall adjusting her riding outfit. "It astounds me that I actually find them enjoyable now. I must be getting old."

"Society requires such events, doesn't it?" I asked.

She nodded. "Yes. Society loves ritual."

"The girls in my class dream of this world. Hunts and balls and beautiful gowns."

"Because they see only the surface. You, in contrast, have been granted a peek behind the curtain. I often think we preserve the elegance only so ordinary citizens may have something to dream about. Not all that glitters here is gold, as you have probably observed already."

"No," I responded. "A lot of it is papier-mâché."

That made the countess laugh. "Just so!"

Hunting horns reverberated in the forecourt, signaling the arrival of the forester responsible for the Lion Hall preserve and his team of beaters. He would do his best to ensure that the riders didn't damage the undergrowth too much.

"Very well, duty calls!" Agneta gave me a friendly nod and disappeared down the front steps.

I watched the mob of riders waiting for the signal to depart. The trampling hooves produced low, rolling thunder. Once they were off, I went to the foyer to check the incoming mail. Some letters had arrived, and one was for me.

I recognized Paul's handwriting. Smiling, I pressed the letter to my breast and hurried upstairs.

At first I took the figure sitting on the window seat in the upstairs hall to be Ingmar. A book lay open on his lap, but he wasn't looking at it. He was gazing into the distance as if searching for something. I realized it was Magnus.

"You didn't go on the hunt?" I asked. It felt too strange to walk past and ignore him. *It does no harm to exchange a few words.*

"No," Magnus answered without bothering to look at me. "Nor did you, obviously."

"I can't bear to see animals killed."

At that Magnus turned toward me. For the first time there was no expression of disdain in his eyes. "I don't care for this savagery either. And despite that, I will maintain the tradition once I become master of this estate."

"One can change traditions, can't one?"

His refusal to respond unnerved me.

"You'd have the authority to make changes," I pressed him.

His face darkened, and I asked myself for the first time if he was really as malicious as he seemed. Perhaps he was just terribly unhappy.

"What is that in your hand?" he asked at last.

"A letter from Stockholm," I replied. "From a friend."

Alarm bells went off in my head. Was he going to interrogate me? He didn't; he sat silent.

"Very well, then, I'm going to my room," I said, but I did turn back for a moment. "Listen, Magnus, there's no need for us to be enemies. I'm here because I had no choice. I don't want anything of yours."

"You said that before." His voice was dismissive again. Had I misunderstood? Or had I surprised him in a rare moment of vulnerability?

I gave him a nod and went to my room. It took me a moment to shake off Magnus's odd negativity, but then I hurried to the desk and opened the letter.

Paul's handwriting shone up at me from the page like a burst of sunshine.

Dearest Matilda,
You have no idea how deeply I desire you! It seems to me that an eternity has gone by! You know I am not so good with words, but I assure you my heart burns with long-ing. Oh, if only these years could end soon!

I closed my eyes and sighed. Warmth spread through my breast. Simultaneously I felt that sweet edge of pain that came each time I thought of Paul. We were so far from one another. I regretted not getting physically closer to him in Stockholm. I wished I'd committed his face more firmly to my memory. I was terribly concerned it might begin to fade away.

> *I was pleased to read that business college is going well. Although I would have been happier to have you in Stockholm, it is good for you to prepare for the future. Father is always saying that I need to take on more responsibility. He is determined to establish a second workshop and insists I complete my apprenticeship and take my journeyman's exams as soon as possible. The day I eventually qualify as a master cabinetmaker, I will be able to provide very well for the two of us. And who knows, perhaps the idea of a furniture store will work out. Do not worry, for I will not lose sight of my goal.*
>
> *Oh yes, and don't be surprised if Daga's letters come less frequently. After she finishes at the seamstress's shop, she has energy for very little. She complains of back pains and needle pricks, but she is determined not to give up. Mother says she should look for a good husband instead, but Father rejects that idea and insists she keep learning. You know already how he is . . . I have instructions to greet you warmly from them and send you their affection.*
>
> *A thousand kisses from me, warm hugs, and the tenderest of thoughts,*
> *Your Paul*

I traced the curve of his signature. His letter made me feel he was near, maybe only in the next room. Yet my heart was heavy, knowing I wouldn't find him there.

In any case, now that the hunting party was away, I would have the time and quiet to write back. I went to the desk.

Dearest Paul,

Your words are a warm embrace on a cool autumn day! I miss you so much, though life here leaves me hardly a moment of calm. I am answering you immediately because today is Saturday and the countess has excused me from schoolwork because of the estate's great autumn hunt.

We have received many people from all over the country. You should have heard all the political discussions last night!

And just imagine, the king himself is among the guests. Yes! Our old King Gustav, who we always saw on the palace balcony during the royal birthday celebrations! I had never expected to see him close up and in person.

He asked my guardian if I wanted to be a debutante. Agneta explained it to me, and I gather a debut means that from that moment on one is obliged to dance to society's tune. That does not interest me. I'm no aristocratic little puppet. I have no desire to go around to one ball after another. I want to be with you, surrounded by sawdust. I can hardly wait until that day arrives. I will not be seeing the king then—instead I will see you every day for the rest of my life. I cannot imagine anything more thrilling.

I am so delighted you will soon take your exams and that, despite the distance between us, you have not forgotten how close you lie to my heart. Tell me when the exams are scheduled, so I may keep you in my thoughts and send you good luck.

Say hello to Daga from me. I miss her so much. At school I talk sometimes with a girl named Birgitta, but it is not the same. Daga has far more sensible views as far as husbands are concerned. Birgitta will not be satisfied with anything less than a prince or a film star! Birgitta seems a bit superficial, but her company is better than none at all. I will certainly not abandon my beloved Daga for her. But I will write that to Daga directly.

If you were here to ask what I am doing today, I would tell you I am preparing to attend this evening's ball. More about that in my next letter.

I send you a tender kiss and a warm embrace. That may not be much, but I hope they give you the strength to hold fast to our dreams.

With love,

Your Matilda

The sun was setting by the time the hunting party returned. Torches lined the drive and the front steps. The fragrance of pine needles, earth, moss, and smoke enveloped the triumphant arrivals, some of whom also trailed the scent of aquavit. Apparently the bonfire had not been quite enough to warm them up. The guests paid no attention to me as I watched from the dining room doorway and overheard exclamations such as, "That was a tricky stretch!" and "Did you see what that clever vixen did? She really fooled the hounds!"

Eventually, Agneta appeared. Her hair was a bit disorderly and her clothing was splattered with mud, but she was laughing wholeheartedly. She immediately caught sight of me, waved, and came over.

"How was the hunt?" I asked.

"Wonderful! The people had their fun, nobody fell off a horse, and none of the hunters got caught in crossfire."

I opened my eyes wide in astonishment. "Does that happen?"

"From time to time. Back in my father's day, one hunter mistook another for a wild boar and blasted his rear with a full load of buckshot. Dr. Bengtsen had his hands full dealing with that, and we were glad the man had not been hit higher up. Fortunately, the victim held no grudge against his hunting companion. But he never went hunting with us again either." Agneta smiled. "But I do not mean to bore you. You had best go upstairs and get ready for the ball. I think there will be plenty of amusing anecdotes to hear later on." She hurried past.

Hours later everyone was gathered in the ballroom. I again wore my beautiful dress, and Lena had worked my hair into an intricate, artful bun low on my neck. Even so I felt quite plain when I saw the other women's gowns—gold brocade on black fabric, brilliant purple, flaming red, and, here and there, dazzling white with sparkling silver threads. Some had shown off their jewelry the day before, and this evening even more did so. I had the impression they'd stepped out of the films Daga and I sometimes went to on Sunday afternoons.

Agneta and Lennard had the good taste not to flaunt their wealth. Agneta wore an elegantly tailored gown in blue-green silk with tiny beads, and Lennard added to his sober formal attire a pocket square and cummerbund that matched her dress.

The king showed no particular ostentation either, appearing in the usual formal evening attire, wearing a monocle on a cord, his beard curled, and a dreamy expression on his face. The guests bowed, but he waved away such ceremony. "Do consider me just another member of the hunt," he said and went to the place of honor reserved for him at our table. The fact that Gustav would spend the evening with us made me nervous. What if he brought up the subject of a debut? Or asked me a question I couldn't answer?

Once the tall doors to the banquet hall were closed, Agneta and Lennard got to their feet and the room quieted. The countess thanked the guests for their presence at Lion Hall and the successful hunt, and she and Lennard stepped out onto the dance floor and opened the ball. The orchestra posted on a platform beneath a display of enormous antlers played a waltz.

It was breathtaking to see how elegantly the count and countess moved about the dance floor as if no one else were in the room. They had eyes only for one another. It was obvious they were deeply in love.

Another couple joined them after a time, stepping deftly into the rhythm of the music. I'd never been to a celebration in Stockholm where there was dancing. As far as I knew, my father had never taken my mother out anywhere. She'd never complained about it, but considering what she must have seen here in the mansion, had she ever wondered what it would be like to be invited to such an elaborate affair? Had the life she'd led really been enough to satisfy her?

When I was a little girl, I often dreamed of such a fabulous ball. Now that I was experiencing one, I felt lost, a princess without a prince. Paul was so far away, but even if he'd been nearby, he'd never have been admitted here. And I didn't know how to dance either. Maybe I could ask Agneta to send me to a studio for lessons . . .

The food was delicious. Ingmar and Magnus didn't look as if they were interested in dancing either. It occurred to me they wouldn't be able to avoid it at a royal debutante ball.

I stood at the edge of the room as the couples swirled around the floor and stepped out from time to time for refreshments. I didn't know what to do with myself, and wished I could help the maids with their bustling tasks. But Agneta surely wouldn't have allowed that.

"Balls are not exactly your passion, are they?" a voice suddenly inquired close to my ear. I recognized Ingmar from his red tie. Who else would speak to me so casually?

I glanced over his shoulder at our table and saw Magnus's seat was empty. He'd probably withdrawn to one of his hiding places. He didn't seem to care what his parents might think about his absence.

"I'm not used to such elaborate occasions."

"You have never been to a party with dancing?"

"Only an open-air concert, but that was a long time ago. My father was always working, and Mother preferred to stay at home."

"So you are a little homebody?"

"Not at all!" I replied angrily. "My girlfriend and I went to the cinema in Stockholm all the time! But the only dancing there was on the screen."

"I did not mean to offend."

"I'm sorry, but this is all completely new to me. Next year I'll know what to expect."

"You should try dancing at least once if you want to know what to expect." Ingmar put one arm behind him and bowed to me. "May I have this dance?"

"You're not serious!"

"About dancing with you?"

"Yes."

"In fact, that is exactly my wish. I would not be here otherwise."

My face turned red. "But I—no!"

"And why not? Because you are still upset with Magnus?"

"Because I don't know how to dance."

Ingmar raised one eyebrow. "You cannot dance?"

I shook my head, deeply embarrassed.

He reached out. "We must change that."

"Didn't you hear me?" I replied. "I don't know how. I would stumble all over your feet."

"All that is required is a strong lead," Ingmar said. "Come on, it will be fun. Try it just once!"

"In front of all these people?" Magnus would burst out laughing if he saw me, and tomorrow he'd make one stupid remark after another.

"Believe me, it is easier than you think."

I gave him a distrustful look. "Are you sure you're wearing the right tie?"

Anyone else would have given up at that point, but not Ingmar. "Absolutely sure. Come, the waltz is almost finished."

I was astonished by the elegance and grace of other couples gliding across the parquet. In contrast, I felt like a rock that Ingmar would have to haul.

I sighed and put my hand in his.

"Come here." He took one of my hands and set it on his shoulder. He lightly gripped the other and placed his free hand on my shoulder.

"There, you see? Not difficult at all. Now follow my steps."

Ingmar moved to one side and pulled me with him. As I'd feared, I didn't anticipate his move and stumbled. Ingmar caught me, and I blushed furiously.

"No more!" I cried and tried to pull away.

He didn't let go. "Do you remember the stirrup at your first riding lesson? You tried to mount with the wrong foot and did a nosedive into the sand. But you kept at it. And you didn't even fall this time. So?"

"I'll never be able to dance."

"If you give up right now, you certainly will not. Let us try it one more time. I will tell you what to do."

He told me to step to the left, and I did. Then another step to the right. It felt nothing like proper dancing. Even though the other guests were focused on their partners, I worried someone would notice me. But Ingmar's hands held me firm. Breaking away from him would attract everyone's attention and probably cause a scandal.

And anyway, I didn't want to run from him. Even if I was berating myself for gross incompetence, it was the first dance of my entire life!

"There, yes, just like that!" Ingmar called, and instantly I trod on his toes. "Ouch!"

"Are you sure about this?"

"You will get the hang of it. Stepping on your partner's feet is an inevitable part of learning."

"Can we move away from the others at least?" I asked. "I don't want to collide with anyone."

Ingmar did his best to maneuver me gracefully to the edge of the dance floor, but I tripped and fell into his arms.

"There, you see? Let's stop before something worse happens."

Ingmar sighed. "Very well," he replied, disappointed. "Another time."

Another time? He had to be joking! I would certainly never step onto a dance floor again!

"Another time." I heard myself echo, and was somehow pleased when Ingmar met that with a smile.

11

I couldn't get the dance with Ingmar out of my head in the days that followed. How good it had felt, even though I'd been so clumsy! It almost gave me a guilty conscience when I thought of Paul. But surely a single dance didn't mean anything. Even so, I wasn't about to let Paul know. He mustn't think that I had eyes for other young men. And especially not for my guardian's son!

I sat in the library for a while after dinner one evening. I'd hardly had a moment to myself the whole day. My homework had taken the entire afternoon.

Since I knew Magnus wouldn't be wandering around at this hour, I took a book from the tall glass-fronted case and settled in an armchair. The crackling and warmth of the fire made me drowsy, but I woke immediately when the door opened.

"There you are!" Ingmar said. "I tried your room, but it was deserted."

"I wanted to read a little," I answered. "What is it?"

"I wanted to make a suggestion."

"And what's that?"

"I would like to help you learn to dance."

"Not such a good idea!" I demurred. "You saw what happened at the ball."

"I thought it went fairly well."

"I—these formal balls aren't for me. Next time I'll stay in my room."

His offer was really very thoughtful, but I was reluctant to get too close. I had an uneasy feeling that dancing with Ingmar would almost be a betrayal of Paul.

"Do you think Mother will put up with that?" he asked. "She will haul you downstairs personally! Whoever lives here is condemned to take part in every formal event."

"Suppose I'm ill?"

"Well, celebrations and balls are sacred in this house. You would just have to sit in a corner with a horse blanket wrapped around you." Ingmar gave me a winning smile. "Oh, come on, you should not be so silly. It is much more fun when you join in. And besides, you will want to shine at your own wedding, I suppose?"

Yes, I would want that, and it hadn't occurred to me. If Paul invited me out onto the parquet, I wanted to know what I was doing, no matter how modest the reception hall.

"All right," I said. "Help me learn."

"Seriously?"

"Yes."

Ingmar lit up. "You will not regret it," he said. "We will start with a couple of simple things, the waltz, probably, and the foxtrot. And if you are really daring, we can practice the Charleston."

"Isn't that the dance they used to do in those American speakeasies? Those women in dresses made of nothing but twine?"

"Well, they wore a bit more than that. Unless you mean Josephine Baker and her skirt of banana skins. They would suit you too."

"No, never! And I'm no flapper anyhow. The simplest things will be enough for me."

"How about the tango?"

"Not yet."

Ingmar nodded. "All right. And you can be reassured I will not tell anyone."

"Not even your brother?"

Ingmar gave a puff of disdain. "Him least of all! But he is not here, is he? No need to fear. So do you want to start tomorrow? About this time? Then you will fall into bed dead tired and will not have to bore yourself to sleep with Plato."

"I prefer other literature," I told him. "But fine, let's start tomorrow."

As agreed, we met the next evening. Ingmar had recruited a stable boy to help move his mother's old gramophone to the library. During our first session he was going to instruct me to the music from my old shellac records.

In his brown tweed trousers, white shirt with rolled-up sleeves, and dark-blue vest, he resembled a picture of a golf teacher I'd seen in one of Lennard's newspapers.

"Now, young lady, are you ready?" he asked with an affected accent and bowed deeply.

It was like a scene from an old film. The only thing missing was pomade on slicked-back hair. I couldn't help giggling.

"What is so amusing?" he asked as he straightened up.

"The way you bowed!"

"That's the custom, unless the man is an absolute oaf," he replied. "Listen to me: never laugh at a man who asks to dance with you. You can turn him down, but never laugh. For us men, a ball is a serious occasion, one that requires a certain amount of courage."

"Courage? I didn't think men had any problem at all speaking to women."

"They certainly do! Especially to women they find attractive, ones to whom they have already lost their heart."

"But asking someone to dance is hardly like proposing marriage!"

"The one follows the other, often enough. Believe me, men will not dance with just any woman. Either they dance with her because they would like to court her, or they have to dance with her, because she is their mother-in-law or sister-in-law. But we never offer to dance with a woman we dislike. At least, not unless we have to."

"Those are pretty funny rules," I said and tried not to show that my pulse had begun to quicken. Ingmar had invited me to dance at the hunt ball. Did that signify something? And how was I to make clear to him I had no desire to be courted, certainly not by him? Should I tell him I was already spoken for?

But maybe I was making too much of this. Perhaps he was just a friend who wanted to teach me to dance.

"Understood. I won't laugh," I said.

"Good. Start over, then." Ingmar bowed once more and asked, "Would you care to dance with me?"

I pressed my lips together to keep from grinning, but I did manage to reply. "With pleasure."

Ingmar nodded. "Not too bad. Now you give the man your hand. Like this." He took my right hand and stretched it out. He gave me a fleeting kiss on the hand. I thought that silly as well, but on closer consideration, it did seem romantic. Provided, at least, that the woman voluntarily surrendered her hand.

"Do I always have to do that?" I asked. "That thing with the hand kiss?"

"Well, if you actually intend to dance with the man."

"And if I'm undecided? Let's say, for example, I like his looks, but I don't know anything about his character. And the dance is a test. Then what?"

Ingmar frowned. "You are complicating things."

"Well, isn't life like that? Lots of times a person doesn't really know if she wants to or not. Why should I let the man kiss my hand if he might turn out to be a fool? Or stuck-up? Or a complete idiot?"

"If he actually is one of those, I suspect you will already know. And if he is conceited, he would prefer to dance with his own mirror image anyway." Ingmar grinned, but didn't release my hand. That made me uneasy.

"What next?" I was anxious to get started, before I got distracted by other thoughts.

"Well, you willingly accompany the man to the dance floor," he said and drew me forward.

Surprised, I tripped over my own feet.

"'Willingly,' I said," Ingmar commented. "Step straight ahead and let your hips sway a little. Surely you have seen it in a film sometime. Do it like that."

"I'm no film star!"

"But you could follow their example. Every girl likes to imagine being a diva."

To be honest, so did I, even though I found the things I read of them in newspapers very odd.

"All right, I'll be a film star."

I held my free hand in a bizarre, affected pose and sashayed my way out onto the floor beside Ingmar.

He shook his head. "If you walk like that, you will look like a chorus girl from the burlesque. Try to tone it down a bit."

"Did someone teach you how to walk?"

"No, but in dancing school it was drilled into the girls."

What kind of dancing school must that have been? One for the offspring of the upper classes? Or did Ingmar and Magnus go to an ordinary dance studio in the city, where the aristocrats were instructed side by side with shopkeepers' daughters? I was sure Magnus would never have put up with that.

"Now we get to what actually happens on the dance floor," Ingmar lectured. "The lady places her right hand in the man's left and her left hand on the man's shoulder. He in turn holds the woman's hand very gently and places his free hand just beneath the lady's shoulder blade. Too many men let their hand slide farther down, especially if they've been drinking, but anything below the waist is strictly out of bounds. The lady has the right to reprimand her partner and push him away."

"I can smack him if he grabs my rear?"

Ingmar grinned. "Indeed, you may. Unless it is the king."

"The king would never force himself upon a lady in that way," I replied. I hadn't seen him dance at all during the hunt ball.

"You are right about that."

"But I can slap anyone else?"

"Yes, provided you are prepared to provoke a scandal. And now let me show you the steps."

Ingmar took me in his arms at an appropriate distance, but I could sense the warmth of his body. That distracted me and made me stumble at the very first step.

"Stay calm," he said. "Simply imitate my movements. We will make a dry run first and then see how it goes with music."

The dry run, as Ingmar termed it, was fairly awkward. I had trouble anticipating the sequence, and I was too nervous to command my legs properly. Fortunately, my teacher was extremely patient.

I felt like a bull in a china shop, but being so close to him was very agreeable. I felt a tiny bit guilty when I thought of Paul. But what harm was there in practicing dance steps?

Eventually, Ingmar cranked the gramophone. My well-used record provided a scratchy rendition of a Strauss waltz, rhythmic and energetic. We achieved nothing like the sweeping grace other couples had shown at the ball, but we moved relatively correctly about the library. Ingmar's assurance and grace impressed me. So did his masterful leading. My clumsiness made it no easy job.

I was soaked with sweat by the time he finally released me. We dropped onto the chairs by the window to catch our breath. The recording again came to an end.

"And that's what people call fun?" I gasped. I ached all over, and my back felt terribly stiff.

"You will get the hang of it over time."

"In a hundred years!" I exclaimed, making him laugh. "When did you first learn to dance?"

"In preparation for my confirmation," he said.

"That was the year before last."

"Correct. You cannot get started early enough."

"That's why you're so accomplished."

"Thanks!" He studied me for a while, then asked, "What about you? Would you ever have learned to dance if you had not come here?"

I shrugged. "I don't know. Maybe. There wasn't any dancing at my confirmation."

"And you would not have been facing the prospect of coming out as a debutante."

"Am I facing it now?" I asked, shocked. "Your mother said—"

Ingmar shook his head. "No worries. Magnus and I will have to dance at court, but you will not. Still . . ." He gave me a smile. "I would be very pleased to have you as my dancing partner."

"Won't you have to dance with daughters of the aristocracy?" I teased. "Maybe your future intended?"

"I hope not! There is matchmaking at those balls, of course, but I have no interest in getting engaged. And neither does Magnus. I cannot imagine him as a married man. Even less than myself."

"Fine, then," I said, and got up. "Teach me how to hold my own with the daughters of the aristocracy."

12

We practiced every day, and I gradually began to gain some measure of confidence. I was still watching my feet much of the time, but occasionally I looked up at Ingmar, forgot my uncertainty, and let him guide me around the room.

"I think we can now begin with the art of conversation," he said one afternoon.

"Tell me: What do people talk about while dancing?"

"Well, that depends upon how well you know your partner."

"In other words, if I don't know him, I talk about the weather."

"Exactly."

"And if he's a business contact, I ask about his wife?"

"If his wife is present, he probably will not dance with you, unless your husband is in the room and invites his wife to do the same. In that case, you ask how his fields are doing and what the prospects are for the harvest."

"And if it's someone else?" I persisted.

"Then you have to consider it carefully. If this is a man you like, you certainly will wish to avoid boring him."

"I tell him about my latest round-the-world voyage? Or the newest jazz club in the city?"

"Something like that." Ingmar concentrated suddenly upon my face. "But that is not quite your style. I would advise you to discuss literature or mathematics."

"That's true, it's not. But those subjects aren't likely to interest him."

"He will find them fascinating. Unless he is a fool." He stopped short, held me, and stared deep into my eyes.

The music ended with a deafening rattle, scratching, and an insistent series of clicks.

Magnus appeared in the doorway, obviously furious. "So this is where you are! I thought you wanted to discuss something with me!"

"I looked for you all day long," Ingmar replied as he released me. "And I have had this appointment with Matilda set up for some time."

"Appointment, is it?" Magnus drawled. "Are you teaching our filthy little Cinderella to dance so she can hunt down her Prince Charming?"

"I forbid you to speak about Matilda that way!" Ingmar said. "She is not a Cinderella. And she needs to be able to dance so as not to disgrace our family."

Magnus glared at me as if I were a noxious insect. "She will always be a disgrace to our family."

I refused to take this anymore. "Go crawl back into your hole! You're not obliged to watch anything you don't want to see!"

"I advise you not to get too infatuated," Magnus snarled. His eyes remained fixed on Ingmar. With a flourish he pulled a paper from his pocket. "*Dearest Matilda, you have no idea how deeply I desire you*' . . ."

Paul's letter! In defiance of his mother, Magnus had gone into my room and rummaged through my things! I flung myself at him. "You have no right! Give me my letter!"

I grabbed his arm, but he held the paper high above my head. Furious, I kicked his shin, but he didn't flinch. He shifted the sheet to his other hand and continued. *"It seems to me that an eternity has gone by! You know I am not so good with words'...."*

"Give me my letter right now!" I screamed. I threw my whole weight against him, but he shrugged me off.

"Magnus!" I heard Ingmar shout. I lost my balance and fell, Magnus's laughter mocking me as he called out words Paul had meant only for me. I clambered to my feet and charged him again, but he ripped my letter to pieces, laughed, and threw them across the logs burning in the fireplace.

I stared in shock at the blackening shreds, then stormed out of the room. For a moment I thought wildly of running to the countess. But what use would that be? She clearly couldn't shield me from her son's attacks.

I ran upstairs to my room, slammed the door behind me, and threw myself onto the bed. Sobbing, I pressed my face into the pillow and screamed in frustration. For a moment I imagined myself strong enough to tear the mansion down, but then a strange weariness invaded me.

There was a knock at my door.

"Matilda?" Ingmar called in a worried voice. "Are you all right?"

I wasn't all right, and I didn't want to see Ingmar, even though he had nothing to do with Magnus's cruelty.

"Matilda, I am so sorry. What my brother did was entirely wrong."

I said nothing. I didn't want to chase him away, but I had no desire to discuss anything. I didn't want to speak to anyone at all.

"Matilda?" He knocked again. I buried my face deeper in the pillow and put my hands over my ears.

I burned with shame. Magnus would probably spread rumors and even tell his mother. In no time at all everyone here would know there was a young man I desired. I felt exposed and vulnerable.

Ingmar gave up after a while and left. I sat up when I heard his footsteps fade away down the hall. My eyes were burning and my throat was raw, but I urgently needed to act.

I looked at the wardrobe. My suitcase was tucked inside. I wouldn't need more than a couple of dresses to get back to Stockholm. My house with its shrouded furniture was waiting for me.

I got my bag and opened it on the bed. I took stockings and underwear from the bureau and then selected two dresses, two skirts, two blouses, and a knit jacket. My pulse thundered in my ears as I stowed everything in the bag and added my other essentials.

I intended to show everyone I refused to be the victim of Magnus's despicable behavior ever again.

That evening I let the servant into my room as usual. Rika was surprised to find me looking so miserable, but she didn't ask why. She laid out my things for the next day, turned back the covers, and wished me a good night. I crept under the blanket. The house gradually fell silent, but Magnus's scornful voice still echoed in my mind.

Could I really do it? I doubted myself at first, but then with every passing minute I became more determined. Finally, at about one o'clock in the morning, I got up and dressed.

My heart pounded as I carefully closed the bedroom door and it clicked shut behind me.

The manor was dark. I hurried down the stairs with my bag in hand and crept across the foyer. A cold autumn wind met me outside, and the sky threatened rain. I hoped with all my might the train station wouldn't be locked, for otherwise I had a chilly night ahead.

I hurried across the courtyard, careful not to make noise. The driver's quarters stood opposite the horse barn, so it was important not to disturb him. If only I knew how to drive a car!

A horse would have to do. I opened the barn door and switched on the light. I grabbed a saddle and went to Berta. She turned to look at me, mildly surprised, but she didn't shy away. I drew the girth tight the way Mr. Blom had shown me and fastened my bag to the saddle. I led the old mare outside.

Not a thing stirred inside the manor, and the windows remained dark. I led Berta across the grassy lawn so no clatter of hooves would raise the alarm.

My heart was in my throat. There would be an enormous hullabaloo in the morning. People would look for me and discover the horse was gone. I was sure Agneta would guess where I was. Perhaps I could stay hidden for a while. Maybe Paul would take me in?

I swung into the saddle at last, urged the horse down the road, and didn't look back.

It wasn't easy to make out the way in the dark, but the rising moon soon lit the road. Berta's hooves echoed loudly in the quiet night. I had instants of panic when I heard cracking and snapping sounds in the woods. I was too old to believe in ghosts and trolls, but I still felt relieved when we were out of the woods.

It took us about an hour and a half to reach Kristianstad. I was shivering like an aspen. My coat offered no real protection against the damp, but at least I had no trouble finding the station.

The city itself was dead quiet, and the public square before the tall redbrick building was empty. There was a light in one window, probably in a room occupied by a guard or the stationmaster. I hitched my horse to a lamp pole and pinned a note onto the saddle saying where the horse belonged.

"Farewell, Berta," I murmured and patted her neck one last time. Then I carried my bag to the station. Was it open?

I cautiously pushed the door, which swung open with a muted creak. The interior was lit but deserted. This was the first time I'd seen an empty railway station. My steps echoed off the tiled walls. I had the impression my own breathing echoed in that space. Lost, I stared around. Maybe I should have waited until later, when other travelers would be there? An oppressive feeling of isolation took hold, and I shivered. The building was as frigid as a mausoleum.

A door creaked. I spun about and saw a man approaching, a uniform jacket thrown around his shoulders.

"The morning train's not for an hour yet," the stationmaster said. "Ye'll catch your death of pneumonia."

"Anything is better than staying home," I replied, surprising myself. Had I really said "home"? Lion Hall wasn't my home! In the best of cases it was just temporary lodging.

The stationmaster sighed. "Well, then, come along with me, young lady. I can't be responsible for yer catching yer death of cold."

I followed him through the empty station. Our footsteps echoed, evoking an odd fluttering in response, no doubt from a pigeon somewhere in the rafters. The faint odor of coffee emanated from the stationmaster's quarters.

I hesitated. My mother had warned me against entering the private lodging of an unknown man. The stationmaster looked like a kindly grandfather, but I knew enough to be suspicious of appearances.

"Come, come, young lady, I shan't bite," he said. "I only wish to offer ye a coffee."

I gathered myself and advanced.

"I'm always up early," he explained to me, "and I check to see if anyone has strayed into the station." He shut the door behind me and went to a little stove in the corner. "Happens often enough I find people here with nowhere to go. I see to it the station door stays unlocked; don't want some poor soul to freeze. Nights are getting cold."

The warmth of his lodging enveloped me like a shawl. The first room was a very simply furnished kitchen. A small table and two chairs stood next to the small stove. Tin boxes and cans were lined up on a sideboard. A curtained doorway led to another room.

He went to the stove and put the kettle on. "Take a seat! Our water will soon be hot."

I sat in one of the chairs. I noticed a photo near the door of a middle-aged woman with a snub nose and soft dark locks.

"My Rosa," the stationmaster commented. "She's been gone for ten years now, but not a day goes by without me thinking of her."

"You live here in the station?"

"Aye, I do," he answered. "And I'll probably die here. Nowhere else to go. When Rosa was alive, I was happy to dash off home. But now that I've brought her here to stay with me, I want for nothing. And if I take a notion to go out into the wide world, I take a day off and travel with the train."

"Isn't it lonely?"

"Lonely? Ye cannot be lonely in a train station. Might even have a young miss turn up. An early riser." He winked at me, and just then the kettle began to whistle.

He shook a little coffee into two enamel cups and poured the boiling water over it. "Turkish coffee. I hope ye like it this way."

"Thank you, I do."

That wasn't entirely true. The cook on the estate served filtered coffee, and Mother had prepared it that way as well. But the strong aroma drove away the leaden fatigue that the warmth of the room had brought upon me.

"Best ye wait a moment, or else ye'll burn yer lips," the stationmaster said and took the chair across the table from me. I looked at the clock above the sideboard. The minute hand clicked forward a notch, but the morning train wouldn't arrive for another forty-five minutes.

The man stared into his cup for a while. "I know how it is with young folks. Something goes wrong for 'em, and they want to go out into the wide world. But my advice is that it's often better to swallow yer pride and just keep at it. The grass isn't always greener on the other side, ye know."

"It has nothing to do with pride," I answered. "It's just that I'm in a place, where—there's someone who despises me. And it's not my home. I'm actually from Stockholm."

"And ye want to return."

I nodded. "To my parents' house. They passed away, but the house belongs to me."

"And the people ye were staying with—what do they say to this?"

"I don't know," I said. "But I have to do it. I have no other choice."

"Do ye have friends in Stockholm, then?"

"Yes. A girlfriend and her brother."

The old man nodded. "Well, I can't tell ye what to do, but I advise ye to go to those two. Don't stay by yerself. Often enough, loneliness brings on desperate thoughts. Especially in difficult times."

"I don't intend to take my life," I replied. "My father did that. He abandoned us. I'm not running away, I just want to go someplace I don't have to see that stupid boy, that's all."

The stationmaster took a sip and sat looking at me. "Does the fool in question happen to be yer friend? Sorry, miss, but we old 'uns are always curious."

"No, not at all!" I responded indignantly. "He just hates me because my mother was a servant, and he thinks he's better than me. He hates me simply because I'm alive."

"Ah, I find that hard to imagine of a young miss like yerself. Perhaps he treats ye so poorly because he's telling himself he has no chance to win yer friendship."

I shook my head. "No, that's definitely not it. He doesn't want me to be there because he's afraid I'll try to take over. While all I really want is to go as far away as possible."

"So ye're doing him a favor, then."

"Yes, if you want to call it that. I don't want anything to do with this bother. I've had my fill and more, and I want peace and quiet at last."

The old man nodded and drank more coffee. "Just so," he murmured, at which I raised my cup. The coffee tasted horribly strong, but I found the fragrance agreeable.

I felt my pulse accelerate as I reflected on the old man's comment. He was right: I was doing Magnus a favor. But how could I defend myself? How could I keep him from snooping through my things and revealing my most intimate secrets? The only way was to stay as far away as possible.

The stationmaster sought to cheer me up by telling me tales of strange people he'd met. A woman with a load of ducks she wanted to put in the passenger car because the creatures were supposedly afraid of the dark; and a man with a suitcase full of bulging cans of *surströmming*, traditional fermented fish, that were on the brink of exploding.

"Think what a stinking mess that was going to be!" he said. "Nothing against the stinky fish itself, I like it, but exploding cans are a terrible problem."

He managed to coax a smile from me with anecdotes like these, and I forgot to watch the clock.

"Perhaps ye should make yer way to the platform," he said finally. "The ticket window isn't open yet, but ye can buy a ticket on board."

I rose. "Thank you very much for the coffee and the kind words."

"Not at all, young lady. But I do ask ye to reconsider yer plan to travel. If ye were to go back now . . ."

"No. My decision is made."

"Well, then, I wish ye all the best. Oh, just a moment—one more thing." He went to the sideboard, opened a drawer, and took out a brown paper bag. He removed a couple of bread rolls, closed the bag, and extended it to me. "For the trip. So ye won't starve before ye get where ye're headed."

"Thank you, that's very kind."

"A person who travels needs the company of a kind spirit. I can't accompany ye, but I can send ye off with a bit of sustenance."

I nodded and tucked the package in my bag. Something occurred to me. "May I ask a favor?"

"Of course. A message for someone?"

I shook my head, knowing he would tell the people from Lion Hall where I was headed as soon as they asked. "Could you please see to the horse that I tied outside?"

"A horse?"

"The horse that I rode here. She belongs to Lion Hall."

"Ye didn't run away from there! Or did ye?"

"In fact, I did. Sometimes a castle is no more than a cabin, and a cabin is a castle. That's what my father used to say."

"Yer father sounds like a good man. I know the church has its notions about a person who takes his own life, but surely he's watching over ye from heaven."

"Thank you, I hope so," I responded. "And the horse . . ."

"I'll see to the beast and make sure she gets safely back to her owner."

"I thank you with my whole heart." Now he had the story of yet another curious encounter that he could tell.

The stationmaster nodded. "All the best, young miss! I hope ye find a place where ye will be welcome."

"I will do my best. Thanks again!"

I took my leave with a smile and a wave. Then I crossed the hall and went out to the platform.

The yellowing advertisement for mouthwash I'd seen upon my arrival that summer was gone. Its place was now occupied by an image of a dapper young man praising a hair tonic. Apparently things did change around here, if only slightly.

Other passengers soon appeared. Some seemed tired, others nervous. One man focused on lighting a cigarette. I looked back at the waiting room a little apprehensively. It was still dark, but the stable boys were sure to be up and about and must have already discovered that Berta was missing. They would have the countess awakened, for they'd assume the horse had been stolen, and then . . . No, I didn't want to think of that.

Fortunately, a few minutes later the loudspeaker boomed that the morning train was about to enter the station. I breathed easier as soon as I saw the locomotive smoke in the distance. They wouldn't catch me now. And maybe I could do something in Stockholm to make sure I'd never have to return to Lion Hall.

13

I hurried from Stockholm's central train station to the bus stop. Lion Hall was probably in an uproar—but let them fret! I would never set foot in a house where I was denied my privacy.

The bus that appeared was completely full. I didn't want to wait, so I started walking. My conscience began to bother me as I trudged southward through Stockholm. My actions were punishing the innocent. Agneta couldn't change her son, and Ingmar was just as powerless to change his brother. But I refused to expose myself to Magnus's attacks for their sake.

I knew Agneta could force me back to Lion Hall at any time, with help from the police if necessary. But what if I found some way to escape? Maybe Paul would be ready to take the drastic step of marrying me and burning all our bridges . . . That would make me his responsibility, and Agneta's guardianship would lapse. And I would be free, living the life I'd dreamed of.

I abruptly changed direction and set out for the Ringström home. The furniture workshop would be busy, but it was late afternoon and almost closing time. I'd be able to speak to Paul in private.

I reached the workshop after an arduous hike through the city. Departing workers paid no attention to me. I went to the residence, rang the bell, and readied myself to face Paul's mother or father. Fortunately, Daga opened the door.

"Matilda! What are you doing here?" She threw her arms around my neck. "What a wonderful surprise! You didn't write you were planning to visit Stockholm!"

I gave her an uncertain smile. "I didn't know it myself until yesterday."

"Why not? Did something happen?" Daga searched my face, her hands still on my shoulders.

"No, I mean, actually, yes . . . there was an unpleasant incident at the manor house. Is Paul home? I have something I absolutely must ask him." I was trembling and didn't want to tell Daga any more than that.

"Don't you want to come in?" Daga asked, bewildered. "Mother's busy in the kitchen."

"No, I really need to speak to Paul first." I forced myself to put on a proper smile. "But it's lovely to see you again. You look marvelous!"

"Thanks, and so do you, but . . ." She shook her head in astonishment. "It's not bad news, I hope?"

"No, but I really have to speak with him. Please, Daga. I'll tell you more later."

I felt the bite of fear deep inside. I hadn't anticipated they'd invite me in. The Ringströms were very hospitable and never let guests depart until they had been well fed. And that meant the very scenario I dreaded. I couldn't face answering all kinds of questions, not right now.

"Well, I'll get him, of course. But then you really must tell me what's going on." She disappeared inside.

This was like standing on a bed of hot coals. What must my friend be thinking?

Paul came to the door moments later, drying his hands on a towel. He must have just arrived from the workshop. "Matilda, my dearest," he exclaimed, "what a surprise!"

I flew into his arms, not caring about his wet hands. "I needed to see you," I said. "You have no idea how I've missed you!"

"I missed you as well," he responded, wrapping me in his strong arms and pressing me to his heart. That moment of affection was worth all the pain and confusion of the flight from Lion Hall. "What brings you here? Are you visiting Stockholm? Or is there a problem with your guardian? Daga seemed worried."

"I can't stand it any longer!" I clutched his shirt. "I want to be in Stockholm. With you." Drowning in desperation, I leaned back to look at him. "Please help me! Marry me! That way I won't have to go back to that house."

"What—what's that?" Paul stammered. His face filled with concern.

"It's horrible there!" I said in a rush. "Magnus stole your letter from my room and read it out loud. He completely humiliated me! And he treats me like a leper!"

Paul shook his head. I couldn't read his reaction. Did he not understand? Or not believe me? I myself could scarcely believe I was telling him this.

"And what does your guardian say to that?"

"Not a word. He's her son!" Even as I was saying it, I knew I was being unfair. Agneta had already spoken to Magnus. Still, I was certain the countess wouldn't really send her son away because of me.

"Matilda, don't get so upset!" he said, resting his hands on my arms. "I'm sure we can resolve this."

I threw myself at him again, and my hot tears smeared Paul's cheek. "I don't want to stay there anymore! I want to come back to Stockholm and I never want to see him again!"

"I understand. But I can't just go out to the mansion and knock his block off." He clenched his fists. "As much as I'd like to!"

I'd seen him take on other boys who'd dared to taunt me. They'd never done that again.

But he was right. He couldn't just set off to Lion Hall. I saw only one hope of escaping from there.

After an awkward silence, he said, "Don't you want to come in? Have dinner with us? You can tell me the whole story afterward without being disturbed."

"No, I don't," I whimpered. "I just want to know one thing: Are you willing to marry me?"

"But—"

"It doesn't have to be today, but sometime very soon. Will you become my fiancé? My only way out is to get married."

Hearing my own words, I realized how shocking they were. But I couldn't help myself.

He embraced me again and held me for a while. He whispered, "Of course, we're going to marry. But not yet. You're still only seventeen. And the countess will be against it. I know I was pressing you before you left, but I've thought about it and changed my mind. It's right for us to wait."

I looked up at him, speechless. His words were a cold shower.

"Listen to me," he said. "Your countess will never allow you to get married now, and you know you have to get her consent."

"You mean I have to go back?" More tears flooded my eyes.

"Tell the countess what happened! I—I would love to get you out of there, but I can't. I haven't reached my own majority yet, so my parents would have to agree. We'll wait until I turn twenty-one. Then I'll ask your guardian myself."

My hopes burst like a soap bubble. He was being rational, but his reluctance hit me hard.

I pulled away.

"Come inside," he said. "My mother will be delighted to see you. And you'll be safe with us."

I shook my head, ashamed and wishing the earth would open and swallow me up. "I'm sorry, but I really have to go. Take care! Give Daga my love!" I picked up my bag and turned away.

"Where will you go?" Paul called after me. "At least stay here with us for a while!"

But that was the last thing I wanted. I strode away through the little front yard before the house and workshop without looking back. Tears ran down my cheeks.

"Matilda!" Paul shouted.

I broke into a run.

I felt so unbearably foolish. The stationmaster was right. I should have stayed. I should have told Agneta. And I shouldn't have turned up out of nowhere to beg Paul to marry me, when I'd rejected that very idea a few months earlier.

I wandered aimlessly through the streets for quite a while, heedless of those around me. I burned with humiliation. What must Paul be telling his family? How would Daga react? Would they all think I'd gone mad?

When I came out of my daze, I realized I was standing on the bridge where my father's lighter had been found. I'd tucked it carefully in my pocket before leaving. Now I found myself staring, entranced, at the spot where he'd dropped it.

Presumably this was where Father had taken his life. I stepped closer to the railing. I'd come here from time to time. Today I asked myself what he'd been thinking. What desperation had filled his heart? It must have been far worse than what I was going through.

I stepped closer to the stone parapet. I could imagine young boys daring one another to balance on it . . .

"Young miss?" I heard a voice behind me. An instant later I felt a hand on my back.

I turned and looked into the face of an elderly woman wrapped in a worn coat with a fur collar. Her tousled gray hair was visible under the brim of her gray felt hat.

"I'm sorry; did I frighten you?" she asked.

"No, you didn't. I—it's not what you're probably thinking."

"And what might that be?" she asked gently.

"I'm not planning to jump," I replied. "It's just that this is the place where my father disappeared. I—I was trying to comprehend how he must have been feeling at that moment."

The old woman's eyes glistened with tears. "You poor thing!"

"It wasn't recent, but I always think of it when I'm here."

"Perhaps you should come with me," she offered. "A young woman shouldn't wander through the city this late in the day."

"You are very kind, but I actually do have a place to go," I answered, picking up my bag. "Be well!"

"You too, my child!" she called after me.

I turned and waved as I crossed the bridge.

Physically tired and spiritually exhausted, I staggered up Brännkyrka Street and took out my key. I knew what awaited me: a house full of shadows, sheets over the furniture, and dust covers tucked around picture frames. But where else could I go? I didn't want to return to Lion Hall; I couldn't. Perhaps I would change my mind the next morning—and face up to my punishment for running away.

I put the key into the lock, turned it, and entered. The air was dusty and cold and smelled of old masonry, but the faint lingering scent of home reminded me I belonged here. I locked the door and carried the bag to my room. The pantry was empty, and the shops were already shut. I had to make do with water from the tap and the last of the stationmaster's rolls.

I sank with a sigh onto the bare mattress of my bed. At least my bedclothes were still here. Miss Grün had stored them in the cedar chest Father had inherited from his grandmother.

I wasn't up to making the bed; I didn't have the energy for it. I stared up at the ceiling. My eyes closed. I was vaguely hoping to hear a pebble rattle against the windowpane. Paul knew where I lived.

I feared a visit from him as much as I desired it, though it would be fruitless. Paul wasn't free to marry. If he'd told his parents the truth about my visit, they'd certainly conclude I was stark raving mad. And Daga? I hadn't explained anything to her. Maybe that had angered her. Or maybe she was worrying needlessly. What a mess I'd made!

My thoughts chased one another in circles for a long time. I slipped into unconsciousness, my body drawn into the depths of the night.

14

The sound of a door opening woke me. In a moment of confusion, I thought Mother was in the house. I half expected to find a steaming bowl of hot milk on my bedside table.

My bedroom door swung open, and I sat bolt upright. The shrouded furniture reminded me I no longer lived here. And there was no hot milk.

My next confused thought was of a burglar, but then I made out the looming figure of Agneta Lejongård.

"Good morning, Matilda," she said in a stern voice. "I am very glad to discover that you are still alive."

I tensed. She hadn't sent the police after me; she'd come herself. I didn't know which was worse.

"I—I'm sorry, I wanted—"

"—to provoke panic, fear, and distress at Lion Hall?" she said sharply.

I struggled up from the bare mattress. "No, it was just—"

"Then why did you run away? Why did you leave without telling anyone? Anything at all might have happened!"

"I rode to the train station, because I—because I didn't know where to go."

"If there was a problem, you should have informed me."

I pressed my lips together. Would that have made a difference? Yes, she'd threatened Magnus with boarding school, but I'd seen how she treated her son—like handling a live grenade. She told everyone that her children were equally precious to her, but she was gentler with Magnus than with Ingmar. I was sure she wouldn't carry out her threat.

"I should not have to emphasize to you that such behavior by a member of my family is not acceptable!" she continued. "We do not run away from our problems. We face them and we solve them."

I'm not part of your family was the resentful thought that came into my mind. *I'm just the ward whom the count's son thinks he can treat any way he likes.* Then I bowed my head. "Forgive me, it was just—"

"What?" she exclaimed. "*What* was it?"

"Magnus read Ingmar a letter I'd received. Out loud. Then threw it in the fire." I was coming across like a petulant little girl, but if the countess was going to insist on knowing what had driven me away . . .

"What kind of letter?" Agneta's voice was still hard. She obviously thought my behavior childish.

"A letter from Paul. I've known him for a long time. He's—" Well, what was he, exactly? The young man who'd kissed me? The boy whose future I wanted to share? The young man who now probably thought I'd lost my wits?

"Your friend?" Agneta prompted.

I nodded.

"Where did you put that letter?"

"In my desk drawer. It was very personal." I was beginning to wonder how personal it really was. Paul's reaction the previous evening had seemed to contradict that interpretation.

Agneta considered this for a moment. "Wash yourself and change your clothes. We are going home."

That's all? I almost blurted. I was expecting a harsh scolding for my foolishness. The absence of one left me confused and terribly apprehensive. Maybe she was going to keep me on tenterhooks and announce my punishment only once we were back at Lion Hall.

The countess left my room, and I dragged myself over to my bag. I took out one of my autumn dresses. Washing with cold water shocked me wide awake. The thick fabric of the dress was welcome, but I was still shivering on my way to the kitchen.

"Do you have all of your things?" was all Agneta said. The tension in the room was intense, like the feeling you have waiting for a New Year's Eve firework to explode.

"I just have to pack my bag."

"Do it! I am waiting."

Was it possible for a guardian to renounce her charge? Was that about to happen? What would become of me if it did? Was I facing life in an orphanage? Feeling oppressed, I dragged my way to my room.

I folded the dress I'd worn for the trip and packed it in my bag, and I gathered the rest of my things. I pulled on my coat and went back to Agneta. She couldn't have followed me by train; she must have taken the automobile. She'd probably driven all night, considering she'd come to get me so early in the morning.

We got into the automobile. I looked back at my house unhappily as it shrank in the distance and disappeared from sight. I'd hoped to stay there, but I probably wouldn't see it again for years.

We drove for a long time in complete silence. The monotonous drone of the motor made me drowsy, but jolts from the occasional potholes kept me from falling asleep. Toward noon we stopped in a little town to eat. My stomach had been growling, but I hadn't dared to mention my hunger. I felt like an apprehended prisoner on the way to trial.

We went into an inn and took one of the tables in the back. The countess ordered water, tea, and two servings of home cooking—meatballs, potatoes, and cranberry jam. I didn't know if I would be able to get it all down, despite the complaints from my stomach.

When at last the countess addressed me, it was in a thoughtful tone. "You know, I am no stranger to impulsive overreactions, such as yours. I too once completely forgot myself and destroyed my own paintings in a drunken rage. I shredded nearly all of them. I regret that now. I wish I had more things to remind me of my youth."

I gaped at her in disbelief. I hadn't expected such calm, much less a description of her own foolish errors. Most grown-ups I'd met never admitted mistakes.

"I greatly regret that Magnus again treated you so shabbily," she went on. "I really do not understand him. His brother's love is steadfast, and the same is true of mine and that of my husband. But my son lives in a world to which he admits no one but Ingmar. And I have the feeling that recently he has been closing the door to his twin as well."

She paused, and I thought of the exchange they'd had in her office as I was listening from next door.

"I am afraid that now I am obliged to carry out my threat. I see no other choice. Perhaps boarding school will teach him elemental decency."

"No," I said. "That's not necessary. I—I overreacted."

Paul's confused expression flashed before my eyes. As did Daga's look of astonishment.

"No, you did not," the countess replied. "You showed me I will face consequences if I fail to deal with the problem. You and I are alike in certain ways. When we are offended or disappointed, a fire within impels us to take direct action and do what seems right at the moment. Even if it is extreme."

She was right.

"I could relent and allow you to stay in Stockholm, of course, but I do not want that. I need you on the estate. No matter where you intend to go once you reach your majority, right now I need you with me. And you need your business-school education. In my role as your guardian, I have the responsibility of equipping you for your future. If that means that I must separate my sons, so be it."

She paused when the waiter appeared with our meals. After he withdrew, she continued, "In any case, it is my duty to punish you. What you did was wrong and caused many people a great deal of anxiety."

"I am sorry."

"You said that already. For the next four weeks you will be confined to the manor. The only exceptions will be to go to school and to attend riding lessons. When not fulfilling those duties, you will remain at home and help me in the office. I have a number of tasks for you."

I nodded. "Yes, ma'am."

"In addition, you are not allowed to write to your friend for a full month. I will have a note sent to advise him so that he does not worry unduly. For that month I will withhold any letter from him that may arrive."

That punishment hit closer to home. But in fact I didn't know whether Paul would write me at all.

"And as for school, you will not receive excused absences for the two days you have missed. I will not request their indulgence. If teachers oblige you to stay after school, you will inform me so I can send the driver at the appropriate time. You are fortunate that the current weather is so uncertain. I was tempted to make you walk to school. But I will not do that for now."

I lowered my head. So many punishments for fleeing from Magnus's attack—but I knew I had no right to complain. Agneta herself had come to get me instead of simply sending the police. That alone was worth a great deal. I would simply have to endure the restrictions until the time was past.

It was already dark when we got back to the estate. My head ached, and my stomach was queasy. How would Magnus react when his mother carried out her threat? Or Ingmar? He knew what his brother had done, but maybe he would hate me too when Agneta sent Magnus away. Why couldn't things have remained as they were?

"Go upstairs. I will tell Rika to bring you your dinner. We will see one another in the morning."

I nodded and made my way upstairs with my bag. I had a tiny hope that Ingmar might suddenly appear and ask about my short-lived adventure. But I saw no one except Rika when she brought up a tray. I felt just as alone as I had the previous evening in Stockholm.

I went down to the kitchen the next morning, put together my own breakfast tray, and vanished upstairs with it. It was Sunday, so I didn't have school. Would it be possible to avoid lunch?

I paced my room the whole morning. From time to time I would stop to look for something to read or glance into my textbooks, but I was too upset to concentrate. The minutes stretched out endlessly, and I felt like a balloon about to pop.

There was no sign of the Lejongårds. I didn't know whether or not to be grateful. On one hand, Agneta might deliver another stern lecture. On the other, perhaps I was being given the silent treatment. It was up to me to reinitiate contact, but I didn't have the courage.

I skipped lunch, for I had no appetite. Lena and Rika checked on me a couple of times, but I told them I didn't need anything. I lay on my bed and stared at the ceiling. What would happen next? Would Magnus truly be sent away? And how would the others act toward me? I'd been so frightfully stupid! I should simply have slapped Magnus's face . . .

That afternoon I decided to go to the library to choose a couple of books. On the way I came across Ingmar sitting in a window niche staring out into the garden. He had a book open on his lap.

"Aha, the fugitive has returned," he said with an easy grin. "You are taking this house arrest fairly seriously. Is that why you did not come to lunch?"

I was afraid to face all of you would have been the truthful answer. "I didn't feel well."

"Well, you look pretty healthy to me right now." Ingmar's comment had a bitter undertone.

"I have begun to recover." And I wanted to flee upstairs.

He put the book down and turned to me. "Do you have any idea what happened here?"

"I can imagine," I said in a small voice.

"Oh? I don't think you can. My mother must have calmed down by the time you saw her."

"I know. And I wish I hadn't done it, but at that moment . . . When Magnus read my letter to you, something in me snapped. I had to do something, and all I could think of was running away. You were there; you heard him!"

"Yes, I was there. And what Magnus did was really mean. But you should not have reacted like that. Father hit the ceiling, and Mother was out of her mind with worry. They thought you had done something to yourself."

"Why would I?" I asked. "I just didn't want to be here anymore."

"And so you stole poor Berta."

"I didn't steal her, I used her for transportation. Didn't the man from the station give her back?"

"Of course he did. But the poor animal was completely confused. One does not just leave a horse tied up outside a train station."

He didn't mention any worry he, Ingmar, might have felt, but I had an intuition he'd been concerned as well.

"I'm very sorry," I said. "I didn't think it would turn out that way. But in the heat of the moment, I just had to get back to someplace familiar. Do you think I don't miss my own house? At least my mother didn't snoop through my things."

"And no one here will do that ever again." He got up from the window bench and gave me a flat stare. "Magnus will leave in a couple of days."

"I'm sorry about that too. I wish it hadn't come to that. I begged Agneta not to do it."

"My mother always keeps her word, whether in good times or bad. Magnus knew what he was getting into when he stole your letter."

"Yes," I admitted, "but I regret it all happened, even so. I would have stayed in Stockholm, but—"

"Mother would never have permitted that. A young woman alone in a house in Stockholm? Now she probably will not let you leave the grounds until the day you get married."

Paul's dismayed face rose before my eyes. I'd realized how stupid I'd been. I could only pray Daga had kept mum and her parents hadn't noticed. If they heard, they'd do everything possible to keep Paul from asking for my hand.

"Were you with him?" Ingmar asked.

"Who?"

"No playing dumb! With your friend, the one who sends you love letters."

I looked down. I didn't want to talk about Paul. He could have saved me from all this, but he hadn't wanted to. Or he couldn't.

"I went to his house. I asked him to marry me."

Ingmar turned to me, visibly piqued. "How could you do something so idiotic? Did you really think my mother would allow you to get married? You are only seventeen."

"I'll be eighteen in three weeks. Anyway, when I marry, I become my husband's dependent."

That provoked Ingmar even more. "And then what? Do you imagine your situation will be better when you're married? When you have children? When you find yourself stuck in one place forever?"

"It won't be like that!" I responded. "I'll be able to move around!" I was suddenly furious, and I didn't know why. Ingmar didn't know Paul. And Paul would never be the sort of man to lock his wife up at home.

"And I thought you felt close to me!"

A sudden realization took my breath away. Ingmar's disappointment wasn't because of his brother. Magnus had spoken the truth: Ingmar had become attracted to me.

"Ingmar," I said helplessly. "I'm sorry if I gave you the wrong impression. I see you as a friend. A good friend. But I've known Paul for years. We promised ourselves to one another a long time ago."

"When? As children?" Ingmar grimaced. "Anyhow, I am glad the fool sent you packing."

"Paul's not a—" I broke off when I saw Ingmar grin.

"Yes, he is, if he does not want to marry you. But, I repeat, I was glad to hear it. And I hope you will concentrate on something else in life."

"On you?"

"Why not? I am your friend, right? And now that Magnus is being banished to boarding school, I need entertainment. And because it is your fault, you will have to go riding with me every afternoon. And we will continue the dancing lessons. How about that?"

"I'm confined to the manor, so I can't go riding. The truth is that I didn't dare be seen in your company, because Magnus would get jealous. As for dancing lessons . . . we want to continue those, don't we?"

Ingmar nodded. I bent over, gave him a peck on the cheek, and left for the library.

15

Three weeks passed. My sentence was nearing its end. And soon after my return, I'd sat through hours of detention to make up for missing school.

My birthday was celebrated simply. I hadn't dared to suggest inviting Paul and Daga because I'd been in disgrace. But on the day, my offenses seemed to have been forgotten.

Countess Agneta gave me a wool coat and an expensive shawl in a brilliant red. It was soft against my skin and made me look less pale. "You will need it if you want to get through the winter here on our estate."

Count Lennard had ordered a dress for me. "For next summer," he explained, when I opened the box and saw that it had puffy arms and was far too thin for winter wear. It was almost the same color as the shawl; Agneta must have given him a hand in finding it. I could have pressed the silky fabric to my cheek for hours. This was the dress—I knew it already—that I would wear to the midsummer festivities.

Ingmar gave me a woven bracelet with glass beads of different colors. He'd made it. It was cool around my wrist and soon became a part of me. I spent hours contemplating the various individual beads.

I heard nothing from Magnus, and that was fine with me. He was at his boarding school and would probably not come back until the Christmas holidays.

I actually had two celebrations on my birthday. With the Lejongårds there was a festive meal with an elaborate menu, and before that there was a get-together with the girls of the household staff. They all chipped in to purchase a blank diary as their present. Despite the painful rheumatism in her hands, Mrs. Bloomquist prepared a special birthday cake. We sat together and chatted, me about my school and the girls about village gossip.

The only thing that lessened my joy was the absence of my mother. My thoughts kept returning to her, and I held back tears all day. A celebration with Mother wouldn't have been so elaborate and the presents would have been simpler, but we would have had one another. She'd have taken me to a café for afternoon coffee and almond cake. We'd have talked about the business school in Stockholm and perhaps about Paul.

I missed him that day. He'd certainly have given me some ingenious bauble he'd fashioned in his father's workshop. And a kiss. That would have meant more than anything else.

We celebrated the countess's birthday two weeks later. The fact that we'd been born in the same month gave me an idea of why she'd said I resembled her in some ways. Daga, addicted to horoscopes, was convinced that people born in the same month were marked by the same astral influences.

Agneta appeared delighted by the number of guests at her celebration. That was one significant difference between us.

Magnus came home for her party. I tried to stay out of his way; he looked as if he wanted to spit on me. Ingmar had mentioned his brother had once collected butterflies. I knew that meant taking the creatures, either live or anesthetized, and piercing them with a pin. I imagined him doing that to me, and the thought sent a shudder through me each time I saw him. But soon he had to go back to school. When he left, I felt as if the sun had come out again.

The first snow fell on Saint Lucia's Day, December 13, and we again received guests for an elaborate celebration. I recognized most of them, although a few faces were new. I shook countless hands and made plenty of curtsies. Many noticed Magnus's absence and several asked jocularly if the family had exchanged him for me. My face blushed redder than Ingmar's cummerbund.

The ballroom was set up as it had been for the autumn hunt ball, but this time the windows and some of the trophies were decorated with palm fronds and red ribbons. The banquet table was beautifully laid with red-and-silver bouquets and tall silver candlesticks. By each invitee's place was set a little box containing a tiny *lussekatt*, the traditional saffron-flavored bun, baked by Svea. The countess and I had packed the boxes personally.

As the guests were taking their seats in the ballroom, the young girls of the Saint Lucia choir streamed into the front hall. With their bright red cheeks and round marveling eyes, they looked like they'd stepped out of a fairy tale.

"It is about time!" Agneta exclaimed. She beckoned to me.

"Excuse us, Countess, we had a couple of problems with Kirsten's robe," said the woman escorting them. "But we will be ready in just a moment."

Kirsten was the chosen Lucia that year. During rehearsal she'd dripped wax on her robe, and the women in the village had been working furiously to remove the wax with hot irons and blotting paper.

"Matilda, allow me to introduce you to Mrs. Sundström, our Evangelical Lutheran priest's wife. She leads Bible study and oversees the village's religious celebrations."

"I'm so pleased to meet you," I said and gave her my hand. We'd been to church almost every Sunday since I'd arrived, but I'd seen only her husband.

"Matilda is my ward," Agneta explained. "She comes from Stockholm and has been at Lion Hall since July."

"You are certainly welcome to join us for Bible study," the priest's wife said. "We have a couple of young persons of your age in the village. You may enjoy getting to know them."

"That is very kind, thank you! I will let you know."

"I do hope you will," the priest's wife said. "Very well, then, let me take a look to see if the girls are ready." She hurried away.

"That was quite diplomatic," Agneta remarked once Mrs. Sundström was out of earshot. "You could have simply declined. Or are you really interested in Bible study?"

"Not at all, but I didn't want to offend her. Lion Hall is important for the people in the area. I don't want them to think badly of us."

Agneta nodded, and I thought I saw a glint of something—pride?— in her eye.

We went back into the banquet hall, where the many conversations had become a busy clamor. Agneta used a bell to call the guests' attention and welcomed everyone. At her signal the lights were dimmed. Hushed whispering continued around the tables.

The door opened and the girls filed in, illuminated by the lit candles our Lucia balanced in her crown. Each girl also held a candle. Their white gowns gleamed in the dimness, and the room fell silent as sweet voices began to sing:

> *Natten går tunga fjät runt gård och stuva.*
> *Kring jord som sol förlät, skuggorna ruva.*
> *Då i vårt mörka hus, stiger med tända ljus,*
> *Sankta Lucia, Sankta Lucia.*

My eyes filled with tears. I didn't know why. The song described how the blessed Lucia drove away the darkness of night, and it moved me immeasurably. A simple song about banishing the dark—how often I'd felt it overwhelming me! I immediately thought of Mother.

The maids hovered at the edges of the festivities, but they weren't excluded; they enjoyed the same meal as the guests. What might my mother have said if she knew I was seeing the same ceremony she once had . . . but from the masters' table?

I quickly wiped my cheeks. I glanced around and saw Agneta watching. I managed a little smile to reassure her.

The girls moved farther into the room and stood before the tables. Their eyes shone; they were clearly relieved to have the first song behind them.

The singing continued. The chorus of voices swelled; girls stepped forward for solos. Several sang so beautifully that you could imagine they were concert performers. Would these girls ever have the opportunity to realize such ambitions?

The guests applauded enthusiastically, and the lights came back up. Agneta thanked them, ushered the girls and the priest's wife to a special table, and declared the buffet open. It included not only the traditional buns, but a wide variety of delicacies appropriate for any holiday celebration.

"This is the last time in the year that we invite our business partners to a holiday event," Agneta told me as the guests went to the buffet. "We have only family for Christmas and New Year's. That is why we make it more elaborate than the Saint Lucia festivals you have probably experienced."

I'd never been to a Saint Lucia celebration. I didn't tell her that; I just nodded my understanding.

16

The dazzling Saint Lucia evening soon faded in our memories. The year 1931 gave way to 1932. Spring brought Easter, and life returned to the estate. The school year reached its end, we held the graduation ceremony, and summer welcomed us with open arms.

Magnus returned from boarding school, of course, but he seemed so determined to avoid me that we didn't exchange a word.

Whenever I saw the postman arriving, I flew downstairs in a tizzy and sorted through the envelopes. One of those afternoons I found a letter from Paul in the incoming mail.

I stared at it, then pressed it to my heart. I went out to the pier at the little lake behind the village. Agneta had warned me against swimming alone there, not aware I was quite a good swimmer. I wasn't there to swim; I wanted to bask in the warm sunshine on my face as I read my letter.

I knew that the nearby swans jealously guarded their new-fledged chicks and it was best to keep out of their way. I was safe on the pier, serenaded by crickets chirping and dragonflies humming in the reeds.

When I carefully opened the envelope, a little flurry of sawdust slipped out. I had no idea whether that was by chance or design. I blew it from the surface of the paper, brushed it from my dress, and began to read.

> *Dear Matilda,*
> *You cannot possibly know how much I miss you. Almost a year has gone by since I saw you last. I am afraid I will not know you now if we happen to come face-to-face in the street. Is there no hope for us?*
> *During this year I learned to drive. My father said it was necessary so I could deliver our furniture to outlying towns. We have more than enough to do, but many of the commissions are from distant parts of Stockholm or nearby towns. The new delivery truck makes it easier to serve those clients. What a marvel! I would so love to take you out for a picnic in the countryside. But you are not here! Can you leave the estate for a while and come to Stockholm? Your house looks so deserted without you. How I wish you would open its front door, speak with me, and give me a kiss! Can you ask your guardian for permission? You are eighteen now, after all. That should be a reason to allow you a trip to Stockholm. Yes?*
> *I cannot wait for your answer.*
> *With love,*
> *Paul*

Those lines made me heave a sigh. How I wanted to see him again! I'd been terribly disappointed he hadn't wanted to marry the fugitive from Lion Hall. But I'd gotten over that. He'd written less often since, but recently he'd sent a photograph. I suspected he was right: he might not recognize me now.

A look in the mirror confirmed the physical changes. I was taller, and my cheeks were no longer chubby—I'd always hated that! I felt much more adult. Maybe it really was time to speak to Agneta about Paul.

I walked back to the manor, gathered my courage, and knocked on the door to her office.

"Come in!" she called from the desk. The air in the room was sticky, and her face was flushed.

"Agneta, are you unwell?"

"No, but I get a migraine headache whenever I have to work on the account books."

"Perhaps I could help? We studied bookkeeping at school last term. It was really interesting."

"Interesting?" Agneta's eyebrows went up. "You are quite an unusual young lady, are you aware of that? I find calculations enervating, even though I know full well they have to be done."

I went to the window and opened it. "Why don't you hire a manager?" It was still quite warm, but the sluggish draft from outside promised to moderate the room's stuffiness.

"I had a manager for a time, years ago, but it did not turn out particularly well. However, if you enjoy sums, you might as well take a look at these numbers . . ."

"May I?" I'd wondered from time to time about the business of the estate. Our teacher had announced that soon we'd be making visits to businesses to see how they were managed. This might be an even better opportunity.

I pulled a chair over next to Agneta, and we began posting the entries of the previous week. It was quite simple if you knew how. "I could do this by myself, if that's all right with you."

Agneta rubbed her temples. "Please do."

I got to work. Less than half an hour later, I posted all the items for income and expenditures and calculated the balance.

"Thank you very much," said Agneta after verifying my arithmetic. "Perhaps I should charge you with this duty all the time."

"That would be difficult once school starts," I replied, but her praise thrilled me.

"But once you finish . . . You are about to start your second year. Once you have your diploma, I would be pleased to have you assist me here. I freely acknowledge that I find all these sums and calculations difficult."

"I'll be glad to," I answered, qualifying it in my mind, *at least until Paul and I establish our own firm.*

"Agneta, may I ask you something?" I ventured at last.

"By all means! You just saved my life. I was on the verge of overheating like our new threshing machine and setting the whole mass of paper on fire."

The incident with the thresher had been really serious. It had given up the ghost from one second to the next, not dying but running amok, overheating and catching on fire. Quick action by the field hands had prevented a real disaster. Now the estate needed a new thresher. That might well be why Agneta was working on the accounts.

"I think you probably remember Paul. The young man who writes me."

"I know who you mean," she replied in a strictly neutral tone.

"I wanted to ask if you'd object to my inviting him to visit here. Or I could go see him in Stockholm. I do so much want to see him."

"It is out of the question for you to travel alone to Stockholm. You would have to be accompanied."

I'd expected as much. "What if he came here?" I asked. "He wouldn't have to stay at the manor. He could take a room in Kristianstad. Or at the village inn."

Agneta's expression became serious. She studied me for a moment, then sighed. "You can see I am having some difficulties with the idea. No doubt he is a fine young man—but are you not too young for a relationship?"

"I don't intend to marry him. At least, not yet."

"In fact, marriage should be the furthest thing from your mind. You are scarcely out of your childhood."

I sighed in exasperation. I was eighteen! Many girls my age were already planning weddings.

"Listen to me," Agneta said. "I am sure you have plans and goals of your own. You should pursue those before fixing your heart upon a man. Look at me, for example: I was well into my twenties and had no intention of marrying even then. Granted, we are different persons, but even so . . . Give yourself some time before becoming involved with men!"

How was I to give myself time when my heart had already belonged to Paul for so long?

"Your mother was a very beautiful young woman," Agneta went on, "but her world fell apart when she became pregnant. Fortunately, Sigurd Wallin, whom she married, was a man of honor. But not every woman has her good fortune. And women fall into misery and distress still today when they get involved with a man at too young an age."

I was shocked when she brought up my mother. We hadn't mentioned her for months. Now it was clear Agneta had known my mother was pregnant when she left the estate. This wasn't the first time my guardian had surprised me. The fact that she'd been aware of it put everything in a new light.

The question of how my mother had met my father filled my mind, but I didn't dare voice it. I didn't even want to think about it. I was asking for a little time with Paul, that was all. "Agneta, I promise I won't do anything foolish. I've known Paul for a long time, and he would never attempt to force himself upon me. We pledged to one another that all of—that—will have to wait until after we are married."

Agneta favored me with an indulgent smile. "I was young once, Matilda. I know what goes on in a woman's heart. Once she is infatuated with a man, then—"

"It's not like that with us! I know perfectly well what the consequences could be. And if I were to weaken and something happened, Paul would marry me without a second thought." I stopped for a moment, because I found this conversation very uncomfortable. It would have been even more so with my own mother.

"Men often fail to keep their promises when there are unexpected consequences." She paused. "But you are eighteen. Perhaps I must learn to trust your judgment. You are not me, after all."

What could that mean? She was certainly no example of untoward behavior.

"I promise I will do nothing with Paul that could cause difficulties. But I would so love to see him again. And if I'm not permitted to travel to Stockholm, I would really like to invite him to visit me here."

Agneta took a deep breath. "Very well. Let him come! But I insist on getting to know him. That is my only condition."

"Do you really mean it?"

"Yes. And I leave to him his choice of lodging. He may stay here at the manor, as far as I am concerned. But that is up to him."

All my hesitation and doubt fell away. I leaped up and hugged her. "Thank you so much, Agneta! This means so much to me."

Agneta nodded. "Go ahead and write him today! Tomorrow we two can go to the city, and you can post your letter then."

"We're going to the city?"

"I think we have earned ourselves a reward after all this work on the accounts."

Paul's reply arrived not a week later. He planned to come the following week. He was reluctant to accept the invitation to stay at Lion Hall, for he had no idea of estate protocol and etiquette. He didn't want to be constantly surrounded by my guardian's family either. He asked me to reserve a room at the inn.

I was pleased, even though it meant that I'd have to return to Lion Hall in the evenings and leave him alone at the inn.

His letter made me doubly happy, for he'd chosen a week Magnus would be away at summer camp with boarding school classmates.

Ingmar, who'd been spending a lot of time with his brother, was very dejected about Magnus's trip. "You could have let me join at least," he complained to Magnus the evening before the departure.

"You know the trip is only for members of my class. You should go to boarding school too. It is so much better than here."

Ingmar glanced at their mother. "You know one of us has to be here."

"Really?" Magnus asked. "Why? It is enough if *she* is here." He didn't point to me, but I knew who he meant.

"Magnus!" said Agneta in a tired voice.

He shot me a venomous look. "Truly, I am glad I got to go to boarding school. At least there we do not have to share a table with individuals who are beneath us."

"Magnus!" Count Lennard said. "Stop that, right now!"

Their son raised an eyebrow. "And what do you propose to do about it? You cannot threaten me with boarding school. I will be happy to be back with my friends."

His spiteful words visibly affected his parents and, even more, his brother. Having to witness the acrimony between them pained me.

"Excuse me," Magnus said and got up at last. "I have to see to my packing."

I'd expected Agneta to keep him at the table, but she didn't. She continued her meal in silence. Lennard looked at her. He probably was just as aware as I was of her suppressed anger—and also of her regrets. If Magnus had stayed at the estate, would it have been any easier to live with him? I doubted it.

I didn't go down to breakfast the next morning but instead asked Lena to bring it up on a tray. As soon as I'd finished and was dressed, a knock came at my door. I called out, and Ingmar looked in.

"Good morning! Just wanted to see how you are doing," he said. "May I come in?"

"Yes," I said and posted myself by the window.

"I missed you at breakfast today. How are you?"

"I decided not to go down. I had no desire to be insulted again."

"I'm really sorry that Magnus is like that."

"So you have said. It is not your fault."

Ingmar looked concerned. "He did not come downstairs for breakfast either. Yesterday we quarreled. He said terrible things about you, and I hit him. If he is angry at anyone, it is me."

"That's too bad," I said. "I didn't want it to come to this."

"Nor did I, but even so, it did . . ." He looked down in shame.

We were silent for a long moment.

"This will never change, will it?" I asked at last. "Magnus and I, we'll always have to avoid one another."

"I hate that."

"It's just for a few more years, at least. Then you'll have peace and quiet at Lion Hall again."

Ingmar plucked at my sleeve. "And if I do not want you to leave? And if Mother does not want you to either? Everybody sees how much she cares for you. You are like a daughter to her . . ."

"But I'm the cause of the disturbance here. And Magnus will inherit Lion Hall someday."

"Well, we will just have to find a solution. Eventually. He is off to summer camp now, and he will spend all his time loafing in the cabin when he comes back. You will see him only at meals. I will make sure he keeps a proper distance."

Ingmar marked that promise with a firm nod, and I knew he would keep his word.

17

The day of Paul's arrival came at last. I was more excited than I'd been for a very long time. I got up at six in the morning and stood before the wardrobe, trying to decide what to wear.

I'd gotten a couple more beautiful dresses on the shopping trip to the city with Agneta. But which would Paul like the most? The white dress with the tiny blue flowers? The red one from Count Lennard I'd worn at midsummer? Or maybe the sea-green one I thought made me look so sophisticated?

My eyes fell upon the bead bracelet at my wrist. Ingmar's gift. Should I take it off before Paul came? I didn't want Ingmar to notice and get upset, and I'd had the nagging feeling that Paul's visit displeased him.

I left the bracelet in place and chose something to complement the colors of the beads: a blue midlength dress with little ruffled sleeves and a scooped neckline adorned with flounces.

I put up my hair myself because I didn't want to bother Lena. She'd taught me how to weave a braid and wind it into a bun. Doing that without help was a challenge, but I managed. Checking my reflection in the mirror, I couldn't decide if I was pleased with what I saw, but I was certain Paul had never before seen me looking like this.

It was still early, so I decided to take a little stroll. Lion Hall shone in splendor at this time of day. The staff was already awake and about, of course, but they moved so quietly you'd think you were all alone.

I went downstairs and out into the park that surrounded the manor. The pavilion had gotten a new coat of paint for the midsummer festivities. I caught a faint whiff of it, for the morning dew had dampened the scents of flowers and grasses.

Walking toward the pavilion, I imagined sitting there and chatting with Paul. Or would we simply be gazing into one another's eyes? Would Agneta allow us to steal away to the pavilion together? She'd told me her parents' wedding ceremony was performed here. I absolutely had to share this place with Paul.

I closed my eyes and let the morning sounds work upon my spirit. The songs of the larks, the cuckoos calling in the distance, the twittering of sparrows jumping about and combing the grass in search of food, a loud neigh from the stalls. I'd never dreamed a place could offer such peace and yet vibrate with so much energy.

Eventually I went back to the manor. The maids were setting the breakfast table. I thought about going to the kitchen instead, but just then Ingmar came downstairs.

"Say, how about taking a little ride?" he said cheerfully and then focused on me. "Oh!"

"What do you mean, 'oh'?"

"You have made yourself so fine for—him."

"Yes, I have," I replied. "Any objection to that?"

"No, I—I was just hoping we could take a ride."

"I can change," I offered. "Paul doesn't get here until midday."

"Never mind, I will go out alone." He started past me, but I reached out and held him back.

"Ingmar, the fact that Paul is coming doesn't mean I have no time for you. Wait here, I'll be right back. All right?"

He nodded.

"Good," I said and hurried upstairs. I came across Count Lennard just leaving the master bedroom suite.

"Good morning, Matilda. My, how nice you look! Is your young cavalier coming to breakfast?"

I resisted the urge to roll my eyes. "No, I was just trying this on." *Do I really look so striking?*

"That dress suits you wonderfully. Your young friend will like it."

I hurried to my room before Agneta turned up to chime in. I slipped out of the dress and into my riding outfit—just the blouse and the trousers; it was too warm for the jacket.

Ingmar, waiting at the staircase, smiled broadly when I appeared.

"Satisfied now?" I asked.

He nodded. "Satisfied! And if you ask me, I much prefer this outfit."

"I know, but your standards are not particularly rigorous!"

"Well, few occasions require a beautiful dress, either here or in the village. Midsummer is past, and the harvest festival is still a couple of weeks away. Your riding outfit is perfectly suitable."

"Granted, but Paul can't ride. He's from the city."

"Then he will be bored to death here. I hope you have warned him we have no bars and no wicked jazz clubs."

"There's an inn. And we should go now, while we still have time before breakfast."

We went to the stalls in what all the people here referred to as "the new barn." I'd learned more about old Count Thure Lejongård, who'd died in the fire along with his son. It was ghastly that the former stable master had set the fire. Fortunately, his replacement, Lasse Broderson, was a man of energy and integrity.

Soon, we led our horses out and rode off. Our ride took us past the village cemetery. The sight of it always sent a shiver up my spine.

"Have I ever shown you our family vault?"

"No, and before you go dashing off in that direction, I want you to know it doesn't interest me in the least."

"Why not? The old mausoleum is pretty impressive. And besides, that way you can meet my grandfather."

"There's a portrait in the foyer, so I've already met him."

Cemeteries made me uneasy. I'd only rarely visited the grave of my parents, or rather, that of my mother—my father's name was inscribed on her gravestone as well. Agneta paid someone to tend the site and renew the plantings there.

"Did you actually know your grandfather?" I asked.

"No. And I cannot remember very much about Grandmother either. I know her portrait well enough, but I was too young to form an impression of her. They say she was quite strict."

"The portrait of her is beautiful."

"It is. My mother sometimes refers to her as the Snow Queen. You know that fairy tale, I suppose?"

"My mother read it to me many times."

"There you go, then; that gives you a good idea of her character."

"She can't have had a heart of ice."

"To listen to my mother, you might think so. But maybe tears could soften it. Like with Kay in the Snow Queen story."

We rode out across the fields, leaving the cemetery behind. We worked our way to the old cabin via a long detour. I hoped to show it to Paul, but decided not to mention that to Ingmar.

At last we returned to the manor.

"You ride like a real Lejongård," Ingmar commented as we were putting the horses away.

"You've only just noticed?" I laughed at him. "I've been taking lessons for almost a year!"

"Imagine that—you arrived here over a year ago! We must celebrate that anniversary, once your gentleman caller has left. I will persuade

Mother to take us all to a fine restaurant in the city. A French one, with more on the menu than meatballs."

"I have nothing against meatballs," I commented as I handed a stable boy the reins of my horse. "But that would be very nice of everyone."

"I hope your friend does not sweep you off to Stockholm with him."

I shook my head. "Don't worry, that won't happen. He's only twenty and I'm eighteen, so it's simply not possible."

The departure to Kristianstad was scheduled for noon. I was nervous about Paul's reaction when we arrived in an automobile to fetch him. I'd have preferred to return by horse, but he didn't know how to ride, and Agneta wouldn't hear of sending the carriage with its bare wooden seats.

Ingmar seemed tense. "Should I go with you? After all, you will be out on the road with a man I know nothing of."

"But I know Paul very well," I countered. "Don't fret, he'd never do anything untoward."

"I am not worried about how he will behave," he said. "But who is to say you will not leap on him like a lioness? You must be lean and hungry after all these months."

"Don't talk that way, please, especially not in your mother's presence. You'll make me look bad."

"Oh, all right, go ahead. But if that young stranger tries anything stupid, you must tell me. I regard you as a sister, and brothers defend their sisters, no matter what."

I knew his feelings for me were more complicated than that, but I was touched by his determination to protect me.

"It won't be necessary," I said and gave him a hug. "Take care!"

I got into the back seat, and the chauffeur set the car in motion.

I almost regretted the fact that I had no one with whom to converse during the trip. I needed a girlfriend like Daga, someone who could share my excitement. I still got along well with Birgitta, but it wasn't the same.

We finally reached the train station. I had a fleeting recollection of riding Berta here the year before in my effort to escape Magnus. I put that thought aside. I certainly didn't want those memories to spoil my time with Paul.

The driver pulled up behind several taxis lined up before the station. I got out and went inside. I still had some time before Paul's train was due.

Not a lot was happening. A few travelers were waiting. I looked around and spotted the door I'd gone through the year before. Would the stationmaster be busy? I hesitated, then gathered myself and went to his lodging.

I knocked. All was quiet for a moment, but then I heard steps and the door opened.

"Hello, I—" My words failed me. The man looking out wasn't the old stationmaster. His uniform was the same, and the interior looked much the same as before, but this man was much younger.

"Yes, miss? What can I do for you?"

For a moment I was too confused to reply. "The—the old fellow who tended the station, I don't know his name—might it be possible to speak with him?"

He gave me a puzzled look, then something seemed to click. "Ah, I see! You mean old Olufsson. He died two months ago. Heart failure. They found him holding a photograph of his wife. Tragic, it was." He gave me a searching look. "Are you a relative?"

"No, I met him last year. He helped me when I was . . . stranded at the station."

"Well, they say he was a very kindly man. I'm sorry I never met him. I was lucky to be assigned to his position."

That was life: one man's misfortune was another's luck. I remembered clearly what the old stationmaster had said about missing his wife. Could he have had an inkling he would be following her soon?

"Thank you very much," I said. "And please excuse the intrusion."

"Not at all," the official replied. "They told me early on that people would often come to me with questions that had nothing to do with trains and schedules. I'm sorry I couldn't give you more agreeable news."

I nodded and wished him a good day. My heart was heavy as I walked toward the platform. I wished I could have assured the old man that things had turned out well.

Before I could brood about that, the station echoed with the announcement of the arriving train.

I stepped back from the edge of the platform like everyone else and watched for the train. A billowing cloud of steam materialized, and in mere moments the great black locomotive powered its way along the track, pulling many carriages behind it. Paul would be in one of them. My heart began to pound.

The train braked, and steam covered the tracks. Figures appeared out of the cloud: men in summer jackets, women in dresses or other colorful garb, some with bolero hats hanging behind them.

I found I was wringing my hands. Where was Paul? From which direction would he appear? I searched in both directions but saw only unfamiliar faces. Had he missed the train?

"Young lady, perhaps you can tell me the best way to get to Lion Hall?"

Startled, I whirled around. "Paul!" I cried. He looked taller. Maybe it was because he was wearing a tweed jacket, a white shirt, and dark trousers instead of his work overalls? His hair was combed back in soft waves, and his eyes shone like those of a male model in a haberdasher's advertisement.

"So you do recognize me!"

I threw myself into his arms. We kissed one another, longer and more passionately than ever before. People on the platform stared, but I didn't care.

"And you recognized me?" I demanded, pressing my forehead to his.

"Of course! I would know you in a huge crowd or even in disguise."

"I'm glad to hear it. Maybe I should have dressed as a circus clown."

"I wouldn't mind! Your appearance doesn't matter. It's your inner self that interests me. Although I do have to admit that the dress suits you very well."

"I chose it especially for you!" I took his arm. It was lovely to have him next to me. I had the feeling he'd brought with him a whiff of my previous life and earlier, carefree times.

We exited the station. He was surprised and visibly impressed by the car.

"Good Lord. Is that a taxi?"

"No, it's the countess's automobile. The driver takes us to school in it every day."

"You and the two sons. Or rather, one son, now. The other's still at boarding school, isn't he?"

I'd written Paul about what had happened.

"Right now his school is out for the summer, but he's on a trip with his boarding school friends."

"I hope his brother isn't such an idiot."

"Don't worry. Ingmar is entirely friendly. He sees me as his little sister, even though I'm more than a year older than he is."

"So he's just a kid."

"No more than I am."

Paul shook his head. "No. You're entirely different. Mother always claims that women mature earlier."

"That may be, but you mustn't call Ingmar a child. That would make him bristle, and how!"

The driver took charge of Paul's suitcase, and we got into the back. I instructed him to go to the village inn.

"Not to the castle?" Paul asked.

"The manor house," I replied. "There's a difference, even if I don't know what it is." I suppressed a giggle. I felt lightheaded in Paul's presence, even a little silly. "You can put away your things and maybe freshen up a bit. Then we'll drive to Lion Hall, where a grand reception awaits you."

"Grand reception?" he echoed, dismayed. "I hope I have the right clothing for that."

I looked him over from head to foot. "Well, since the king sent his regrets, this suit will probably have to do."

"I hope so," Paul said. "It would be terrible if they took me for a stable boy, considering that I'm at a total loss when it comes to horses."

"We can change that. You'll take riding lessons this week with Mr. Blom."

"What?" he said. "Are you serious?" He hesitated for a moment and gave me a searching look. "That's a joke, isn't it?"

I left him hanging for a moment, then grinned. "Yes, of course. I found out quickly that a week isn't enough time to learn to ride. And since there are plenty of automobiles in Stockholm, I'm sure horses are irrelevant to you."

"But you know how to ride," he responded. "That means you could just take one of the horses out of the pasture and ride away."

"Well, maybe we might need to do that, someday when we're married."

"Will you gallop away from me?"

"No, that's not what I meant. But maybe I'll have to go fetch something in a hurry. If I've learned anything in these past months, it's that many times a horse is better transportation than any automobile."

"Father says that all the time, but he bought us a delivery truck anyway."

"And you really know how to drive it?"

"Of course!" he said. "I still need to get my license. But that's just a matter of time. A couple of hours of practice, a test, and I'll be the terror of Stockholm streets."

"I'll be happy to have you as my chauffeur."

"You'll have to be in Stockholm."

I smiled at the thought. Agneta hadn't yet let me get behind the steering wheel, but perhaps I'd be able to persuade her.

18

While Paul stowed his luggage at the inn, I waited downstairs, leaning on the hood of the car, and watched through the doors as the inn-keeper wiped down the bar. I would happily have gone up with Paul, but rumors spread quickly in a village. The locals would certainly be gossiping about the young man who accompanied Miss Matilda. If the young lady in question also went up to his room, there'd be a perfect storm of scandal. I didn't want people tattling to Agneta.

I looked up. The bees hummed overhead, for the linden trees were shedding quantities of pollen. It looked like the beekeeper's hives would provide a bountiful yield of honey this season.

"So, then, what do you think?" Paul asked from the door of the inn. He'd changed his dark trousers for sand-colored ones that were a bit more fitted. He wore a fresh shirt. Only the jacket over his arm was the same.

"You look like a film star," I said.

"Do you think I need a tie?"

"Bring one with you," I answered, for I wanted him to make the best possible impression on Agneta and Lennard.

"Thought so!" he said and extracted a fine, neatly folded tie from his jacket pocket. "I can put it on in the car."

"No need. Everyone dresses casually during the day. We have mirrors throughout the house, so you can put it on before dinner."

Paul took a deep breath. "I'm nervous, you know. I feel like you're about to introduce me to your parents."

"My mother knew you. And found you charming."

Out of the corner of my eye, I saw the driver impatiently shifting his weight from one foot to the other. "Let's go," I suggested. "We'll have time to talk in the car."

Paul nodded, and we got in.

"Meeting your mother wasn't at all the same thing," he said as we rolled away from the village. "These are aristocrats. And I'm just an apprentice in a furniture workshop."

"And I'm a student at business college," I replied. "They respect me here, and they'll respect you too. Agneta once mentioned she'd have been happy to lead a bourgeois life, maybe as the wife of an ordinary man."

"Seems that her family got in the way of that."

"She said it was because of the circumstances. Her father and brother died in a fire, and she was the only heir. She had no choice."

"She could have sold the place."

"Paul," I said, "if you inherited your father's factory, would you turn around and sell it?"

"Probably not. Unless I had entirely different plans for my future."

"But there's no prospect of that, unless there's something you haven't told me."

"Nothing has changed."

"There, you see. You wouldn't sell the workshop, and Agneta didn't want to sell the estate. Each person finds his place."

Those words were scarcely out of my mouth when I began to wonder. Where was *my* place? Here or in Stockholm? Which would I rather give up, the estate or my house on Brännkyrka Street?

I was no longer sure. My parents' house had always been home, but the estate had become increasingly precious to me. If I married Paul and left Lion Hall, I would certainly miss it.

We arrived at the manor, and fortunately there was no reception committee. A couple of stable lads dozing in the afternoon sun took no notice of us.

Agneta, however, seemed to have been watching. She came down the front steps as we emerged from the car. Her skirt was almost the same color as Paul's trousers, and she wore a diaphanous raspberry-colored blouse.

"Welcome to Lion Hall," she said and gave Paul her hand.

Though clearly intimidated, he shook it politely. "Thank you very much for the invitation. This is all very impressive."

"And you have not even seen the interior." Agneta laughed. "Matilda will certainly give you a tour. But first I would like to invite you to join us in the salon."

"Delighted," Paul answered and followed her into the manor. I saw he was feeling overwhelmed—hardly surprising, considering the array of framed portraits staring down at him. I remembered very well my own reaction upon stepping into the entry hall for the first time.

Agneta gave him a moment to look around, then led us toward the salon.

"This was my mother's favorite room," she said, stepping through the art deco doors that had recently been given a new coat of green paint. "I must admit that at first I didn't care for it. Probably because Mother's friends, who often visited, were not particularly well disposed to me. I was a bit too . . . progressive . . . for their tastes."

"Were they against your driving the automobile?" I asked.

"Oh, it was much later that I learned to drive. But there were many aspects of my young life that were unusual for those times. For example, I was still unmarried at the ripe old age of twenty-seven."

"That would be unusual today as well," I responded. "Many young women want to get married as soon as possible."

"And why is that, really?" Agneta asked. "We campaigned back then against the obligation to marry. Or at least not to be auctioned off like breeding stock."

I hid a little smile when I saw Paul's shocked expression. Agneta had once commented that there were different worlds for men and women; many women could feel quite at ease in the men's world, but very few men could deal with the women's world. I didn't know if she was right about that, but Paul's sudden discomfort was evident.

"Countess Agneta was a suffragette," I explained to him.

"Indeed I was, and proud of it! Unfortunately, life here has not allowed me much time to act on those convictions, but we certainly celebrated when women were finally granted the vote."

She brought us to the table in the center of the room with old-fashioned basket chairs grouped around it. A coffee service awaited us on the glass tabletop beside a display rack with seven varieties of pastry.

"In this very spot in 1914, a couple of women asked my opinion of the assassination of the Austrian archduke," she said as she settled in her chair. "Charming, yes? But have no fear, Mr. Ringström, I will not torment you with such talk. Consider this simply a welcome to my home. You must be quite fatigued. The trains are faster these days, but the trip still requires almost a full day."

"Thank you, I feel fine," Paul said as he seated himself.

I took on the task of serving coffee and sat opposite him. The place at Agneta's side belonged to Lennard, and when he was absent, she sat alone on the sofa. *"With my mother's ghost,"* she'd once explained with a smile.

"I'm happy to get away from Stockholm," Paul added. "I'm usually in the workshop all day. My family doesn't like to travel."

"And you?" Agneta inquired. "When I first met Matilda, she told me she would like to see the world."

"So would I. Especially in her company."

Agneta gave an almost imperceptible nod, then took a sip of coffee. "I would have liked to travel as well. But when one has an estate, one cannot afford to absent oneself for long."

We chatted about this and that for almost an hour. Paul was wary, like a traveler forced to cross an unsteady bridge that might give way at any moment, although Agneta gave him not the slightest reason to feel that way. Warm and friendly, she responded with great interest to whatever he had to say.

At last we'd emptied most of the pastry rack and finished the pot of coffee as well.

"Is there anything else you would like, Mr. Ringström?" Agneta asked. "May I offer you more?"

He shook his head. "No, thank you! I've had more than enough already."

"That being the case, I would suggest you two take a little stroll. You must have a great deal to say to one another." She winked at me, gave Paul a warm smile, rose, and went to the salon door.

I was greatly relieved. I had Paul to myself at last!

"The countess is very impressive," he said as we crossed the garden and made our way to the pavilion. The bees buzzed in the blue lupine flowers that bloomed in profusion all about the manor. "She towered over me like a mountain I would never dare to climb."

"And you'd better not try," I teased him. "Unless you're looking for trouble with the count!"

"I've never met a woman so decisive and so intelligent."

"What about me?"

"You're intelligent too, but in a different way."

I raised my eyebrows, which made him run a hand nervously through his hair and scratch the nape of his neck. "Sorry, I guess that sounds kind of funny. The countess is—is like a mother-in-law a person would really like to impress, but then he realizes he has almost nothing to offer."

"She'll never be your mother-in-law," I replied. "After all, she's not my mother. When she's no longer my guardian, if all goes well, she'll be a good friend. And you really have nothing to fear from a friend." With those words we climbed the steps to the romantic pavilion. We sat on the wooden bench, and I leaned against him. My heart filled with warmth. "I've missed you so much. All these weeks and months . . ."

"I wish you could come back to Stockholm."

I shook my head. "It's not that simple."

But I knew what Paul meant. Separation was horrible, and I sensed it had created a gulf between us. That distance could be resolved only by writing more frequently or, better, by wandering together through the park every day.

"We'll see," I said finally, speaking more to myself than to him. "I'll concentrate on my studies and we'll see how things develop."

I had a notion he was going to suggest I ask his father for a job. Mr. Ringström spent a great deal of time doing his accounts. I was sure I could polish off that work much more quickly. But Paul didn't suggest it, and I was thankful.

"What do you say—shall I show you the horse barns? Even if you don't know much about horses, I'd like to give you an idea of my surroundings."

"I'm happy for you to show me whatever you like," he said with a smile as he took me into his arms. I was a bit shy at first, for I was afraid Agneta might be watching. Her office window had an unimpeded view of the back gardens. But then I threw caution to the winds and sought his lips with mine.

As we walked to the barns, I told Paul the story of the great fire and described the momentous birth of the most recent foal.

"But aren't horses born all the time on an estate like this?" Paul asked.

"That's true, but the births of really valuable animals, those with pedigrees, are always celebrated. Agneta never misses the opportunity to attend. A veterinarian is called in specially, and the horse immediately gets a name."

Paul gave me an astonished look.

"What is it?" I asked.

"A year ago I wouldn't have believed it possible for you to get excited over such things."

"Nor would I," I admitted. "But the foals are simply too cute for words! I'll show you, if you like."

We ran into Ingmar just before we reached the stalls. He came around the corner of the barn wearing riding breeches, a checkered shirt, and rubber boots.

"Oh, Ingmar!" I said. "This is Paul Ringström."

"Pleased to meet you." Ingmar smiled, but I saw a dangerous light in his eyes, similar to his twin's cool regard. "I am Ingmar Lejongård. Lejongård-Ekberg, actually, since my parents decided to give us both names. But for simplicity's sake I use Lejongård."

Paul was obviously bewildered. He glanced at me, then responded, "It's a pleasure."

"Just call me Ingmar. Any friend of Matilda is a friend of mine."

"That's very kind of you. You can call me Paul."

"All right, then. Have to go now, Paul! We will see one another at mealtime."

Ingmar tossed a smile in my direction, turned around, and disappeared. I was sure he had nothing urgent to attend to, but I was relieved that he was discreet enough to leave me alone with Paul. I'd been afraid he would dog our steps.

"He is practically a child," Paul whispered once Ingmar was gone. "And a pretty stuck-up one at that."

"Ingmar's not stuck-up. He was explaining things, that's all. Count Lennard's last name is Ekberg, Countess Agneta is a Lejongård. The children's double last name has ancestral reasons more than anything. That way neither name will die out."

Paul shook his head. "These people have completely different concerns."

"That's true, and you and I can hardly imagine them. And I have no intention of dubbing our children Wallin-Ringström. We're ordinary people and can be happy we don't have to worry about whether our family names are preserved or not."

"Well, Father would be pleased to have Ringström grandchildren, but lots of people have that name. Lejongård, on the other hand—that's one I've never come across."

"If it's up to me, your father's wishes will be fulfilled," I said and escorted him to the pen where the mares delivered their foals.

After I'd shown Paul the stalls and some of the pastureland, we went back to the house. He put on his tie, and I excused myself to put on the red dress Lennard had given me.

We found our way to the dining table, and Paul's place was next to mine.

The count shook Paul's hand. "Aha, so this is the young man our Matilda has told us so much about!"

"Thank you very much for inviting me. Matilda showed me some of the estate, and I must say that it is very impressive."

"Just wait, then, until you see our fields," said Lennard with an amiable smile. "I expect that a man from the city might find estate life somewhat monotonous. The compensation is that we have fresh air and all the quiet we want. You come to appreciate that when you are my age."

We seated ourselves, and an awkward silence settled over the table.

"Well, I think people have a mistaken idea of city dwellers," I began. "We too have our refuges. Parks, for example. Or terraces along the shore. Often we simply wander through the old town."

"Oh yes, it is really charming," Agneta replied. "I often went there with my friend Marit." She turned to Lennard. "I really believe we should invite her here again."

"With pleasure, my love," the count said. He rang a little bell to signal that the maids could begin serving.

I hadn't seen Agneta's friend Marit in all the time I'd been here. The countess mentioned her often and recounted anecdotes of their times together, but her most recent visit must have been quite some time earlier.

The servants came in one after another, bringing bowls laden with potatoes, vegetables, and sausages. We didn't get such a variety every day. I was pleased that Paul was being treated to a special meal instead of just the traditional *pyttipanna* hash the cook often prepared from leftovers.

During the meal I had the feeling that Ingmar and Paul were keeping an eye on one another, sizing each other up. It was laughable. Paul was twenty, and Ingmar had turned seventeen in the spring, so there was a world of difference. Paul was right; opposite him, Ingmar did look boyish. As I thought about it, I saw that in Paul's eyes Ingmar must have an advantage: he lived in the same residence with me, while Paul was far away in Stockholm.

"Well, Mr. Ringström, how are things in Stockholm these days?" Agneta said, seeking to get a conversation started.

"Oh, there have been many recent changes," he replied. "There's construction everywhere. Parts of the city that used to be sparsely settled are now pulsing with life. One has trouble believing the rest of the world is having economic problems."

"Do you follow the news reports?" Lennard asked.

"Oh, of course! We often discuss politics over the dinner table."

I saw Agneta's eyebrows go up. Just for a moment, but I was sure of it.

"And what do you think of developments in Germany? Support for the German chancellor seems to have eroded. And the unrest continues to spread."

"My father is concerned about the growing strength of nationalist forces," Paul answered. "He thinks nothing good will come of the gangs fighting one another. Hitler strikes a chord among the needy, and Father sees that as dangerous."

"Your father is interested in events abroad?"

"We have some clients in Germany. It wouldn't be good for us if the unrest became general or war came. There would be financial consequences. My father is very pragmatic."

"Your father sounds like a wise man," Lennard commented. "But I think his concern for his enterprise may be unwarranted. The development of the residential construction industry here offers great opportunities. Those apartments have to be furnished, after all."

"That's true, and my father and I are optimistic." Paul gave me a quick glance, and I blushed. "One day I expect to open my own branch of the business. Or even my own independent firm."

I'd been waiting for him to say that. I smiled as I felt Agneta's sharp eyes on me. Was she watching for some sign of my feelings? Was she trying to discern whether we were really suited for one another?

She turned to Paul once more and began discussing art. I hadn't thought my friend cared about painting at all, but he made me proud by valiantly holding up his end of the conversation.

I accompanied Paul to the car after dinner. I'd have liked to be alone with him, but I didn't want to cross the boundaries Agneta had defined.

"That was a pleasant evening," Paul said, holding my hands. "The Lejongårds are good people. I'm content that you're with them."

"I'd rather be with you," I said. "But you're right, they're upstanding and admirable. They treat me like a daughter."

"And you've earned it too. Your mother would be proud."

I nodded and regretted that here in the manor lamplight I couldn't give free rein to my emotions.

"We'll see one another in the morning, won't we?" he asked.

"Yes, we will. I'm going to ask Svea, our cook, to prepare a picnic basket. We can walk in the meadows or go to the lake."

"That sounds fine."

"And not too boring?"

"Nothing could ever be boring with you." He pulled me to him and gave me a kiss on the lips. Not as passionate a kiss as on the train platform, but the memory of it would stay with me in my dreams.

He climbed into the automobile, and it pulled away. An enormous longing washed over me. He was no farther away than the neighboring village! And yet I had the impression that a part of my soul vanished with him in the darkness.

19

Early the next morning I asked for my horse to be saddled and went to the kitchen. Svea had promised she'd have the picnic basket ready before breakfast.

The maids were whispering together when I arrived.

"Good morning," I said, provoking an instant silence. Rika's face was red. What was going on?

"Good morning, Miss Matilda," Lena said. "You must be here for the basket."

"Yes, and I see it's ready. Where is Svea? I'd like to thank her."

"She's caring for Mrs. Bloomquist. Our old cook has taken a turn for the worse since yesterday. Svea's taking her some soup."

"Then I'll thank her when I get back. Please say hello for me!"

"I will."

The whispering recommenced behind Lena.

I understood their excitement had to do with me. "Is something going on?"

"No," Lena said, embarrassed. "The girls are going on and on, trying to decide whether the young man who visited yesterday is your fiancé."

Aha.

"No, he's a friend from Stockholm. I've known him almost all my life." Paul was much more than that, but it would've been inappropriate to describe him as my fiancé when we didn't have permission from his parents or the countess. "He's visiting for a week."

The girls hid their reactions, but I knew they were disappointed.

"Too bad," Rika commented. "It would really be wonderful to have another wedding at the estate."

"I'm sorry, this is partly my fault," Lena said. "I described the countess's wedding to them not too long ago. I was very young in those days. There's been no wedding on the estate since then, and the girls are hoping for another."

"They'll have to wait a while longer," I said. "But if that day comes, I can imagine getting married here. The pavilion is gorgeous."

"They say the gracious lady's parents were married there," Lena said. "She would certainly be delighted."

They gave me hopeful looks.

"Well, then, I'd better go," I said, not wanting to give them reason to launch into wedding plans for me.

I turned away. The girls managed to control themselves until I'd mounted the stairs, and then the discussion burst out again. Were they debating what kind of dress I would wear?

"You are not staying for breakfast?" Ingmar asked as I made my way to the door, picnic basket in hand.

"No, and I probably won't get back until this evening," I said. "I spoke to Agneta and got her permission."

Ingmar didn't hide his skepticism. "And where do you two intend to go? Surely you are not going to that fellow's room!"

"That is no concern of yours," I responded. "And besides, he's not a 'fellow.' His name is Paul."

"I remember. But I think I should know where you two are headed. One never knows; he might still turn out to be a cad."

"Paul is no cad! I forbid you to talk about him that way!"

Ingmar raised his hands to pacify me. "Just joking! In this weather, I assume you will go to the lake or to the meadow with the big willow tree."

"That may be," I said. I'd been intending exactly that. And what if Ingmar suddenly turned up? If he did, I hoped he wouldn't provoke a confrontation.

"Then enjoy yourselves, you two," he said. "And if it should enter his head not to behave like a gentleman, then . . ."

"Then I will correct him," I said. "I'll see you this evening!"

Outside, I fastened the basket to the saddle. It looked a bit precarious, but I wasn't going to be riding at a gallop. I swung up and headed out through the gate.

The morning was splendid. I was bubbling with anticipation. I'd never had so much time alone with Paul before!

Not much was going on in the village at this time of day. The people were in the fields, seeing to the wheat and the root crops.

I hitched the horse up outside the inn and went inside just as Paul came downstairs.

"You're incredibly punctual!" He gave me a kiss. The innkeeper was watching us from behind the bar, and I was sure the news would spread like wildfire.

"They say it's going to be very warm, so I'd like to get us into the shade as soon as possible."

"And how are we to get there? You didn't happen to bring a carriage, did you?"

"No, my horse. And a picnic basket."

"But you know I can't ride!"

"We don't need to ride. I'll lead the horse. The estate meadows aren't far from here."

I'd actually wanted to go to the lake, but after the exchange with Ingmar, I was willing to bet he'd turn up there sooner or later. The meadow was a bit more secluded.

"And we can get there on foot?"

"It'll take maybe half an hour." I took his hand. "Come on, I have everything we need."

I drew him outside and unhitched the horse. The village street remained deserted except for a cat on a fence assiduously licking itself.

We walked at an easy pace until we reached the place I'd chosen. I knew the meadows of the estate as well as the contents of my own wardrobe. This spot would remain in shade all day long.

Svea, who'd thought of everything, had folded a blanket over the picnic basket. I spread it out under the huge willow.

The basket was packed with cunning little pastries, bread rolls, hard-boiled eggs, baked goods, some jam and butter, and fruit. She'd included a jar of pickled strawberries and a thermos of coffee.

"We have everything we could ever want," I said after I'd laid it all out. "Now, don't tell me you get a feast like this every day."

Paul pulled me to him with a smile. "No, this is anything but ordinary." He kissed me and we settled back onto the blanket. "It outdoes even Daga's efforts to please her beloved."

"She has a beloved?"

"Yes, Arndt. He works in an office. If you ask me, he's a good match. Unfortunately, his parents live all the way out in Småland, a long way from Stockholm. They own a glassworks."

"Daga loves glassware!"

"Indeed. I hope Arndt can get them a big house. She'll fill it up!"

"So you think she'll marry him?" Daga hadn't told me she had a boyfriend! I realized I needed to work harder to stay in contact with her, despite her heavy workload in the seamstress's shop.

"Probably. Daga's like you—once she sets her sights on a man, she's not going to let him get away."

"I'm not quite like that," I replied.

"That's what you say! The two of you are like the little shepherdess who wants to marry the Danish prince," he declared and added in a falsetto, "'Just watch; I'll catch him soon!'"

I recognized those familiar lines from the fable. "I hope Arndt has the magic stone his true bride will have to tread upon. Life in fairy tales is so much simpler."

"But less predictable." Paul picked a grape and popped it into his mouth.

We ate slowly and savored every bite of Svea's picnic, then we lay embracing on the blanket and looking up at the ceiling of sheltering leaves. The quiet rustling in the branches overhead lulled me. There was no place I'd rather be.

"You know," I said, wanting to stay awake so as not to waste a single moment with Paul, "this morning the girls in the kitchen asked if we were going to get married on the estate."

"Really?"

"I told them I didn't know yet. And besides, we're still too young to get married."

"Is that right? You had a different opinion just nine months ago."

"You were right not to agree," I told him. "I was desperate, ready to do anything to get away. But I know it wouldn't have been good for us. At least one of us has to be an adult in the eyes of the law. Otherwise everyone else can tell us what to do."

"You're right about that. Do you think the countess will give us her consent?"

"That depends entirely upon your behavior here."

"Did the lady say anything? I was pretty nervous yesterday."

"No comments were made, but I have the impression Lennard likes you."

"And the countess?"

"She didn't express an opinion."

"Not so enthusiastic, I guess." Paul plucked a stalk of grass and twisted it between his fingers.

"Agneta thinks I shouldn't allow myself to become attached too soon. I'd risk suffering the same fate as my mother."

"Life as a servant?"

"Getting pregnant out of wedlock. People don't talk about it, but it turns out my mother was pregnant when she left the estate. I have no idea how my father managed that. They won't discuss that either."

"And how about the maids at the mansion?" Paul asked. "Did they know your mother?"

"Lena did. As did old Mrs. Bloomquist, I'm sure. But she won't say much. She's much more interested in the kitchen and her recipes. She never married."

"And your Lena isn't interested in getting married?"

"I don't know. We don't talk about such things. And I'm glad we don't."

I turned to Paul. His features had changed since I left Stockholm. His face was more rugged and manly, more squared off. He'd lost the look of adolescence even more definitely than I had.

Paul returned my gaze and raised the wisp of grass to my face. He ran it gently across my cheeks and then along my upper lip. It tickled at first, and then I felt a different sensation. A subtle warmth spread through my abdomen and crept upward to fill my heart and breast. I felt a sweet tingling, an edge of impatient expectation.

Paul sensed it. I saw him gulp and heard his breathing quicken. He dropped the stalk of grass, bent over, and kissed me as never before. His lips pushed against mine, and his tongue slipped into my mouth, soft and yet demanding.

I pressed myself to him and returned that kiss. His hands gripped my body, and I threw my arms around him. His hand ran down my side and around my hip, and he grasped my thigh.

As he caressed me, my heart pounded so wildly I thought my chest would burst. I felt a throbbing between my legs, a sensation I'd often had when thinking of Paul. I clamped the blanket between my legs in an effort to suppress it and to keep from imagining our wedding night.

Passionate longing overwhelmed me for a moment, but then I remembered Agneta's warning. I was an inexperienced virgin, but I could see where this was heading. My mother got pregnant before she married, and I had to avoid that at all costs.

I grabbed Paul's hand. "Don't, please," I whispered. "We mustn't!"

He rolled away with a gasp. His face was flushed. He stared at me, uncomprehending at first, and then sank back. I sat up, my heart hammering furiously. I'd never wanted anything so urgently, and never in my life had I been so frightened.

"I'm sorry," Paul said and sat up as well. "I just thought—"

"Shh!" I'd suddenly heard something.

A rider was approaching. I recognized Ingmar and rolled away. I didn't want him to see me in Paul's arms.

"Here you are!" he called. "I have been looking for you everywhere!"

"Why?" I asked. "I told your mother where I was going."

"Right, but who knew whom you might be meeting?" He gave Paul a defiant look.

"I expect you recognize me," my visitor commented.

"Of course he does!" I got to my feet. "What do you want, Ingmar? Is something wrong?"

"No. I just thought I might swing by and make sure things had not gotten out of hand. I am not disturbing you, am I?"

"Yes, in fact, you are!" How much had he seen? And if Paul and I had actually . . . I couldn't bear to think of the consequences. "Ride back home, Ingmar. I wouldn't spoil your fun if you were out somewhere with a girl."

"Right, then," he said. "See you tonight!"

His resentment was obvious. Why were men like this?

He yanked his horse around and spurred it viciously. The dapple gray reared and dashed off in the direction of an irrigation ditch that wound its way through the meadow. It wasn't particularly deep or wide, but the edges were steep and slippery.

I realized Ingmar intended to leap the ditch.

"Is he always like that?" Paul asked, getting to his feet beside me.

I was transfixed, unable to do anything except stare at that ditch. My riding master had warned me about it. Ingmar was a far more experienced rider, but there was no need for this foolhardy exploit.

"I don't know what's gotten into him." I shook my head and turned to look at Paul, but then heard a loud cry.

I spun around. Ingmar had disappeared. And there was no sign of the horse either.

"Damn!" I took off running.

"Where are you going?" Paul called.

I paid no attention to him. My heart was racing.

"Ingmar!" I shouted. "Are you all right?" I ran so hard I got a tremendous stitch in my side and could hardly breathe.

I reached the ditch and screamed in horror. Ingmar and the horse were at the bottom. The animal must have broken its neck. Worse, it had fallen on top of Ingmar, who lay motionless beneath it, his legs and torso in the shallow water.

"Paul!" I shouted. My friend was a few steps behind.

"What's—" he began, but the awful spectacle took his breath away.

"We have to get him out from under the horse! Quick!" I leaped into the ditch and tried to grab Ingmar under the arms but couldn't get a proper grip.

"Can you budge the horse a little?" I asked Paul, who stood there like a pillar of salt. "That's the only way we can free him!"

Paul slid down and braced his shoulder against the animal. It didn't move at first, but when he put his feet against the wall of the ditch for leverage, he managed to displace the horse's weight just enough for

Ingmar's body to slip a couple of inches. I tried to pull him free, but he was far too heavy for me.

"Help!" I cried. "I can't move him."

Paul abandoned the horse and came to me. I moved aside, and he grabbed Ingmar under the armpits. I wanted to help but had no idea where to seize the inert body.

Paul hauled forcefully, grunting with the effort. Ingmar's drenched legs came into view. I didn't want to touch them for fear they might be broken. But Paul couldn't move him all alone.

"Hold him upright for just a moment," Paul said. "I'll haul him up onto the grass."

I wrapped my arms around Ingmar's torso, and gritted my teeth as Paul clambered up out of the ditch.

"Hurry! I can't hold him much longer!"

"Coming!" Paul cried, stretched out on the ground, and reached for Ingmar. He managed to get a grip and pulled with all his might. I tried to push up Ingmar's legs to help him. Once I saw my friend succeeding, I climbed up after them.

"Careful!" I cried as Paul stretched Ingmar out on the grass. "He might have broken something."

"Entirely likely."

I squatted down next to the boy's head. "Ingmar?" I called and patted his cheeks. "Ingmar, wake up!"

But he didn't react.

I felt for a pulse and found it, but it was very feeble.

"I'll get the doctor. Keep watch over him!"

I jumped up and ran to my horse. My heart thundered so loudly in my ears that I didn't hear whether Paul replied. I untied my brown mount and glanced at Ingmar's fallen steed. Its head was twisted horribly. Why the hell had Ingmar insisted on showing off?

My stomach contracted painfully, and I was quaking with anxiety by the time I reached the village. I had no idea where the doctor's office was, for he always made house calls for us. He was the son of old Dr. Bengtsen, who had passed away a couple of years earlier. Agneta had told me how pleased she was that the practice remained in the same family.

I was lucky enough to come across a man in the village who gave me directions, and moments later I leaped down from the saddle outside the office. It was open for consultations; two elderly women and a man sat in the waiting room. Voices were audible through a closed door, but I couldn't wait.

I tore the door open. "Dr. Bengtsen, please come right now!" I begged the astonished doctor, who had a stethoscope applied to a patient's back. "Ingmar Lejongård has fallen with his horse. He's unconscious!"

The doctor stopped his instinctive objection in midsentence. "Where?" he asked, tearing off his stethoscope.

"In the meadow by the little lake."

"Are you on horseback?" he asked.

"Yes," I said. "I can take you with me."

"That's not necessary; I'll follow you. Please wait outside. I'll be right there."

I nodded and abandoned the consultation room. The people there stared wide eyed at me. I dashed outside.

Moments later the physician led his own horse out of its stall. I saw a bulky saddlebag that must contain his instrument case. He mounted and we galloped away.

I pushed my horse as fast as I could and lost no time worrying that I'd never ridden this fast before. I reached the site of the accident and ran to Paul and Ingmar.

"Has he come to?" I cried. I pressed my ear to Ingmar's chest. I heard his heart beating, but what if he had internal injuries?

The doctor was with us immediately. He opened his case and methodically began examining Ingmar.

"Please ride to the manor house," the doctor said. "We need an automobile. The chauffeur should bring it as close to here as possible. We must get this young man to the hospital."

I gave a despairing moan. Was Ingmar that badly injured? Fear paralyzed me.

"Please go, miss!" the doctor shouted at me. "Now!"

I spun around, catching a glimpse of Paul's chalk-white face. I had no time to hug him. Agneta needed to know what had happened.

I was blinded by tears and deafened by my pounding heartbeat all the way to the manor. I passed through the estate gate—no thanks to me, but because the horse knew its way home. I urged it to the circular drive and leaped down from the saddle. My knees gave way as I hastened up the front steps; I sank to all fours but forced myself back up and continued.

The girls in the entry hall were shocked when they saw me.

"Miss Matilda, what happened?" Lena asked.

"The countess," I wheezed, "is she in her office?"

"Yes, of course."

"Thanks!" I hurried up the steps. My knees shook, and for a moment I thought I wouldn't be able to speak. I rushed in without knocking. "Countess, Ingmar had a bad fall with his horse!" I cried and only then did I see the count was with her.

Lennard spun around and Agneta jumped up.

"I got the doctor. We need the car. He has to go to the hospital."

The countess paled. "Oh my God!" she gasped and ran to the door, the count close behind.

"Where did this happen?" he asked as we raced down the stairs.

"In the meadow close to the lake. He was trying to jump the ditch, but the horse slipped and fell. We got to him right away."

"We?"

"Paul and I. We were having a picnic, and Ingmar came by."

Agneta seemed not to hear any of this. Her eyes were dead, and she moved like an automaton.

She took the wheel and beckoned me inside. The motor roared to life. "Show me where!"

The count joined us and Agneta stepped on the gas. The tires spun and kicked up gravel.

I guided the countess to the meadow. Agneta left the road, turning onto a track through the grass that horse-drawn wagons had made. The automobile bounced and groaned in protest, but soon we saw the ditch and then Ingmar, Paul, and the doctor. My stomach clenched in fear.

Agneta yanked on the hand brake, killed the motor, and leaped out. I'd never seen her move so fast.

"Dr. Bengtsen, how is my son?" she cried.

"He's alive, but I fear his back may be broken. He may have a concussion as well. In any case, I can't be sure; we need X-rays. He must be taken to the hospital."

I looked at Paul. He stood there stunned, avoiding everyone's eyes. I went to him and grasped his arm.

"Did he wake up?" I whispered.

Paul shook his head. "No. The doctor tried to wake him, even put smelling salts under his nose. But he didn't move a muscle."

Worried, I looked back at Ingmar. *Come on, wake up!* I silently pleaded. *Sit up and tell us that you just stepped away for a moment. Tell us you're all right!*

His eyes remained closed, and his mouth didn't twitch. His face was deathly pale. I saw no sign of blood, but that meant nothing. Blood didn't always show.

"Count Ekberg, will you please help me get the young man into the car?" the doctor said. "We must drive very carefully to avoid any damage to the spine. We would lose too much precious time if we waited for the ambulance."

"I will drive him personally," Agneta said.

"Are you sure?" Lennard asked, but his wife's glare silenced him.

"Good. Then place your arms beneath him so as to support the body, and I'll do the same from the other side." He looked toward Paul. "And you, young man, please help us with his legs."

Paul looked as if the doctor had just demanded he leap into the fiery pit of hell, but he obeyed. All together they lifted Ingmar. Even though they were three grown men, they had difficulty carrying the inert body to the car. I ran ahead and opened the rear door. Fortunately, the top was already folded back, which simplified the task of arranging him. They placed Ingmar on the upholstered rear seat, careful to keep his spine properly aligned.

"I will stay here next to him," the physician said and worked his way into the narrow space between the front seats and the back.

"Can you manage?" Agneta asked, for the doctor's position looked awkward and unnatural.

"Yes, it's fine. The important thing is to keep the young man from rolling out of position."

Agneta nodded. "Matilda, will you come with me?"

"Yes, gladly, but . . . wouldn't it be better if the count went?"

"My husband has to go back to the manor. We are expecting an important call from the royal stable master. I will phone him with an update from the hospital and he will join us there later."

I'd heard that Clarence von Rosen had inquired about a pair of breeding stallions.

"Good, I'll come with you then," I said and went back to Paul. I was so terribly upset. We'd expected a completely different afternoon.

"I'm accompanying the countess to the hospital," I explained to him. "Can we see one another when I get back?"

Paul nodded. "We can."

I hugged him and felt him trembling. Or was it me?

I pulled away and ran to the car. Agneta was giving Lennard instructions. "Pack a bag for him, please, he will certainly have to stay at the hospital for a while."

"I will. Do not worry, my love," Lennard replied. "Just stay at his side."

I hopped into the passenger seat. It occurred to me that this was where Magnus had always sat on the way to and from school. Agneta started the motor.

"Everything all right back there, Doctor?" she asked, glancing into the rearview mirror.

"Yes, gracious lady, everything is set."

With that she moved off with great care, as if driving on eggshells.

20

As we made our way down the highway at moderate speed—Agneta avoided the potholes at all costs—I looked back at Ingmar again and again.

I hoped against hope he would at least come to, but his condition remained unchanged. He looked asleep, but his pallor was alarming. I was frustrated that I didn't know more about human biology. What sort of injury would drain his face of all color? I was horribly frightened, and I wasn't the only one. Agneta drove with great concentration, but desperation crouched in her eyes. She clutched the steering wheel so tightly that her knuckles were white.

We reached Kristianstad after an hour that seemed an eternity. Traffic became dense, and some drivers honked when they couldn't get around us quickly. Only now was I realizing how hectic city life was and how impatient urban dwellers were.

We reached the hospital at last. From afar the tall white building with many windows looked like a hotel. The reek of disinfectant reached us as soon as we rolled through the gate. Agneta drove straight around to the back. The alternate entrance was wide and level to facilitate delivery of injured persons.

The doctor gave a little groan as he climbed out of the car but immediately straightened up and hurried inside.

Agneta sat for a moment behind the wheel, then pulled herself together and climbed out. She opened the rear door and reached in to put her palm on Ingmar's forehead. "Wake up, my boy," she whispered. "You must not leave us. What would I do without you? What would any of us do?"

A tear trickled down her cheek as she bent down to kiss him. I felt like bawling but tried to control my emotions. Agneta needed strong support, just as I had on the day they carried my mother's body away. There'd been no one for me then; the neighbor women were no help at all.

Dr. Bengtsen was soon back with white-uniformed men and women trundling a wheeled stretcher.

The following moments stretched out bizarrely. Agneta stepped aside and wiped away tears with the back of her hand; the orderlies carefully lifted Ingmar from the back seat and placed him on their trolley. His head lolled to the side. What if his neck had been injured? I didn't know what a person with a broken neck looked like, but I was horribly afraid.

They wheeled him through the wide entry. Half-heard scraps of consultation fluttered behind them like birds. The earth beneath my feet seemed to tilt. I felt a hand on my shoulder.

"Come, Matilda." It was Agneta.

"Please," I said, "I'm not feeling well. I'd think I'd best stay here for a minute."

She nodded, and followed Ingmar and the attendants. The great mouth of the rear entrance swallowed her up, and I squeezed my eyes shut. A low buzzing filled my ears. *Don't faint,* I told myself. *Don't you dare faint!*

I stood there with my mind blank for a long time, unaware of my surroundings. At last the buzzing faded, lost in the thunder of my furiously pounding heart. I felt blood infusing my limbs. I opened my eyes.

By some miracle I was still on my feet beside the automobile. Someone had closed its doors. I went around the car, entered the hospital, and encountered a labyrinth of stairs and corridors.

One of the nurses directed me to a second-floor corridor lined with folding chairs. I dropped onto one. It was quiet there, but muffled noises came from the other side of the swinging doors. Was Ingmar really here? What could the medical staff be doing?

I squeezed my wrist without thinking and was shocked to find that Ingmar's bracelet had disappeared. Had it been torn off as we struggled to free him from beneath the horse? I had an irrational urge to go look for it, but good sense prevailed.

Tears filled my eyes. What if the loss of the bracelet was a bad omen? Ingmar would be furious! But why was I worrying about that while he was probably struggling for his life?

The examining room door swung open, and Agneta came out. Her hair was in tangles, she shambled like an elderly woman, and her arms hung lifeless at her sides.

I jumped to my feet. "How is he? Is he all right?"

She dropped heavily into a chair. "They took X-rays, and now all we can do is wait. He has a severe concussion, in any case. We will not know if anything is broken or whether he has internal injuries until the plates are developed. We have to wait."

He was still alive, but what if he could never walk or ride again?

"I'm so upset!" I placed a hand on Agneta's arm. "I feel like it's my fault."

Agneta shook her head. "No, you should not feel that way. I only wish Ingmar had been more careful. What could have possessed him? He must have known that ditch was much too wide to jump."

I could have told her what had possessed him. But why cause her more pain?

"You know, I have mixed feelings about hospitals," Agneta said, staring blankly at the light-green walls. "A hospital is meant to preserve life, but things go wrong all too often."

She continued staring. "My brother died here. So did my mother. We brought her here for a heart condition, but it was too late. There was no longer any hope. But I suppose it would be unfair to claim that this institution fails to sustain life. Ingmar and Magnus's births were difficult. I am afraid I would not have survived, had I not had the sense to arrange to deliver here. Still, enormous anxiety afflicts me whenever I enter."

"I understand that," I replied. "But death comes at home as well. My mother died in our house in the middle of the night. I found her the next morning. I wish I'd had the chance to take her to a hospital. Maybe doctors could have helped. She was far too young to die."

"Yes, she was. And the same was true of your father. All too often, life subjects us to trials and burdens that seem too much to bear."

"And often it's not just 'seem,'" I responded. "They *are* too much. That's when you feel like screaming."

Agneta looked at me. "Do you feel like screaming now?"

"Later," I answered. "When I'm alone in the forest. It wouldn't be appropriate right now. I might scare the patients out of their beds."

A wry smile flickered across Agneta's face.

At that moment Dr. Bengtsen came through the swinging door. He had his jacket over one arm, and his shirt was soaked with sweat. His face was flushed.

Agneta rose. "Are the X-ray plates ready?"

"No, but they will be soon. I discussed his case with my colleagues. Their preliminary examination eliminated the possibility of a broken neck, for which we can all be grateful, but we have to verify the condition of his spine. The young man may have to spend weeks or even months in a plaster cast. My colleagues will make that decision. Excuse me now, for I must return to my practice."

"Take my automobile," Agneta said. She glanced at me. "And would you be so kind as to drive Matilda to Lion Hall?"

"Naturally."

"But I want to stay here!"

"You are welcome to come back later," she told me. "For the moment there is nothing you can do. Make sure my husband packs a valise for Ingmar. If he has not, help him do so."

I nodded.

Agneta handed Dr. Bengtsen the car keys. "Take good care of yourself and Matilda. We will discuss the matter of your fee when I return."

We left the waiting area and went downstairs. I wanted to pester the doctor with questions, but I didn't dare.

We climbed into the automobile, and the doctor knew exactly what to do. He handled it as confidently as if it were his own.

"I learned how to drive in the army," he explained. "One of the best lessons I took from there. Would you like to get a driver's license someday?"

I was in no mood to discuss driving, but I could tell he was making small talk to distract me from my worries.

"I certainly would," I answered. "The countess's driving skills impress me very much."

"Yes, Countess Lejongård is a remarkable woman. My father was close to the family, and I certainly understand why."

The doctor drove faster than Agneta had dared because of Ingmar's injuries, so we reached Lion Hall in only forty-five minutes. Dr. Bengtsen's horse stood tied in the courtyard in the shade of one of the trees; Lennard must have ridden it there.

The doctor turned off the motor and gave me the keys. "Greet the count for me and ask him to keep me informed. I greatly hope the young man's injuries will turn out to be not too serious."

"Thank you, Dr. Bengtsen," I replied and shook his hand. I climbed the front steps as he rode away.

Count Lennard was pacing in the office. He was startled to see me. "Matilda!"

"Your wife is still at the hospital. Dr. Bengtsen drove me. Ingmar has been X-rayed."

"Were they able to tell you anything?"

"His neck is not broken, but unfortunately there's no other news for the moment. Your wife says they have to wait for the results of the X-rays. Those will probably be ready by the time we get there."

"Fine. Will you please pack a bag for him? I have some things to work through."

"Of course. Anything I can do to help."

I stood in the doorway of Ingmar's room, frozen with fear. I didn't care if Ingmar was angry with me; I just wanted him to live without crippling injuries. I shook my head to push away those thoughts and forced myself to concentrate on the task at hand. What did he need? Fresh clothes, pajamas. Underwear? His toothbrush? A book to keep him entertained?

My eyes fell upon the airplane model, now almost finished. I'd been so preoccupied with Paul that I'd forgotten it.

I opened the wardrobe. It smelled of cedar and soap and Ingmar himself. When I touched the trousers hanging there, it was like touching his body. Suddenly that was terribly painful. I chose one pair and took a shirt from its hanger. What else did he need? It was summer, so he wouldn't want a sweater. How about undershirts?

Fortunately, Lennard appeared a moment later. "So what do we have here?" he said. "I see you have already set out some things."

"I'm not so familiar with young men's clothing," I apologized.

"I will take care of the rest. Perhaps you would like to go choose a book for him. He will certainly be pleased to have something to read."

I was turning to go when Lennard's shoulders suddenly sagged. I went to him and placed a hand on his arm. "Are you all right?"

Of course, he wasn't all right. Nothing was all right.

"Yes, I can manage," he said. "Go quickly and get a book. I will finish with this."

My anxiety increased with every passing minute, but the task of doing something for Ingmar distracted me. It took a while, but I finally found something I thought he would like: Jules Verne's novel *Five Weeks in a Balloon*, about a scientist who invented a new kind of dirigible to circumnavigate the globe. The book was fairly old, and I didn't know if Ingmar had already read it.

I found Count Lennard descending the stairs. His face was red, so he'd probably been weeping. Worry about Ingmar was about to tear me in half, but I did my best to appear calm.

"Have you picked something?"

I showed him the book.

"A fine choice," the count declared. "Ingmar is fascinated by flight. I did not know we had that title in our library. You have keen eyes. We are ready to go now, I think?"

I followed him to the car.

On the ride over, I caught Lennard wiping away a tear, and racked my brain for a topic that might distract him from his concern.

"How was the call with von Rosen?" I asked.

Lennard's laugh came out sounding like a bark. "The noxious man wants a pair of breeding stallions, but only if we're prepared to sell to his German business partners as well. Perhaps my worry over Ingmar made me speak too rashly, but I told him that Lion Hall does not sell to Germany. Things went badly after that."

"You don't sell to Germany? Why not?"

Lennard stared straight ahead. "Agneta refused to sell to the Germany military in the Great War. And we have other, personal reasons."

A couple of white-uniformed nurses came out as we entered the hospital, obviously at the end of their shift. The stench of carbolic acid sent a shudder through me. The count carried the valise, and I accompanied him with the book tucked under my arm. We'd hardly exchanged a word during the drive. I heard him sigh deeply as we stood before the hospital's main entrance. I wanted to say something reassuring, but I couldn't; I was filled with despair.

We hurried through the corridor. Count Lennard had gotten a nurse to guide us to Ingmar's private room. Agneta was at his bedside when we entered.

They'd put Ingmar into a white hospital gown with tiny blue dots. One leg was in a plaster cast and propped on a stack of blankets. His eyes were still closed.

The countess saw us, got up, and embraced her husband. "It is so good to have you both here!"

"And what do the doctors say?"

"He has a concussion and severe neck strain. His leg and two ribs are broken."

"Has he been awake?"

Agneta nodded. "Yes, but I doubt he really knew what was happening. They gave him morphine. The physicians say he will not be able to respond coherently until sometime tomorrow."

I took a deep breath when I heard that. He'd woken up. His injuries sounded serious but not life-threatening.

"He was very lucky," Agneta added. "If he had fallen slightly differently, he would have died."

I tightened my lips. I was so relieved he'd escaped the worst. I would give him a real scolding once he got back home.

I placed the book on the bedside table. It looked as if he'd be staying for quite a while.

21

It took me a long time to get to sleep that night. Each time I closed my eyes, I found myself reliving Ingmar's accident. We'd avoided the direst consequences, but I shivered, knowing what could have happened.

Finally, I couldn't stand it. I threw off the covers, got up, and paced around the room. I wanted—no, I *had* to do something. But what?

I went to the window, pushed the curtain back, and stared out into the night. It was pitch-black out there. All I saw was my own face reflected in the windowpane.

For some reason I thought of Magnus. He would be at summer camp with his classmates for another week or so. In the confusion, no one had thought of him. Did the boarding school have a telephone? If so, Agneta could call and inform Magnus. But would that be enough? Shouldn't someone send him a telegram? Or should we just wait until he got back? I almost went to get my pen and stationery, but I realized I had no address for him. Anyhow, a message from me was probably the last thing he wanted.

I rode to the village in the morning. Just as I arrived at the inn, Paul stepped out carrying his suitcase.

"Paul?" I asked, confused.

"Good morning."

I pointed at his case. "What is this? We booked your room for a week."

"That was before," he said. "I should leave."

"But why? Ingmar had a concussion and he broke a leg and two ribs. Obviously, he'll have to stay in the hospital for a while, but—" My words died away when I saw Paul's expression.

"Matilda, I can't."

"What can't you do?" It took me a moment, but then I realized. "No! You're not jealous of Ingmar, are you?"

Paul's mouth became a grim line. I tried to embrace him, but he pulled away.

Vexed, I glared at him. "What is your problem? I had to tend to him! He was injured!"

"It has nothing to do with the accident. It's the way he was behaving toward you. Toward us. Treating me as a rival."

I felt a stir of anger. "Don't be ridiculous!"

"Is he in love with you?" he demanded with a dark look.

"No! Ingmar is like a brother, but that's all."

"Well, apparently he has a different opinion. Otherwise why would he have done such a stupid thing?"

"I have no idea. It was idiotic. It doesn't mean I like him better than you!"

"But he's here. I'm far away in Stockholm."

Something tugged at me deep inside. Was Paul blaming me for living on my guardian's estate? This attitude was completely different from what he'd written to me.

Then it clicked. He was afraid! He feared I might fall in love with Ingmar, who was there all the time. And he probably assumed I'd prefer a grand estate to a furniture workshop.

"Paul, I beg you! Ingmar is very nice, and he's helped me adjust. But there will never be anyone for me except you."

Paul's look of disbelief hurt me terribly. I fell silent. As did he.

"How do you plan to get to Kristianstad?" I asked finally.

"A farmer is giving me a ride."

I swallowed painfully, burning with disappointment. I saw that nothing I could do or say was going to change his mind.

"Please don't be angry," Paul said. "I was enjoying my time here. But I can't just pretend that nothing happened. And neither can you. We'll make up for the lost days, I promise. Maybe now you can finally get permission to visit Stockholm. That way we won't have to witness another disaster like the one yesterday."

I sighed, heavy with dull disappointment. I had plenty of time for Paul now, despite everything. And Ingmar was alive!

"All right," I heard myself say. "We'll make up for it."

Paul smiled and took me in his arms. He gave me a kiss, but it was radically different from before. There wasn't a trace of the passion I'd experienced under the willow tree.

I followed him outside. There was no sign of the farmer who was supposed to drive him.

"Won't you please reconsider?" I asked, struggling to control my emotions. I didn't want to let him go. And I didn't want him thinking I had feelings for Ingmar.

"No. The wagon will be here soon. By the way, I left your picnic basket with the innkeeper."

He kissed me one more time, but I pulled away to keep him from seeing the tears flooding my eyes. I went straight to my horse and swung up into the saddle.

I left, but rode only a little way. I hid behind a tall, thorny hedge at the edge of a field for a few minutes, and at last a wagon came jolting by. The driver didn't see me, but I recognized Paul, sitting in the bed of the wagon and gazing at the fields on the far side of the road. He looked lost in thought. What was going through his head? Was he wondering whether I was being honest? If I was worth it? His desire for me had been unmistakable—but that was yesterday.

I began crying. *Damn it, Ingmar,* I thought. *Why did you have to go and spoil everything?* But I was glad that nothing worse had happened. Ingmar was still alive, and his injuries would heal.

Perhaps Paul was right. Maybe I did love Ingmar. But it wasn't the same!

After the horse-drawn wagon disappeared down the road, I wiped away my tears and rode back to Lion Hall. I took a shortcut that Ingmar had shown me.

The automobile was parked on the circular drive before the manor. Lennard and Agneta appeared as I climbed the steps.

"Why have you returned so quickly?" Agneta asked.

"Paul left. He didn't want to stay after what happened."

The count and countess exchanged a glance. "Well, I must say that is a little unusual," Agneta said after a moment. "After all, Ingmar is doing well. There is no reason—"

"He just didn't want to stay!" burst from me, louder than I'd intended. "Excuse me," I said, embarrassed. "May I come with you to visit Ingmar? I really do not want to sit alone in my room."

"Of course," Lennard said. "Would you like a moment to change clothes?"

I looked down at myself. I was dressed well enough in my riding breeches and blouse, but I wanted to shed them as soon as possible. "Yes. Just a moment, I will be right back."

"Take your time," Lennard said. Agneta gave me a nod.

A few minutes later I stepped into the car, wearing the red dress Lennard had given me. This time the count was behind the wheel, and the countess was in the passenger seat. I had the back seat to myself. I couldn't help remembering how I'd ridden back from the train station with Paul. The memory brought a momentary smile to my face that quickly gave way to the image of him in the back of the farmer's wagon. I began to feel uneasy as we rolled toward Kristianstad. What if we caught up with him en route? Should I ask Lennard to pull over and give him a ride? Maybe he'd refuse to get into their car. I squirmed throughout the trip as if on a bed of glowing coals.

Agneta noticed. "Is there something you would like to talk about?"

I shook my head. "No. Everything is fine. I—it all happened so suddenly. I hadn't thought he would want to leave. I mean, Ingmar will get well, and—"

She turned to look at me. "Perhaps he is jealous?"

"That may be. But Ingmar is like a brother to me, so there's no reason for Paul to worry. When Ingmar was lying there in the ditch, I had to do something!"

"If he is angry with you for helping Ingmar, he is not the right man for you," the count said. "Your help was vital in minimizing Ingmar's injuries."

"Paul helped too," I said defensively. "Without him I'd never have been able to get Ingmar out from beneath the horse. That's why I don't understand. He was there; he saw everything."

Lennard sighed, and I saw him glance at his wife. His eyes returned to the road. "Men are often hard to understand. They may feel themselves threatened in situations where there is no menace whatsoever."

"It will be best for you to discuss it with him," Agneta said. "He will come to his senses once he returns home. You can write and assure him that we will welcome him back. Next time he need not stay at the inn."

I nodded, but I wasn't going to invite him to visit anytime soon. And I knew I wouldn't be allowed to travel to Stockholm alone.

Maybe that was how things would have to be. It could be a test for us. We would come together if the fates desired. I hoped with my whole heart that they did.

When we got to the hospital room, Ingmar was sitting up, waiting for us. His neck was in a brace and his leg, in its plaster cast, was in traction. The pain medicine they'd administered seemed to be effective enough to permit him a smile when we entered.

Agneta embraced her son, and so did Lennard. I gave the family their moment, then I came forward and kissed his cheek.

"It was all worth it," he told me, "just for that!"

"Don't talk such nonsense!" I protested. "Nothing is worth breaking your neck."

"Yes, pay attention to Matilda," the countess said. "That is the very truth!"

Ingmar gave us an ironic smile.

After a while Agneta and Lennard stepped out to consult the supervising physician, and I was left alone with my friend.

"I expect you're going to be angry with me," I murmured.

"Whatever for?"

"I lost your bracelet. It probably came off when we were getting you to the car. The beads must be scattered in the grass."

"Hardly matters," he said and took my hand. "I will make you a new one when I am up and about again. There is no lack of beads." He paused a moment. "Is he gone?"

"Paul, you mean?"

"Yes. Paul."

"He left for Stockholm. It was frightfully stupid of you to try to show off to him like that, you know."

"Yes, it was. But I achieved my goal. He's gone."

"Yes, and he's furious. He thinks you want something from me."

"And if I do?"

"Stop it!" I gave him a stern tap on the shoulder. "We two are practically brother and sister. I could never think of you any other way."

Ingmar made a face. "You can be glad that my bones ache too much for me to take that to heart."

I smiled. If my own heart hadn't belonged to Paul already, I'd have given it to Ingmar.

"I need to sleep now," he said. "Will you promise to come back to see me tomorrow, dear sister of mine?"

"I will see what can be arranged. The driver may not be available."

"I am sure my mother will look in on me tomorrow, so you can come with her. And if need be, you can always ride to Kristianstad. You did it once before."

I closed my eyes. "Don't remind me! But as soon as I'm old enough, I'll learn to drive. Then I can take the car all by myself."

"Provided Mother or Father is not out on business somewhere."

"Maybe they'll get themselves a second automobile. I intend to learn to drive, one way or another."

"After that you can learn to fly. We can take lessons together."

"First things first! When a person drives, at least there's solid ground under the wheels. You can't say that of an airplane."

"Well, a pilot has solid ground under the wheels for a moment or two. And then he soars free."

We looked at one another.

"Thank you," he said finally, again taking my hand.

"For the book?"

"For everything. Especially for not just leaving me in the ditch."

"Never, you ninny," I said. "And besides, I couldn't have managed you without Paul's help."

"Oh, right, Paul again," Ingmar murmured. "I had almost forgotten him."

"Ingmar—"

"No, never mind. He is your friend. And I am grateful to him as well."

"Will you do me a favor?" I asked.

"Name it."

"If Paul visits me again, please don't ever get carried away like that. You could have died, just like that poor horse! I don't want anything to happen to you. You know I care for you, and that won't change when

I'm with Paul someday. Permanently with him, I mean." I recalled that moment under the willow tree—Paul's hand running across my hip and my body aching for him.

Ingmar shook his head. Was he declining my request?

"He is not the one for you. But I will keep out of it from now on, and I promise that next time I will not break my ribs for his sake."

"Thanks!" I lifted his hand and gave it a kiss. "Let me live my own life, all right?"

"As you wish. But if anything goes wrong, I will always be there to help you."

I smiled at him. "I make you the same pledge. I will always be there to help you, no matter what."

PART II

1934

22

The year 1934 arrived in a dazzling shower of stars. Agneta had ordered a wonderful fireworks display for New Year's Eve. It astonished the villagers. As glistening fountains shot up and formed a cathedral of glittering light, I sent a quiet wish up to the heavens: *Let Paul want to marry me.* I wanted so much for him to propose on my twenty-first birthday in November.

I knew I'd have my work cut out for me persuading Agneta to give her consent. Paul hadn't been back to Lion Hall since the disastrous visit a year and a half earlier, but I still clung to my hopes. He mentioned no other woman in his letters and continued to proclaim I was the only one for him. Perhaps he'd decided to avoid the subject of marriage as long as I was attending school.

A cold, rainy winter was followed by an exuberant spring, and the summer promised to be mild. I'd gotten my diploma magna cum laude in May, which pleased Agneta to no end. My mother would have been proud. I'd been living in a sort of suspended animation since then, taking care of estate business. Agneta seemed to be in no hurry to change that, but my heart was still set on living with Paul and establishing our own firm.

This was the year that fate would reveal its intentions. I would turn twenty-one at last, become independent, and have the option of leaving Lion Hall.

The estate broke out in flower. Even though the national economy faced severe difficulties, life ran at a different pace in the countryside. Agneta had many mares bred, and the harvests at the Ekberg estate were bountiful. Count Lennard's sister was recovering steadily from a severe influenza that had unnerved us before Christmas.

Ingmar and Magnus were rarely at the estate, coming home from university to visit Lion Hall only on weekends or holidays. Relations between Magnus and me did not improve. He did his best to avoid me. I was always apprehensive when he was there, expecting some nasty trick. Even so, things remained calm, and he spared me from further torment. Might it be that he was gradually getting used to me?

In any case, I enjoyed time spent with Ingmar. He liked to tell stories about Stockholm and his studies. Previously he'd thought agronomy would be boring, but now he spoke enthusiastically about crop management, artificial fertilizers, and plant hybridization. I absorbed it all, and in return I kept him informed about the estate, the new horses, and village gossip the maids brought back from their Thursdays off. I would surely miss all that when I left to marry Paul.

Now, we all had our hands full getting ready for the midsummer festival. I'd learned the routine over the years, but I'd had very little to do with the guest list. Clients and business partners were on it, and only very rarely was anyone's name removed. The seating arrangements had become an increasingly delicate balancing act, for we had to keep in mind both friendships and enmities.

"Matilda, could you make time to ride to the village tavern and give the innkeeper instructions for the supply of aquavit? The errand boy is not here, and I have matters I must tend to in Kristianstad."

"Of course. I'm happy to help." I smiled, more than happy to escape stifling confinement in the office. It was perpetually warm there, even though we kept the windows wide open. After a while, that organized wilderness of files and accounts got to be more than I could bear.

The countess was apologetic about assigning me minor errands, but I enjoyed riding to the village. I had a fleeting hope I might run into that odd old man. I'd intended to speak to him ever since our first encounter, but our paths hadn't crossed. I'd made the acquaintance of a number of other people, though: the priest and his wife, the shopkeeper, most of the farmers and their families, and, of course, the innkeeper. Olaf Björnsson had purchased the inn after the death of the previous owner some years before. For quite a while it looked as if the inn would stand empty, but then Björnsson and his family turned up. He won the hearts of the villagers in a matter of weeks.

I went downstairs and out to the stables, where I found Lasse Broderson instructing a stable boy. "Miss Matilda, to what do we owe the honor?"

"I must ride to the village. Could you have a horse saddled?"

"Which would you prefer?"

"Any of them will do, really. As long as it won't throw me." I'd ridden old Berta for a long time, but she'd since been put out to pasture. After that I'd rarely ridden the same horse twice.

"You should choose for yourself," Broderson replied and gestured to the stable boy to attend to me. "The gracious lady always rides her favorite."

"I like them all," I replied, for I had no desire to tell him I'd soon be leaving. Paul still hadn't proposed, but I was sure he would do so in advance of my birthday and my return to Stockholm. The assumption at Lion Hall was that I would stay forever. I didn't want to disappoint them, so I said nothing.

"But I will consider your advice," I added. "How are our pregnant mares doing? Do you have an idea of when they will give birth?"

"Gunda could go into labor at any time. We're keeping a close eye on her, and we'll put her into the stall as soon as there's the slightest sign."

"Do let me know when that happens."

"At your service, Miss Matilda!"

I thanked him and took the horse the stable boy led out. Linus was a dark-brown gelding I enjoyed riding because he had steady, reliable instincts when faced with unfamiliar situations. Perhaps I should designate him as my favorite. I swung up into the saddle and rode away.

The warm air enveloped me as we trotted to the gate. I closed my eyes and enjoyed the breeze. Once off the estate, I let Linus canter and hunched down close to his back. I could scarcely remember that first clumsy mistake of mine when I put the wrong foot into the stirrup. Riding had become second nature. I would sorely miss it after returning to Stockholm. But Agneta would probably let me visit from time to time.

The wheat was ripening. Count Lennard had given instructions to sow American maize and flax in newly plowed fields.

The church bell was tolling as I approached the village. Had someone died?

I rode on and caught sight of a funeral procession. Men were carrying a simple wooden coffin on their shoulders. Passersby removed their hats and bowed their heads. I dismounted and bowed briefly as the coffin passed.

"Who passed away?" I asked Thea Brickholm, the wife of one of our tenants.

"Old Korven," she answered. "He's finally at rest after all the misery he had to endure."

Korven? That name echoed in my mind. Suddenly I saw myself again, seated in the lawyer's office as Mother's will was unsealed. She'd been born a Korven.

"What sort of misery?" I asked.

Thea's face took on a woeful expression. "Well, his daughter got pregnant and disappeared overnight. His wife hounded him for the rest of his life, saying he should never have allowed her to go work on the estate. That's where she met the rascal who did it."

"Did what?" I asked, thunderstruck.

"Made the child, of course! The man who got her pregnant. No one knows who he was, because she refused to say. And then she up and disappeared."

An icy chill ran down my spine.

"Yes, and once the daughter was gone, old Mother Korven raised a terrible fuss. Some said she wanted to take the lady of the estate to court, but nothing ever came of it. The old man was stuck with that evil-tempered wife always pestering him. She died a few years ago, but Korven never recovered. He was completely addled when he died. Terribly sad situation. He has his peace at last, thank God."

I stood there, petrified. I didn't know why Mother had left for Stockholm, but clearly she'd wanted nothing more to do with her parents. Whenever I'd asked about it, Agneta gave me vague answers, so after a while I stopped trying to find out. Had my mother simply disappeared one dark night? Why did the villagers think Father was a rascal? He married her, after all! But maybe people here didn't know that.

I was so upset that I didn't notice when Thea left.

What if that confused old man actually was my grandfather? That thought squeezed my heart. Why had I run away? Why hadn't I asked him? On the other hand, would I have been ready to accept that revelation?

I came out of my haze after a while and remembered I'd been on my way to the inn. I led my horse along the street and hitched it to a linden tree.

A shiny new motorcycle was parked in front of the inn. I'd seen similar machines in Stockholm. Paul was fascinated by them. Who here in the village could afford such a thing?

I went up the steps. In summer the innkeeper opened the public rooms just after noon so thirsty travelers could stop for refreshment. More and more tourists were visiting Skåne province to enjoy its mild weather and natural beauty. Agneta did not object to hikers crossing her lands, as long as they didn't get in the way of the farmhands or bother the horses.

"Good day, Miss Matilda!" Olaf Björnsson called. "It's been quite a while since last we saw ye here!"

Ingmar had brought me there during his semester break, and Björnsson had served us strong coffee and homemade cake.

"There is much to do at the estate," I explained and came closer. Most of the clientele were tourists. The motorcycle outside must belong to one of them. "We are already busy preparing for the midsummer festival. That is why I am here."

"Ye're not here to invite me, are ye?" Björnsson teased.

"No, not today! But I fear that this year there will be so many guests that we will need a bit more aquavit. Perhaps half again the usual amount. I hope you will be able to supply us."

Björnsson put a speculative finger to his lips. "Well, let me think about that . . ."

"Oh, come, Olaf! I know you have enough. Especially for Lion Hall!"

"Aye, ye've caught me out! Of course I do. And since ye're such a lovely maiden, I'll even make ye a special price for it."

I gave him my best smile. "Thanks so much, Olaf. The countess will be pleased, and she will show her appreciation."

I stepped outside and took a moment to luxuriate in the sunshine. The cheerful exchange with the innkeeper had let me forget for a moment the old man who'd died that day. I decided to ask around on the estate to see if he'd had some connection with my mother.

"Excuse me, young lady? If you please?"

Startled, I opened my eyes. A man I'd seen in the public room stood beside me. I looked him over. His dark hair was marred by a wide streak of white, and his face was deeply wrinkled. A long, clearly ancient scar crossed one cheek; it glistened snow white and ran straight up into the brown of his hair.

His face was small and his hands were slightly deformed. He wore a tattered coat that looked as if military insignia had been ripped from it. All in all, he was definitely a shifty character.

"Yes? What is it?" I responded despite his appearance. There were people around; I could call for help if necessary.

"I don't quite know where to begin . . . Do you happen to be from the estate? Or do you know something about it?"

"Why do you ask?"

"Well, the fact is, an old acquaintance of mine lives there . . ."

"Who is this acquaintance?" I demanded. Could this day get any more bizarre? First the funeral of a man with Mother's last name, and now this oddball inquiring about the estate.

"That I would prefer to keep to myself. I do not know how she would take it if I turned up unexpectedly . . . But I would be grateful to hear what has happened there over the past years. Perhaps I will drop in on them after all."

"I have not been on the estate for very long. Only three years."

"Do you work there?"

"Yes." A little voice warned me not to give away too much.

"Well, it is not the worst place in the world, as I know quite well. I advise you not to walk away from it."

I detected a twitch in his face. Was he suffering from some nervous affliction? Was he about to ask for something?

"I am afraid I cannot help you." I turned away, but the man grasped my arm.

I gave him a sharp look, and he released me immediately. "Please forgive me, but—Countess Lejongård—is she still mistress of the estate?"

"Yes, of course."

"And—her husband? I mean, she has a husband, does she not?"

"She does. And two sons. And if you want to know more than that, you will have to call at the estate and ask directly. Good day!"

I turned my back and strode to my horse. I was wound up tight.

Why was this man asking these strange questions? Anyone in the village could have told him the countess was married and had children. Why did he single me out?

Fortunately, he made no move to follow. I looked around for him when I reached my horse, but he'd vanished. I got into the saddle, mystified.

The estate was deserted when I rode in. Agneta must have departed for the city. I wished I'd had the opportunity to ask her about old Mr. Korven.

I went to the kitchen for afternoon coffee. Perhaps I could beg a treat or two from the cook. Agneta had continued the tradition of afternoon coffee breaks, even though she didn't invite lady friends to the salon as her mother had.

Lena was alone in the kitchen. Had something drawn everyone away?

"Ah, Miss Matilda! You're back."

I liked the fact that Lena didn't address me as "gracious miss," the way the younger girls did. I'd expected that annoyingly formal usage to die out, but it hadn't.

"Yes, and I see that everyone is out."

"The gracious lady took Mrs. Bloomquist and two of the girls with her to Kristianstad. But there's no need for you to miss your afternoon break. I have fresh-brewed coffee."

"Do you mind if I sit here for a while? I've got so much on my mind and don't want to brood about it all alone."

"With pleasure! I'm happy to have company."

Lena poured two big cups of coffee and put out a plate of pastries. I wasn't particularly hungry, but the smell of coffee revived me.

"Lena, may I ask you a question?" I began, my eyes riveted upon my reflection in my coffee cup.

"Of course, Miss Matilda. What's on your mind?"

"I was just in the village. I saw a funeral pass by."

"Oh dear, that's sad. Did you find out who it was? I haven't been back there since my mother died."

"A woman called him Old Korven. I'm wondering now . . ." The words died on my lips as I saw Lena's expression. She clamped her mouth shut, and there was a hint of anguish in her eyes. "My mother's maiden name was Korven, and I'm wondering if he was somehow related to me. And to my mother."

Lena sat looking at me but said not a word.

"A couple of years ago," I went on, "an old man spoke to me in the village. That was the day my clothes disappeared from the wardrobe, and I was wandering aimlessly. He called me 'Susanna.'"

Lena looked at her lap and took a deep, shuddering breath.

"What's the matter?" I asked.

"It's so—I—"

"It's something else my mother didn't tell me, isn't it?"

"It seems so," she admitted. "You need to understand those weren't easy times for your mother, what with the pregnancy and having to leave the estate. There was a lot of worry and confusion."

"You mean when my mother left the estate to join my father?"

"Yes," Lena said. I saw her thinking hard. "Your mother's parents—I don't know how much she told you."

"Very little," I admitted. "Or, to be truthful, nothing at all. It didn't seem too important to me back then, but now I'm wondering if the man I met is the one who just passed away. And if he—"

"—could be your grandfather?"

"Yes."

Lena nodded. "I'm afraid he was."

"Afraid?" I raised my eyebrows. Her confirmation struck me like a blow. Why hadn't anyone told me my grandfather was living here?

"Well, the way Susanna was treated by her parents was . . . Something terrible must have happened. Otherwise she wouldn't have fled from them." Lena seemed to be looking into the past. "The gracious lady made arrangements for Susanna to go to Stockholm and get married there. I was very young then, and I wasn't informed of the details. But Susanna wrote me and begged me not to let her mother or anyone else know where she was. She was determined to disappear."

I saw the old man's face again. I'd been frightened of him, despite his pitiful appearance.

"My own mother told me," Lena said, "that the Korvens didn't regret their daughter's disappearance. And they made no effort to look for her."

"Could it be that—?" I stopped. Did I really want to know what had happened between my mother and her parents? Mother had surely had her reasons. But still, I was curious. "Is there anyone who can tell me more?"

"I'm afraid only Susanna and her parents themselves knew. And once she was gone . . . It was odd, but there was almost no talk in the village. The Korvens railed against the estate, but after a while that stopped. The woman died, and the man let himself go and gradually lost contact with the world. That's all. I have no idea if the Korvens ever took anyone into their confidence. It's probably better not to root around in the past."

I stared down into my cup as if it were a magic mirror that could reveal the truth. The coffee was lukewarm now, but my fingers were like ice.

"Thank you, Lena," I said.

"Happy to help," she replied and got to her feet. "I have to get back to work. Don't take things too much to heart. Your mother was a fine person, and she deserved to get away from the village. Things would have gone badly for her there if she'd stayed. Perhaps she'd have died and gone to her grave even before her mother did." She left the kitchen.

I sat there for a while longer and gazed through the open window high in the kitchen wall. The heavens were an innocent blue, and a bee buzzed endlessly about, trying to decide whether to come in or stay out. It finally opted for the exterior. Would it be good for me to do the same? To stay outside and ask no more questions?

"You are so quiet this evening," Agneta commented at dinner. "Is there something you need, Matilda?"

As so often, we two were the only ones at dinner. Count Lennard had gone to Ekberg to tend to business but more importantly to visit his sister, who'd had health problems for some time.

I shook my head, still full of what I'd learned from Lena that afternoon. "No, I am quite all right."

That was true in one sense but completely false in another. I was confused. The grandfather I'd never known had been buried that day. A part of my life had been withheld from me.

"You seem to have something on your mind."

I saw I wouldn't be able to avoid explaining. But should I question her about my mother? On one hand, I wanted to know what my grandparents had done, but on the other, I feared learning something horrible. My mother had tried to protect me with her silence. Why should I expose myself to harm by bringing to light whatever secrets she'd been concealing?

"There was this strange man," I finally responded, turning instead to that bizarre encounter. "He spoke to me after I left the inn."

"The inn?" Agneta reflected for a moment, and then she remembered. "Ah, yes, the liquor. What did the innkeeper say?"

"He will supply us with as much as we require. Since I was the one doing the asking, he will give us a good price. At least that's what he said."

"That old charmer. Watch out for him!" Agneta smiled, but then turned serious. "But what is this about a stranger? Was he rude to you? Should we notify the police?"

I shook my head. "No, he was not impolite. At least, not the way you are thinking. He wanted information. For example, he asked if you were married and how things on the estate had changed. He was very odd. He gabbled something about how I shouldn't give up life on the estate."

Agneta put down her fork. She swallowed painfully and stared at her plate. "What did this man look like?"

"Well, a little run-down, I guess. He wore an old coat and there was a long scar on his face. His hair was turning gray, and he had blue eyes."

"And did you tell him anything?"

"No. I mean, no more than what everybody knows. That you have a husband and two sons. Then I got out of there, because he seemed a bit unhinged."

"That was the right thing to do," Agneta said.

Did she have some idea of who he might be?

23

The next morning Agneta and I were at breakfast when a stable boy came running. "Gunda's about to have her foal!"

The countess and I exchanged a glance, put our napkins aside, and hurried to the door. We crammed our feet into rubber boots, for there was no other footwear downstairs, and we rushed to the stalls.

The lads had already brought the mare to the birthing pen. She lay on her side in the straw, snorting. The veterinarian squatted next to her, his stethoscope on her belly.

"Well, Doctor? How does it look?" Agneta asked.

"Good," the vet answered. "It will take a while longer, but the mother is sturdy, and the foal's heartbeat is strong."

"We will just have to wait." Agneta looked the mare over, reflecting. Then she turned to me. "In the old days, an old horse wizard from the village would come to us. Did I ever tell you about Linus?"

"Linus? Like the horse?"

"The horse was named for him. It was born only a few days after he passed away. Linus always said he intended to be reborn as a horse. He loved our animals." Pain flickered in her eyes. "I decided to honor him. And who knows, perhaps his soul really is in there somewhere."

"I hope not," I said. "I like riding Linus. I wouldn't like to think that I'm sitting on a horse wizard."

"I hardly think it would bother Linus to have a young lady's tender rear upon his back."

"Madame Countess!" My feigned shock provoked a hearty laugh from Agneta.

"You will be legally independent in a handful of months," she said after a moment. "Perhaps you might give a thought to how you would like to celebrate that birthday."

"Perhaps it is a bit early for that?" I asked. "After all, my birthday is not until November!"

"True, but it is not just any birthday. You will be twenty-one." I heard a hint of sadness in her voice. As of then she would cease to be my guardian. Agneta smiled. "We should make it a proper celebration."

"I will consider it," I said. "But, really, it would be enough to celebrate just as usual. A lovely little meal . . ."

"Are you sure? We could all organize a wild and whirling ball!"

"For all our clients and business partners?" I smiled and shook my head. "No, by no means. But I would be pleased if I could invite my friend Daga and her brother."

"That Paul from two years ago?"

"Yes, that very Paul," I confirmed.

Agneta's forehead wrinkled in concern. She leaned on the stall door and looked at me. "I have the impression your Paul has made himself relatively scarce since then. And given his rushed departure after the accident . . ."

"That is all in the past," I declared. "I would be very happy to invite him. And his sister too."

Agneta took a deep breath and released it. "Very well. You may invite them both, as far as I am concerned. It is a significant day for you. When the sun rises on your birthday, you will be permanently entitled to make your own decisions. I remember very well how it was for me on that day—although I had to wait until I was twenty-five for the court to approve my petition for independence. Women in this country have achieved a great deal in the past twenty years."

"Thank you," I said. "And I will make sure that Ingmar does not act like a fool in Paul's presence."

"My son has grown up a good deal since then," Agneta commented. "I think he is capable of mastering his emotions. He still tends to see you as a little sister and feels obliged to protect you."

"There is no need. I am older than he is. And Paul is truly a good man."

"I trust your judgment." Agneta paused and sighed. "When I contemplate the fact that my boys will also attain their majority soon . . ." Another flicker of pain crossed her face. "But that is how life goes. Children are born and leave home to put their own children into the world."

No sooner had she said that than the mare got to her feet.

"Oh my, here we go!" Agneta said and turned to watch the birth.

Baron was the name she gave to the little black stallion born that afternoon. He was up on his own thin legs in just a few minutes and surveyed the stall with a lordly air. His mother showed touching concern for him. I only reluctantly separated myself from this little wonder.

I mused over Agneta's remark about children. I'd never thought of it that way, but it was true; before you knew it, you were an adult obliged to make your own way in life. Horses had it easy. Pride meant nothing to them, and no one forced them to make choices.

That evening on the way to my room I happened to overhear Agneta's raised voice in the salon. For a moment I thought she and Lennard were quarreling, so I continued down the hall to give them their privacy. Through the closed door I heard Agneta insist, "It is not possible! He cannot have returned. He simply cannot!"

I stopped in my tracks.

"Well, the description may tally. Who else would have asked Matilda about you?"

"He died!" Agneta exclaimed. "He is dead!"

"You have never received any evidence of that."

"But the detective! He wrote me that—"

"That man's name wasn't exactly the same. And perhaps he could have been using a false name. Is that possible?"

I wondered who this odd stranger could be. Lennard had been away for several hours during the day. Had he gone to the village to make inquiries?

"It is a shame that I did not find him," Lennard said, confirming my suspicion. "With a closer look I might have determined whether it was possible. But he probably feared getting into trouble after he spoke with Matilda."

"Under what name did he register?"

"Holm. Ivar Holm. It is not an uncommon name. Perhaps he has gotten more cunning. But I have a feeling that something is amiss. He wants something."

"But why now? Our sons are almost grown, and we've been married for a long time. That was twenty years ago!"

Agneta sounded distraught. Could the stranger have had something to do with the fire that had caused the deaths of the old count and Agneta's brother? Had the former stable master now finished his prison term? Was he intending to take revenge on the Lejongårds?

A wave of misery and regret washed over me. I should just have ignored the man! What if he resorted to arson again?

I tiptoed away and decided to take a walk around the estate to clear my head.

I couldn't forget the discussion I'd overheard. I couldn't ask either Agneta or Lennard, but I went to Lena the following day as she was going through Agneta's extensive closets to identify items in need of repair. We'd decided to recondition garments and auction them off at midsummer to benefit charitable causes.

Agneta had suggested that museums and theatres could use such garb. It was no coincidence that this year's guest list included two theatre directors, the business manager of the Royal Opera, and the head of the National Museum.

"It would be remarkable to see my mother's clothes in a new piece on the stage. Or in an opera. By Puccini or Verdi, no doubt."

"I'm sure she would be pleased," I'd answered.

Agneta had sniffed. "No, she would hate it. Too frivolous. And that is the very reason I plan to dispose of them this way."

Since then the pile of clothes Lena had heaped upon the Empire sofa had become a small mountain.

"Lena?" I called and peered into the jungle of hanging garments.

"Here I am, Miss Matilda!" she replied, emerging with a voluminous green dress over one arm.

"Good Lord, who would have worn something like that?" I exclaimed.

"I don't know much about fashion," Lena said. "But I assume the gracious lady's great-grandmother, no less, stepped out to a ball in this one. The moths have been at it for a very long time, unfortunately." She showed me lace on one sleeve that was so chewed away that it looked like the vestiges of a spiderweb.

"Lena, may I ask you something?"

"Yes, of course!"

"You remember you told me about the stable master who set the fire in the barn."

Her expression became grave. "Yes. What about him?"

"The day before yesterday, after I saw that funeral procession, a stranger came up to me and wanted to know about the countess. When

I told her later, she seemed very upset. Is it possible the arsonist was let out of prison?"

"Langeholm? I heard back then he'd been sentenced to prison for a very long time. That's all I know."

Langeholm . . . Lennard said the stranger had used the name Ivar Holm and suggested it was probably false. The two names weren't all that different.

"Would he have any reason to want to revenge himself on the countess?"

"Lots, probably," exclaimed Lena. "But the gracious lady wasn't to blame. He was blackmailing her father and was also responsible for the deaths both of the father and the son." Her expression changed. "It was all because of the man's love, a woman who'd been put off the estate. Juna Holm, her name was."

"Juna Holm?" I echoed her. My pulse accelerated. How could I share my suspicion with Lena without admitting I'd eavesdropped on the count and countess?

"Yes, Holm; that was her name. We never heard from her again. The newspapers speculated that she changed her name after the trial."

"He could have done the same, couldn't he?"

"Of course!" Lena looked at me with great concern. "Take to your heels if you see that stranger again. He did your mother wrong, and you'd better not remind him of it."

"My mother?" I went hot and cold all over. "What did he have to do with my mother?"

"Well, word is that he threatened her. I don't know all of it, but there was definitely something going on. Your mother left the estate, and the police arrested him not long after that."

I stared at Lena. My mother had been involved with the arsonist? Why hadn't Lena told me that before?

"It would be best to stay out of his way. Please be careful!"

"I will be." Shaken, I left the clothes closet, my mind full of uncertainties. What had happened? Langeholm had known Mother. And he'd approached me!

I was quaking with fear. I'd been thinking of going to visit Old Korven's grave, but now it seemed far more prudent to avoid the village and stay out of sight.

24

That afternoon, the countess and I pored over the account books. I'd introduced a new system to track expenditures and revenue, but we still had piles of paperwork to deal with.

Something was bothering Agneta. I wished I could ask her about it, but I was wrestling with my own difficult thoughts, particularly the fear that some malicious stranger might be skulking around outside, targeting the estate and me as well.

We were distracted by a rap at the office door.

"Come in!" Agneta called.

Lena entered. "There is a young man who insists on speaking to you, Miss Matilda."

I sat bolt upright. *Who can this be?* I checked with Agneta, who nodded, then I followed Lena downstairs.

And in fact a young man in a pin-striped suit was standing in the entry hall. I almost didn't recognize him.

"Paul! What a surprise! What on earth are you doing here?"

I flew to him, hugged him, and kissed him. He returned the hug and kiss, although not as ardently as I'd desired ever since we'd last seen one another.

I gave him a searching glance. "You aren't happy! Has something happened?"

He cleared his throat. "I am happy," he maintained, which obviously wasn't true. "But I'm afraid I won't be able to stay for long."

What a strange thing to say! I took his arm to guide him out to the garden, but he didn't budge.

He frowned. "I must speak to you, Matilda." That wrinkle between his eyebrows was a sign he was about to deliver bad news.

"Don't you think it might be better to go to the garden?" I suggested, again trying to move him out of the manor. The servants had no need to hear whatever it was he had to tell me. Secretly I was hoping that he would finally—finally!—propose to me. Maybe he was nervous? Or was something else on his mind? My stomach contracted in apprehension, and my heart pounded like mad.

He hesitated. "Well, I don't mind going to the garden."

We left the manor in silence and descended the steps. I halted as soon as we reached the park. "All right, then, tell me what's going on."

Paul took a deep breath. "My father is sending me to Norway. He bought an old furniture factory there and wants me to manage it."

It took me a moment to absorb this. Norway! That was unimaginably far away.

"Fine, then, I'll go with you."

My immediate response brought a pained expression to his face. "I'm afraid that won't work."

"Why not?" It was more of a gasp than a question.

"Father won't consent to a marriage. He wants me to concentrate entirely on the business. I'm not allowed to have any distractions."

"Distractions?" I echoed. "I'm a distraction?"

He looked down, unwilling to meet my eyes. I felt as if I'd just stepped off the edge of a cliff.

"Matilda, try to understand . . ."

"I understand perfectly. You don't want me anymore. You're betraying me, breaking your promises, and giving up on everything we wanted to build together."

"I am not!" he countered. "But, Matilda, I—yes, we talked about getting married. But we were just children."

"You were nineteen."

I felt my heart tearing apart. All these years I'd set my hopes on the day we'd announce our engagement. Now he was leaving me behind.

"But I was just a boy! And believe me, you're very important to me. But don't you think a marriage has to be based on something more than just letters? We're only pen pals! We should have seen one another more often. My parents hardly know you."

"This is coming from your parents?"

"Matilda, it's really a matter of the business. I'll have to work both day and night."

What a feeble attempt to avoid hurting my feelings!

"I can help you in your office. After all, I have my business-school diploma! I was the best in my class. The countess is always saying I know everything about bookkeeping, and—"

"Matilda!" The tone of his voice stopped me short. He took my hand, which was icy. "It won't work. I can't marry you. I'm going to Norway, and only time will tell what'll become of us." He looked around. "As far as I can see, you've settled in very well. You should stay. Think about what you want to do with your life. Forget me and our silly childish pledge. We will come together again if it's fated. Let's hope we live that long. And we can keep writing."

I stared at him as if he'd just slapped my face. All these years I'd been preparing to share my life with him and to build a business. Maybe I'd been foolish to think he ever intended to marry me.

He was right about one thing: we'd seen one another hardly at all. Physical proximity had been denied to us. But I was incensed that he was going to cut me out of his life except for an occasional letter.

"Fine, then, go to Norway! I wish you all the best!" I pulled away from him and stamped the full length of the garden. Tears shot into my eyes. I was hurt, abandoned, and betrayed. Everything I'd so joyfully anticipated had vanished in an instant.

"Matilda," I heard him call behind me. "I'm so sorry! We can still—"

I turned and shouted, "Remain friends?"

"Yes!" he said, but I spun around and kept going. How could I possibly appear before Agneta like this? He should have sent me a letter instead!

I stormed upstairs to my room. Sobs shook me, but I didn't dare wail. I didn't want to attract anyone's attention or have to explain. I didn't want to have to admit that the young man I'd expected to become my husband had just shattered my dreams.

I paced around my room, crossed my arms across my chest, and tried to control myself, but it was impossible. When I shut my eyes, I saw Paul's face; covering my ears couldn't stop the echo of his words in my mind.

I leaned against the door for a time and then decided to go back to the office before Agneta came looking for me.

The countess didn't look up from her work. "So, then, who was the visitor?" she asked.

It was no use pretending. "Paul. My friend Paul." Deep disappointment spread its bitter taste through me. "My former friend, Paul."

Agneta straightened up and removed the spectacles she'd recently taken to wearing. "He came to visit? The one you wanted to invite to your birthday?"

I nodded. Yes, the same Paul who was here when Ingmar had his horrible accident. The Paul whose letters had become less and less frequent. The one who'd once wanted to build a business and a life with me.

"There is no need to invite him now. He is going to Norway. And he sees no reason to take me with him."

Agneta put down her pen and frowned in concern. "Had he promised to take you?"

"We—" I couldn't continue. I didn't want to break down before the countess, but I couldn't help it.

Agneta got up. Gently she took me in her arms. The sleeves of her dress quickly became wet with my tears, but she seemed not to mind. Her embrace did nothing at all to relieve my misery.

"We wanted to build a business together," I sobbed. "We wanted to marry and have children. We wanted a future! But now he's leaving. He could marry me—after all, he's already twenty-three—but he won't!"

Only now did it become clear to me that over recent months and years our plans to marry had remained undiscussed and perpetually vague. He hadn't brought them up, and I'd failed to remind him.

I cried my heart out, leaving myself overheated and my eyes swollen. Agneta held me the whole time, but I hardly noticed. I desperately wanted to wash away my disappointment, but it was no use. It had taken my soul as fast in its claws as a hawk seizing a little rabbit.

Only after a very long time did my tears ebb to a mute whimpering, an occasional shudder, and a hiccup.

Agneta maneuvered me to a chair. She squatted down and looked into my eyes. "I know what it is to be betrayed," she said. "I know it all too well. There was once a man I wanted to marry, but he disappeared from my life. That is the greatest, most painful injustice they can inflict upon us: encouraging our hopes and then disappointing them."

She brushed a strand of hair from my face. "It may seem stupid of me to say this but let me assure you that this too will pass. Even if you cannot believe it now, there will certainly be another man for you. One who will protect you and stand by you, who will forgive your mistakes and stay with you, no matter what happens. You are young, Matilda, and you will find love, or it will find you. Go ahead, weep and lament as you must, but keep your eyes fixed on the future. A whole world, a whole life, awaits you."

That evening I took out all of Paul's letters. A deep calm descended upon me, which seemed odd after all my weeping, and the pain in my breast subsided to a dull ache. I couldn't understand why I was feeling better. I'd lost the man I wanted to spend the rest of my life with!

I laid out the letters in chronological order and saw for the first time how few he'd sent in recent months. The stack for the past year was much shorter than those from my early years at Lion Hall. Had I written less often as well?

I hadn't kept copies, but I knew I'd answered each of his.

I was well aware that estate business had dominated my days in recent months. I enjoyed the work and liked the people. I especially liked Ingmar and felt the same way about Agneta and Lennard. I still hated Magnus, but he didn't live at Lion Hall anymore. The story was that he was studying literature and planning to become an author. I wondered how a person like him could write fiction. What kind of stories could he possibly invent? Crime novels in which a countess's ward meets some gruesome end?

I didn't care. When Magnus became the next Count Lejongård, I'd have to leave Lion Hall. He wouldn't give up the title to continue dabbling in literature. But it was likely that many years would pass before that happened.

Had I given up my dream of a life with Paul without even realizing it? Had I unconsciously signaled that I wouldn't accompany him? That there was no great love between us after all?

But if so, why did it hurt so much? Maybe because it meant losing the last connection to my childhood, my very last link to Stockholm . . .

I gazed at the piles of letters, nonplussed. My correspondence with Daga had also fallen off. Was that because she had a fiancé to occupy her time? Or was it because I had shifted my attention to Lion Hall?

I found no answers to my questions, but I was haunted by the feeling it was somehow my fault that Paul was going to Norway without me.

25

Midsummer and the festival finally arrived and drove Paul out of my thoughts. The strange man who'd come up to me outside the village inn didn't show his face again. I'd overheard Lennard telling Agneta that he was gone.

"It was probably nothing at all," he said. "Or he got cold feet. Either could be the case."

I still wondered if the stranger could actually have been the arsonist.

Ingmar and Magnus returned home the day before the midsummer celebration.

Magnus greeted me in his usual crass manner. "You are still here? I thought that you would have run off with some rotten man by now. At your age you should have had a boyfriend long ago."

"Mind your own business!" I snarled.

Over the years, Magnus, already a loner, had become more and more eccentric. He was present physically, but his thoughts were always far away. We treated one another as complete strangers who happened to be lodging in the same residence. We had no reason to speak. Magnus camped out in the former estate manager's old cabin most of the time he was home. Ingmar told me his brother was writing a novel.

Ingmar's presence was a bright spot. I was bursting with news for him.

We were strolling in the garden the evening before the festivities. Sunflowers loomed over us and sweet-smelling roses enticed the bees. The bandstand was already in place. Colorful crepe paper streamers were stretched all around, and the maypole was impressively tall.

"Did your mother tell you about the strange man who came up to me in the village?"

"A man spoke to you?" Ingmar asked. "Who?"

"If only I knew!" I confessed that I'd inadvertently overheard his parents.

"Maybe it's time for you to come to Stockholm," he said. "This tale of yours bothers me."

"Your father would have taken action if there were real danger. And if that man really is the arsonist, what connection could he have with me? I think your mother should be the one to go to Stockholm to investigate."

"She wouldn't want to leave the estate unattended."

"I just wish I knew what my mother had to do with that man," I said.

"Your mother?" Ingmar frowned.

"Lena hinted at something like that. But no one's given me a clear answer."

"You need to ask my mother outright."

I shook my head. "I can't."

"You're afraid of what she'll say?"

"Yes, I am. Each time I raise the subject of my mother, something new comes out. It's like peeling away the layers of an onion. If I ever get to the center, I'm bound to be in tears."

"But only if you take it the wrong way," Ingmar countered. He took my arm in his. "You really should consider coming to Stockholm. For a while at least. It took me some time to admit, but it really is a beautiful city. Exciting and completely different from the sleepy countryside."

"You just want to have me nearby."

A quick smile crossed his face. "Naturally! Then I could promenade with you and make my classmates envious. If your Paul would allow it."

"I don't think he's my Paul anymore," I said, toying with the bow of my dress.

"Why do you say that? Did you quarrel?"

"His father sent him to Norway."

Ingmar stared at me in astonishment. "And so? What prevents you from going to him there? It's not as if you're stuck with inheriting an estate."

"I have a house in Stockholm."

"Sell it! Take the money and then off to Oslo with you!"

His attitude surprised me. First he suggested I come to Stockholm, and now he was encouraging me to go to Oslo?

"Paul doesn't want me there," I murmured.

His eyes widened. "He doesn't want you?"

"You heard me. He thinks the plans we made were childish. He has to make his own way in Norway now, and he has no use for me there."

"What a fool!" Ingmar growled and then hugged me. "I'm always here for you. Do you hear?"

"Thanks," I said and placed an arm around his shoulders.

"And what do you say—shall we dance at the midsummer fest? You remember how?"

"Of course," I said. "And I'm happy to dance with you."

"Then I have something to look forward to," he responded cheerfully.

The guests arrived the following afternoon, and within hours the empty garden was transformed into a festive meadow where midsummer was celebrated with food, song, and dance.

Surrounded by talk and stories, I forgot about Paul and even stopped brooding about the strange man, although I did scan the garden from time to time. Many faces were unfamiliar, but I would have recognized his.

Magnus kept out of sight, and I danced a lot with Ingmar. As the daylight slowly faded, everyone got a bit tipsy. Even Agneta and Lennard had a couple of drinks.

I went to the kitchen. Old Mrs. Bloomquist was there, chatting with the serving girls. They tittered when they saw me, which distressed me a bit. But I wasn't going to rebuke them; I wasn't their employer, after all.

"Ah, here's Miss Matilda!" the old cook exclaimed. "You look so thin, dear. Are you eating properly these days?"

"But of course, Mrs. Bloomquist. And how are you?"

"Oh, it's up and down for me, I never know," she said. "There are times I feel I could tear up trees by the roots, and sometimes I want to sleep all day long. That's probably my age."

"Still, it's lovely to have you here." For a while that had seemed unlikely. Mrs. Bloomquist's back and legs gave her trouble, and her memory wasn't always the best. Agneta had finally persuaded her to retire, for she didn't want to take the risk that the cook would forget what she was doing and injure herself.

"Ah, well, Lion Hall isn't just my former place of employment. It's my home. I started here as a wee young girl. Did you know that? Here in the kitchen is where I always wanted to be."

That impressed me. I hoped someday to find a job or profession that suited me just as well.

She was the oldest employee the estate had ever had, now two years senior to the coachman who'd passed away just before my arrival. If anyone knew Lion Hall, she did.

I had an idea and took the chair beside her.

"Do you perhaps have some idea of what was going on between my mother and the stable master back then?"

"Your mother?" she asked, slightly confused, but then remembered. "Oh yes. Susanna."

"That's right, Susanna," I echoed.

"There was plenty of talk in those days. I must declare I didn't believe any of it, for most such gossip is from evil tongues and only hurts people."

"What did they say about my mother?"

"Well, some claimed she had an affair with Langeholm, not long after his little lover was discharged and sent away. Servants weren't allowed to get mixed up with one another in those days. A messy business. He must have been looking for a replacement."

I stared at her, unable to believe this.

"Of course, that was before she married your father," the cook added. "And as I said, it was just a rumor. Don't take it to heart."

What? My mother was rumored to have had an affair with the arsonist?

If only Mother hadn't kept events so hushed up! If only she'd told me directly what had happened!

I gave Mrs. Bloomquist a sideways glance. I'd have liked to quiz her some more, but the elderly cook's eyelids drooped. Moments later she was snoring softly.

Agneta came into the kitchen as I was leaving. "Oh, here you are! I had assumed you were taking a stroll."

"I needed a moment of quiet," I replied. "Mrs. Bloomquist seems to have found me boring. She fell asleep at the table."

"You are anything but boring, Matilda. It is late, and Mrs. Bloomquist is no longer used to staying up. I wish she had gone out to mingle with the guests, but she is so attached to her kitchen. She misses it."

"Did she never plan to marry?" I asked. It seemed a shame for a woman to bind herself to a manor house and at the end of the day be regarded as nothing more than a former employee.

"I have no idea. I cannot peer into the human heart. She was already here when I was a child, but as far as I know, there has never been a man in her life. If there was, she hid him very well."

"Agneta," I said, "may I ask you something?"

"Anything!"

"That stranger who spoke to me . . . could he have been the arsonist? The one responsible for the deaths of your father and brother?"

Agneta looked alarmed. "Are you still worrying about him?"

"Yes. In fact, I can't get him out of my mind."

"And what makes you think he might be the arsonist? Langeholm will sit in prison for the rest of his life."

Her comment amazed me. Hadn't she thought the same thing? Hadn't she discussed it with Lennard? I felt myself blushing furiously.

"I heard a rumor," I said. "A rumor it might be him. And that he had something to do with my mother."

Agneta shook her head but at first was speechless. Finally, she muttered, "That is—not possible. No. It cannot be."

"Are you sure? Maybe he was released."

"No, he was not the arsonist. Langeholm is in prison."

"Then who was that stranger?"

"I cannot tell. I did not see him, after all. Probably a lunatic. Or a reporter. Maybe a spy from some rival horse breeder. We have heard of such people asking questions in the village from time to time. You would do well to forget him."

"I can't possibly do that."

She stroked my arm. "I know. But now you should go see to the guests. The night is still young."

I nodded, then hesitated. "Did my mother have anything to do with the arsonist?"

Agneta's expression became extremely serious. "Don't believe what people say. Langeholm was a terrible person, beneath contempt and not worthy of discussion. And your mother was a good woman. Nothing else matters."

I nodded but sensed she wasn't telling the whole truth. Something was hidden, something she didn't want to tell me. Was the old cook right? How could I possibly find out?

"Thank you," I said and headed outside. I didn't join the celebrations but withdrew to a quiet corner of the garden and stared up at the stars.

Are you there? I silently appealed to my mother. *Can you help me discover the truth?*

26

Late that summer I received a letter from Daga. I had a moment of hope that Paul might send news through her. He might say he wasn't bold enough to write me directly and confess he'd made a mistake.

No. It was a wedding invitation.

Within a flowered border the golden script gleamed:

> *Mr. Arndt Vessel and Miss Daga Ringström announce that*
> *on Saturday, October 6, 1934, they will be joined in the holy*
> *bond of matrimony.*

Shocked, I stared at the invitation. The wedding was scarcely a month away, on the same weekend as the estate's autumn hunt.

I tottered across the room and dropped onto my bed. I felt as if I'd been shot through the heart.

We'd once promised we would be each other's maid of honor, but there was no mention of that here. I'd heard from Daga only sporadically since Paul left for Norway. I'd known about Arndt, but not that they intended to marry so soon.

I didn't know what to do. As happy as I was for Daga, I couldn't decide whether to accept the invitation. I'd be just another guest, invited as a matter of courtesy. And Paul would surely be present as well. My eyes flooded with tears. First Paul and now Daga! I'd lost them both.

I shoved the letter into my skirt pocket and went looking for some quiet place to think things over.

I found it under an enormous apple tree so ancient that it bore almost no fruit anymore. Its trunk was clad in bark so furrowed and uneven that it looked like an elderly man's face.

I'd had my doubts when Ingmar first suggested hanging a swing from this tree. But that swing had borne my weight without complaint ever since. It rocked back and forth so gently and in such a wide arc. I shut my eyes. The wind caressed my face and ruffled my hair as if to console me.

Suddenly I sensed I wasn't alone. I looked around.

"Nice to see you still enjoy this spot."

Ingmar reached up to pull off a very green, extremely sour apple from the tree.

I stopped the swing, mortified he'd seen me doing this. After all, I wasn't a little girl anymore!

He took a bite of the apple. "What's going on?"

I didn't want to talk about it, but I knew he wasn't going to give up. "My girlfriend Daga's going to be married the weekend of the autumn hunt."

"That's grand! Let me guess—you have no idea what to wear!" He gave me a grin, but it disappeared when he saw my reaction. "What? You look like you want to tear me limb from limb."

"Daga is Paul's sister."

"Ah, the scoundrel who ran off to Norway."

"Don't talk like that about him," I said. "I'd prefer not to speak of him at all. And I probably won't go to this wedding."

"And why not?" Ingmar asked. "You could take me along and pretend that we're engaged."

"He wouldn't believe it," I responded. "Anyway, I don't want to. I don't want to see him."

"And your girlfriend? What about her? Is she still important to you? If so, you absolutely should attend."

I looked at him. "Well . . . I'll speak to Agneta. After all, she has to give me permission."

"I'm sure she will. And if you want, I'm available to serve as your escort. I'll be back at school then; no autumn hunt for me!"

I shook my head. "It's lovely of you to offer, but I have to go by myself to see if the friendship can be salvaged. I'll do my best to avoid Paul."

"Understood," Ingmar said. "My offer still stands, though. If you change your mind, you know where to find me."

"Thanks, Ingmar." I gave him a big smile.

Stepping out of the Stockholm central train station three weeks later was entering a different world. I wished I'd traveled a day earlier so I'd have had time to rest, but perhaps a single night's sleep would be enough.

I tossed and turned until late. I was astonished by the number of sounds in my old house. I'd almost forgotten how distinct the various creaks and groans could be. I imagined the ghosts of all former inhabitants gathering to hover over me.

Eventually, I sank into a completely dreamless sleep.

When I arose the next morning, the ghosts were gone and the house was still. Sunshine poured through the windows and lit the swirling dust motes.

There was no warm water, so I had a very quick wash, then put on my dress and seated myself before the tarnished mirror. I'd pulled the sheet off it the previous evening.

I wasn't as expert as Lena at fixing my hair, but the result was acceptable. I applied some makeup and inspected my reflection. Would Daga recognize me? It had been so long since we'd seen one another . . .

Preparations finished, I tucked the wedding gift into my bag and set out. I had a distinctly uneasy feeling in my gut. What should I do when I saw Paul again? Surely there'd be no way to avoid him entirely.

A well-ordered line of vehicles was parked along the street outside the Ringström place. It looked as if guests had traveled there from all across the country.

I went to the door, braced myself, and pressed the doorbell. It opened quickly.

"Good day," I said. "I don't know if you remember me . . . Matilda Wallin?"

"I know you, Matilda," their mother replied, completely transformed, for she wore a dark-blue dress with polka dots instead of her familiar housewife's attire and apron. She'd spent time with the hairdresser, for her gray-flecked hair lay in elegant waves. "Come in. Daga is almost ready."

Smells from childhood welcomed me when I stepped inside. I remembered very well the marvelous cakes from Mrs. Ringström's kitchen. She must be very pleased that Daga had found the love of her life.

"Where should I put the gift?"

"It's best to leave it with me," said the mistress of the house. "We're taking all of the gifts to the reception hall."

"Thank you," I said and handed her the pasteboard box wrapped in bright green paper and tied with delicate white ribbons. It contained a modern hand-cranked kitchen mixer like I'd seen Svea use. "Is Daga in her room?"

"Yes, go right in!" Mrs. Ringström said as she vanished into another part of the house.

I crossed the living room on my way to Daga's room. All sorts of guests were congregated there, including a couple of young women in matching white dresses. I didn't know a single one.

Paul was nowhere to be seen. I greeted those present and continued on my way.

Daga was seated before her mirror, fidgeting with her veil.

"Just leave it," an older woman, presumably her hairdresser, counseled. "After all, you don't want it to come loose on the way to the altar." Neither had noticed me.

I studied Daga for a moment. She wore a snow-white dress gathered at the waist. The veil billowed around her carefully pinned and braided hair. She was stunning, and every man present was bound to envy Arndt.

"Don't worry, Mrs. Sörensen, nothing will happen," she said. "Thanks very much!"

She caught sight of me in the mirror. "Matilda!" she cried and flew toward me. "How lovely you were able to come!"

"I couldn't possibly miss my friend's wedding."

"It's wonderful to see you again. It seems like ages since we were in school!"

"Yes, it's been a really long time," I said. "Now you've turned twenty-one, and I will too, before long."

"And then you'll be independent, won't you?"

"Yes, I'll be set free and can leave Lion Hall. But I'll probably stay there after all. I don't really have any other plans."

Daga looked stricken. "I'm so sorry about Paul."

"It's all right." I didn't want to discuss it. "Things are going well for me, and I'm here to celebrate with my friend. Is Arndt still the man you thought he was at the beginning?"

"No! He's even better. He's so sweet and takes such good care of me. He's even letting me keep my job."

I was careful not to appear surprised by that. Could a husband refuse to allow his wife to work? Paul's views on the subject had been completely different—or so I'd thought.

"That's very considerate of him," I said a little awkwardly. I felt completely out of place here. This was my Daga standing before me, but I had the feeling that the link had loosened so much it scarcely bound us at all. Still, it was good to see her.

"Your dress is breathtaking," I said and reached out to touch a sleeve. "You look like a princess."

"Yes, I'm so delighted! Mrs. Vagström, my employer, made it for me as a wedding gift." Daga took both my hands and looked at me. "And when you get married, I'll sew your dress."

"That's darling of you," I answered, hiding my doubt. I'd have to find a husband first. And by the time I did, if that ever happened, I probably wouldn't remind her of the offer, for she'd be busy with house-keeping, work, and children.

A young woman rushed into the room in a great fret. "Daga, it's almost time! You need to get ready!"

She was obviously the maid of honor, for she wore a white dress and had flowers in her hair. I felt another pang of envy.

"All right, we must talk more later." Daga took my hand and pulled me out of the room.

Five bridesmaids stood lined up before the bride's vehicle. Daga walked through the arbor, as dignified as royalty in her glorious dress.

"Matilda, would you like to ride with us?" someone asked behind me. I turned and recognized Mrs. Ringström. "Paul is running a little late, but he promised to join us at the church."

"Yes, Mrs. Ringström, thank you." I followed her, greatly relieved by that bit of news. It would have been very uncomfortable to sit in the same car with Paul.

We got in. Mr. Ringström put the car in motion, and his wife looked me over. "You've become a proper lady," she commented.

"So grown-up and elegant! Life on that estate seems to suit you wonderfully."

"It does," I replied, wondering what she could possibly be getting at.

"It's really a shame your mother is no longer with us. But it looks to me as if you've found a good substitute."

She'd never even met my mother. I'd always gone alone to visit the Ringströms. Her remarks were just small talk, meaningless syllables to fill the silence.

"Yes, the count and countess are very nice, but not a day goes by that I don't think of Mother."

"She would have been very pleased to see how you've turned out."

I nodded. Mrs. Ringström turned to look forward, and I took the opportunity to study her. A slight smile played about her lips, but her eyes were hard.

Those comments left me uneasy. How had she seen me back then? As the pitiful daughter of an impoverished widow whose husband had committed suicide? As a child of doubtful origins? I was beginning to feel unwelcome.

Fortunately, the church was not far. The groom would already be inside, as was the custom. We got out. I lagged behind as the bridesmaids lined up and Mr. and Mrs. Ringström hurried to escort Daga.

Her face was bright red with excitement, something makeup couldn't hide.

I was happy for her, but I found myself suddenly wishing I weren't there at all. I should never have let Ingmar talk me into this.

There was no sign of Paul. I'd expected the worst: that he would be best man to his future brother-in-law.

I was glad that Mrs. Ringström took no further notice of me.

I went into the church along with people who looked like distant relatives. I settled in one of the rearmost pews and watched the bridesmaids, envious of the maid of honor. *That should have been you,* a little voice whispered bitterly. *You were her best friend. And now all those girls have usurped your place.*

I turned away and gazed toward the front. I didn't recognize any of the men. Paul must be sitting in the first pew with his parents.

The organ played a brief prelude and then it was time. The wedding march filled the church. The whispering crowd fell silent, and all eyes turned.

There she came, our Daga, solemnly pacing up the middle aisle, as gorgeous as a fairy princess. The congregation rose. As did I.

We caught one another's eye. I smiled. Daga was trembling slightly, which was no surprise. A woman's wedding day is the most beautiful day of her life. No one could blame Daga for feeling somewhat intimidated, for the bride was the center of attention.

She arrived at the front, and the man waiting for her at the altar smiled and gave her his hand.

Arndt was a handsome young man. His hair was dark and curly, and the wire-frame spectacles perched on his nose accentuated his remarkable features. We'd used to make fun of men with glasses, but on Arndt they seemed quite sophisticated. He looked intelligent. I just hoped he would make her happy.

After the ceremony, everyone drove to a reception hall. I got a ride with other guests.

The happy invitees frolicked and danced in honor of the newly-weds. I sought out a corner away from the crowd, for I wasn't feeling well. The buffet food was very good, and there was more than enough to drink. I could have turned to liquor to dull my thoughts and deaden my emotions, but I didn't want to.

Maybe no one else sensed it, but it seemed to me that a strange shadow lay over the festivities, as if my presence wasn't wanted. Despite happiness and celebration wherever I looked, my heart was heavy.

How long was one obliged to stay at a wedding reception?

I held on hour after hour, drifting to the buffet table from time to time to nibble something. Finally, I went out into the courtyard for a breath of fresh air. I was glad I'd worn a thick knitted jacket, for the evening chill was settling in. Perhaps my gray wool jacket possessed magical powers to keep me warm and render me invisible. Perhaps no one would notice if I slipped away. I sighed and went back in.

Daga was dancing her shoes to tatters. Paul stood with the other men, probably boasting about the Norwegian firm's successes. I saw no one I wanted to speak to.

Night fell at last. I went to say farewell to Daga. I knew that nothing awaited me but an empty house full of ghosts and shrouded furniture, but I needed time to digest the day's experiences and orient myself.

"You're going already?" my friend exclaimed. We hadn't found a single moment for conversation, and I certainly hadn't wanted to intrude. She was so happy, surrounded by many good people, and I didn't want to spoil her mood by speaking of my disappointment that Paul had let me down.

"I don't feel entirely well," I said. "The long train trip seems to have affected me. And I have to get up early tomorrow."

"But I'll toss the bridal bouquet an hour from now! I thought you might want to try to catch it."

I nearly snorted in scorn. Why would I be interested in a bridal bouquet? Who would I marry? Never mind the fact that her bridesmaids would elbow one another madly as they fought to be the lucky one.

"That's quite all right. I wouldn't want to deprive your other friends of the opportunity."

I must have sounded put out, for Daga looked at me, distressed, and reached for my hand. "I feel I've neglected you. I'm very sorry."

"There's no need. Above all, I want you to be happy. And I really think you will be." I looked toward Arndt. He seemed very nice. If he and Daga had children, they would be very good-looking.

"Yes, he's wonderful." Daga's look was adoring. "And I'm sure someday you'll find a wonderful husband too."

"I promise to invite you to the wedding," I said, hoping I didn't sound too bitter. Daga wasn't to blame for her brother's decisions.

"That would make me very happy. And I promise I'll write much more often. You're still living on the estate, aren't you?"

"Yes. That's not likely to change anytime soon." In different circumstances I'd probably have told her about the strange man and the midsummer festival, but this was no place for confidences.

"Fine! Then let's stay in touch, all right?"

"Yes!"

She gave me a hug. For a split second we were those same girls who'd gone to school together, but then we stepped apart, grown women once more, one married, the other abandoned.

"I wish you all the luck in the world," I said, trying to keep from bursting into tears.

"The same to you," she replied and turned away. I didn't look to see if she watched me leave or devoted herself to the guests instead.

On the way out, I came face-to-face with Paul.

"Oh, hello," he said, a bit embarrassed. "I—it's lovely that you've come."

I felt my face distort into an unhappy smile. "I'm on my way home."

"Really?" he asked in surprise, although I was wearing my coat and had my bag on my arm. "But the party is far from over."

"I have to catch the early train," I told him. "And besides, I have a headache from the trip. I really just need to go sleep now."

Paul stuck his hands into his trouser pockets. "Well, then . . ."

I stood looking at him for a moment. His transformation was almost more affecting than Daga's. She'd embraced me at least. He wasn't moved to do the same.

"Take care, Paul," I said and pushed past him. I remembered how I'd sat in my room with the stacks of his letters and come to definite conclusions: he'd grown distant; I'd done the same.

"You too!" I heard him say, but I didn't look back.

The noise of the party followed me some way down the street, but soon I was embraced by darkness and silence. A dog howled somewhere in the distance. That was all.

I had no headache. My only pain was deep in my heart. For a moment I considered dropping in on Ingmar, for it would be only a short taxi ride. But I decided against it.

I got to Brännkyrka Street, locked the door behind me, and switched on the lights. For the first time, I used Mother's bedroom instead of my own. I stretched out on the bare mattress and for a brief moment imagined I was sensing her scent and her warmth.

She'd been gone for years now, but I still felt that familiar dull ache of grief. I would never stop missing her. Just as I would always miss Paul.

The time had come to map out a new path for myself. If Paul and Daga could do so, why couldn't I?

I got up very early after a long, restless night, packed, and went to the nearest bus stop. I wasn't going directly to the train station; first I was going to visit Woodland Cemetery.

The place was almost deserted at this early hour. Sun streamed across the treetops, where birds twittered their morning songs. The gate was open. I trudged through.

I hadn't been here for a very long time. I'd have brought flowers, but the shops weren't open yet and my train wouldn't wait.

The intense quiet worked upon me as I neared the stone engraved with the names of my mother and father.

The ivy had flourished and almost completely covered their plot. Moss had made its way into the letters engraved on the stone—hardly surprising, considering the profusion of trees and greenery all around the graves. I rubbed the inscriptions clean with my handkerchief.

"Hi, Mama," I murmured. I found it difficult to speak to her there, even with no one else present. Some people suggest imagining the face of one's dear departed, but when I'd tried that, the image that presented itself was of Mother in her coffin. I didn't want that.

I gave my mother a hushed account of what had happened in recent months, from Paul's departure for Norway to Daga's wedding. I told her I was about to become an adult fully responsible for myself.

I contemplated my father's name. It would be no use trying to speak to him, for he wasn't there. He was somewhere out at sea, probably floating through seaweed in the depths. Or, more likely, his body had completely dissolved.

Why did life have to be so full of loss? Parents, friends, loved ones—they all vanished eventually.

I heaved a sigh and ran a hand across the top of the gravestone in farewell. As I walked out through the main gate, an elderly woman, hunched and wearing widow's weeds, came hobbling the other way. How long ago had she lost her husband? Were children of hers interred here as well?

I greeted her, and she looked up in astonishment. I set out for the central train station.

27

A cool autumn wrapped the woods in white mists. My birthday was approaching, but the event I'd looked forward to for so long caused me only distress. Everything had changed.

My childhood was gone. All the people I'd once thought important had vanished one after another and hovered unreachable in the shadows. Daga had promised to write more often, but I didn't expect much. She had her husband and her women friends, all of whom were entitled to more attention than I was.

I'd drawn a red circle around November 2 on my calendar as soon as I'd brought it home from the stationery store. All Souls' Day was the day of my freedom, and now it had come.

I ran a fingertip across the date and smiled. As of this morning I was legally an adult—no more guardian to watch over me and no obligation to stay. I could go wherever I liked and do whatever I pleased, even if I didn't have any idea of where my path would lead.

A knock on the door interrupted my brooding. "Come in!"

It was Agneta.

"Good morning, birthday girl!" she said and brought a little package out from behind her back. "I wanted to be the first to congratulate you."

"You are!" I responded with a broad smile.

She took me firmly in her arms. "I wish you every imaginable good and all possible joy in your newest year of life," she murmured into my hair. "You are almost a daughter to me, and that is why I brought you this."

She handed me the package. Had Agneta herself wrapped it up so artfully? She watched me expectantly as I undid the ribbon and carefully removed the paper. My heart thrilled; I had the feeling something special awaited within.

The little box was covered with velvet. I opened it, and gasped, dazzled. It contained a string of pearls and a pair of earrings set with diamonds. And, even more striking, both the earrings and the gold necklace clasp were shaped like lions' heads. The eyes were diamonds; additional gems gleamed in the manes. The pearls weren't ordinary white ones but pinkish in tone. They must have cost a fortune. If I were to wear them to my wedding or to some magnificent formal occasion, ladies would go pale with envy.

"Do you like them?" she asked, beaming. "I had the earrings and the clasp made especially for you and picked out the pearls myself. I did not want any old-lady pearls; this shade seems far more appropriate for a young woman."

"They're indescribably beautiful!" I exclaimed, overwhelmed. "Thank you so much, Agneta!"

"It is my pleasure." We embraced one another again. When she released me, I saw tears glistening in her eyes.

"Well, now, we have gotten through it at last," she said and held my hand. She was trembling as she tried to control her emotions. "You are responsible for yourself now, and you can go wherever you like."

"Yes," I replied, my heart still heavy. There was nowhere to go. I had the house in Stockholm, but Paul wasn't in the capital anymore. I could follow him to Norway, but that brief encounter at the wedding had made it clear that our relationship was definitely over.

"I wanted to tell you how much I value and love you. And how happy it would make me if, despite your new freedom, you would consider staying at Lion Hall. I know you dream of having your own firm, but here on the estate you have given me invaluable help. No, in fact, that is a gross understatement; you are far more than an assistant. I would be truly pleased if you would stay here and formally take on the responsibility of managing estate business. You are already managing a great deal of it."

I stared at her. "Do you mean that in all seriousness? Should I take it as a job offer?"

"Yes. And it is also an invitation to remain a member of our family. Perhaps you may need some time to consider it."

"I will do that," I said, but I knew instantly that I would accept.

She was right; I was involved in a great deal of the business. And I'd seen how much good it had done Agneta to be relieved of some of the tasks. Meanwhile, Magnus continued to devote himself to his literature. I could tell that his choice worried Agneta, but she let him decide, probably because she'd once studied art and knew what it was like when parents sought to dissuade a person from pursuing a dream.

But this was not the moment to contemplate the future. I wanted only to celebrate the fact that I was a grown woman at last.

The birthday party was a small gathering, just as I'd wished, even though Agneta had offered to host something much larger. An intimate celebration seemed only right, considering I'd turned down the offer of a debut at the royal palace. Still, I couldn't entirely put aside the thought that she was doing her best to find a mate for me.

Marriage didn't interest me in the least. I'd met the sons of her friends and business partners. Not one of them did I find appealing. And besides, I wasn't about to allow myself to get swept up in a fantasy that was sure to come to nothing. I would concentrate on my own life and find my place in the world.

Dinner was elaborate and delicious. I took a walk with Ingmar afterward, very pleased he'd come home for the occasion. But why had he brought his brother? I pictured Ingmar lecturing Magnus about the importance of decency and good manners.

"And how are you feeling?" Ingmar asked. "You're a free woman now. You can decide anything and everything for yourself."

I had an idea where he was headed. "Honestly? I don't feel much different, even though everything around me seems to be. But I'm learning that's how life goes. Everything changes. I'm lucky there are one or two things that haven't."

"Correct. Me, for example."

"Right. You!" I responded and looked at him. I knew if I gave him the slightest encouragement, he'd start courting me, but I didn't want to lose my only real friend. Everything was fine just as it was.

A twig snapped behind us. We stopped and turned.

It was Magnus. Apparently he'd been following us for a while.

"What are you doing here?" I felt a sudden tightening in my chest.

"I have something for you," he said and came closer. He held a small package in one hand.

I stared as if expecting it to bite me. "What is this?"

"Your birthday present."

I had a very bad feeling about this.

"Oh, go ahead," Ingmar said. "See what it is."

I looked at him. Did he know what was going on? Had he pushed his brother to come up with a gift, even though Magnus had been avoiding me all day long? Or had Magnus inexplicably had a change of heart?

Hesitantly, I accepted the little package. "Thank you."

I felt obliged to open it, but first I asked, "Why are you giving me something? I thought you couldn't stand me."

"Well, to quote you, things change. Did you not say that?"

I disliked his snarky tone, but I tore open the package anyway. It held a little box that looked very old. It must have once held something valuable.

I was touched for a moment, but that uneasy feeling wouldn't go away. I raised the lid and found a neatly rolled scroll. I took it out and untied the little ribbon.

It was a train ticket to Stockholm.

Bewildered, I looked at him and then at Ingmar.

"You are free to leave here at last," Magnus said. "Far be it from us to stand in your way. With this you can take the first train tomorrow."

I stared at him in shock. Ingmar appeared just as taken aback; out of the corner of my eye, I saw him shaking his head. Magnus leered.

I was glad he hadn't given me this earlier in the day. He was obviously provoking me in expectation of a negative reaction he could relish for a long time.

A great calm settled over me. Seconds ticked by as I pondered. Inspiration struck.

"How sweet of you!" I cried with the biggest, happiest smile I could plaster on my face. "With this I can visit you two in Stockholm! That's so extraordinarily thoughtful!"

Magnus's features went rigid. He must have been expecting me to burst into tears. But I was no longer a child, so there was no reason to run to Agneta. I was an adult, and it was high time for Magnus to treat me as one.

"Ingmar, look at this!" I said. "Your brother has just spared my savings. Now all we have to do is decide on a date for my visit!"

Ingmar gaped at me, then laugh lines crinkled up around his eyes. He was barely able to keep from guffawing.

Magnus gave me a long, dead stare, then stamped away in a rage.

I covered my mouth to contain my mirth. There was nothing funny about the situation, of course, but a marvelous feeling of triumph did settle over me. For the first time I'd managed to give Magnus as good as I got!

Ingmar sighed. "And I really thought he was finally going to do something nice."

"He did!" I responded. "It's my choice: I can take this ticket as a command to go away forever, or I can use it the way a good bookkeeper would, to avoid an expense. Train tickets are expensive. I'll use this one the next time I visit Stockholm."

Ingmar gave me a doubtful look. "Or you could give it back to him."

I shook my head. "No reason to. Magnus will never like me, and eventually I'll leave the estate. But when that day comes, I'll walk away because I decided to, not because someone gave me a ticket."

Ingmar nodded and put an arm around my shoulders. "Let's go inside and drink a toast to that. I'm sure Magnus has crawled off somewhere."

"If not, we can invite him to join us. I'm not going to let him get to me anymore."

I didn't tell Agneta or Lennard of Magnus's latest trick. I ignored the giver's intention and stored the ticket in my desk drawer.

The following day Silja brought me a letter on a silver tray. "This came for you, Miss Matilda."

Puzzled, I picked it up. "Thank you!"

My heart made a little leap. I thought it might be a letter from Paul since he knew my birth date, and I had a lingering hope he'd send his regards. My pulse changed sharply when I saw I'd been mistaken.

The return address was that of a law office in Stockholm.

I hefted the letter for a moment before picking up my opener. The stationery was heavy and smooth, the typewritten address precise and sharp. The letterhead on the enclosed sheet bore a printed coat of arms that looked almost royal but in fact was that of Ole Malmström,

Esq., of Stockholm, who requested I visit him in his office on Tuesday, November 6, concerning a matter of inheritance.

Not a word more.

A matter of inheritance? Who could have left anything to me? I stared hard at those typewritten lines as if hoping the letters would magically reformat themselves to reveal the significance of this message.

Perhaps Mother had made some arrangement for me? Would I receive a last letter from her? But why would she have gone to an attorney other than the one she'd used for her last will and testament? Could this be belated news of my father?

She hadn't taken me to the reading of Father's will and had told me nothing afterward. I'd wanted to ask what the attorney had said, but I didn't dare. I heard her sobbing quietly to herself late that evening.

I'd struggled all night long with fear and speculation, worried that we were about to be evicted, and only in the morning did I work up the courage to ask.

"Don't worry, darling," she said, running a hand through my hair. *"We're not going to lose the house. Your father deeded it to me, and it will be yours once I'm gone."*

But she still seemed upset. I never learned why, and after a while I stopped wondering.

What did this portend? Certainly not that I was going to lose the house. Was there something else Father had wanted to bequeath or communicate to me? Something that had to wait until I was legally an adult?

I wrestled all day long with the question of whether to tell Agneta of this strange summons. She wasn't my guardian anymore, so she had no automatic right to be informed. I felt the strong urge to confide in someone, but whom? I knew Agneta would offer to accompany me. Perhaps I could get away with telling her I had business in Stockholm.

"I'd like to go to Stockholm on Monday," I informed the count and countess at dinner. "I'll be back on Tuesday evening."

"By all means," Agneta said. "Could you tell us why?"

"I received a letter that probably has to do with my father. Apparently there's something that requires my presence."

Agneta nodded and glanced at Lennard. I couldn't read the significance of the look they exchanged.

"Is it really all right?" I asked.

"Of course it is." She hesitated. "I will go with you if you like."

I shook my head. "Thanks, but that's not necessary. I'll tell you all about it when I get back."

Agneta nodded again, but her eyes were haunted.

I retired to my room early that evening. My stomach was queasy. I studied the attorney's notification again but found no clue to indicate whether the matter had to do with Father. Still, I thought that had to be it. Had he left me a farewell letter? Perhaps a note revealing why he intended to take his own life?

I was afraid, but I also wanted to know. This perpetually unsettled matter was a blank space in my life. I'd never been able to say goodbye to him. I'd never found out what had actually happened, why he did something so terrible.

I went to my desk, opened the drawer, and took out Magnus's birthday gift. I hadn't expected to use it so soon.

28

Three days later I approached the attorney's office in a high state of agitation. I wished I'd brought Agneta. I might be an adult now, but her support would have been welcome.

I went up the steps, passing two men on their way down. I rang the bell. A young woman in a gray suit and bright blue blouse opened the door.

"I have an appointment with Mr. Malmström. My name is Matilda Wallin."

She smiled at me. "Step right in, Miss Wallin! Take off your coat and have a seat. I will inform Mr. Malmström immediately."

I nodded. The law office was decorated in the traditional style with dark wooden paneling and heavy furniture, but the secretary's desk had the latest model of typewriter and a gleaming black telephone.

The telephone rang shrilly, startling me. I looked around guiltily. I was used to ringing telephones, of course, but you'd never believe it, the way I jumped like some foolish country girl.

The secretary came back right away. "Mr. Malmström is ready for you. Would you please come this way?"

I got up. My knees were like jelly.

"Good morning, Miss Wallin," the attorney greeted me. He was a portly, kind-looking man with extravagant sideburns and a medium-size bald spot. "Please have a seat! I hope you had a pleasant journey." "Thank you; everything went as planned." I folded my clammy hands tightly in my lap. I had a tingling feeling in my chest as if it were filled with soda water.

"I am pleased to hear it. Very well, let us get down to business. Do you have a document with which to identify yourself?"

I nodded and took out my identity card. I looked extremely young in the photograph. He examined it, glanced at me, and handed it back. He then picked up an envelope from his desk, broke the wax seal, and took out two sheets of paper. His secretary was posted with a pen and notepad on a chair just inside the door to record the session.

"Present in the office today for the matter of the Lejongård inheritance is Matilda Wallin, whose identity has been authenticated with her national identity card."

The Lejongård inheritance? Before I could recover from my surprise, Malmström continued, "I now read the instructions of Countess Stella Lejongård, made and attested on August 21, 1917."

My eyes opened wide in astonishment. Stella Lejongård? That was Agneta's mother! What could she have to say to me? How did she even know of my existence? She'd passed away years before I came to the estate. And then, the date—this was written when I was less than four years old!

"On August 21, 1917, Countess Stella Lejongård appeared before me and made out the following handwritten instruction: '*Miss Matilda Wallin, born on November 2, 1913, will when she attains her majority be given full authority over the bank account cited hereafter, currently with a balance of fifteen thousand crowns.*'"

I sat there petrified. Countess Agneta's mother had entrusted me with a bank account? Fifteen thousand crowns was a fortune! The lawyer continued, "In addition, she instructs me to read the following appended remarks."

Dear Matilda Wallin,
We have never met, and by the time this letter is read to you I will have been gone for many years. I do not know if my daughter has ever presented herself to you, but if not, today is the day for you to learn the truth about your origins and your father.

My father? This made no sense!
Malmström went on.

This matter has troubled my soul for a long time. Perhaps I write because my conscience bothers me. Whatever the case, the reason you are here is that you—although you bear a different surname and grew up far from Lion Hall—are a member of my family.

Some years ago a maid named Susanna Korven was employed in our house. She became pregnant without benefit of marriage, and after a further incident, she was discharged.

That should in fact have been the last I heard of Susanna: her dishonor should have resulted in her exclusion from all society. However, due to the bullheaded intervention of my daughter, Agneta, you grew up as you did. Your parents were viewed as respectable persons.

I have no obligation to contact you, for in fact you have no legal claim upon the family.

But there were photographs. Images of you as a child. I never admitted it to my daughter, but you remind me very much of my beloved son. Hendrik, Agneta's brother, was your father. I find it difficult to write this, but the photographs your mother sent to my daughter touched my heart. You have Hendrik's eyes. That is why I have made the decision to designate part of my fortune as yours.

    I leave you a relatively modest amount. The truth, however, is worth far more.

    It is not possible for me to legitimate you. That would have been my son's responsibility, but he was in no position to do so. Even so, I depart with the consolation that I have arranged for you to learn of your ancestry.

    Live well, long, and in peace,

    Stella Lejongård

There was absolute silence after the attorney finished the text. The only sound was the ticking of the grandfather clock to my left. Feeling the attorney's eyes on me, I turned to see the secretary putting the last touches on her notes.

Realizing I'd been holding my breath, I let it out in a long, slow sigh. I became aware of my racing pulse.

How should I take this? The tingles and twitches of my chest and gut had disappeared. I'd become a block of stone.

My mind rejected what the attorney had read out to me. Stella Lejongård claimed I was the daughter of Agneta's brother, Hendrik—whose death had put an end to the countess's plans for an independent life as a painter!

That couldn't be. My mother had been involved with the son of a countess?

It wasn't possible.

But why on earth would Stella Lejongård invent such a thing? And leave me so much money, to be revealed only when I reached adulthood?

"May I see the letter?"

"Naturally. I will provide you the original and keep a copy here in my office, as is customary." He handed me the document, and I read through it, word for word.

There was nothing other than what I'd already heard. This declaration in the woman's elegant handwriting, delivered from beyond the grave, did not alter when I read it for myself.

She claimed I was Hendrik Lejongård's daughter! That made me cousin to Ingmar and Magnus. And niece to Agneta and Lennard.

"Do you accept the bequest?" the attorney asked me, the faintest touch of impatience in his voice.

Did I want it? It was tied to the truth, at least according to Stella Lejongård.

I couldn't reject truth.

"Yes," I said. "I accept it."

Moments later I tottered out to stand stunned on the sidewalk. Automobiles rattled by in the street, and the wind ruffled my hair. Damp air crept inside my coat. I hardly noticed; I was numb.

Mother had had a liaison with the heir to the estate! She'd become a fallen woman and was forced to leave. But how had she come to marry Father?

I couldn't believe she'd kept these secrets from me!

My head ached and pounded. Only my mother's death had been a greater shock. What should I do?

I had a wild impulse to rend my clothes and scream, but people would have taken me for a madwoman and called the police. Violent trembling shook me. My hands clenched into fists. *No, stop! I mustn't let anyone see my consternation.*

Summoning all my willpower, I started walking. Then I broke into a run and ran faster than ever in my life.

There was only one thing I could do. I had to go back to Lion Hall, confront Agneta, and demand an explanation.

29

I fidgeted, twisted, and turned on my seat in the train compartment all the way back to Kristianstad. I went over the attorney's words again and again. I read the letter he'd given me over and over. There I had it, black on white: Stella Lejongård had declared I was her grandchild.

But why hadn't anyone told me? Because they didn't know? I found that hard to believe. Agneta knew. Stella had very deliberately mentioned that in the letter. Why had Agneta concealed this? Because she'd feared that it would cast doubts on property arrangements for her own sons? Surely not—she must know there was no way I could be validated as an heir.

The closer I got to Kristianstad, the angrier I felt. I'd discovered earlier that Agneta had deceived me by hiding the fact that Mother was employed at Lion Hall, and I'd forgiven her. But now? And why hadn't her brother married Mother? Because she wasn't good enough? Because he'd have to face the censure of people around him?

It was evening when the train pulled into Kristianstad. I hadn't told Agneta when I expected to be back, so of course there was no driver waiting; but that was fine with me. I took a taxi. It was quite expensive, but money was the least of my concerns.

It was dark by the time I got to Lion Hall, and I was determined to corner Agneta and Lennard. I burned with anger and scorn. No more lies or secrets! I stamped my way up the front steps. The letter in my bag seemed to burn like a torch of truth.

"Miss Matilda, good evening!" Rika said as she passed me in the foyer.

"Good evening!" I said and strode directly to the dining room. Lennard and Agneta were already at dinner, little expecting what awaited them.

"Good evening, Matilda! Back already?"

I was trembling from head to foot. "Agneta, I have to speak to you!"

She got up. "For heaven's sake, what has happened?"

"*This* is what happened!" I snatched her mother's letter out of my bag and slapped it onto the table.

"Do calm yourself, Matilda," Lennard interjected, but I ignored him. Agneta froze at the sight of the letter.

After a long moment she reached for it, very gingerly, as if the sheet of paper would snap at her like a rabid dog.

Go ahead! Read it! I felt like shouting, but I was too angry to get a word out.

Agneta's face lost all color. She took the letter between her fingers ever so tentatively, lifted it, and instantly clapped one hand to her mouth. Her eyes remained fixed on the declaration that had shaken the very foundations of my being. Stella Lejongård's words had ripped years of my life away and left nothing behind.

"What do you have to say to that?" I demanded. I didn't know how much she'd read, but it must have been enough. "Tell me . . . *Aunt* Agneta!"

I refused to cry.

"Well? Cat got your tongue? When were you planning to tell me? When were you going to confess you threw my mother out because your brother got her pregnant? Because he didn't marry her, as he should have!"

"Matilda, please hear me out," she said, trembling. "It is not what you think. The circumstances back then—"

"*What* circumstances and back *when*? The circumstance that my mother wasn't good enough for him? The circumstance that she was good enough for his bed? Why did you make her suffer through that? Why?"

My voice failed me. A roaring filled my ears and my knees shook. I felt faint, but I refused to swoon in the face of such duplicity. Anger blazed through me.

Agneta was at a loss for words. "Your mother—she—"

"She was just a servant, wasn't she? Not good enough for you people. And that's why I wasn't good enough either, not good enough to deserve the truth."

"Matilda—" Agneta began, but I was fed up.

"Don't bother!" I hurled those words at her and ran to my room.

I slammed the door and crossed the room in long strides. Standing at the window, I had no idea how to vent my rage. By screaming? Raving? Smashing a windowpane? I'd been lied to all my life! Tears finally gushed forth.

Everything I'd known lay in ruins. Daga was married and had dropped me, Paul had vanished, and now I'd had it forced into my face that the man who'd drowned himself and whom I missed so terribly hadn't been my father at all. My mother had been impregnated by the scion of Lion Hall and fired from her employment on the same estate that took me in after she died, the estate to which I actually should have always belonged.

Weeping, I went to the desk for my father's lighter. How I wanted in that moment to burn the whole place down!

And I did click the lighter. Instants later my thumb felt a sharp pain. I stood there, imagining what would happen if I sent everything here up in flames, including myself.

The pain became intense and brought me to my senses. I dropped the lighter and flung myself onto the bed.

Nothing would come of destruction. Instead, I should begin a new life. I could use my business diploma and escape. I had to do that. Immediately.

I'd accepted the bequest, but Stella Lejongård's money was the only thing I would take with me into my new life.

A knock came at the door. I wanted them to leave me alone, but I responded automatically. "Come in!"

Agneta appeared in the doorway but didn't enter. "May I?"

"It's your house," I replied and sat up. My eyes were swollen, and my throat was raw.

Agneta carefully closed the door behind her and approached. She pulled a chair over next to the bed and seated herself. "I am very sorry, Matilda, that I did not tell you. I could not. I was afraid, so terribly afraid."

"Afraid of my reaction?" I countered. "Don't you think it would have been better if you'd told from the first?"

"Very likely," she admitted. "The truth is that the circumstances were complicated."

"They're no better now!" I glared at her. "Did you know your mother set this up?"

Agneta shook her head. "No. I did not have the slightest idea she had a place in her heart for you. The date—she died not quite three months later. Shortly before Christmas. We didn't celebrate the holidays that year . . ."

"So you were never going to tell me?" I shouted. "You'd have left me forever in the dark about my true identity?"

"I—I was afraid. Afraid to lose you!" Agneta raised her arms as if to plead but dropped them when she saw my expression. "I was afraid it would destroy you."

"Don't you think a life of lies was worse?"

"You are probably right." She sighed heavily. "I believed no one would ever know. But truth almost always will out; there is no way to bottle it up. I wish to tell you the whole story. I am sure you will still be angry with me, but at least I can give you the truth to which you are entitled."

I gave her a disdainful look. What guarantee did I have she wouldn't sell me another pack of lies?

"In fact, you should have grown up here," she began in a broken voice. "You really should have inherited the estate. But your mother was a servant and not married to my brother. I have no idea of Hendrik's intentions when he started their relationship. But it would be naïve to suppose he would have renounced his inheritance for her sake. And that would have been the only acceptable way to marry a woman not of the same class."

I snorted in derision. *Not of the same class!* When would the world stop thinking in such terms?

"You should have told me!" I hissed. "I see Mother was trying to protect me, but *you* should have told me the truth as soon as you became my guardian."

"Yes. I see now I should have done just that, but that is not all there is to their story. My brother loved your mother, I am sure of it, and he probably failed to consider where that love might lead. He may have persuaded himself they had a chance, but he was never able to pursue it or provide for your mother. He died before he found out about you." A bitter, strangled laugh escaped from deep in her throat. "I never told you why the portraits in the entry hall are separate. My father and my mother . . ."

I had no idea what that had to do with anything, but I let her continue.

"My father died almost twenty-two years ago in the fire you have heard about. The roof fell in on him as he tried to protect my brother with his own body. Hendrik—" She couldn't go on for a moment. "My brother, Hendrik, was in the hospital for two days after that. We expected him to survive. I was counting on it. I had planned a different life for myself. I wanted to become an artist, a painter. I wanted to conquer the world. But Hendrik died, and my world collapsed. I tried to convince myself I could simply bring my former life here with me, but that was a delusion. I lost everything. In order to fulfill my obligations, my duty as the heiress to Lion Hall, I had to give up my art. The man whom I had loved abandoned me. I destroyed almost all my paintings and became the woman I now am."

Her eyes wandered, and she stared into the darkness beyond the window. "Weeks later, your mother collapsed while on duty. It turned out that she was pregnant. She refused to name the father. I was bullheaded, just as my mother wrote to you. My duty was to discharge Susanna, but I refused. I wanted to find a solution."

"You mean you looked for some dolt to take responsibility?"

"No, not someone stupid. Things were different in those days. We women had to petition the court to obtain our independence. We did not have the right to vote. There was no thought at all that a pregnancy was also the man's fault. When such a thing happened, everyone automatically deemed the woman a tramp, a prostitute. In truth, things have changed very little since then. As you know, my friends and I were deeply engaged in the campaign for women's rights. We were suffragettes."

I saw deep melancholy in her eyes. "We also took in women who had become pregnant. We found husbands for them. Volunteers. Men who needed wives so as not to be outcasts from society."

"What do you mean?" I asked. My father—or at least, the man I'd thought was my father—had been a respected citizen and breadwinner. How could he have been disgraced?

"They were men who really were not looking for wives. Men who risked going to prison for their affection for other men."

"No!" I burst out. "My father wasn't like that!"

"I have no idea; I never met him. All I know is that he was a kind and righteous man, a man who assumed the responsibility for Susanna and her child. Susanna agreed to the arrangement; she had no choice, for even if Hendrik had wanted to marry her, he was no longer alive to do so."

"Not that it made any difference," I said bitterly. "You people would have kept him from marrying her anyway."

"Do not underestimate my brother, I beg you. He could be just as stubborn as I was. But that is a moot point. Your father, Sigurd Wallin, freely took Susanna in and gave her and her child his own name."

"When did you find out your brother was my real father?"

"When I searched out your mother to help her. I said I needed to know who had fathered her child. And she told me. I was bowled over, but not for a second did I doubt she was telling the truth. The morning after his death, I had seen her in his room, sobbing her heart out. I did not realize what it meant at the time. I helped her, and out of gratitude she kept in contact with me."

Tears filled my eyes. I still wanted to vent my anger, but suddenly all I could feel was the great weight of misery and unending grief.

"She and I decided not to tell you of your true identity. We wanted you to live a normal life. It never occurred to us what might happen, if—Well, I stupidly trusted my mother with the secret and showed her your baby pictures. She seemed completely indifferent. Never in my wildest dreams did I imagine she would write to you. Or leave you a bequest. It seems each and every one of us in this family conceals secrets."

A long silence followed. Her words filled my mind like the deafening clamor of church bells.

In a different society, I'd have grown up at Lion Hall. I'd have had a family, cousins. Instead, first I'd lost my father and then my mother. I'd been abandoned and denied.

And now I'd learned I actually did have a family, and they didn't want me. Worse—they'd done their best to make sure I'd never learn where I came from. The monstrous behavior took my breath away.

I was confused and bewildered. We sat across from one another, neither speaking, and I cast about for some way out, escape in any possible direction. A life with Paul was impossible now, and I wanted nothing to do with Lion Hall. Why would I want to be the poor niece receiving crumbs from their table, when my life could have been so different?

Sigurd Wallin had claimed me as his daughter, so I had no legal recourse and no way to prove otherwise.

I was determined to leave the estate of the faceless man who'd sired me. "I will go to Stockholm," I declared at last. "I will forget Lion Hall and make a life for myself there. I'll use your mother's money, but not unless I have to."

Agneta almost collapsed. I was legally free to do as I pleased. And what I wanted to do more than anything was to hurt her as badly as she'd hurt me. I knew very well she was hoping I would stay, and for that very reason I intended to refuse.

I remembered how from the first she'd expressed the hope that I'd consider Lion Hall my home.

"I have my own property, a business degree, and experience; I can use all of that. I refuse to live in this haunted house. Who knows what else you're hiding?"

Agneta bowed her head. She could have denied it, but she didn't. There had to be more.

"I am very sorry to hear that."

"Yes," I replied. "And we should just leave it at that. What's done can't be undone. I have to put Lion Hall behind me." I took an angry satisfaction from seeing her take each word like a slap in the face. She deserved this punishment.

A moment later she got up without a word and went to the door. Then she turned back. "When do you wish to go?"

"First thing tomorrow morning. I'll take the bare minimum and send for the rest of my things later. That is, if you permit it."

Agneta nodded and left.

I took a long, shuddering breath. My thoughts ran in circles. My childhood and youth had been a lie. A lie lived by my loving mother and never revealed.

What should I do now? I'd presented a brave front, but I hadn't the slightest idea.

30

Sleep eluded me until very late, and uneasy dreams plagued me when it came. My father thrashed in the water and sank; I leaped to rescue him and grabbed for his hand. He slipped away in the torrent. I tried to scream for help but couldn't make a sound. Sigurd Wallin sank deeper and deeper and disappeared in the dark-green depths.

I bolted upright, frantic and soaked in sweat. Gasping, I scrabbled in the bed table drawer for my father's lighter and pressed it to my breast. It had lost its magic; the chill of its metal surface in my clammy hands repelled me. Panicked, I threw it back in the drawer and huddled in bed.

An oppressive black sky lay heavy over the manor house. Rain pattered quietly against the windowpanes. Sunrise was far away, but I knew I wouldn't be able to sleep.

I got up and began packing, as I had before my frantic escape three years earlier. I'd never expected to do that again. Magnus had remained surly, but I'd gotten used to his foul moods. This time the perfidy wasn't his but his mother's. I still found it incredible that her brother was my real father.

Half strangled by sobs, I piled winter clothing into the case. Agneta must have loved Hendrik deeply—at least her words and expression suggested as much. That made it even more perplexing that she'd hidden the truth. Surely her brother would have been furious if he'd found out.

I tossed blouses, skirts, stockings, and underthings into the suitcase. I pulled out the steamer trunk and packed away summer clothes and more. I left the ball gown in the wardrobe. I would have no use for it in my new life.

I'd finished packing by the time the maid knocked. My face felt swollen and my pulse was loud in my ears, but I was ready to go and glad of it. Sleep could wait until I got back to my own house.

Rika's eyes opened wide. "Are you going on a trip, Miss Matilda?"

"No," I answered. "I'm leaving for good. Could you please inform the chauffeur?"

"For good?" she echoed. "But why?"

I could have snapped that it was none of her business and sent her away, but then I'd have been like *them*. Like Stella. And Agneta.

"The gracious mistress will explain it to you later today. Be so kind as to bring me breakfast. I will not be going downstairs."

"Gladly, Miss Matilda," she replied, bewildered, then curtsied and left.

She was bound to tell the kitchen staff. Rumors would run wild. I didn't care, for I was never coming back.

After breakfast, I set my suitcase out in the hall, along with everything I needed for the trip.

Magnus had always intended to drive me out. Let him celebrate if he wanted!

Ingmar, however, was different. He'd been my friend—my only friend—and had tried to make my life easier. I would miss him. I'd have to tell him what had happened. But I didn't know if I could admit him into my life in Stockholm.

I had to run the gauntlet of departure first.

I went downstairs, certain that Agneta and Lennard were still at breakfast.

And sure enough, I heard the murmur as they discussed business. They weren't talking about me. I put my suitcase down in the foyer, took a deep breath, and stepped into the dining room.

Lennard saw me and immediately put down his coffee cup. He wished me good morning. Agneta turned and did the same.

"I came to say goodbye."

Agneta rose and came to me. "You do not have to leave, you know," she said apologetically. "We can sit down and talk this over."

"There's nothing to discuss," I replied. "I intend to turn the page on everything here. Please allow me that."

Agneta nodded. "Very well, if that is your desire. But wait just a moment; I have something I wish to give you."

She left the room, and I heard her go upstairs.

Lennard got up. "So you really do want to leave?"

"Yes. But I want you to know it isn't because of you. It's because of Agneta and the secrets she keeps concealing."

Lennard sighed. "I am sure she really did mean it for the best. For your sake."

"Did you know?" I asked.

Lennard nodded guiltily and bowed his head. "Yes. But she begged me not to say anything. There were many times I wanted to tell you."

I pressed my lips together. It was understandable, I supposed, for him to respect his wife's wishes. Even so, it would have been better if he'd confided in me. We'd have been spared this painful scene.

"I am very sorry that you had to learn the truth in this way. My mother-in-law was often somewhat—difficult. She never told us of her intentions, even though she often reproached us for not keeping her informed."

I remembered the portrait of the beautiful, elegant woman. I'd have liked to have known her, but I'd been deprived of that chance by their decision to keep me in the dark, a decision imposed by class snobbery and absurd views of morality.

Agneta appeared and held out an envelope.

"Your letter of recommendation," she murmured. "I know you do not wish to accept anything from me. But take this at least. Perhaps it will help when you apply for employment."

We contemplated one another for a moment before I took the envelope and shoved it into my purse. "Thank you."

I had the feeling she wanted to try again to persuade me to stay. I was grateful she didn't.

"I hope you will find happiness," she said finally. "But always remember that this house is your home. You are free to return anytime."

"A home that wanted nothing to do with me," I said ruefully. "All the best to both of you!"

I turned and made my exit. Agneta gasped and sobbed behind me, but I ignored her.

The skies over Lion Hall were overcast as I got into the automobile. The chauffeur closed my door, took his place at the wheel, and moments later we got underway.

Throughout all the years at Lion Hall, I'd looked forward to leaving and wondered what it would be like to be free at last. My only feeling now was the sorrowful weight in my breast.

I was free. And I had nowhere to go.

The train sped along, and the countryside unrolled before me. I leaned my forehead against the window and stared at the scenery. We'd long ago left behind the woods and fields around Kristianstad.

Cradled in the palm of my hand was my father's lighter—or, rather, the lighter that had belonged to the man who took in my pregnant mother. He knew I wasn't his own flesh and blood. If only I could ask him to explain why they'd never given me a clue . . .

Many things were clearer now.

For example, Mother's frequent distraction. She must have been thinking of her true love, a love that could never be fulfilled, a love I reminded her of.

And Father? Had her distant attitude driven him to suicide? Could he no longer stand being compared to a rival on the far side of the grave? I would never know. Hendrik Lejongård's ghost must have lived in our house. It was probably waiting for me now.

As I brooded, my self-righteousness faded. The farther I traveled from Lion Hall, the less sure of myself I felt.

What was awaiting me in Stockholm? Which way should I turn, what goal should I pursue? I had Stella's bequest, but I didn't want to depend on her money. I could get by for a while with my savings from the salary Agneta had paid me. But after that? There were no estates to manage in Stockholm. Should I try to relocate to the countryside, maybe somewhere in the north?

And then there was the house I owned, my safe harbor despite its ghosts.

Maybe I could work in an office, or as a bookkeeper for a large store or shipping concern.

These questions hounded me all the way to Stockholm.

I felt a bit better when the city's familiar skyline came into sight. I was home again. Of course, I couldn't deny that Lion Hall had also been a home to me. That was part of the reason I was so upset that Agneta had lied.

I picked up my suitcase and stepped into the corridor. The conductor smiled but luckily for me he wasn't moved to chat.

The train pulled into the platform, engulfing the people there in smoke and steam. I straightened up. The conductor opened the door and stepped back. I blinked up at the gray November sky. A stray shaft of sunlight peeked through the clouds. Passengers streamed past and jostled me, but I didn't mind. I made my way to the stairs.

The Ringströms came to mind. For a moment I considered visiting them. Their house's scent of glue and sawdust had always had a calming effect.

But the friend of my youth was now a married woman living all the way across the city. Paul was in Norway, and Mrs. Ringström had acted so oddly on the way to the church. There would be no comfort for me in sawdust and wood glue and the high, keen shrill of the mechanical saw.

My childhood was over, and worse, it had been a lie. A father who wasn't my father, a mother who'd been just as mendacious as my guardian. I would miss Lion Hall, but it was no longer part of my life. I should never have been there, and if Susanna Wallin had survived, I'd have known nothing about it.

Stella Lejongård had made sure I would learn the hard truth. Perhaps because she had a guilty conscience, as she'd claimed. But maybe she had intended to punish the woman she saw as having seduced her son. Her letter and bequest would have forced Mother to explain. That might have torn the two of us apart.

The only good thing was that Mother hadn't been subjected to that cruelty. She was spared the humiliation of confessing the secret she took with her to the grave.

The gray clouds still hovered overhead, but a narrow shaft of sunshine as brilliant as a spotlight dazzled me momentarily as I stepped out of the station. I took it as a sign. I wasn't going to give up.

31

Morning sunlight awakened me. My eyelids were heavy. I'd thrashed in my bed and woken repeatedly from half-remembered dreams. In the last of them, I'd stood on the parapet of the bridge from which my father had leaped to his death. I climbed up and was about to dive after him, but something grabbed me. I looked down and saw tendrils of ivy had twisted about me, wrapping my legs up to the knees.

I sat up. Bright light flooded my room and revealed thick layers of dust. I hadn't expected a sunny morning after the previous day's grim weather.

The clock had stopped years before. I checked my watch. It was just after ten o'clock.

At this time of day, I would be sitting with Agneta in the office after my daily stroll around the Lion Hall grounds.

I got up, washed, and dressed. After breakfast I set out for the university.

Normally I would be reluctant to approach Ingmar in front of his friends, but he needed to know what his mother had done, and he had to hear it from me.

I took a bus and then wandered about the university grounds for a while. They were more extensive than I'd expected, with many annexes in addition to the main building. The campus was stark and barren in the November light. The trees were bare and the grass was dead. Crows cawed from the rooftops.

Morning lectures were still underway. I peered through windows at the lit interiors where students sat in steep rows listening to their professors.

Settling on a stone bench, I pulled my coat closer about me and wondered if I was doing the right thing.

I thought back to the day Agneta had hauled me back to Lion Hall. That humiliation had left a bitter aftertaste. Ingmar had been my staunch supporter afterward. He'd always defended me; he'd always been there for me. I recalled rescuing him after his catastrophic accident. Later he'd persuaded me to go to Daga's wedding, where I learned the valuable lesson that friendship is perishable. Should I simply avoid him? Could I simply put our relationship on ice?

There was no bell to signal the end of class. Countless knuckles rapping on wooden desks generated rolling thunder.

Seconds later, students streamed out of the lecture halls and noisy chatter filled the vast square. They carried piles of textbooks and wore jackets of all different qualities. Most had their hair combed to one side in the fashion of the day.

Ingmar appeared, gesturing emphatically as he explained something to a couple of his classmates. When he noticed me, he froze, quickly said something to his friends, and then hurried over. "Matilda, what are you doing here?" he exclaimed. "Did something happen?"

"You could say that. Do you have a moment? I'd like to have a word. Just the two of us."

"I have another lecture right now, but—" He glanced at his classmates. "My intrepid young comrades will share their notes. Come on!"

He took me to a nearby café frequented by students. It was almost empty at this time of day. The brown paneling was redolent of coffee and tobacco. Newspapers fixed on wooden batons hung from a rack, and their odor of printer's ink filled my nostrils. A display case offered different sorts of cakes, but I had no appetite. This encounter was crucial, too important to our friendship.

We ordered coffees, for the grumpy proprietress wouldn't let us sit there without ordering something.

"So now tell me, please," Ingmar said. "What brings you here?"

"Something happened," I said. I took the attorney's letter from my purse and with it the pages in Stella Lejongård's handwriting. "Read these!"

Ingmar took them. He wasn't surprised by the attorney's invitation, but as he read through his grandmother's text, the creases on his forehead grew deeper and deeper.

"This can't be!"

I shivered involuntarily. "Apparently it can."

"That makes us—"

"Cousins," I said. "Imagine that."

Ingmar leaned back in the chair and released a noisy breath. He stared blindly before him, then turned to me. "And my mother knew this?"

"She did. She told me the whole story. About time too."

"And how are you feeling about it?"

"Terrible." I looked down. "I left Lion Hall for good."

"What?" Ingmar exclaimed. "But why?"

"I don't want to live in a place full of secrets where they hid my true origins. Agneta can't tell me what to do anymore. And as your— our—grandmother's letter tells you, I can't be legitimated because my real father is in your family crypt." I got choked up and had to pause a moment. "Your family never wanted anything to do with me, not even before I was born."

"That's not true!" Ingmar cried. "Why do you think my mother agreed to become your guardian?"

"She probably felt guilty."

"I don't think so." Ingmar reached out and touched my cheek. "Mother is not a bad person. She has her secrets, but her intentions are good."

Tears filled my eyes. "She should have told me. Don't you think?"

Ingmar couldn't meet my tearful gaze. "Yes. She should have."

"I—I really don't know how to say this," I told him, trying to hold back sobs. "Lion Hall should have been my home. Instead they sent Mother away, and for twenty-one years everyone pretended Sigurd Wallin was my father. I believed them! I was devastated when he killed himself. I was deceived for all those years, and I'd still be living a lie if your grandmother hadn't decided to enlighten me. Do you really think Agneta eventually would've confessed? She didn't even tell the two of you!"

My voice had risen to a hysterical pitch, and I suddenly felt light-headed. I'd thought I had myself under control, but my disappointment was a beast capable of ambushing me at any moment.

"I agree that what she did was wrong." Ingmar gently placed his hand on my arm. "She should have told you."

"She should never have sent my mother away!"

"Matilda. It's not that simple. Your mother would have been disgraced. People would have pointed fingers and condemned her; you'd have been born into scandal. I'm sure my mother wasn't planning to keep it a secret forever."

"When was she going to tell me? When the lawyer read Mother's will to us, why didn't she say she was my aunt?"

Ingmar found no answer to that. "I can't tell you why. Maybe she wanted to protect you. You were grieving; perhaps she wanted to avoid inflicting even more pain."

"I wish she had! Nothing could have hurt me then. I'd already lost everything!" I slumped. My emotions gradually ebbed, leaving me empty inside.

We sat together in silence for a very long time.

"I'm not going to change my mind," I declared in a scratchy voice. "I won't go back to Lion Hall. I intend to make my own way in the world. And I want to ask you something."

"What?" he asked. "I mean, you don't need to go away. We can find a solution. I'll speak to Mother."

I grabbed his hand. "Ingmar, please listen!"

"Very well," he said with a sigh. "I am listening."

"It's not like those other times. No one's reading my personal mail, and there's no housemaid's dress in my wardrobe. This is worse, it's inexcusable. Nothing your mother does can make up for the fact that she hid my paternity. I need time to think things over, time to get myself in order. On my own. I'm asking you not to contact me."

"But why?" He snatched back his hand. "It wasn't me! If I'd learned we were related, I'd have told you right away. I'd have helped you clear up things with Mother. Even though I'm furious with her."

"I understand that, of course, and I'm not saying I'll never contact you again. You'll always be my friend, but for now I want to cut ties to Lion Hall. Your mother might try to use you to persuade me. I can't take that."

"May I say something?"

"Of course."

"That's pure nonsense!" He shook his head. "We've known each other for years, and I really thought—maybe I was mistaken—that we liked one another."

"Yes, we do, but—"

"And now you insist I break off all contact with you? Because my mother hid the fact that you're my cousin? Can't you see how idiotic that is?"

I felt myself being swayed. He was right; my decision was punishing him. But I couldn't begin a new life unless I put Lion Hall entirely behind me. And I was sure that sooner or later Ingmar would try to entice me back, directly or indirectly.

"Maybe it is too severe," I admitted. "We—maybe we can make a pact: give me a year. Let me see what it's like simply to be myself, Matilda, all alone in the world. Once that year is over, I'll write. And then we'll see one another again."

"A year!" Ingmar echoed. "Do you think that will change anything? You're a Lejongård. It's in your blood!"

"According to your grandmother! But there's nothing official to prove it."

"But there is *this*," he said, tapping his chest over his heart. "Why do you think the two of us get along so well? That's why! For a long time I thought I was in love with you, but obviously it was a different kind of attraction. You are what I will never have in my twin brother, despite what they say: a kindred soul."

I took a deep breath and wanted to flee, but that would have been useless. Ingmar knew where to find me. And I didn't want to run away from the problem. I needed a solution.

"It's only a year, Ingmar," I reasoned with him. "That's enough time for my anger to cool down. Then we'll write one another and meet. In Stockholm. I'll never set foot in Lion Hall again."

I saw a tear trickle down his cheek and reached for his hand again. "I like you very much, Ingmar. You're like a brother to me. And we won't lose one another forever. But you have to give me some time."

He stared at me, the blue of his eyes even more intense than usual. It pained me to see how wounded he was, but I was sure I was doing the right thing.

"All right," he said. "One year. But not a day longer, you hear? Otherwise I will be knocking on your front door."

I smiled, got up, and hugged him. "It's a promise. One year, then I'll write. Promise me, though, that you won't tell your mother any of this, all right? She should be left in the dark, just the way I was. She mustn't get any news of me."

"I promise," he said, then stood and planted a kiss on the crown of my head.

We parted before the university. I watched Ingmar walk away until he disappeared into the university grounds. My heart ached. I would really miss him.

I hadn't intended to compromise; I'd really intended the separation to be forever. I was glad anyway, for this would give me time to work out what I was going to do in life.

32

That same day, I went to the cemetery to visit my mother. I brought a fistful of flowers, though I knew that they'd wither quickly in the November weather.

"Why did you keep it all from me?" I asked the gravestone. "Why was it you never let me know there was a different man? One you really loved?"

I paused, then added, "And you, Father, wherever you are, why did you let me believe it? Why did the two of you think I had no right to know?"

My voice rang out in the quiet of the graveyard, but it was no use asking questions of the dead.

I left but didn't go directly home, for I had no desire to brood, cooped up inside my parents' house. I took a bus northward, intending to stroll in the heart of the city. The King's Garden, Stockholm's central park, was relatively quiet this time of year, but there were cafés and art galleries and enough people around to take my mind off my troubles.

When I got out of the bus near the royal palace, I caught sight of the Grand Hôtel, one of the many classical-style edifices in the city center. The flags displayed across the roof and the castle-like facade made it stand out.

I stood there, thunderstruck. I'd been in a hotel only one time in my life. The bustle of arrivals and departures had fascinated me. Could I hope to get a job there? It wouldn't exactly match what I'd been taught, but I was pretty sure I wouldn't mind working there, maybe even as a chambermaid. I simply wanted to banish my memories of Lion Hall. After all, hadn't I dreamed of the wide world when I was a child?

I couldn't travel the world, but perhaps at the Grand Hôtel the world would come to me. And I'd never be alone.

I gathered my courage and stepped inside.

A young woman at the reception desk, dressed in a smart blue suit and with a cascade of blonde hair framing her face, gave me a friendly smile. "How may I help you, madame?" No doubt she was expecting me to ask for a room or to contact one of the guests.

"What must I do to obtain employment here?"

"Excuse me?" She frowned, then looked around as if seeking someone to translate.

"I would like to apply for a position."

"What sort of position?"

"Any position at all."

The woman's expression suggested I was raving mad. And maybe I was. Maybe I'd had a nervous breakdown that morning and hadn't noticed.

"Well, it is not up to me to say," she answered. "But I could call Mr. Viselundt, our personnel director."

"Please do so," I said with a warm smile. "My name is Matilda Wallin."

The desk clerk kept her eyes on me as if afraid that I might pull out a knife. She picked up the telephone. She didn't let me out of sight as she spoke to someone about my request.

She hung up. "Please have a seat over there for a moment."

"Thank you," I said and went to the sofa area. As I sank into the soft upholstery, I realized the folly of what I was doing.

I must be out of my mind! I was asking for any position at all in Stockholm's largest and most elegant hotel. I hadn't written an inquiry or filled out an application form; I'd acted entirely on impulse. I half expected the uniformed doorman to tap me on the shoulder and order me to move along.

A couple of minutes passed. I studied the lobby's gorgeous chandelier. Its crystals sparkled with light as the crown jewels might have done.

"Miss Wallin?" a male voice asked. "I am Bert Viselundt, the institution's personnel director."

In his late forties with a receding hairline, he wore a dark-blue pin-striped suit.

I got up and offered him my hand. "I am very pleased to meet you."

He took it. "Please accompany me to my office."

We went past the reception desk, the clerk gaping in disbelief. The head of personnel was actually offering me an interview, even though I didn't have an appointment. Was this real, or was I sitting on a bus, lost in a dream?

No, it was happening and was as real as the strong cigar odor in his office. He motioned me to the visitor's chair. "I understand you are seeking employment." He seated himself behind the desk. "And what position were you imagining for yourself?"

"Well, in fact I don't really care. I would gladly work as a chambermaid. I will take any job that needs doing."

"Where were you previously employed?"

Wasn't that irrelevant? The realization that I'd have to mention Lion Hall sent a wave of unease through me. But so what? Probably no one here knew Agneta Lejongård.

"At an estate called Lion Hall. Not far from Kristianstad."

"And what were your duties? Were you employed as a servant?"

No, but my mother was, I almost declared. *She had an affair with the count's son.* Fortunately, I wasn't that rash.

"I worked in the administrative office. It is a huge estate dedicated to horse breeding."

"I gather you come from somewhere around there?" The man examined me from head to toe, probably assuming I was a simple village girl. It was ironic to think that, when I'd left Stockholm, people had assumed I was incapable of living in the countryside.

"I was born in Stockholm," I told him. "After my mother's death I resided on the estate for several years. I attended Kristianstad's business college, and I can provide my diploma if you wish."

"You graduated from business college?" Viselundt asked. "And now you want to hire yourself out as a chambermaid?"

"Well, I did not say that I had my heart set on working as a chambermaid. I meant only that I would accept any sort of employment."

"And why here, pray tell?"

"I need a new challenge. And I have just returned home."

"Home? To your parents?"

"To my parents' house. It belongs to me."

The man nodded and considered this for a while. "And what about your employment at the estate? Were you discharged?"

"No, it was my decision to leave." For reasons that were none of the personnel director's business.

"Was that by mutual accord?"

"Yes," I replied as decisively as I could. I sensed Viselundt's growing annoyance. Maybe I should give up and get out. This was a crazy idea.

I remembered the letter of recommendation in my purse next to the letters I'd shown Ingmar. I didn't want to use whatever Agneta had written, but it couldn't be helped. Maybe the contents would win him over.

"Here is my employer's letter of recommendation," I said. "If that might interest you."

He accepted the envelope a little reluctantly. He appeared to have come to the same conclusion as the desk clerk. Even so, he unfolded the note and read Agneta's text.

At that moment I really wished I knew what was in it. No; in fact, I wished I'd never entered the hotel. I should have thought before acting. I should have drafted a letter of application. And why on earth had I set my sights on a hotel? Me, Matilda Wallin, who'd wanted to be a partner at Paul Ringström's furniture factory. Had Mother's ghost lured me here?

Mr. Viselundt leaned back in his office chair. Something about him reminded me a bit of Ingmar. Perhaps it was because he looked just as bewildered as Ingmar had during our conversation earlier that day.

"I will be frank with you," he began. "The truth is that we have no open positions. The staff here are hired because they were recommended to us. It is extremely rare that we publish employment opportunities. This institution is one of the best hotels in Sweden and beyond a doubt the best in Stockholm. The clientele that pass through these doors include crowned heads, wealthy aristocrats, celebrated artists, and owners of great estates."

He gave me a moment to let that sink in. "Yet you simply appear here and give me the impression you have not spent even five minutes considering this. You ask for any position at all, even though you have a business-school degree and worked in the administrative office of one of the country's most famous estates."

He folded his hands in front of him on the desk. "Young lady, you should ask yourself what sort of work you seek before you come in here to waste my time. I cannot hire someone who will take any position at all."

I bowed my head. My hopes were dashed. Agneta's letter had done me no good. I probably shouldn't have shown it to him. I probably shouldn't have accepted it from her.

"Go home!" Viselundt exclaimed as he returned the letter to me.

I nodded and put the letter back into its envelope. My cheeks flushed in shame.

"And when you get there," he added, "sit down at your desk and write out a proper letter of application. I want your references as well as a description of your background. This is not a country inn where people hire staff the way shipping companies hire sailors. A business college graduate with your experience would be qualified for employment as an assistant in our administrative offices. But only if she went about the process properly. Do you understand?"

My eyes widened. "Yes, but—you will entertain my application?"

"That I will. As I do any employment request delivered in good and due form. But you are not to show your face here again until such time as I invite you to do so. Is that clear?"

Warmth filled me. He hadn't turned me down! Yes, he was being quite brusque, but what had I expected? To be taken in with open arms? At least he was going to give me a chance!

"Yes, Mr. Viselundt," I answered. "I will have the application letter delivered to you as quickly as possible. Thank you!"

I rose and put away Agneta's letter. Just as I reached the door, Viselundt spoke again. "Why, exactly, our hotel?"

I smiled. "It was an inspiration. I was on my way to the park, but suddenly I realized this was where I was meant to be. I want to work here."

Aboard the bus back home, I fumbled through my purse for Agneta's letter. My temples were pounding, and I felt oddly elated. That morning I'd been terribly depressed by what had happened and because of Ingmar's dismay. Now I was tingling with anticipation.

My first instinct was to tell Ingmar, but I reminded myself to obey my own rules.

What had Agneta written that had worked such magic? The light in the bus wasn't particularly good, but it was adequate to decipher the contents.

I certify that Matilda Wallin was a member of the staff at Lion Hall estate for four years. In that time she not only acquired a comprehensive knowledge of bookkeeping and business administration, but she also collaborated in the preparation of seasonal events at which we received His Royal Majesty along with other notables. I always found her work highly satisfactory. Matilda Wallin is discreet, diligent, quick-witted, and pleasant of character. She is ready to devote herself to any operational task, taking full initiative while reacting to difficulties rationally and with good judgment.

Any employer will be fortunate to hire this young woman to work on the staff of his or her enterprise.

Signed,

Countess Agneta Lejongård

I put the letter away, cringing. I'd shouted at her and accused her, but she'd given me a sterling recommendation. For that I owed her deep gratitude.

I had no idea if this hymn of praise was accurate or if Agneta had drafted it to mollify her guilty conscience. Maybe she'd counted on provoking these feelings of confusion, regret, and sympathy.

Should I telephone to thank her? Should I at least write?

No, I decided. *I cannot do that.*

I worked on the application letter all through the night. I'd gotten names of other hotels from the telephone book, but my hopes were fixed on the Grand Hôtel.

The more I considered it, the clearer it became that I was perfectly suited for the Grand. I knew all about hosting high-ranking guests. I was accomplished at bookkeeping, and business school had taught me that the differences between various types of enterprise were minor. Whether it was a question of renting rooms or selling horses and grain, the interplay of expenditures and income was treated identically in the accounts.

Furthermore, I'd enjoyed organizing the midsummer celebration, the hunt, and the Saint Lucia festival, as well as the lesser receptions and the crown princess's summer holiday at our manor. I'd probably had more direct exposure to influential people than any other applicant would have.

Yes, I was suited to the job. I'd had no tutoring in applying for employment, but I did my best to put all this into my draft.

I looked down in the early morning light at the scrawled sheets on the desk, the crumpled pages I'd discarded, and the clean copy of my submission. I was dog-tired but satisfied. I flirted with the idea of allowing myself a little sleep but decided to go to the hotel instead. I put my application letter in a brown envelope along with the Lion Hall letter of recommendation and a duplicate of my business-school diploma, grabbed my coat, and set out.

The bus was crowded with laborers, government workers, and employees. A couple of women in inexpensive but chic coats carried on a lively conversation about office politics and people at work. They fluttered their mascara-daubed lashes and provided splendid lipstick laughs perfect for advertising images.

I was stepping into a new world. My time at Lion Hall had transformed me into a provincial maiden no longer familiar with the big city.

And that was about to change.

My stop came. I left the bus and marched straight to the reception desk. The same young woman sat there. She recoiled when I addressed her.

"Please deliver this to Mr. Viselundt," I requested and handed her the envelope. "And I beg you to excuse my intrusion yesterday. I was so exhilarated that I forgot myself. I did not wish to frighten you."

She took a breath and then smiled tentatively. "Oh, call it water under the bridge! That is very thoughtful of you."

"Not at all. It's kind of you not to hold it against me. Could you please give me your name?"

"Tilda."

I broke into a big smile. "What a coincidence! My name is Matilda. And I hope we will soon have the opportunity to be colleagues."

The desk clerk didn't know what to say to that, so I simply wished her a good day and left.

PART III

1939

33

The attack on the Gleiwitz radio station on August 31, 1939, and Germany's subsequent invasion of Poland greatly alarmed the Stockholm public. Twenty-one years had passed since the Great War in Europe.

Those were almost the only items on the broadcast news, and of course everyone worried about the possibility of another war. Many feared that Sweden wouldn't escape unscathed this time, as we had two decades before.

King Gustav declined to criticize the German leaders. Some of those around him were actually fascinated by Hitler. Sweden had remained at peace for more than a hundred and twenty years, but the country had maintained cordial relations with Germany throughout. Maybe the old hands who warned of impending war were right; perhaps Sweden would soon be awash in blood and horror.

That morning, the concern was evident at the Grand Hôtel. In this luxury haunt of countless very important persons, news spread fast—both good news and bad.

I'd been employed for almost five years at the hotel with the beautiful facade, the elegant dining room, and the glittering chandeliers. I'd seen many faces in my time there. I'd vicariously experienced joy and sorrow, romance, and scenes of scandal and conflict. It was rare we had to carry a guest out feet first . . . but it had occurred. And every year a handful of deadbeats skipped out on their bills; our doorman, Mr. Clausen, was particularly angered by their irresponsibility.

I'd never regretted my abrupt decision to apply for employment here.

It pained me a little that the days of Nobel Prize banquets at the Grand were past. The first had taken place in 1901, the last in 1929. Mr. Clausen, who'd worked at the Grand for more than twenty years, sometimes reminisced about those splendid fêtes. Now the annual gala dinners took place at Stockholm city hall.

The Grand Hôtel was nonetheless the setting for countless splendid occasions. I especially enjoyed the glassed-in garden, one of the newer additions, and I often lingered there after hours to listen to jazz. As a teenager I'd dreamed of smoke-filled clubs, but this was far better, even though staff members had to stand discreetly in the back.

I'd never seen our customers as agitated as today, three days after the Gleiwitz attack. The lobby was crowded, all chairs and sofas were occupied, and many people were absorbed in newspapers with great black headlines. Others were engaged in heated debate. I heard Hitler's name mentioned more times than I could count.

The staff were in a tremendous dither. Bellboys told us the navy feared for the safety of our Baltic shipping. Chambermaids debated whether to stockpile coffee and sugar against possible rationing. I was ready to bet my last crown that they'd storm the shops as soon as they got off duty.

I felt no panic; I had everything I needed, and I didn't believe that the king would allow Sweden to be drawn into war. He hadn't taken sides in the Great War, even though the late queen had been German. He was unlikely to change his policy even in the event of a second Europe-wide conflict.

"Miss Wallin, it looks like we have a problem." Tilda was running her finger down the list of reservations. "We are overbooked. I have no idea how that could have happened, but we are in a fine mess."

I frowned. Overbookings created difficult situations, as we quickly had to come up with acceptable alternate accommodations.

"Are you sure that all our esteemed guests will be coming?" I took a look.

"I am afraid they will." Tilda hunched her shoulders slightly. I doubted she was responsible for the error. The tired night clerk probably hadn't checked the records when he took the reservation.

"Let me see . . . I think there is a bit of a gap between the Hornebys and the Wildströms. The Haraldssens leave on the fifteenth, freeing up their room. We can put the guests from overbooked room twenty into that one and ask them to change to their own room once the Wildströms leave."

Tilda groaned. "There will be complaints."

"Yes, but it will be better than sending them to another hotel. We can make the bad news more palatable if we present them with a bottle of champagne."

Tilda nodded and got to work on the arrangements.

I couldn't help recalling our first encounter. We'd often talked about the madwoman who'd stamped into the hotel demanding to be hired. How quickly the time had passed!

I stepped behind the reception desk. Among my duties as administrative assistant was checking with the housekeeper to make sure the staff were behaving properly and to see if any guests had complained. By maintaining the highest possible standards, we justified our prices.

I looked out and was struck as if by lightning by the sight of an arriving guest. A man was headed for the reception desk, a woman in a red woolen coat at his side.

"It can't be," I said to myself.

Tilda had disappeared somewhere, so I took her place at the desk. "Good day to you." I did my best to appear as unmoved as possible.

"Good day. My wife and I have a room booked," he said. "My name is—"

"Paul Ringström."

He stared at me in great surprise, then it clicked. "Matilda? Is that possible? Matilda Wallin?"

That smile I'd always found so disarming lit up his face.

"Yes, at your service." I couldn't help smiling back. And suddenly the memories crowded into my mind, images from the old days, especially of the day we'd sat under the willow tree.

That brought other things to mind as well.

It had been a long time since I'd deliberately thought of Lion Hall. I'd generally succeeded in keeping the estate out of my mind.

Since joining the staff of the Grand Hôtel, I'd lived only for this institution, its employees, and its customers. The hotel took me on wholeheartedly and rewarded me with a status that flattered me. There was underhanded business here, of course—swindles and secrets, such as when an affluent guest appeared with his attractive secretary, supposedly on a business trip, but spent the whole day with a Do Not Disturb sign hung on the door to his room. Or when a couple awkwardly claimed to be spouses, though an alert observer might notice that their wedding bands didn't match. The hotel staff was used to such peccadillos and found them amusing most of the time. We enjoyed a bit of gossip, for we got along quite well, sharing information as well as our own joys and heartbreaks. We were frank with one another; if somebody disliked something, he or she was free to say so.

Paul had no idea of my musings. He beamed as if welcoming a wonderful apparition. "How long is it now? Five years?"

"Yes, I think five years is just about right." Along with those recollections came one of the day he'd arrived with no notice and announced he was going to Norway. I'd heard nothing from him since; our brief encounter at Daga's wedding didn't count. And not a word from Daga either.

Despite the smile, Paul was embarrassed and tongue-tied. He suddenly remembered he wasn't alone. "Oh, you haven't met Ingrid!" He turned to the woman beside him. "This is my wife, Ingrid. Ingrid, this is my old friend Matilda Wallin."

She smiled sweetly and extended her hand. "So pleased to meet you!" She had a slight accent.

"Thanks, I feel the same. You speak excellent Swedish."

"Our languages are not so different," she commented, blushing. "You are a friend of my husband?"

"A childhood friend," I replied. "We have known one another since middle school." I glanced at Paul, who avoided my eye. He remembered very well the promises we'd made.

"Ingrid and I are on a business trip," he declared to break the momentary silence. "She works in my firm. She's a star."

She smiled, pleased by his praise, and stepped closer to him.

I was stunned. My expression had stiffened to a mask. "In your firm?"

That embarrassed Paul even more. Was he remembering the hours we'd spent spinning tales of our future?

"Yes. Ingrid helps me manage my business."

He didn't explain, but I understood she was a bookkeeper. That was my profession, the reason I'd gone to business school.

A leaden weight settled in my abdomen. How nice for him. He'd realized his dream. Our dream—except that I had no place in it.

"That is lovely," I commented, in a voice far too saccharine to be taken as honest. Neither seemed to notice. Evidently the years at Lion Hall and in the hotel had perfected my acting skills. "I hope you have a pleasant stay in Stockholm. Miss Lundt will take care of your room reservation. Unfortunately, I must excuse myself. I do hope you will understand; those of us in the front office have endless paperwork to deal with!"

Tilda popped up as if summoned by magic. I gave them another smile and turned away. I'd have very much liked to have seen Paul's expression, but I kept myself from looking back. I didn't want him to see my eyes or perceive my deep disappointment.

I walked intently to my office even though it was the last place I wanted to go. I felt my composure crumbling, and I didn't want anyone to notice.

I shut the door and leaned back against it. My temples throbbed and my eyes burned. Helpless fury raged in my gut.

Paul and Ingrid! I could imagine what their wedding invitation had looked like. Just like Daga's.

I'd blamed myself for the fact that Daga and I had lost contact. But shouldn't Paul have written to inform me of his engagement, if only out of a sense of decency?

I took a deep breath, and something occurred to me. Maybe he had—but he would have written to Lion Hall. Perhaps Agneta had forwarded the wedding invitation, and I hadn't opened her letter.

My sudden misgivings made me want to hurry home to check, but I couldn't get away. I had a full day of work ahead, and I'd be lucky to escape before eight o'clock that evening. I certainly couldn't leave.

Still leaning on the door, I tried to order my thoughts. The press of everything I had to do that day helped me focus.

It took a while, but eventually I had myself more or less under control. I left the office and caught myself hoping, just a little bit, to see Paul. But he must already be in his room with his wife and his luggage.

He's a hotel guest like any other, I told myself. *I probably won't see him again.*

34

I was so tired by the time I got home that I could hardly see straight. Night fell much earlier at this season, and I usually went to bed early to try to clear my mind of the day's events. But I knew that was no use. I was exhausted, but my mind was wide awake.

I switched on the light, put down my purse, peeled off my coat, and kicked off my shoes. I went into the living room and turned on the radio I'd purchased after my first year at the hotel. It had cost a small fortune, but this immense wooden box with the fabric-covered loud-speaker and the buttons and switches captured music from all across the world. It was well worth the price.

Soft jazz surrounded me. The torch singer complained of her lost love, and I really understood what she meant for the first time. What was worse than an unexpected encounter with a lost love?

The plaintive tune followed me into the kitchen as I searched the pantry for something to eat. I had very little, for I usually stopped by a corner grocery on the way home unless I'd brought leftovers from the Grand. The hotel owner didn't mind, for he hated waste.

Paul was a childhood infatuation, but now that I'd seen him again, I couldn't get him out of my mind. I'd thought I had my emotions under control, but that afternoon I'd caught myself pacing outside the door to his room. My eyes had filled with tears when sounds of a muffled conversation came through the door.

Damn it, why didn't I keep a closer eye on the reservation list? How could I overlook the name Ringström?

Without much appetite, I took bread, butter, and cheese from the pantry. I carried them to the living room, where I sat on the sofa and put my legs up on a hassock. I was in the habit of picking up a book to read a few pages, but that evening I was too restless. The image of Paul rose before me, along with memories of Lion Hall.

After finishing my meager meal, I went to the little desk at the window where my mother had written her letters. Probably including some to Agneta Lejongård.

Had Agneta forwarded Paul's wedding invitation? I had to find out whether he'd included a note.

I opened the drawer where I'd piled Agneta's letters, all unopened. For many months she'd tried to make contact, despite what had happened.

I wanted to know if Paul had thought of me when he met and eventually married this woman. Maybe with that knowledge I could put him behind me once and for all.

I slit open letter after letter. I glimpsed the familiar handwriting of Agneta and Ingmar; one was from Lennard. I paid no attention to the contents once I'd confirmed that no invitation was enclosed.

My hands started shaking. *Damn it, Paul, why did you have to turn up now?* My Stockholm life had been easy—I had my work at the hotel, I had my house, and I needed nothing more. I'd had an occasional fling with an attractive man, but none of them meant anything to me. And now here I was, hunched over a pile of letters I'd never wanted to open!

I came across a thick envelope and hesitated. By then I'd strewn around me a profusion of torn envelopes. This ominous one had been at the bottom of the pile. Why hadn't it aroused my curiosity? Why had I shoved it into the drawer with the rest?

I opened it carefully and found a second envelope inside. My name was inscribed in precise script. The writing wasn't Paul's, that much I knew, nor was it that of anyone at Lion Hall.

The sender was simply *Paul Ringström, Oslo.*

Sudden knowledge struck me, and I almost dropped the letter. This had been written by the woman who was now his wife.

I stared at the envelope, aware my heart was pounding.

I pulled myself together and opened it.

As expected, it contained an invitation, just as straightforward as the one from Daga.

> *Mr. Paul Ringström and Miss Ingrid Rubinstein are pleased to announce that they will exchange their vows on March 22, 1937. You are warmly invited to celebrate their wedding at the reception immediately afterward.*

The invitation included directions to the hotel where the reception was to take place. Ingrid's parents were Sarah and Schlomo, Jewish names. The civil wedding was at city hall and a rabbi was to perform the religious ceremony.

There was no personal note. Invitations like this one must have gone out to many friends, relatives, and acquaintances. It had taken place two years earlier.

I felt as if it had just happened.

I told myself I should be happy for Paul, but I couldn't be. I shoved the invitation back into its envelope, planted my elbows on the desktop, and tried not to wail.

Paul had gotten married, but I was twenty-five years old and still alone. I'd lost my innocence to some random youth who'd been kind to me my first year back in Stockholm, though I should have given it to Paul. No one but Paul.

After a while I picked up the sheet of stationery that had been folded around the invitation. It contained a single sentence.

I think this may be of interest to you.

    A

Agneta must have given up. She'd gotten the message, loud and clear, that I wanted no further contact. That was exactly my intention, but this confirmation made me miserable.

I abruptly gathered the letters and stuffed them back into the drawer. I threw the wedding invitation in after them. Maybe it was just as well that I hadn't seen it. I wouldn't have gone in any case. I wouldn't have wanted to witness Paul's bliss. I wouldn't have wanted to speak to him.

And now he'd turned up at my hotel. Was that fate or pure chance?

That night I tossed and turned. When sleep finally came, I dreamed of a wedding celebration. The reception hall was draped with gauzy fabric and blue garlands, and arrangements of bizarre blue flowers stood on the tables. I saw a bride and groom but couldn't make out the face of either one.

"May I have this dance?" a voice behind me asked.

"With pleasure," I answered without bothering to look.

We stepped onto the dance floor, and he took my hand. I raised my eyes and found myself looking into Ingmar's face. He was terribly changed. His hair was gray and his face was wrinkled.

Alarmed, I tried to pull away, but he held me in his grip and began the dance. He swung me about so energetically it scared me. I cried out, but no one came to my aid. I glanced down and saw I was wearing a wedding dress that was soiled and tattered.

I awoke stifling a scream.

Gasping, I looked around. It took a moment for me to realize I wasn't in that eerie blue room, dancing with an elderly Ingmar. My heartbeat gradually returned to normal. My nightgown was sticky with sweat.

I fell back with a sigh of relief and stared at the ceiling. What was the meaning of this? Was the dream telling me to marry Ingmar? Was it warning I'd have to wait until he was old and gray?

No, that made no sense. After some thought, I remembered that Ingmar had offered to accompany me to Daga's wedding. That must have been the source of my tangled nightmare. I needed to forget it and banish both Ingmar and Lion Hall from my mind or I would begin to regret my departure.

But that horrid vision haunted me, for I felt guilty about treating Ingmar unfairly.

I'd written him when the year was up, as promised. I'd had lots to report about my job at the Grand Hôtel and my experiences there. Writing it down, I realized in retrospect that I'd succeeded, and I felt a glow of pride.

His reply was proof that things had changed in the interim. He reported in wooden prose that he would soon be taking the exams for his diploma. Ingmar mentioned in passing that Magnus had a good deal of work ahead to complete his degree in literature, so he'd be at the university for a while longer.

He knew I didn't want to hear about Lion Hall, so he didn't mention the estate. His note was maddeningly brief. After all, Ingmar's life was bound up with Lion Hall, so what did he have to tell me? And he knew all too well that Magnus was of no interest to me.

We continued to correspond and from time to time he asked when I'd be coming back. I ignored that and responded by describing the hotel and the great pleasure I took in my work.

I didn't mention Agneta's letters. He probably guessed I wasn't reading them. I was pretty sure he was sharing with Agneta whatever I told him.

I had to admit to myself that that year of enforced silence had greatly affected our friendship, and not for the better. The proof of that came when I saw him in the city. His mind was elsewhere, and he hadn't raised the question of a return to the estate.

We lost touch after that. My last letter brought no response. I'd worried briefly that he might have had an accident, but Agneta would surely have found some way to notify me. No word came, so I put him out of my mind.

And now, this nightmare. Was it a warning to get back in contact? What was the meaning of his apparition as an elderly man?

35

I'd put thoughts of Paul and the wedding invitation mostly out of mind by the time I stood outside the driving school two days later.

I shifted nervously from one foot to the other. I'd been attending evening classes, one of only two women there. Our male classmates smiled at us patronizingly, and some teased us by asking if we wanted to become chauffeurs. We ignored them as best we could. And now the big day had come. If everything went as expected, soon I would be allowed to pilot an automobile through the Stockholm streets.

Perhaps I was being superstitious, but I'd worn my best dress despite the cool weather. It was mauve and high waisted with a wide, loose-fitting ruffled skirt that reached just below the knee. It was sleeveless; my upper arms were veiled in gauzy fabric. It was really a summer dress, but I had the feeling it would bring me luck, despite the knitted jacket that concealed it.

Another student's exam was still in progress. After waiting for what seemed an eternity, I saw the car come around the corner. What score would the candidate have obtained?

The car pulled up, and the three men remained seated in the vehicle for a while. What were they discussing? I tried not to stare. Eventually, the examinee left the vehicle.

"Well?" I asked. "How did it go?"

He said nothing, but his gesture was one of discouragement. He strode down the street.

I felt a tightening in my chest. What if the examiner was in a bad mood? Maybe he was even more demanding than our driving instructor!

The door opened, and our instructor, Mr. Drugesand, leaned out. "Miss Wallin?"

He'd pressed me fairly hard in recent weeks and hadn't hidden the fact that he believed women didn't belong behind a steering wheel. But he'd taken my money and given me the same lessons as other students. I hoped never to see him again after taking the exam.

"Here!"

"Get in."

I obeyed his command and settled into the upholstered front seat. A tang of sweat lingered in the air, presumably from the young man just tested. I glanced in the rearview mirror at the examiner behind me, a policeman with his thinning hair in a comb-over. A pince-nez with round lenses perched on the bridge of his nose. He didn't look up from his clipboard.

"Very well, Miss Wallin, show us what you have learned."

The examiner's voice made my pulse accelerate a little. I glanced over at the instructor in the passenger seat, though I knew I couldn't expect any help from that direction.

I stepped on the clutch and started the motor. I engaged first gear slowly but smoothly, following the sequence he'd drummed into my head, and the vehicle rolled forward. These were moves I'd practiced countless times, but I had the panicked feeling that I was forgetting everything.

I moved out into traffic, feeling like a drowning person surrounded by sharks. The motor vehicles weren't the only problem; I also had to watch out for horse-drawn wagons, bicyclists, and pedestrians, any of which might suddenly move out into the street.

The route cut diagonally through the city and toward the neighborhood that included my own steep residential street. The instructor had me drive up the sharp incline, stop and set the hand brake, then release it and resume my route uphill. I managed it better than I'd expected. The auto had to work a bit on the steep hill, but then we were off and away. I breathed a sigh of relief.

Back in city traffic, I guided the vehicle as carefully as possible through the hurly-burly of rushing cars. A couple of times someone with an obvious death wish stepped out in front of us, but fortunately I knew where the brake was. And it even worked!

Back at the school, I found my hands wet and clammy. I left them resting on the leather-wrapped wheel for a while so that the instructor and the examiner wouldn't notice that my convulsive grip had left the leather soaked.

"Well, Miss Wallin, I find your driving style relatively sporty," the examiner commented. "I have no doubt you could make a career for yourself on Berlin's closed-circuit racetrack if women were allowed there."

I shut my eyes. Had I driven too fast? I'd felt like I was flying, but I'd kept my eyes on the speedometer. Was he of the opinion that women should drive slower than the speed limit?

"That being so, and since I have the impression that you're confident and capable with the vehicle, I will issue your driver's license."

I looked around. "Really?"

The examiner gave me a stern look. "Did you not feel that you were in control of the vehicle?"

"Oh, on the contrary, of course I was!"

"Then do not question my verdict."

I pursed my lips. The examiner scribbled something on his clipboard and then handed me the license. My photograph was already attached.

Look at this! My very own driver's license!

"Congratulations," the examiner said. "In addition, your address is quite a notable reference for Stockholm's driving schools."

"How so?" I asked. I'd never heard that Brännkyrka Street had any particular significance.

"Well, that is where in 1907 the first woman ever to be issued a Swedish license demonstrated she had mastered driving skills. She performed the same maneuver with the hand brake that you did today. Alexandra Gjestvang, a very interesting woman—she passed away just last month, unfortunately. She even became a race car driver. Perhaps you plan to follow in her footsteps."

I shook my head. "No, in fact, I don't. I'm employed at a hotel, and from time to time there are tasks more easily carried out with an automobile."

"I am certain you are right about that." A smile flickered across the examiner's face. "So, then, I wish you happy driving!"

I got out and said goodbye to the driving instructor. I was authorized to drive! The world was my oyster!

Shortly afterward I paraded into the hotel with my newly issued driver's license. I was floating in the clouds. Forgotten was the nightmare about Ingmar, as well as the fact that Paul was staying there.

"How was it?" Tilda asked, her cheeks glowing with excitement.

"To tell the truth, when I saw the expression of the young fellow ahead of me, I almost turned around and walked away."

"He failed the test?"

"No idea. He didn't say a word. And then I saw the examiner."

Tilda pressed her hands together the way she did when listening to a cops-and-robbers drama on the radio.

"He wore a uniform and had nasty little spectacles." I embellished a bit to please my audience. "He held a clipboard full of papers. And then he challenged me to show what I could do."

Tilda's eyes grew larger and larger. "And then?"

"I put the car in gear and away we went, quick as the wind, like the car chases in the movies. And then came the high point: I had to drive up Brännkyrka Street. It seemed even steeper than usual."

"How could it be steeper?" Tilda asked. "Since you live there, you must know it well."

"Yes, but in a cranky old driving-school vehicle the city becomes a different landscape. The street where I was born, even more so. The examiner sent me climbing the hill, and halfway up he told me to stop and set the hand brake. Imagine it: headed uphill, I carefully release the brake, slowly engage first gear, and step on the gas. For an instant the car seems about to roll backward, but then it starts moving and grinds its way up over the cobblestones. It snorts and clatters, but eventually we reach the top!"

Tilda's eyes lit up. "How exciting! I can hardly wait to learn how to drive too."

"Well, when you've saved up the tuition, tell me. I can recommend a driving school. The instructor is a bit grumpy, but no more so than many of our guests. And then you'll be ready to go."

"I hope so!" she cried and hugged me. "I am so happy for you. And I hope you will take me out on a picnic in the countryside sometime."

"It will be a pleasure!"

I went toward my office. Someone stepped into my path. I went rigid when I recognized Paul. Had he been waiting for me?

"That was an impressive story," he commented. "Maybe you should consider a career in radio theatre!"

"I took my driver's license test today."

"And?"

"Passed!"

"Heartfelt congratulations!"

"Thank you!" I gave him a sharp look. "Did you need something?"

"Matilda, may I have a word?"

I froze. I'd just been about to hug the whole world; seeing him now made my heart freeze in my chest. "Why?"

"I want to explain something. I—I have the feeling that you're avoiding me, and that's why—"

I took a deep breath. Something in my face silenced him. "All right," I said. "Come with me!"

I took him to the restaurant, which was mostly empty at that time of day. The coffee hour was long past, and the evening meal wouldn't be served for another two hours.

We took a secluded corner behind some greenery. This nook with a small table and two chairs was often sought out by couples eager to nuzzle in private, but I wasn't in the mood for that. I folded my arms across my chest. "Well?"

"Matilda, please." He took the place across from me. "I need to explain. I—I sent you an invitation." He bowed his head. "I'm very sorry."

"I know. I found it. The day before yesterday. Agneta—"

I found it difficult to pronounce her name. I felt anger stirring in my breast and yet a painful yearning for the days I'd run through the meadows of Lion Hall. For the years I'd helped in the office and the way she'd encouraged me to stay as part of the family. I hadn't known then that I was already a Lejongård by birth . . .

I pushed those thoughts aside. "Agneta forwarded it to me, but I was so angry with her I never opened her letters. I only just located it."

Paul looked at me in astonishment. "You were angry with your guardian?"

"She's not my guardian anymore. As far as I'm concerned, I'll never see her again and I'll probably burn her letters. But never mind that. You wanted to tell me something?"

Paul sighed. "Everything turned out differently from what we imagined as children, didn't it?"

I shook my head. "It did, but I'm satisfied with my life. I made my own way."

"Are you married?"

"No."

"Why not?"

"Does it make a difference?"

"No, of course not."

We sat in silence.

"How did you two meet?" I asked him. "I assume it was at your firm."

Paul gave me a funny look. "No. In a bar. At a jazz concert."

I lit up. "We have jazz concerts here too. Will you still be here next Friday? We'll have a group from the United States."

"That would be lovely, but by then we'll be on our way back home. Ingrid and I . . . It was love at first sight."

"And you had the bright idea of hiring her for the firm."

"Her father's a merchant. She grew up helping with the business."

His words pelted down on me like great hailstones. He'd found himself a merchant's daughter. I hadn't been good enough.

"I have a business degree. And I'd have gone to Norway with you."

"Really? And what if we'd been deluding ourselves? If you'd found it wasn't the life you wanted?"

"It *was* the life I wanted. I didn't care if it was in Stockholm or in Oslo."

"But you'd changed completely. You were the ward of a countess, and you lived on an estate. She would've had to give her permission. It was too much for me, all that. And besides, when that boy had his accident—I saw how you acted around him. How you took care of him. It looked to me as if you were in love—"

"Paul!" I exclaimed. "I liked him a lot, that's true. And the truth is, I still do, because he wasn't in the least to blame for his mother's mess. But Ingmar is my cousin."

"Your cousin?"

"Yes. I found out about it just after my twenty-first birthday. Agneta's brother got my mother pregnant. I'm Agneta's niece. That was why I left. I wasn't going to be lied to anymore."

Paul thought that over. "How did you find out?"

I shook my head. "Never mind that. In any case, Ingmar disappeared from my life two years ago. He got his degree and went to live on the Ekberg estate he's going to inherit."

"The contact is completely broken off?"

I nodded. "Yes. We corresponded some in the beginning, but not anymore. He probably has other things on his mind. He was never a good letter writer anyhow. But that's irrelevant as well, isn't it? We're talking about you and me."

"Yes." His eyes fixed on mine. "You and me."

Suddenly he was very close, and the intensity of his gaze thrilled me. We were lying together again on that blanket under the willow. The way my body was reacting was totally wrong, but I couldn't help it. Without wanting to, I went around the table to him and our lips found one another.

That kiss had none of the innocence of our young years. Paul pulled me passionately into his arms, and I was helpless; I had to return his embrace. I was keenly aware of what he wanted, and at that moment I wanted the same thing.

But we were in the restaurant, and anyone might walk in.

"Paul, please," I said as he caressed my neck. "We can't do this. Think of Ingrid!"

His wife's name immediately brought him to his senses.

Breathing hard, he pulled back and rubbed his face. It took him a while to overcome his arousal.

"I'm very sorry," he said at last in a shaky voice.

I nodded. My heart pounded in my throat. How I'd wanted to give in to his passion! But he'd chosen another. And we were in the hotel. I could lose my job.

"You should go," I said then. "Your wife will be wondering where you are."

"Matilda, I—"

"It's all right. Go. Let me do my work."

"Of course."

He left. I saw him disappear beyond the screen of plants and then leaned against the table with my head in my hands and my eyes closed until my pulse returned to normal.

Damn it all, what is happening?

I waited a moment longer and then left. Fortunately, Tilda was busy with a new arrival. I shut myself away in my office and hoped I wouldn't have to leave it anytime soon.

36

That evening, I went home crestfallen. Fortunately, Paul hadn't shown himself again. I could have asked the doorman if he'd left the hotel with his wife, but I really didn't want to know.

I picked up the mail and stepped inside, noticing that I needed to remove spiderwebs and trapped flies from the ceiling lamp. When had I last cleaned the house? And why was I noticing it at precisely this moment?

I took a seat at the kitchen table. This time I didn't turn on the radio; I listened attentively to the surrounding silence instead. Only the muted ticking of the kitchen clock was audible.

Five years earlier I'd left Lion Hall. What would my life have been if Paul had taken me to Norway? The announcement of Stella Lejongård's bequest would certainly have been relayed to me in Oslo, but there I'd have had someone at my side. Instead I'd been alone, just as when Mother died.

Gloom settled over me. I would have been in Ingrid's place, but now I was alone and he was with his wife in my hotel. They had their life together, and all I had was my parents' house. My life had been at a standstill since the day I came to work at the Grand Hôtel. I had no husband and no family, only a weather-beaten house and a profession that took up almost all of my time.

That thought filled me with anger. I could have done something about it; I should have started looking for a husband years ago. Then I'd have had someone to flaunt when Paul turned up. I could have shown him I didn't need him. What did I do instead? I kissed him! I was deeply ashamed.

My thoughts ran in circles for a long time, and finally I gave up and went to bed. I was hoping for the merciful oblivion of sleep, but instead I stared at the ceiling.

A pebble struck my windowpane, startling me. Then another one.

I went to the curtain, my heart pounding.

And lo and behold, there he was. Not a ghost from the past, but a real person of flesh and blood.

I opened the window.

"Looks like it still works!" he called out with an embarrassed smile.

"Why are you here?" I demanded, my voice rougher than I'd intended.

"To see you. I've been walking all through the city, and—"

"—and now you need a place to spend the night?" I sensed my heart hardening against him. "I suggest you go back to the hotel."

"That's not what I meant. I wanted to talk to you."

"We did that already. This afternoon."

"Yes, but—I wanted to apologize."

"Don't go out of your way!"

"Please, Matilda . . ."

I felt torn. There were no spying eyes, no one scandalized and ready to tattle to parents.

His parents . . . Why had he and his wife come to our hotel instead of staying with his parents?

"Just a moment," I said and stepped back from the window. I really didn't want to let him in, because I didn't know how I'd react if he tried to take liberties. But I put on a dress and slippers and opened the door.

Paul was still out in the street. I beckoned to him.

"And Ingrid?" I asked as soon as the door shut behind him. "Where does she think you are?"

"I told her that I was going to meet an old friend."

"Do you think it's right to lie to her when you go skulking to meet an old girlfriend?"

"There's no harm in that, is there?"

No harm! He was traveling with his wife on business. And by all appearances, she'd never heard of me before they checked in at the Grand Hôtel. But who would confess to his wife that there'd been a girl he'd encouraged to hope—and whom he'd replaced?

We went into the living room.

"Would you like coffee?"

"Yes, please."

I hurried into the kitchen and put the kettle on. The blue flames flickered beneath it. I stared at them for a while, then took the coffee can from the pantry. I knew that coffee in the evening was inadvisable, almost poisonous, for it would keep me awake all night.

But preparing the coffee gave me the chance to brace myself to deal with Paul. Why did he want to apologize? For kissing me behind the restaurant shrubbery? For abandoning me so long ago? I tried to convince myself that was over and forgotten, but I couldn't, for it still provoked anger and pain deep inside me. I hadn't forgiven him.

The kettle's shrill whistle interrupted my thoughts. I poured the boiling water into the filter and watched it drain through. I placed the full coffeepot and two cups on a tray. He had no reason to expect an elaborate coffee service at this time of night. I added sugar and some condensed milk anyway, since I didn't take my coffee black. When I came back to the living room, Paul was standing in the center, looking around.

"You really need to have the ceiling seen to," he commented. "A couple more months, and you'll have paint flakes falling on your head."

"Never mind. I'll take care of it when the time comes." I put the tray down on the coffee table and poured two cups. "Well, then, what did you want to say?" I did my best to resist the spell of his gaze but felt myself giving in. His face had become handsomer, and his young self was still visible only in his eyes. His body had changed. His shoulders were broader and his arms more muscular, doubtless because of the rigors of his profession.

"Back when I left the country—" He sought the words as he cradled the coffee cup in both hands. He didn't seem to notice it was scalding hot. "There were plenty of times I wondered if I'd done the right thing. I couldn't forget how hurt you were. I asked myself if I'd led you on, promised you too much."

"In point of fact, you promised me nothing at all," I replied. "Those were childish dreams, and I'd gotten wrapped up in them. Since then I've found my place and I'm happy in it."

I didn't want to show him how I really felt. Particularly not if he was looking for absolution.

"You have no idea how happy that makes me," he said. "But I still feel like I walked out and left you in a difficult situation. You know, back when my father had the idea of buying the Norwegian firm, I was against it. I even told him you were the reason I didn't want to go."

I was astonished. "You did?"

"Yes. I know you won't like it, but my mother convinced me otherwise. 'Somebody like her, living with the nobility,' she said. 'You won't be good enough for her now. You won't be good enough for that countess either. It'll be better for you to concentrate on your own business.'"

I stared at him. I'd noticed his mother's strange attitude at Daga's wedding, but I'd assumed it was because she saw me as a penniless orphan. I was wrong—what I'd seen was envy, because she thought I'd managed to get above my station. If I'd only known then that I really was related to the Lejongårds . . .

"And you listened to her."

Paul looked down. "Yes, I did. After what happened with that boy, I was filled with doubt, and eventually I accepted Mother's and Father's advice. I thought that Lion Hall was the best life for you."

I took a deep breath. *Her envy had such terrible consequences . . .*

He took a swig of coffee. "I would really like to ask for your forgiveness. For not listening to my heart. For abandoning you."

He put down his cup and reached for my hands. Everything in me shouted to disengage, but I couldn't.

"Are you happy with Ingrid?"

"Yes. But now I see that part of me will always belong to you. In the last few days, while I was showing her around Stockholm and we went to all our business meetings, I wondered constantly what it would have been like to have you at my side. With your charm, you'd have instantly won people over."

"Ingrid doesn't?"

"She's not like you at all. She's very shy and content to stand in my shadow. You would have been a partner. I knew that the instant I saw you again."

We looked at one another in a silence that stretched into minutes. He had no notion how his words had moved me. All the years of separation, that afternoon at Lion Hall, and the guarded encounter at Daga's wedding—all that seemed to drop away, leaving only the two of us just as we'd been. Teenagers strolling through Stockholm, but more experienced.

He took me into his arms. It felt so right that I made no effort to resist. We kissed, and suddenly it was as if we were again lying in the shade of the willow tree on that summer day.

"Paul," I whispered as he lifted his lips from mine. My whole body was on fire for him, though I knew it was wrong. I didn't have the strength to break free. I clung to him instead, and our lips hungrily sought one another.

I drew him with me into the bedroom.

You shouldn't be doing this, a tiny voice warned me. *He's a married man, and he lied to his wife. And who knows, this is probably the only reason he came—looking to get at last what he'd been denied before.*

But I had to have him.

We peeled the clothes from our heated bodies. My fingers clawed his back, my breasts pressed against his chest. He wrapped his arms around my waist, bent to gather me up, and then laid me on the bed. We made love as if there'd been no years of separation. I spread my legs willingly and he thrust between them. I gave a huge gasp as our bodies united.

An orgasm overwhelmed me, and Paul shuddered and released himself. I wondered why I hadn't yielded to him before, why I'd allowed other, lesser men to do this.

I'd thought it was right at the time, but now I understood that it had been wrong.

For me there was only Paul, no matter what had happened.

I came to my senses as he collapsed, panting, on top of me.

"Get out of here!" I cried.

"What?" he asked groggily and pushed himself up on his elbows.

I slid away and squirmed out of bed.

"This can't be, it's not possible!" I paced, terribly agitated.

"Matilda—" he tried to reply, but my burning glance silenced him.

My body was on fire. On one hand, the sensations following my climax were better than any I'd ever experienced; on the other, I was flooded with guilt.

"No!" I shrieked, without knowing what I was denying. Distraught, I grabbed my dress and threw it on, as if I were suddenly ashamed to be naked.

"Matilda, please, calm yourself! What's gotten into you?"

"Into me?" I asked in return. "I've just gone to bed with my childhood friend. We've deceived your wife, and you've betrayed her!"

"She'll never know."

"Oh, really?" I challenged him. "Maybe that's not important to you, but how about me? It means something to me. I should never have done this . . ."

I moved about the room in a frenzy. Paul got up and tried to embrace me, but I pushed him away. I knew I'd give in again if our bodies came into contact.

"Why, oh why, did you come here?" I cried with a cold, furious look. "If only you'd stayed at the hotel!"

Paul looked hurt—and that's exactly what I wanted. I wanted to hurt him just as much as he'd hurt me by turning up with this Ingrid of his. Just like when he'd left without taking me to Norway.

"Then this just now meant nothing to you?" he asked.

"This just now?" I stabbed a finger at the bed. "Do you really believe that *this just now* was something we should have done?"

He didn't answer.

"We need to forget all this!" I went on. "Unless you intend to get a divorce and take me to Norway."

"Matilda . . ."

Damn it, how many times is he going to call my name?

I wanted to scream, but I was breathless and close to collapse. I sank down on the edge of the bed.

Paul moved as if to sit there too, but he held himself back. Instead he gathered his things and dressed.

I stared into the void. I was completely confused. So much pressure, so much to say, but my throat closed up. I knew he'd tell me he couldn't seek a divorce. He couldn't give up his business in Norway. He was going to return to everything he'd achieved. He hadn't come to

Stockholm to trade his wife for another woman. Even though he'd done exactly that, however briefly.

"You had better leave," I heard myself say dully. "Ingrid is probably waiting up."

In my peripheral vision I saw him nod.

"Darling—" Suddenly his voice was congested. He cleared his throat. "You should know that I—I've always had feelings for you. That's why I came here."

Feelings for me. And what use were they?

"Good night, Paul!" I said. I couldn't manage any more than that. I could have lectured him or made demands, but I wanted nothing except for him to disappear. For the dark of night to shroud me and let me forget what had happened.

37

I was afraid to go to work the next morning. I blamed Paul and cursed myself for letting him in. I should have known what he had in mind.

But there was no way around it; I couldn't call in sick. My heart was in my boots, but I was no coward. If I saw him, I'd treat him as a stranger, just another guest who'd booked a room with us.

I glanced at my mauve dress. It had brought me luck with my driver's license. But that's where my luck had run out.

Instead, I picked out a dark-blue dress with white polka dots. After a quick cup of coffee, I donned my coat and left the house.

The bus was crammed, as always at this time of day, and I had to stand. One of the seated passengers was deep in the daily paper. By leaning over, I made out a headline reporting the Germans had occupied Krakow. The woman next to him had a basket on her lap stuffed with empty cloth bags and shopping nets. She was probably on an expedition to buy as much coffee and sugar as she could find.

The jovial doorman greeted me. "You're not driving yourself, Miss Wallin?"

"Mr. Clausen, you know very well that I don't have a car. Yet!"

"Then you should ask the proprietor for a raise as soon as possible!"

His playfulness relieved some of my tension. "In these times of war, that hardly seems wise."

"But Sweden's not in the war."

"No, but who knows what lies ahead? I prefer to put my coins in the piggy bank and take the bus."

I knew Mr. Clausen had laid in provisions. So had everyone on the staff, except for me. I didn't need much, and I figured that I could always dig up the little I required. Unlike others who had to take care of a family.

I entered the lobby, where several guests were already lined up at the reception desk. Tilda left them and came running as soon as she saw me. She seemed upset.

"Matilda, good morning, do you have a moment?"

"Of course I do."

Her agitation made me suddenly uneasy. What could she possibly want that was so important she'd abandoned all those guests?

"The Ringströms left ahead of schedule, early this morning."

I raised my eyebrows. "Were they displeased with our service?" I tried to hide my misgivings. Was it because of me? Had Ingrid seen through his excuse? Had he been stupid enough to confess our tryst? I tried to hold myself steady.

"It seems they had to go because his firm called him back. Mr. Ringström asked me to give you this."

She handed me a sealed envelope addressed simply to *Miss Wallin*. I recognized Paul's handwriting.

"Thanks," I said. Tilda returned to the desk, and I walked numbly to my office. Scandal was the last thing I needed.

Trembling, I tore the envelope open. It held one of the correspondence cards the hotel supplied to its guests. The envelope was ours as well.

Paul's note was brief.

Dear Matilda,

Our encounter yesterday evening is among the most beautiful experiences of my life, but there is no way for me to escape the fact that my actions have hurt you. Please forgive me! I have decided to leave so as to avoid sowing more chaos in your life. You were right to reject me—I would never divorce Ingrid, for I want to avoid hurting both her and you. I am leaving, and I hope that your life now will be as full and rich as you deserve. You have earned it. I wish you all the happiness in the world.

Paul

I stared at the card for a long time. It was clear that my worry that Ingrid knew something was unfounded, but his admission struck me harder than any ambiguity.

I would never divorce Ingrid.

I needed to forget him, despite what my heart told me. How foolish of me it had been to believe even for a fraction of a second that I could have what I'd so ardently desired.

I felt something had been ripped out of my chest. Paul was gone forever. I should have been grateful for that, but I still felt the pressure of his lips and the touch of his body upon mine.

I crumpled up the card. Our hotel had central heating, so there was no stove or fireplace in my office. I shoved the wadded-up note into my skirt pocket and went to the kitchen, where the assistant chef was busy preparing the day's menu.

"Hello, Sören. Would it bother you if I burned this?"

"Not at all, Miss Wallin," he said, focused on dicing a celery stalk that filled the air with its distinct aroma.

I opened the cover of the oven's firebox and watched the card go up in flames, eliminating all traces of our relationship—all tangible traces, at least. The intangible scars I would still carry, but even those would eventually fade.

38

Disturbing reports came thick and fast as the year wore on. Hitler's army rolled east, encountering scarcely any resistance. Poland surrendered. Germany and the Soviet Union divided it between them. Swedes were shaken by the Soviet incursion into Finland. The many deaths and injuries caused by the war there evoked a swell of sympathy. Many Swedes volunteered for the Finnish forces.

That wasn't the only front where danger threatened, unfortunately. The native fascist forces controlling Norway had laid the country wide open to the Germans.

Swedes soon felt surrounded. Power outages became common, and rationing was instituted. Rumors that Swedish-flagged freighters had been sunk in the Baltic raised a furious outcry.

Sweden changed its status from neutral to nonbelligerent, an announcement that only confused the public. Was the king about to conclude an alliance with the Germans? Would he send Swedish troops abroad for the first time after so many decades of neutrality?

On a day in late March 1940, shortly after a truce ended the Winter War between Finland and the Soviet Union, my morning routine was abruptly interrupted. I was standing before the mirror getting ready to leave for work, smoothing my somber gray winter coat and checking my hair, when I was startled by a knock at my front door.

A woman in a brown checkered outfit stood outside. Her hair was streaked with gray, but her face was quite youthful. Was this some charity dame seeking donations?

I looked around the edge of my front door. "What is it?"

She looked me over for a moment. "Are you Matilda Wallin?"

When I nodded, she continued, "Please excuse the intrusion. My name is Marit Hallmark. I don't know if the name means anything to you. My maiden name was Andersson."

I could scarcely believe it. "I know who you are."

I'd never seen Agneta's friend, but the countess had mentioned her from time to time. The two had been young suffragettes together. They hadn't seen each other often after Marit got married, but they'd kept in touch with letters and telephone calls.

Now she stood outside my door evoking memories of Lion Hall, just as Paul's sudden appearance had done less than a year before.

"I'd never expected to come face-to-face with the girl whose mother I carried off to Stockholm," the woman said. "I see you're still living in your parents' house."

"What do you want?" I wasn't interested in a conversation about my mother, whether this woman had been involved with her or not.

"I have information for you from my friend Agneta."

She reached into her purse and took out an envelope of fine, champagne-colored stationery. Such an object seemed unbelievable in our times of rationing and penury. Paper was often in short supply, even though Sweden had vast forests.

"She told me you'd refuse to open anything from her you received in the mail, so I volunteered to deliver the message."

She held out the envelope. It was imprinted with the Lejongård coat of arms. My stomach cramped at the thought of news from Agneta.

I could have shut the door in her face, but my hand reached out of its own volition and accepted the letter. "Thank you." I looked at her. Was she aware of everything that had happened between Agneta and me?

"Please read the letter," she said. "It is very important."

"Why aren't you telling me what your friend wants?"

"I'm not the sort to open other people's mail. Whatever Agneta has to say concerns only the two of you. I urge you to read it. Dresser drawers are deep and convenient, but all too often they swallow up news one eventually regrets not receiving."

This woman seemed weirdly threatening. How could she possibly know I'd stuffed Agneta's letters into a drawer?

"Very well. Are you expecting me to stand here and open it in front of you?" The resentment in my voice must have been obvious.

"Not at all. Do so in private and at your leisure. And no matter what Agneta has to say, you should reply. It is really extremely important." She nodded in farewell and walked away down the street without another word.

I stood looking after her. The letter was a dead weight in my hand. Should I open it? What difference would it make if I just tucked it away with the others?

I'd said I would read it. And I had a queasy feeling. Agneta hadn't written for three years, and now she was trying to reach me. She'd even persuaded her friend to deliver it, so something serious must be afoot.

I took the letter into the living room. It was almost time for my bus, but this couldn't wait. I sat on the sofa, opened it, and read.

Dear Matilda,

I know that right now and probably for the rest of your life I am the last person from whom you wish to hear. Your continued silence despite my letters was proof that you no longer wished to hear news of Lion Hall. And that you will never forgive me.

I accepted that and hoped only that you would find happiness in your new life. But now something has happened that forces me to ask for your help.

As you already know, Magnus is little inclined to assume responsibility for Lion Hall's businesses and welfare. He is in Stockholm, devoting a great deal of time to seeking a publisher for his novel. Unfortunately, Lennard is suffering extremely serious health problems. His condition has deteriorated noticeably. I shall not beat around the bush; I must appeal to you directly: I need help. Help with the estate and with other matters.

First, the estate—do you recall Clarence von Rosen, the man who accompanied the king on our hunts? You commented that he looked like an "egghead." But there is nothing amusing about him now. He is an ardent supporter of Germany, and it appears he has disparaged us to the king. We received notification out of the blue that the palace would no longer be purchasing horses from Lion Hall. As royal equerry he cites the war and current economic conditions as the excuses, but I know his decision is political. My source of information concerning his politics and business undertakings is very trustworthy.

And if that were not bad enough, Ingmar traveled to Norway not long ago, and it does not appear that he will return anytime soon. I cannot say more in this letter. In any case, the result is that I am overwhelmed and unable to manage both Lion Hall and the Ekberg estate. I need the assistance of a person who has always demonstrated more business sense than I possess: I need you!

I can only pray you will forgive me insofar as possible and come here. On my knees, I beg you: help us! If not for my sake, then for Lennard's. He is constantly asking when you will come home, especially when intense pain makes him delirious. I beseech you, put aside your grievances and come back! Speak to me, talk to Lennard. I am at the end of my rope; there is no one else to whom I can turn.

If you are willing to return to Lion Hall, I will be overjoyed to arrange things and get you settled. I will happily reimburse your expenses and any losses. A brief note from you is all I need; that will be enough.

With love, as ever,

Your aunt,

Agneta

Stunned, I examined the letter for minutes on end. The lines were irregular and Agneta's handwriting was little more than a scrawl. As far as I could remember, her handwritten documents had always been precise. They'd appeared almost printed.

I didn't know how to react. The familiar anger at her deceptions roused itself within me, intensified by grief and scorn. We'd broken off communication long ago—and now here she was, insisting I return. How dare she!

I read the letter again and couldn't overlook the tone of pure desperation. The palace's refusal to do business with Lion Hall was a severe blow. The royal stables had always paid promptly, and the relationship had brought us clients from all over the world. Now outsiders would start to wonder why Lion Hall had been cut off. And at a time of such pervasive economic problems.

And Ingmar—what in heaven's name was he doing in Norway? And what was this about Lennard being ill?

I dropped the letter into my lap and covered my face. What should I do? Go there to get an idea of what was going on? Find out why Ingmar had left? Why he'd abandoned his parents in these difficult hours? And why Magnus was neglecting his family duties?

Magnus.

I again felt the sting of his disdain. He must have been overjoyed by my abrupt departure. How would he react if he saw me turn up again? He must have learned since then that I was his cousin.

But never mind about him. I was concerned about Lennard most of all. He'd always been so kind. He'd welcomed me into his home and family. If he was in such poor health, who was I to deny his wish to see me again?

I got up, stowed the letter in my purse, and set out for work. I needed time to think.

That was a day of wild confusion at the hotel. Luggage had been mishandled at the central railway station, and several guests had received the bags of a family who'd gone to a different hotel—and worse, it was in a distant suburb. Our driver had his hands full sorting out the luggage and getting the misdirected pieces to their owners. And to top it off, a trunk belonging to a musician had disappeared, and he was due to play that evening in our glassed-in patio.

All that pushed Agneta's letter out of my mind, but once the confusion had been straightened out and I was back at my desk, her pleas loomed again before me. Lennard and Ingmar worried me terribly— what could possibly be going on with them? Had Agneta understated the seriousness of their situations?

I allowed myself a few minutes at the evening jazz concert, where I leaned against the wall behind a couple of potted palms and soaked up the sounds.

Just then I noticed a man and woman and mistook them for Agneta and Lennard. Their bodies were similar, and so was the cut of their hair. It was only upon a second, closer look that I saw I'd been mistaken. I was gripped by sudden panic. I tore myself away from the concert and rushed back to my office. One of the cleaning ladies was already there, emptying the wastepaper basket. I waited until she left and then went to the telephone.

I asked the long-distance operator to be connected to Lion Hall. She transferred me, and moments later I heard ringing at the other end.

The telephone was in Agneta's office, quite distant from the salon and the bedrooms. It would take her time to get to it, assuming she heard it at all.

My disappointment grew with each ring, but so did my distress. What if Lennard was so ill that she had no time to spare for anything else? And what were things like at the estate? I thought of all the people employed there. If everything came crashing down, they would lose their livelihoods.

The ringing persisted for several minutes, and the operator returned. "It seems that your party is not answering. Should I try to reconnect?"

"No, don't bother," I told her. "Thanks very much!"

I left my office, extremely concerned. Music was clearly audible in the lobby, but I didn't return to the concert. I collected my coat, grabbed my purse, and said good night to Jan, our night porter.

There was little activity in the Stockholm streets. I took the first bus that came along. As it rolled toward the bridge over Lilla Värten, I couldn't get Lion Hall out of my head. Bankruptcy would have frightful consequences for the employees, the villagers, and many business partners.

I knew Agneta. She was an expert in breeding horses and negotiating contracts, but her bookkeeping skills were mediocre at best. What sort of plight were they in? And what would happen to the staff? The younger ones could certainly find some sort of work in the city, even if the demand for servants wasn't as strong as in the past. But someone like Lena, with no husband, would be left destitute. How could I stand by and watch that happen?

The bus rolled toward the southern sector of the city. After all, the only person I despised was Agneta. Granted, she was the mistress of Lion Hall, but the estate was so much more than its owner. It astounded me that she hadn't made Magnus do his share. Was he really without a clue when it came to running two estates?

I was sure it was stupid of me to return, even if only for a few days, but it wouldn't be the only stupid mistake I'd made. I had many unpleasant memories of the estate, but I'd also experienced many marvelous things there. I couldn't just let it go to ruin.

By the time I walked up to my front door, I'd made my decision.

39

It was no easy task to convince the hotel owner to give me two weeks off. By insisting stubbornly that my uncle was gravely ill, I was finally able to win him over.

I stood on the train platform at Stockholm Central waiting for the morning train to Kristianstad just as I had many years before. The breeze blew dry leaves across the tracks, and a couple of weary sparrows pecked about in search of food. Here and there the blanket of clouds overhead parted momentarily to reveal a hint of blue sky. The sun struggled up in the east.

I'd sent a telegram to say I'd arrive that evening and that there was no need to pick me up.

The train appeared on time. I got aboard, put my valise up on the shelf, and sat down.

This trip offered me plenty of time to go through Agneta's letters. That had been my intention, for I wanted to find out if she'd mentioned Lennard's illness, but I just couldn't bring myself to take them out. My hands were cold, and I felt as if by reading them I was about to throw the door open to something horrible lurking in the dark.

Only hours after leaving Stockholm did I gather the courage to pick up the first letter. Her lines were precise and her handwriting was clear.

November 15, 1934
Dear Matilda,
I hope you are doing well. Ingmar tells me that you two spoke in Stockholm. I was very relieved to hear that you arrived safely and are looking for appropriate employment.

Ingmar also said that you asked him to give you a year before communicating again. I find that reasonable, but please do let him know how you are doing from time to time. He is very concerned about you, as is everyone here. That includes me. Not an hour goes by that I do not blame myself for failing to tell you the truth. Why, oh why, did I fail you? I often wish I could turn back the hands of time.

Then I recall that my aim was to protect you. I did not want to tear you away from the life you knew. I did not want to destroy the truth you thought absolute. You never knew a father other than the man who was so important to you. I know he was good to you.

When your mother and I came to our agreement, I vowed never to detract from Sigurd Wallin's generosity by telling you he was not your father. If Susanna and Sigurd had not passed away in such an untimely fashion, you would never have needed to know. I was taken completely by surprise when my mother reached out from beyond the grave and threw our lives into such confusion.

But you know all that, and it makes no difference now. You are certain to hold a grudge against me, for you are a true Lejongård.

My brother was a gentle man, but he could be mer-
ciless when someone did him an injustice.

Ah, well. Christmas holidays are fast approaching,
and as always, we will have a Saint Lucia fest to cele-
brate the return of the light. It breaks my heart to know
that your seat at the celebration will be empty. But please
know that we think of you every day. Perhaps someday
you will find your way back to us. I desire that so fer-
vently. I am more than willing to give you the place in
the family that belongs to you by right.

With love,

Your Agneta

I read one letter after another and witnessed a succession of disasters. Von Rosen wasn't the only one to blame for the estate's difficulties.
Other problems had emerged long before he brought about the termi-
nation of the business relationship. Agneta was in over her head and
had lost control; the estate's affairs were in drastic decline.

There'd been a time when I'd have taken malicious pleasure in that
news. But my anger had cooled, and I worried for the people who
depended on the estate for their jobs and sustenance.

I finally got to the last envelope.

July 14, 1937

Dear Matilda,
This is my last letter to you. Since you have not answered
any of my letters in the last three years, I have to accept
at last that it is useless to try to reach you. It seems likely
that you did not even open my earlier letters.

I can understand that, at least a little. There was a time when my relations with my parents were deplorably bad. I ignored their letters in the same way, and I very often wished I could break ties with them entirely. I never succeeded. Lion Hall forever drew me back, and the deaths of my father and brother guaranteed I could never leave.

Your situation is different. You had a different life before you came to Lion Hall. I do hope—and I mean it sincerely—that your life is going well and you have found happiness.

Although I fear I write these words only for myself, I want to tell you of recent events.

We celebrated the midsummer fest, as always, but given the prevailing uncertainties, spirits were somewhat dampened.

Shortly after that, a violent storm wreaked considerable damage on the Ekberg estate. Ingmar had his hands full saving what he could. He is gradually making progress, and we hope he will be able to join us no later than the weekend of the autumn hunt.

Lennard's health has deteriorated alarmingly of late. His liver is causing him severe problems, though never in his life has he imbibed excessive quantities of alcohol. The physicians tell us that with careful attention to his diet and activity he should have many years ahead of him, but we must be constantly vigilant to see that his condition does not take a turn for the worse.

I know that Magnus is no great concern of yours, but since he received his university degree, he has been working assiduously at making a career for himself as a writer.

A newspaper has published a novel of his in installments, and he is at work on another.

As you know, I would prefer for him to follow in my footsteps, but Lion Hall interests him far less than his typewriter. I leave the choice to him. I know that if I were to demand that he take charge of Lion Hall, that alone would drive him away forever. He is very like me, and I know that only a disaster would be sufficient to oblige such an individual to take on these heavy responsibilities. Let us hope that any such catastrophe can be kept from our doorstep as long as possible.

Well—you have not forgiven me and probably never will. In my earlier letters I emphasized repeatedly how much I regret not taking you into my confidence from the beginning. I will not harp on that. But I will be so bold as to make a request. If, contrary to my expectations, you should read this letter, please reply, however briefly. At least through Ingmar, or via anyone at the estate with whom you feel an attachment. I know that I forfeited any right to be part of your life, because of my failure to speak, but I do truly and sincerely wish to hear that you are doing well. That knowledge will put my soul at peace.

Receive a heartfelt greeting from

Agneta

I lowered the page and stared at the passing countryside for a very long time. Tears came to my eyes. The forest along the tracks blurred into an impenetrable wall of green. Agneta had done me an injustice, but her reports moved me nonetheless. I felt remorse, and I was almost disappointed that she'd given up. I'd pushed her away from me for so long, but now I was forced to contemplate a difficult question: whether the consequences of my behavior had been worse than the consequences of hers.

Kristianstad's streetlamps were illuminated by the time I crossed the main hall of the train station. I had an odd feeling of homecoming, especially when I caught sight of the little door to the quarters where the elderly stationmaster had lived. His young successor must have forgotten me long ago.

I left the station and made my way to the taxi stand. I looked around for Agneta's automobile just in case, but she'd respected my wish and refrained from sending the driver.

I climbed into a taxi and gave the driver my destination. Memories flooded back as we drove through the city. I saw myself standing before the business college and seated with Ingmar in the car as he tried to finish his homework at the last second. I remembered dashing through the city with Birgitta when classes were out; I saw myself going to the cinema on Sundays with the rest of the girls, after I'd pleaded long and hard to convince Agneta to let me. I'd spent nearly four years of my life here. It was part of me, even though I'd done my best to forget it.

We left Kristianstad and drove into the dark countryside.

The taxi driver was taciturn and kept his attention entirely on the road. I was glad for that. Thick mists rose from the fields and drifted through the headlights, sometimes veiling the road in white. Animal eyes glimmered in the night from time to time but quickly disappeared.

Half an hour later the manor appeared in the distance, little more than a point of light. It grew rapidly as we approached.

We came to the front gate. "Shall I drive you up to the house?" the driver asked.

I was just as familiar with the approach to the manor as I was with the street outside my house in Stockholm.

"Yes, please," I replied. We passed between the gate's massive pillars.

"That's quite a place," the driver commented as we entered the circular drive. "Are you part of the family?"

"No, I—I'm here on a visit, that's all."

Had I just denied it? I actually was part of the family, but that was far too complicated to explain, and besides, the driver didn't need to know.

I paid, got out, grabbed my valise, and stepped to the driver's side of the taxi. "Have a good trip back!"

The taxi was disappearing into the dark when it occurred to me that I should have asked for his telephone number so he could pick me up two weeks later.

I stood motionless for a moment, taking in the sight of the glowing manor windows, then I went up the front steps. I was halfway up when the door opened. It was Rika. I almost didn't recognize her, for the tender young thing had become a strikingly attractive woman.

"A warm welcome, Miss Matilda!" she called. "The gracious lady is expecting you."

"Thank you," I said as I shed my coat and handed it to her.

Agneta met me in the former smoking room, which had long before been converted into a sort of reception area. When one stepped through the door, one could still catch the faint whiff of the cigar smoke that had been blown into the air those many decades earlier.

I knew why Agneta liked this room. The lingering tobacco odor reminded her of her father. I took it as significant that she'd decided to receive me here.

The prodigal child was coming home—at least that's what she hoped.

"Good evening, Agneta!" I tried to keep my voice strong and neutral, so as to hide my turbulent emotions: resentment and confusion, poignant memories, terrible nervousness, and—even though I didn't want to admit it—a touch of exhilaration.

Agneta gave me a sincere smile. "How lovely to have you here once more!"

"I won't be staying long. My employer gave me two weeks' leave. I'm here for Lennard more than anything else."

Agneta nodded. "I understand. Nevertheless, it is lovely to see you. You are a bit of light in the darkness."

An uncomfortable silence followed. I knew she was watching me, hoping for a sign that reconciliation was possible. I wasn't going to give her that satisfaction, even if she was facing dark days.

"Your old room is ready," she said at last. "And when you are settled in, I will give you a full picture of everything that has happened here."

"Let us wait until tomorrow," I said, even though I was aching to have news of Ingmar and find out why he'd left his family to go to Norway. "I'd like to unpack and look in on Lennard."

"Of course." Tears glinted in her eyes.

I had a momentary urge to take her in my arms, but the familiar resentment welled up and held me back. She deserved no comfort.

"I will inform him you have arrived. Perhaps you two can have a few words together in the salon."

"That would be lovely. Thank you," I said in the same neutral tone I used with the hotel staff. I turned my back on her and went upstairs.

40

How strange it felt to enter my former room! I'd lived a wonderful existence there, but it had also been the scene of some of the worst days of my life. Still, satisfaction filled me as I pulled the door closed.

The maids had set it up wonderfully. I felt as if I'd never been away. There were no musty smells and none of the stiff, cold bedclothes I'd found in my parents' house. The room seemed to have been under a magic spell, waiting for me to reappear.

I ran a hand across the pink flowered comforter that invited me to stretch out and relax. I glanced at the wardrobe. Were my clothes still there? I'd never sent for them, hoping Agneta would dispose of them at the charity auction.

My hand trembled as I reached out to open the wardrobe, recalling the day that Magnus had played his horrid trick on me. Had he heard I'd visit? Would another maid's outfit be hanging inside?

I yanked the door open but found neither billowing dresses nor a uniform. The closet was bare except for the blocks of fragrant cedar that kept moths away.

Relieved, I opened the other doors, unpacked my valise, and hung up my things. I'd finished by the time a knock came at the door. I tensed, expecting Agneta.

"Come in," I called and turned to face the caller.

The first thing I saw was a tray loaded with food. I looked into a familiar face.

"Lena!"

"Good evening, Miss Matilda," she greeted me with a shy smile. "The gracious lady thought you might be hungry."

"That's very kind," I replied somewhat stiffly. "Please put it down on the dresser."

Upon my arrival in Stockholm five years earlier, I'd wondered if Lena knew why I'd left, and whether she'd always known the truth. I'd eventually concluded she was as little to blame as Lennard—less, really, given her station.

"We're very pleased you're back," she said, rubbing her hands nervously as she began to withdraw. I noticed subtle strands of silver in her hair.

No doubt she expected me to say something like *I'm glad to be back*, but I couldn't. It wasn't entirely true.

"Silja got married," she volunteered. "And Mrs. Bloomquist—" Her expression turned bleak. "Mrs. Bloomquist died last year. Cancer. We were all very sad."

"I am very sorry to hear it." My throat tightened. I remembered the elderly cook very well.

Lena nodded. "Svea was hoping to have an assistant cook, but the way things are, they've even had to let some of the stable boys go."

"Is Lasse Broderson still there?"

"Oh yes, he is. Constantly complaining he needs more hands for the job. But these days almost no one is buying horses. The gracious lady could sell animals to Germany, of course, but she says that she refused in the last war, and she isn't about to change her mind now."

"That sounds like the countess," I said, realizing that I'd almost called her "my aunt."

A little silence ensued. I wasn't sure what to say. Perhaps I should mention that I would be staying for only two weeks, to prevent the staff from assuming I was home for good. I couldn't bring myself to say the words.

"Well, then, enjoy your meal," said Lena. "Please tell me if there's anything else you'd like to have."

"Thank you," I said as she turned to go. "Oh, Lena . . ."

"Yes, miss?"

"I am very happy to see you again. When you have time, can we talk about my mother? Now that the truth is out . . ."

"Of course," she said and smiled. "I'd love to."

I'd assumed I wouldn't have any appetite, but my stomach growled in response to the tempting smells from the dinner tray. Svea had prepared traditional Swedish fare: meatballs in brown sauce, potatoes, and lingonberry jam. I couldn't resist.

I went down to the salon afterward, where Lennard sat on the rattan sofa next to his wife. The two broke off their conversation when they saw me.

Agneta rose. "Hello, Matilda. Please have a seat," she said, fidgeting. "Are you properly settled?"

"Yes, thank you," I answered. "And thank you for the meal!"

"I thought you might need a bit of something."

I nodded while trying to hide my horror at Lennard's appearance. The man I'd once known had withered away. He was feeble, almost gone. Lennard was only in his fifties, but his yellowish skin was as wrinkled as that of a man several decades older.

"Matilda!" he said and struggled to his feet. "It is lovely to see you again."

"I'm happy to see you too." I embraced him.

"You are quite adept at concealing your alarm," he said with a wry smile. "I know I look like a ghost. And the worst of it is that I do not know what I have done to deserve it. I was never much of a drinker, yet my liver is all but gone."

Tears choked me. It just wasn't fair. This man had given his all for his family, and fate was punishing him with a creeping infirmity that sooner or later would deliver him to death's door.

"Sit down and tell me about your life in Stockholm. I am pleased that Agneta was able to reach you."

I glanced at his wife; her face remained impassive.

"I believe I will leave the two of you alone for a while," she said.

"Whatever for?" Lennard asked. "You do not want to hear what Matilda has to tell us?"

Agneta looked at me. "I am sure she will inform me later." She turned and left the salon.

I watched her go.

"You have not forgiven her, have you?" Lennard said softly. "Five years have passed, but you are still angry."

"It is not easy to forgive what she did. Paternity should be hidden from no one, regardless of the circumstances."

Lennard nodded. "I understand, but things were different when we were your age. Society's moral codes controlled every aspect of our lives. That is why people often shielded children by concealing uncomfortable truths."

He paused, then patted the seat next to him.

I settled beside him, ready to burst into tears.

"Your aunt's reasoning often confounds me," he confided. "I frequently ask myself what else she may be concealing."

"To tell the truth, I haven't the slightest desire to know," I commented. "I'm here now to do what I can to help the estate. And I'll persuade Ingmar to come back home."

"That will be no easy task, I fear," Lennard said. "Have you discussed it with Agneta?"

"No, that can wait until tomorrow. Unless there is something you think I should know right now."

He shook his head. "I will not get ahead of her. Much has happened. Things that surprised us, even things that came close to driving a wedge between the two of us."

"You?" I stared at him in disbelief. Agneta and Lennard had always stood together as one. What could have divided them?

"I am afraid that one of the secrets Agneta and I guarded has cost us one of our sons."

"In that case maybe you should tell me. Otherwise I face a sleepless night."

"No, Matilda, I prefer to leave that to Agneta. I prefer simply to enjoy your presence here. How long will you stay?"

"I took two weeks' leave."

"You are employed, then! Did you set up your own business?"

"No, I work at the Grand Hôtel. I'm the assistant manager for accounting and events."

Lennard nodded, impressed. "A position of great responsibility."

"It is. And I enjoy it."

"I am sure you have gotten to meet many influential persons."

"Oh yes. Musicians, politicians . . . Once we hosted an Arabian prince. He was in Sweden because he wanted new blood for his stable of racehorses. I never had the opportunity to recommend Lion Hall, unfortunately."

"That is too bad. But in the prevailing circumstances we would have had difficulty satisfying any new client. Agneta now finds herself responsible not only for Lion Hall; she also must worry about the

Ekberg estate. A couple of weeks ago she actually fainted from overwork and distress. That is why I pressured her to try to contact you once more."

"Agneta fainted?" I was shocked.

"Yes, and she will probably scold me for telling you. But the days for secrets are past. I am sure you agree."

"I would welcome that change."

Lennard gave me a big smile. "As would I. And now, I think, it is time for bed. You are here at last, I am reassured, and I can devote myself to more pleasant thoughts."

"You haven't worried about me, have you?"

Lennard nodded. "I certainly have. Since the day you left. Particularly because you never acknowledged Agneta's letters."

"Didn't Ingmar keep you informed?"

"He did, more or less, as long as the two of you were in correspondence. But then there was this incident, and . . ." His voice trailed away.

I wished I knew what had happened. Had Agneta provoked Ingmar somehow? Why hadn't he come to me?

I decided it had to wait until morning, for I saw our conversation had fatigued Lennard.

"I apologize for not responding. I was furious with Agneta."

Lennard nodded. "I believe you. But even if that anger never goes away, promise me one thing: write to us from time to time. Tell us how you are. I would like to know."

I took his hand. "Yes, sir. Understood."

"Good. Then get some sleep. The important thing is that you are here. The rest can wait for tomorrow."

I helped Lennard up and accompanied him out to the hall. I expected to see Agneta there to meet him, but she was nowhere in sight.

"I can manage it from here," he said and gave me another hug. "Good night, Matilda! And welcome back to Lion Hall!"

41

The morning dawned slow and dreary, and even the wonderful bird-songs failed to entice the sun out from behind the heavy clouds.

I woke with bones like lead, as if I'd walked all the way from Stockholm. Could it be the change in climate? I got up, yawned, and stretched. Once again, I was astounded how at home I felt here. Except for this incredible lethargy.

A shared breakfast was ahead of me that morning. Perhaps I was dreading that.

As in earlier days, I got up and went to bathe before the maids showed up. The tap water was cold, but it jolted me awake. I took a skirt and a pullover from the wardrobe but changed my mind and chose blue trousers instead. An idea had formed in the back of my mind: maybe it would help to take a horseback ride. I hadn't gone riding since my departure, and times of solitude with nature had always done me good.

I had a quick cup of coffee in the kitchen with Svea, then left for the horse barns. The hands were already mucking out the stalls; one of them pushed a heavily laden wheelbarrow down the walkway. Lasse Broderson was up early as well.

"Good morning!" I greeted him as I entered the main barn.

The men who'd been chatting stopped short and gaped at me as if I were a ghost.

"Miss Matilda," Broderson exclaimed happily, "you're back!"

"Since last night," I said and shook hands with him and the others. "And I was wondering if I might take Linus out for a ride."

"But of course!" the stable master replied and sent one of the boys to saddle the horse. "Are you planning to live here from now on?"

"I'm just visiting, to see how the count is doing."

"Well, the gracious master and gracious lady haven't had things so easy in the past few years," Broderson said. "If I may be permitted to say so, it seems as if good fortune abandoned the estate the day you left."

Was that punishment for what Agneta had done to me? Did the people here know what had happened? I doubted it. If they hadn't known it at the time, Agneta would have had no reason to make it public afterward.

"Maybe I can bring back a bit of luck," I said. "I'll take a look at the accounts. But I'll have to get back to my position at the hotel."

"Hotel?" Broderson was amazed. "What would you want to do in a hotel? You're much better qualified for the estate."

"It's the largest and best hotel in Stockholm. And believe me, I feel more than qualified for the responsibility."

The stable lad appeared and handed me the reins. Linus gave me a nuzzle of recognition.

"Thanks so much! I'll be back after a little tour of the grounds."

Lasse nodded and stepped out of our way.

I led Linus outside and mounted. It felt odd, for I hadn't been on a horse in five years. But all those skills came back. I clicked my tongue, pulled on the reins, and guided Linus with my knees as Mr. Blom had taught me.

I rode through the main gate and urged Linus to a faster pace. I realized how much I'd missed the wind in my hair and the animal moving powerfully beneath me. No automobile ride could compare.

I rode past fields still fallow at this time of year, where soon wheat would sprout and rapeseed would bloom.

With no particular goal in mind, I followed the road. It led to the village, of course, but also to the meadow where Ingmar had his accident. Not to mention the great willow that had sheltered Paul and me on our blanket—but never mind that. I didn't care to relive that experience.

Fortunately, the folly of going to bed with Paul had resulted in no physical consequences. I'd vowed to put him out of my life. Paul could run his Oslo business, and I would pursue my star in Stockholm. And if he should ever be so bold as to book another room at the Grand Hôtel, I would make sure to be on leave.

As I cantered toward the village, a rider came in the opposite direction. She sat on a dapple gray and wore a tightly cut black riding outfit on her thin, almost gaunt body. It was Agneta. She reined in her horse.

I hadn't expected this encounter, but there was no way I could avoid it.

"Matilda," she said.

"Agneta," I acknowledged.

The countess's appearance had completely changed since the previous evening. She'd seemed weak and mournful then, but now she resembled an angry Amazon. I'd rarely seen her bristle like this during my time at Lion Hall.

"Neither of us is a child anymore. We need to talk. At the cemetery." She turned her horse.

A discussion in a cemetery—who could possibly have expected such a thing, especially after returning to a place she never wanted to see again?

By the time I got there, Agneta had already tied her horse to the pillar at the entrance. Swarms of crows cawed loudly from the tops of the tall trees surrounding the holy ground.

I dismounted and hitched Linus up. "Fine. Let's talk."

Agneta shook her head. "Not here. We are going inside. Your father should be present for our discussion."

My father is somewhere deep in the Baltic, I was tempted to point out.

Agneta opened the gate, which gave way with a reluctant squeal, and she strode straight ahead through the rows of tombstones. I suddenly remembered the day I'd seen the funeral procession of the old villager who was probably my grandfather. Why had I never visited his grave?

Agneta halted. When I caught up to her, I realized she stood before the final resting place of that same old man and his wife.

"Your maternal grandparents."

"What is this?" I demanded in a nasty voice. "A guided tour?"

"No. I am making up for what I neglected back then."

"And you think that'll set things to rights so I'll forgive you?"

She flinched, then straightened again. "I know you do not intend to forgive me, despite what I am about to show you."

I took a deep breath. "Fine, then. Show me my grandparents' graves."

"They disowned your mother when they saw she was pregnant," Agneta said after a moment of contemplation. "I went looking for her; your grandmother and grandfather shouted at me and blamed me. An old herb woman finally told me where she was staying: a little shack on the lakeshore. Your mother was suffering, but her parents did not care about that. They were obsessed by the shame they thought Susanna had brought upon the family. You have no idea what a satisfaction it was to shield her from them."

"Well, you did manage that much." She'd helped Mother; that I couldn't deny.

"But it cost everyone dear," she replied. "The Korvens never learned of your existence. They never knew Susanna had married an upstanding man. She was dead to them from the moment she confessed she was pregnant and refused to name the father. She told no one but me."

"You and your mother!"

"No. My mother learned it from me. She continued to consider Susanna beneath contempt. But I did all I could to awaken some sympathy in Mother's heart, some feeling for you. I tried to show her photographs; she must have given in and looked at them when I wasn't there. I never imagined she would be moved to make that bequest. But she must have had an idea of how I would react to it." She took a side path. "Come. We will continue."

She walked away, but I remained standing there. I saw the old man before me once again and remembered him calling me by my mother's name. "Susanna?" If I'd known of my origins then, how would I have replied?

After a moment I followed Agneta to the Lejongård mausoleum. Ingmar had once pointed it out when we were riding by. It was imposing, a fortresslike edifice. A grilled iron gate barred the entrance.

Agneta took out a key and opened it.

I hesitated. I was uneasy about walking into a crypt. It was like entering a room full of unfriendly strangers.

Agneta picked up a lantern that stood just inside. She lit it. "Come on. There is nothing to fear. No one lying here will do you harm."

I was tempted to flee, for I had an intuition of her intentions. She probably thought she could bind me to the estate with spells from my ancestors.

I was determined to resist, but I followed her with a shrug anyway.

The crypt smelled of mold, earth, and decades of dust. Dead leaves that the wind had blown through the barred gate were heaped in the corner. The dead lay in compartments marked with stone tablets. The years chiseled into those stones were unbelievable. People who had lived a hundred, two hundred, even three hundred years before were interred here, a huge family united in death. I shuddered at the thought that someday people might want to seal me away in here with them.

Agneta led me to the far reaches of the crypt. She put the lantern down on a little pedestal. A marble vase there held withered flowers.

She put her hand on the plaque covering one niche. "This is your father."

I looked at that alien-sounding name. *Hendrik Lejongård.* He'd been thirty years old, not much older than me when death snatched him away.

"I often wonder how things would have turned out if he had survived. I would not be here now, and you—"

"I would not either," I replied. "Because my mother would have been driven from Lion Hall. I'd probably be living in the gutter somewhere. If I was alive at all."

It finally dawned on me that I also owed to Agneta the fact that I'd had a safe home and a good education. She'd seen to it that my mother married well; she'd sent me to business school.

I felt a flush of shame, and for the first time I wondered if it'd really been so terrible of her not to confide in me.

"That could be. Your mother was in a terrible state when I found her in that hut by the lake, starving but too proud to beg. The old herb woman was the only one watching over her. That old crone could easily have acted as an 'angel maker.' But you were not unwanted. By Susanna—or by me."

She sighed. "My brother would have loved you. And I believe I knew him well enough to say he would have stood up for you and your mother. The scandal would have been unprecedented. My father might have disinherited him, but Hendrik would have done the right thing. He must have loved her very much. And, indirectly, he lost his life because of her."

I stared at her. Was she blaming Mother for the death of her brother?

"Once, years ago, you asked me how your mother was involved with Langeholm, the arsonist," she went on. "Well, he had discovered the relationship between my brother and Susanna. He blackmailed her.

363

Used her carnally, even though she was pregnant. He forced her to steal for him. She obeyed because she did not want my brother's reputation to be blackened."

I shook my head. "My mother wasn't a thief!"

"She tried to steal. In fact, that was why she was discharged. Up until then I had done my best to hide her condition. But when she was caught with my mother's brooch, I had no choice; she had to go. Later I found out Langeholm had forced her, but it was too late. She could not be admitted onto the estate. Not with the child. You know how society is. A woman who becomes pregnant without a husband is seen as a whore, never mind that the man is equally to blame. He is even more to blame most of the time."

An enormous weight settled on my breast. My mother, a thief! I'd thought nothing more could shock me, but once again Agneta had proved me wrong.

"I know I made a terrible mistake," she continued. "I should have told you who you really are."

"You said that before."

She nodded. "True, I did. And since then not a day has gone by but I have wondered when would have been the right time to do so. And when you would have been able to accept it." She regarded me.

"The day we first met!"

"Really? You had just lost your mother. The man who had become your father had died not long before. Would you have been able to take the truth then?"

"I confess, we'll never know." The stifling weight on my chest threatened to crush my heart. "But looking back on it now, after all this time, I still think I should have been warned. What hurt most of all was that you probably intended never to tell me. Or am I wrong?"

Agneta bowed her head. "I do not know. I wrestled with that question during all the time you were living on the estate. I was looking for the right time, and often, I must admit, I was tempted just to let the whole matter drop. *It is better that way,* I told myself. *She has a good life, so why should I deprive her of her childhood?* No one knew the whole story except my mother and me. I had not yet married Lennard back then. So, after my mother's death, I was the only one who knew exactly what had happened."

"You weren't aware your mother had visited the Stockholm attorney?"

"Toward the end of her life my mother went to Stockholm several times. She must have written out the instructions for the bequest on one of those trips."

"And no one noticed that fifteen thousand crowns were missing?" I could scarcely imagine how Stella Lejongård could simply withdraw such a huge sum.

"My mother had her own money in a separate account, and she often spent extravagantly. I did not look into her expenditures when the account came to me after she died. She also had a safe deposit box where she hid her own secret, one she kept from me for years. Her motivation for concealing it was probably the same as mine concerning you."

What kind of secret? Clearly the old proverb still held: *the apple doesn't fall far from the tree.*

Agneta looked into my eyes. "What is done cannot be undone. I can do nothing but beg your forgiveness. I have learned my lesson, and from now on I will always be honest with you."

If only she'd made that promise earlier! How would I react if my own daughter was furious with me? Or, as in Agneta's case, my niece? Would I be willing to humble myself and beg forgiveness? Surely I would. Would I want to receive that absolution? Of course.

Could I forgive Agneta? Only time would tell, but in the meantime we could treat one another with respect.

"Very well," I said. "Tell me how things stand at the estate."

Agneta looked crestfallen. She'd probably been hoping I would forgive her. But for me, just agreeing to speak to one another like adults still felt like an enormous concession.

"It looks bad," she answered and studied the plaques for her father and mother. "Germany's war has thrown many things into disarray. I should have foreseen that, but I did not. From one day to the next I lost half of my business partners, either because they were Jews whose possessions were plundered or they were fanatical supporters of Hitler. I refuse to support that man's ideology as von Rosen obviously does. As a proud, loyal Swede, I owe allegiance only to my king."

Her eyes flashed and she paused. "Unfortunately, our Swedish, Finnish, and Norwegian clients have distanced themselves. There is growing fear everywhere that Sweden may not be able to keep out of the war. Not to mention that our ships are no longer safe in the Baltic. I am sure you remember how precariously our accounts were balanced."

I nodded.

"Despite my best efforts I have been unable to preserve that balance; we are now on the brink of ruin. And to make things worse, I am not at liberty to focus on business affairs. It breaks my heart to see Lennard like this. He puts on a brave face and does his best to help, but his liver is withering away. The doctors were optimistic and said he still had a couple of years, but—a couple of years, Matilda! Only two years! Lennard is not even sixty yet! Neither Ingmar nor Magnus is married, and it is entirely possible Lennard will never see his own grandchildren."

She pressed her lips together, and tears trickled down her cheeks. She quickly wiped them away. "And there is the problem with my sons . . ."

I stared at her. The younger Matilda would have rushed to take her into her arms, but the woman I was now wasn't sure how to react. Agneta might need comforting, but I couldn't bring myself even to touch her.

"What is this about Ingmar? Why has he vanished? And why isn't Magnus lifting a finger to save the estate he's going to inherit?"

"The matter is complicated," Agneta told me. "Perhaps Ingmar himself will tell you one day. I do not know if I am entitled to reveal what happened. In any case, we quarreled. It was frightful, the worst quarrel I have ever had with him. Magnus has always seen things differently, but Ingmar was beside himself. He refused to speak to me for weeks. Then, in March, just before I wrote to you, he announced that he was going to Norway."

"Norway? Why Norway?"

"He claimed he wanted to help two friends, former classmates of his. He refused to say anything more, and we have not received word of him since." She sighed. "It is astounding how alike the two of you are. One would almost think the two of you were the twins."

"But that makes no sense. He had to help them? With what? And why now, when his father is terribly ill and Magnus seems unwilling to take any responsibility?" I experienced once again my old disgust with Ingmar's brother. Now that I knew we were related, I was even more outraged with Magnus.

"You will have to ask Ingmar. I keep hoping for a letter, but he seems to have cut off all ties. I cannot even be sure that he is still alive."

"He must be. Otherwise the police would have informed you. Or his friends would have."

"In other words, you are saying every day without news is a good day."

Agneta's expression was so woeful that despite myself I placed a hand on her arm. "I am sure he will write. And if you like, I can ask Paul to keep an eye out for him."

"Paul?" she echoed, then made the connection. "Ah, the cabinet-maker who went to Norway."

"He has a furniture business in Oslo. He took a room at my hotel a couple of months ago, so we should have his address on file."

She looked as if my job at the Grand Hôtel was news to her. But perhaps she was only surprised to hear I was still in contact with Paul.

What I'd heard made it impossible for me to keep sulking, though it would be a long time before I found it in my heart to forgive her.

"Listen, Agneta," I said with a sigh. "Times have changed. I've made a new life for myself. Sooner or later I'll have to return to Stockholm, because if don't, I'll lose my job. The hotel has been good to me and I'm happy there. But I'm here now and ready to help, provided you keep your promise to be absolutely honest. When I go back to Stockholm, I'll try to help you from there, but right now we need to get Ingmar to return and make Magnus do his share. He's got to stop lolling around with his head in the clouds. He can do that someday when he's the owner and has a good manager. For right now, he has to help his mother."

Agneta reached out and took my hand. I fell silent. I didn't like this; I didn't want her emotion.

"Thank you," she said. "For being here. You have no idea how much it means to me."

Fortunately, she didn't ask again for forgiveness.

42

I went directly to Agneta's office as soon as I got back. The chaos there was appalling. I picked up the phone and asked the operator to connect me with the hotel.

Tilda sounded surprised to hear from me. "Is everything all right? Are you okay?" I heard the worry in her voice, even though I'd mentioned I was going on holiday, nothing more.

"Yes, thanks, Tilda. I'm doing fine. How are things at the hotel? No problems?"

"Oh, same as ever. Nothing particular to report—other than a couple of missing hand towels and some potted plants that need watering."

"I'm glad to hear it. Listen, could you please get me the address of Paul Ringström? You know, the man who left me the note."

"Why do you need it?"

Giving out addresses was against house rules, but as the general manager's administrative assistant, I was the enforcer of those rules.

"I have news of a mutual acquaintance and would like to pass it on. Would you help me out?"

"But of course!" Tilda put down the telephone. Longing crept in as I listened to the usual hubbub in the background. Guests' voices, the rumbling of luggage trollies—how lovely it would be to be watching the usual activity!

A rattle as the phone was picked up. Tilda gave me the address.

"Thanks so much. You're a treasure!"

"Nice to hear! But please take some time off. If you're out there in the country with your uncle, you should be enjoying the fresh air."

"I will. That's a promise." I said goodbye.

I immediately took the address I'd scribbled down and carried it to the desk in my room.

Paul would be surprised to hear from me. And it would astonish him when I asked him to look for the man he'd been jealous of a few years before.

We weren't tender young things anymore; we were adults. I stressed that in my note and said his help would be a great favor to me.

After all, Paul owed me. He'd come back into my life and made me do something I immediately regretted. He'd tampered with my deepest emotions.

I finished the letter and addressed it to him. It was early enough in the day to get it into Kristianstad's outgoing mail. I took my coat and purse and went to Agneta's office.

She stood lost in thought before the window, as if the pile of documents and files on her desk didn't exist. She seemed very far away.

"Agneta?"

I'd startled her. "Yes?"

"I'd like to take the car to Kristianstad."

She nodded. "Yes, just tell the driver."

I smiled. "No need. I've had my license for several months. I prefer to drive myself, but I need your permission. After all, it's your automobile."

She blinked in astonishment. "You got your license?"

"It seemed prudent," I answered. "We have a hotel vehicle. I often use it for errands."

Agneta smiled. "Excellent! But be careful! And take care when you're shifting. Our car is far from new."

"Thanks." I withdrew.

Agneta hadn't exaggerated; the car's best years were clearly behind it. I felt how loose the gears were as I maneuvered it out of the garage under the astonished gazes of the stable boys.

"Miss Matilda!" the chauffeur cried, pulling on his jacket and running after me. "You didn't tell us you wanted to go to town!"

"I do, in fact, but I'll drive myself. I have the countess's permission."

"Of course—but you'll put me out of a job!"

I waved and stepped on the gas.

As the car jolted along the road, I thought back to all the times I'd ridden to school with Ingmar and Magnus. How carefree those years had been, even though I hadn't thought so at the time!

In Kristianstad I parked on a side street lined with small businesses. The post office was close by. I wasn't planning to buy anything, but I did want to see if the shops I remembered were still operating.

The line in the post office moved quickly, and my turn soon came. The young postal clerk looked haggard.

I paid and left. The sun peeked out from the clouds. I stood just outside for a moment and lifted my face to the sun. It was surprisingly warm outside.

"Matilda?" came a voice behind me.

I spun around.

"I can't believe it's you!" Birgitta came forward with open arms, and before I could react, she hugged me just as she used to do in school.

"Birgitta!" I said, smiling broadly. "What are you doing here?"

"Well, what do you think? I run my father's store. With my husband." She proudly displayed the gold ring on her hand.

"So you found your Cary Grant?"

"Much better than that!" she exclaimed. "Karl is a dear, and he's a good businessman too. A couple of months ago we enlarged the shop and even set up a little mail order business serving the countryside." She paused for a moment and beamed at me. "And how are you? I haven't seen you since graduation!"

"I'm assistant to the general manager of the Grand Hôtel in Stockholm."

"You're not at Lion Hall anymore?"

I shook my head. "Not for quite a while. I was drawn back to the big city. I'm here on a short visit." The rest was none of her business.

"Oh my, that's exciting! I'll have to convince Karl to take me to Stockholm so we can stay at your hotel. Is rationing causing you problems? People say public institutions and hotels always have priority."

"Well, we do the best we can," I replied mildly. We faced the same supply difficulties as everyone else, for many consumer goods were no longer being imported.

She seized my hand. "Say, are you in a terrible hurry? May I give you a tour of our shop?"

"Why not? I had something to mail, and I've already been to the post office."

"Great, come with me!" Birgitta said. "I'm really proud of what we've done with Father's business. And maybe you'll find something you need!"

Her father's enterprise had been a mystery to me during our school years. We'd gone to the cinema together a number of times, but Birgitta had never invited me home with her.

She brought me to two immense buildings as big as warehouses. The store housed in one of them featured household goods. The other was probably for the stockroom and offices. Two large delivery trucks stood in the courtyard.

"We hope the army won't commandeer our trucks," Birgitta commented when she saw my expression.

"Do you think that mobilization is likely?" I asked. So far there'd been no sign that Sweden was likely to go onto a wartime footing.

"Nothing on earth is certain just now. But we're not going to let that spoil our afternoon, are we?"

She pulled me into the shop and showed me their offerings: housewares, enamel bowls, dish towels and hand towels, brushes, and even Dutch wax fabrics. But the array was less extensive than one might expect, given the expanse of storefront.

"You've really built something impressive, Birgitta," I said after the tour.

"Working in a famous hotel isn't bad either. Do you still plan to set up your own business?"

"Well, we'll see," I told her. "I don't know."

"And what about your admirer?" she asked with a meaningful look. "Paul, I think his name was. Isn't that right?"

"Nothing came of it. He settled in Norway years ago to manage the Oslo branch of his father's furniture business."

"And you didn't go with him?"

I shook my head. "We'd grown apart. Or maybe I should say we grew up."

"That's a real shame. And how about that good-looking little aristocrat you rode to school with?"

"That's a bit more complicated." I wished I could vanish in a puff of smoke, because I knew Birgitta was going to pester me with questions.

"How so? Did you two fall for one another?"

"No. He disappeared. Men seem to flee from me and run off to Norway. It's probably a curse."

"Oh, pooh!" Birgitta exclaimed. "The right one's bound to come along someday. Probably right there in your hotel."

We walked on, and Birgitta showed me through the spacious living quarters behind the store. Her parents had retired and gone to live in the north, deeding the business to her and her husband. Birgitta and

Karl hadn't yet been blessed with children, but she remained optimistic on that score.

We returned to the store, where I adamantly refused to accept any gift. "I really don't need a thing, Birgitta, but thanks very much! But please remember that the two of you are welcome in the Grand Hôtel at any time. I will make sure they offer you a special discounted rate."

Birgitta smiled in delight and hugged me again. "It was lovely to see you again, Matilda. Keep in touch and let me know when you'll be back. We can spend an afternoon together, just like old times."

"Just like old times," I echoed with a smile. "Of course I will, Birgitta."

And with that she set me free. I gave her another wave and turned away.

I enjoyed a gorgeous sunset on my way back to the estate. Getting away had done me good, but as I entered the manor, I became aware of a pervasive gloom I hadn't noticed when I first arrived. I encountered Agneta as I was hurrying to my room to change for dinner.

"Well, did you take care of everything?" she asked.

"Yes, thanks, it was a pleasant drive." Agneta nodded and continued down the hall, but I called her back. "I wrote to Paul. He lives in Oslo, and I asked him to try to locate Ingmar. Maybe he can find out something."

Agneta was surprised. "I thank you for that. Come down to dinner, if you like, and we can talk about it. Lennard is not feeling well, so it will be just the two of us."

"I'll be right there."

I noticed a radio was on the sideboard. That was new.

"Switch it on if you like," Agneta said as she came into the dining room behind me. "Lennard and I enjoy listening to a bit of music at dinner."

My eyebrows rose. "You never tolerated music during a meal. Unless we'd hired musicians for a special event."

"There, you see—times have changed." Her smile was bitter. "It is often better to float away with the music than to brood."

Did she and Lennard really have nothing to say to one another? Or did their conversations inevitably come back to illness? Was the sight of her husband a harrowing reminder that he was slowly dying?

I pressed a button and a moment later heard a clarinet playing a gentle melody. It lent a different atmosphere to the room. Agneta lingered by her chair, her eyes closed as she enjoyed the music.

A few moments later an announcer informed us it was eight o'clock—the usual hour for dinner at Lion Hall.

I realized that, while Agneta might appreciate the music, she'd put a radio here for an entirely different reason. The newscast that followed the clarinet described the latest war developments, including the German offensive in France and provocative actions in the Baltic. The English had begun sowing mines to hinder the German navy.

Agneta lowered herself into her chair, fully intent on the news reports.

I knew she must be thinking of Ingmar. As long as Norway was at peace, she could feel he was not in danger.

I was glued to the broadcast as well. Agneta breathed a sigh of relief when the weather forecast ended the program. "No news from Norway," she commented. "That is good."

I knew that there'd been a clash with German naval vessels just off the Norwegian coast. The newspapers had been reporting on the growing power of nationalist forces there.

I'd have liked to declare *They won't dare attack Norway,* but who could tell? My stomach cramped as I remembered how swiftly the Germans had triumphed elsewhere.

43

Over the following days, I did my best to put out the fires that menaced Lion Hall from all sides. Agneta's explanation that she hadn't had time to attend to estate business was a gross understatement. In my absence the disorder had again reared its ugly head and had gotten considerably worse.

In addition, there were the difficulties caused by Clarence von Rosen. He'd said nothing to Agneta and there'd been no open conflict, but his pro-Nazi sympathies had enormous consequences for us.

I was infuriated by our apparent helplessness. Couldn't we get around the man?

"We must speak to the king," I told Agneta, at my wits' end. "He'll understand that von Rosen is being unjust. Maybe he isn't even aware that our contracts have been terminated."

"He knows," Agneta said. "I wrote to him, asking for clarification. I begged him to pardon us if we had somehow offended him. I received no answer."

"I'm sure he's very busy. People are appealing to him from all sides."

"The Bernadotte family has never been too busy to respond to their loyal supporters. His silence is significant; it means that the royal stable master is more influential than we are. We have fallen into disgrace, merely because we are unwilling to sell our horses to those making war." She was furious.

Anger welled up in me as well. They couldn't possibly punish us this severely for our refusal to deliver horses to the war. Sweden was still "nonbelligerent," after all, with a market economy!

I'd thought I'd left the estate behind, but now I realized how angered I was by this injustice. It affected not only the Lejongårds but also the people who worked for us and those who depended on us.

"I could write him another letter on our behalf."

Agneta shook her head. "No, please! We Lejongårds may have been favored by the king, but we will not stoop to beg now that we have lost that status. We are the most ancient noble line in Sweden, far older than the royal family. We sacrificed ourselves and shed our blood in the Thirty Years' War!"

Agneta's fierce outburst startled me, but I understood her pride. We shouldn't apologize. By declining to do business with aggressors, we were not infringing on Swedish national policy in the slightest.

I was seized by the desire to travel to the royal palace to give the good folk there a stern lecture. But I knew that Agneta would never permit it.

"Then we'll have to get along without the king," I replied resentfully. Agneta knew the royal family far better than I. But my experience running a hotel had taught me that it was important to counter malicious rumors. Maybe we could do something to offset the damage.

"If anyone can find a way out of these troubles, you can." Agneta reached out and took my hand. I felt her shiver. "You have no idea how much everyone here has missed you."

Her words touched me, but I quickly regained control. I wasn't going to stay forever; I was here to deal with the crisis, that was all. My life was in Stockholm. I would do what I could to help, but Agneta would have to face up to her responsibilities.

Putting the accounts in order was the first step. Maybe I'd come up with something in the process.

The deeper I immersed myself in the task, the greater became my concern that Magnus hadn't lifted a finger for his parents. He'd never tired of bragging he would inherit Lion Hall. So why wasn't he here? He could surely dabble in his writing while tending to estate business.

"What actually is the matter with Magnus?" I asked Agneta on Tuesday morning. An idea had occurred to me the previous night as I lay awake, unable to sleep. "Why doesn't he live on the estate anymore? Has he crept off to spend all his time in that horrible old cabin?"

"Magnus has an apartment in Kristianstad. He moved there after the quarrel, and he has shunned us completely since then." Agneta's expression was woeful. "But at least I know where he is."

"Have you written to him about your problems?"

"No, but he was perfectly aware of the situation. He may act as if Lion Hall means nothing to him, but he knows."

"And can't he get off his high horse and come home? Maybe he's waiting for you to apologize."

If only I knew what had caused the quarrel . . .

"I hardly think a simple apology will set things right," she said. "I have the impression that I do not know my sons anymore. That is particularly the case with Magnus."

"Maybe I should talk to him," I surprised myself by saying. Until very recently, I'd have considered such an offer proof that I'd lost my mind. But times had changed. I was an adult and had lived through things far more difficult than Magnus's taunting.

"I scarcely believe that he would listen to you."

"Well, I can try at least."

Agneta's expression was dubious. "After all that has passed between the two of you?"

"We were children. Maybe his time in Stockholm knocked a little sense into his head."

Agneta reflected for a moment. "Very well, you might as well try! But do not expect very much. Magnus has devoted himself to art. He is the son of two fiercely determined individuals. It will take more than a conversation to move him to assume his responsibilities."

"But perhaps he'll make his demands explicit and tell me what sort of apology he wants."

I drove to Kristianstad shortly afterward. I had Magnus's address from Agneta, and I was familiar with the neighborhood. I hoped I'd find him awake and dressed. Many artists were known to stay up late and get up only in the afternoon.

I parked and walked to the apartment building. It reminded me a bit of some along Brännkyrka Street—immense, white, and three storied. The stucco had peeled off in places, but the front door appeared recently painted.

I scanned the buzzers and finally located the one labeled *M. Lejongård.*

I pressed the button and looked out at the street. A delivery truck rattled past. Radio reports had suggested that controls would soon be imposed on automobile traffic so as to preserve fuel for national defense. There was still gasoline available for Agneta's car, but I foresaw a day when we'd have to take our horse-drawn coach to visit Kristianstad.

Minutes passed. I buzzed again and wondered if Magnus was home. He might have traveled back to Stockholm. Or was he still asleep under his comforter? Perhaps he wasn't alone?

At last I heard footsteps. I turned around and saw Magnus thrust his face through the opening of the front door. He still resembled Ingmar, but he'd had his hair cut extremely short and now there was a little scar on his cheek. Had he joined a dueling club during his student days?

Magnus took a moment to recognize me.

"Hi, Magnus," I said.

"Look here—the maid's daughter honors me with a visit."

I felt a kick of adrenaline, but I controlled myself. I'd had to deal with the occasional arrogant guest at the Grand Hôtel, the sort who would treat the staff with contempt. I'd learned to hide my emotions and face down such persons. I threw his insults back in his teeth. "Look here—the man who doesn't give a damn about his own estate!" No longer was I the child to be mocked and insulted. "Shouldn't you, rather than I, be tending to Lion Hall business?"

Magnus tilted his head with a sneer. "Is that why you came? To tell me that? If so, you might as well leave now."

"And you should mind your manners," I snapped. "Are you going to let me in, or do I have to force my way?"

My aggressive tone surprised him. Instead of slamming the door in my face, he stepped aside. "All right, then, come in."

"Thank you!" I stalked past and then followed him up two flights of stairs. The steps were covered with sisal mats that muffled our footsteps. The place smelled of straw with a whiff of cat stink.

Magnus's apartment was crowded with art objects and paintings. It looked like a private museum. *Entrance price: twenty cents,* I thought.

"Are you expecting me to offer you something to drink?" he asked in a mocking tone. "Unfortunately, this is my manservant's day off."

"Don't bother. I just want to talk."

He somewhat reluctantly showed me to the living room, furnished much like Agneta's salon although much smaller. Through the beautiful glass-paneled door that led to the rear of the apartment, I saw an unmade bed. He certainly could use a manservant.

"Very well, let us get down to business," he said. "I assume you want me to come back to the estate."

"Correct."

"Why should I? The place will be mine someday, but that does not mean that I should let it ruin my life in the meantime. Besides, my mother seems to think you are much more capable of managing it. She never tired of saying that, all the time you were gone."

"Her brother was my father," I replied. "Surely she told you that?"

"She did, but as far as I am concerned, you were an unfortunate mistake."

I knew he was trying to provoke me, but I wasn't going to allow it. Not today.

"I doubt you ever knew your uncle well enough to be the judge of that. Unless, of course, he whispers to you from the crypt."

Magnus's eyes narrowed.

"But that's irrelevant. I don't want your estate. But I did come to help. I'm appealing to you: go lend your mother a hand! She needs it all the more, now that Ingmar has vanished."

"Oh, so Ingmar has vanished?"

"Don't play dumb. Your parents certainly must have told you."

"Well, they have an unfortunate habit of failing to communicate things, as you well know."

"But that's no excuse in this case," I snapped back, pleased that conflicts at the hotel had prepared me for confrontation. "Tell me, are you planning to move your lazy bones back to Lion Hall or not?"

"No!" His reply was like the flat crack of a pistol shot.

"Why not? Because you enjoy a life without responsibilities?"

"Because for most of my life my mother has not particularly cared for me, if you want the truth."

"She hasn't cared?" I asked. "That's nonsense!"

"Who was packed off to boarding school? I was! And for no more than a couple of pranks I allowed myself to play on her ward. There was no way for me to have known the deplorable creature was my uncle's bastard."

I swallowed the insult. Magnus hadn't changed a bit. He was still doing his best to shame me for my origins.

"Those were no mere pranks, Magnus," I said. "And I did nothing to deserve them. I've never hidden the fact that I'd have preferred to stay in Stockholm. And besides, you were warned. Don't pretend your mother didn't care about you. She wanted the best for you."

"And showed it by banishing me? *You* are the one she should have gotten rid of!"

I sighed. "That was a long time ago. And it isn't as if Agneta was blameless when it came to me. But here I am, at her call. Unlike you. Even if a man can't forgive everything, he should pull himself together to help his parents in their time of need. Your father is deathly ill, Magnus! And your mother is overwhelmed!"

"As if I could change anything. Let her hire a manager. Or you can take over, if you are so enamored of the place."

"I can't stay there. I'm not Agneta's daughter; you're her son."

He erupted. "And that means nothing at all!"

"What did she do, Magnus?" I pressed him. "And what can she do to get you to forgive her?"

Magnus's lips became a mean straight line. "She sent you. Right?"

"I insisted on coming to see you," I replied. "What is it? What must she do before you'll finally stand at her side?"

"I am not demanding anything. I am simply not interested. It is time for you to go now. I am sure you have more important things to do."

"I'm not leaving here until I have an answer."

"An answer that suits you, you mean." Magnus snorted derisively. "I have already made my wishes absolutely clear." He took a noisy breath. "You seem to have no idea what this is all about. That is typical of my mother. She knows how and when to hush things up. Tell her I will come back when she has closed her eyes forever and the estate belongs to me. Not before. And if she wants to retire, she can deed it to me sooner. I will take care of it once it is mine, and not before."

I was shaking with rage once I was outside on the sidewalk. What a huge waste of time! Incensed, I climbed into the car and put it in gear. Damn it, why did Agneta still drive this ancient piece of junk?

Then I realized the obvious: the estate couldn't afford a new car. I ignored people's stares as I drove through Kristianstad.

I'd calmed down somewhat by the time I got back to the estate and put the car into the garage. I went into the manor and found Agneta waiting for me.

"Shall we have a coffee?" she asked. "Svea has fresh pastry."

"Yes, please," I replied. "Let me just freshen up."

I hurried upstairs. I washed my face and hands and changed my dress, then returned. I'd expected Lennard to be there as well, but the little table in the salon was set for only two.

Agneta waved me to a seat. "Did you have a pleasant drive?" The smell of coffee perked me up, and my stomach responded with a rumble.

"I did, thank you! Though it's probably about time for you to think about getting another automobile. This one has gotten to be quite a rattletrap."

She sighed. "Gladly, but we do not have the resources at the moment."

"You could buy a secondhand car. They're less expensive than brand-new ones, but more reliable than our old museum piece."

"I will think it over." Agneta served the coffee. "Did you speak with Magnus?"

"I did. And since you know your son, you can imagine how he responded." I briefly described his refusal. I included his final comments verbatim, to be sure she got a clear picture. I was quivering with anger again by the time I finished. But it was clear Agneta was even more deeply affected.

"I'm sorry," I said. "I felt I had to be totally honest. I have no idea why Magnus is so hateful, but honestly, he really shocked me. I very much doubt I'll ever see him again. Looking back, it seems a miracle that he didn't grab me and throw me out."

"Never mind," Agneta said, fumbling for a handkerchief. "There is nothing you can do about the way he is. You did your best, and I greatly appreciate that."

I ached to know what had caused the quarrel. Had her sons demanded she turn over the estates early? I couldn't imagine such a thing, at least as far as Ingmar was concerned. But who knows how he could have changed in the intervening years? Agneta looked so miserable that I didn't dare ask.

She excused herself after a while and left. I watched her go, helpless. Maybe I should have held back some of the harsher details.

No! She needed to understand what sort of man Magnus was, even if it was a painful lesson. Perhaps this would motivate her to concentrate at last and plan for the future of the estate without outside help. She'd certainly been self-sufficient in the past.

44

I didn't see either the count or countess the rest of that day. Lennard had been in pain, and Agneta had crept off somewhere and hidden, obviously wanting not to be disturbed.

The next morning, I made my way to the dining room and joined them for breakfast. I summarized the previous day's events for Lennard, choosing my words more carefully than I had with Agneta.

He shook his head in disappointment and took my hand. "How good it is to have you here, Matilda. Perhaps I should adopt you."

"That will not be necessary," I replied. "I will take care of essential business right away."

Following her new custom, Agneta had turned on the radio. She seemed to have calmed down. It was almost time for the newscast.

All I needed was a quick cup of coffee before getting down to work. I wanted to have a clear picture of all the accounts by the end of the next day.

A sequence of tones announced the news. Agneta put her cup down and sat up straight.

"Yesterday, Tuesday, the German navy attacked the cities of Trondheim and Narvik. Additional troops landed on the southern coast and marched toward the capital. Combat is ongoing. We have word that King Haakon VII has fled. The Swedish regime condemns this deplorable intervention while stressing that the country is determined to remain neutral and will take no action against the German forces in Norway."

Those words turned my blood to ice. Ingmar was in Norway. No one knew where, and we had no idea what he was up to. Anger filled me. Why hadn't he contacted his mother? Even though they'd quarreled, he shouldn't follow my example.

Agneta sat petrified for a moment and then covered her mouth with one hand. She was torn by a tortured sob.

"Agneta, stay calm," I said as I got up. "I'm sure Ingmar is fine. Surely he didn't join the Norwegian army."

"How can you be sure? He—" She broke off abruptly, as if to keep from blurting out something I wasn't supposed to know.

"Did he say that was his plan?" He had been interested in flying . . . but surely Ingmar, with his peaceful temperament, wouldn't ever put on a uniform.

"No, but anything is possible in a German invasion!"

I shuddered. I'd never lived through a war, but I'd heard the ongoing accounts of the vast conflict in Europe. Thousands had died, and millions more were at risk. There were rumors of gas attacks and starvation. Agneta was right. If the Germans could overrun Norway the same way they'd seized Poland, who was safe? Especially when plenty of Norwegians were welcoming them with open arms!

I hadn't forgotten how the Germans were treating Jews. When I'd read newspaper reports about Kristallnacht in Germany, I wondered about the fate of poor Miss Grün, my governess for those four weeks in Stockholm. And Paul's Norwegian wife was Jewish. What would become of the two of them if the Germans took charge? What chaos was threatening their country?

I got up and threw my arms around Agneta. "It will be all right," I said. "Ingmar is clever. Maybe he's already on his way back to Sweden."

"He could have telephoned," she sobbed, pressing a handkerchief to her eyes.

Days earlier I couldn't have imagined embracing her. But I didn't want to abandon her to those fears, for they were hounding me also.

"He'll send word, I'm sure. Maybe he has no way to do so right now. But he'll contact us somehow."

Agneta blew her nose and slumped against me. "If he dies, my world ends. I will never have the chance to apologize for what I said. I want to do that more than anything in the world."

"He's not going to die! He's strong, and he has friends. Besides, I asked Paul to look for him. He's not alone. Just give it a couple of days or weeks, and we'll hear. Maybe he'll turn up at our front door."

Agneta nodded, plainly not convinced. "Can you stay longer? If you are not here, I will not know what to do."

"I still have a couple of days."

"That is not enough. If only Ingmar—"

"Agneta"—I tried to calm her—"don't upset yourself so! He'll be back, especially now that there's war in Norway. He would never be stupid enough to put himself in harm's way."

"But what if they do not allow him to leave? If they close the ports?"

"He'll travel overland. He'll get in contact, I'm sure. After all, he knows you're worrying."

Agneta broke out in tears anew. "I wish I had told him," she sobbed. "Both of them!"

I still had no idea what she meant, but that didn't matter just then.

"Ingmar will return." I took her hand. "I know it. He'll get away from them. Maybe he's already on his way."

I wanted to believe my own words, but fear crept through me. What on earth was Ingmar up to in Norway? Who were these friends of his? He was a Swede; surely the Germans couldn't touch him. But on the other hand, who knew what he was helping his hosts with?

A tense silence prevailed in the manor throughout the day. I worked on the accounts and racked my brains for ways to find new customers, taking a break only to check on Lennard, while Agneta stayed in the dining room by the radio. The maids who went to clear the breakfast table were surprised and confused to find their mistress still there.

The news repeated itself and offered no grounds for hope. Confirmation came at lunchtime that the Norwegian king had made his escape. The right wing National Unity Party led by Vidkun Quisling was proclaiming a new regime.

My blood ran cold. Where was this going to end? With Norway under Nazi rule? There was little news out of Germany, but we'd heard rumors the Nazis were harassing Jews and rounding up opposition figures. The brownshirts were known for unspeakable cruelty. What would happen to Paul and his wife? I desperately hoped he would answer my letter and tell me what they were going through.

Much too belatedly that afternoon, I came up with the thought of simply telephoning Paul. Why hadn't I thought of that earlier? I called Tilda, who was equally shocked by events in Norway, and she gave me his number.

"We're all paralyzed with fear," she said. "Be very careful and come back soon, all right?"

I promised I would and entreated her to be equally careful. While trying to reach the operator a second time, it occurred to me that many of the hotel's male employees might soon be called to military service. All those gallant young men . . . I didn't want to think what war would do to them.

I finally got the operator, but her efforts to connect with Norway failed. She finally came back on the line only to tell me that all connections with the country had been cut.

Damn it, Ingmar! I thought as I restlessly paced in the office.

It became clear by evening that the Germans were in control in Norway and Denmark. The Norwegian government had gone into exile. No one knew where the king was.

Agneta looked exhausted. She sat slumped before the radio, a prisoner of the endlessly repeating news. The newscaster had probably gone home and left a recording. She didn't switch off the apparatus until the station signed off and nothing but static was to be heard.

I rubbed my face and stretched. I had to sleep. Perhaps there would be better news in the morning.

45

I tossed and turned all night. What should I do? Tomorrow morning would be Thursday, and I'd have to leave on Sunday at the latest to be back at work on Monday. But could I leave for Stockholm with a clear conscience?

And if I opted to stay at Lion Hall, what then? I'd made Stockholm my home once more.

But everything would break down if I turned my back on the estate. Agneta was distracted and distraught, Lennard was dying, Ingmar was in danger, and Magnus continued to boycott the estate. He was probably lounging in bed without a thought for his family.

My thoughts chased one another in mad circles. What would I be doing if I hadn't responded to Agneta's appeal? I'd never have guessed that Ingmar was in Norway. I wouldn't know to worry.

I wasn't the woman I'd been only six months earlier. I'd come to accept that the world never stopped spinning, and loyalties could change. I'd despised Agneta when I abandoned Lion Hall, but now I couldn't bear the thought of leaving her solely responsible for the estate or of turning my back on Lennard. I was terrified something might happen to Ingmar.

War in Norway would swiftly spread to Sweden if Parliament forced it upon the king. The Germans were claiming they'd occupied Norway because the country had infringed on the terms of its neutrality. What would happen if they accused Sweden of doing the same?

I finally got out of bed, wrapped myself in my robe, and left the room. Maybe a glass of warm milk would help me sleep. I went downstairs and crossed the hall. In the darkness it seemed wider than I remembered.

A light was on in the kitchen. Was Lena up already? Or Svea? I preferred to be alone, but I went down the stairs anyway.

To my absolute astonishment Agneta was weeping alone at the kitchen table.

Why had she come belowstairs? To hide her misery from Lennard? She could have holed up in the office . . . but perhaps she wanted to avoid the mountain of work awaiting her there.

"Agneta?" I whispered. She looked up slowly. Her face was terribly haggard. "Why are you down here?"

"I love this place. I spent a lot of time here as a child. It is strange— often the plainest room in a house is the most comforting."

"The kitchen is the heart of a house." I settled beside her. "One of my associates says it's the room that holds the family together. People always go to the kitchen when life gets to be too much for them."

A long silence followed as Agneta brooded. "Were you wondering what could have caused my sons to quarrel with me?"

"Yes," I said. "Of course. But I didn't want to put any pressure on you."

"I promised I would always tell you the truth about family matters, and you are cousin to them both. You should hear it directly from me."

I watched her. She fidgeted as if trying to pull invisible rings off her fingers. She had something she wanted to tell me; maybe this was a step toward reconciliation.

"I appreciate that, but if you find it too painful . . ."

Agneta shook her head. "It does not pain me; it fills me with shame. It will probably horrify you. And for that very reason, you should hear it from me."

I sat up straight and placed my hands in my lap. What was coming?

"Do you remember the stranger who accosted you at the inn? With a white streak in his hair and a long scar across his face?"

"Yes, I do." Her words immediately brought an image of him to mind, even though at least five years had passed. "Did he come back?"

She nodded. "Late last January he came directly to the estate and insisted on speaking to me. I assumed it was just someone looking for work, but I almost fainted when I saw him."

"You knew him?"

"Oh yes, very well. More than twenty-five years ago, he presented himself to me under the name Max von Bredestein. He became my estate manager—and my lover."

Lover? Agneta had betrayed Lennard with the estate manager?

"Did Lennard ever find out?"

"Lennard knew. This happened before Lennard and I married. I had fallen in love with that man, Max, and really believed he was the man of my dreams. But when the Great War broke out, he disappeared. I heard nothing of him after that. I even sent a detective to look for him, but all that turned up was the information that a man with a similar name had died in a battle in Italy. Imagine it: there Max stood in my salon. Much the worse for wear because of the war and a hard life, but I would have recognized him even with my eyes closed."

She stopped for a moment, apparently lost in memories. "I have to explain that the man did not vanish entirely without a trace. He left something behind. Shortly after he disappeared, I discovered I was pregnant."

I had an unwelcome premonition. "Did you miscarry?"

She pressed her lips together and shook her head. Shame colored her face. "Ingmar and Magnus are from him. And just as was the case with your mother, a good man—Lennard—undertook to marry me so as to shield me and the children from scandal."

Magnus and Ingmar weren't Lennard's sons? A haze settled over me as I struggled to follow her confession.

"There I was, paralyzed by the sight of that man. He claimed he was happy to see me again. I did not know what to say. He had been dead to me for so many years! Even though the detective had not located any conclusive evidence, for years I had been convinced he was no longer of this world."

"What happened?"

"We quarreled. I accused him of abandoning me, disappearing and running off to play at war. He tried to justify himself, but I refused to listen. I reproached him for insinuating himself here and using a false name for all those years, for that is exactly what he had done. He had pretended to be his own brother so he could hide out in Sweden. Then he said, *'Your sons . . . they are mine. Confess it! I investigated and found the date of their births. I was on the estate when they were conceived. You had no other lover, so they must be mine.'* My world collapsed. The worst possible scenarios went through my mind. Was he going to blackmail me? Did he want to install himself on the estate?"

I recalled Agneta's alarm when I'd told her of the bizarre stranger at the inn.

"He said nothing; he just stared at me. He was waiting for me to confirm it. I insisted they were Lennard's sons. He demanded to see them and insisted I tell them the truth. And, worse, he wanted to take them away with him to Germany, because he had no other children. I refused and vehemently ordered him out of the house.

"Just then Lennard appeared. He was furious. He stormed into the room and ordered Max—or Hans, since that is his real name—to get out. The intruder sneered. *'Do you even know that she cuckolded you? That your sons are my children?'* I have never seen Lennard so enraged. He grabbed von Bredestein by the collar and physically threw him out.

Lennard was already ill, and he is not the sort of man who uses physical violence. I was shocked to see he was capable of it. He struck von Bredestein, threw him down in the foyer, and threatened to kill him if he ever set foot on Lion Hall grounds again. I ran out trying to separate them, but Hans was already on his way out. *'You are going to regret this,'* he snarled and left our house."

I found it hard to imagine Lennard attacking that stranger. I'd never seen him lose his temper. He'd always seemed placid, particularly in contrast to Agneta.

"What did he mean, 'you are going to regret this'?"

"I have no idea. At first I dreaded he would go to the newspapers to peddle his story and cause a scandal. Then I remembered Langeholm, and I was afraid von Bredestein would take his vengeance on the Lion Hall stables. A couple of my people still remember him; Lasse worked for him. But his revenge came via different means."

She paused, distracted, not noticing she was clawing the tabletop as if trying to gouge tracks in it.

"Both Ingmar and Magnus were at Lion Hall. Ingmar had been helping me for a while, and Magnus turned up from time to time to hide out in the old manager's cottage. As if he sensed that his father had lived in it and the boys were conceived there."

I remembered that horrible old hut and how Ingmar had ridden there to show it to me. I'd never been attracted to the place, especially after he told me it was Magnus's favorite refuge.

"I did not know Magnus had heard all this and told Ingmar about it afterward."

I had a momentary vision of Magnus eavesdropping. Typical!

"The boys came to us and demanded an explanation. Lennard did his best to calm them, but Magnus said, *'We know you are not our real father. We want the truth.'* It was like that terrible time you came back from Stockholm with my mother's letter. My world fell apart, and I wanted to run away. I lost you, and now I was about to lose my sons.

Lennard tried to intervene, but I finally told them the truth—their real father was a con man who had wormed his way into the job at the estate.

"Ingmar was beside himself. He said I'd lied to them as I had lied to you. He refused to accept that the situations were different. I had thought Hans von Bredestein was dead. Why would anyone confuse children with tales of a dead man, when they already had a loving father who never treated them as anything but his own flesh and blood?"

She looked at me. "You will lecture me now and say they had a right to know. But what use would that have been? I was certain they would never find out about the man who had engendered them."

"I'd have assumed the same. Yet even so, I felt I had the right to know."

"Yes. I understand that now. I was misled by my own experience. I myself never had the desire to meet my real father."

"Your real father?"

"My mother's husband, the man whose portrait hangs in the foyer, is not my real father. A riding accident had rendered Thure Lejongård sterile. I am the offspring of a military officer on the royal chamberlain's staff who had a brief affair with my mother. Strictly speaking, the Lejongård line died out with Thure and Hendrik. And yet here we are."

These revelations took my breath away. Were all the women of this family condemned to carry the burden of unspeakable secrets?

"I remember quite clearly the evening my mother told me the truth. She was very ill and saw death approaching, and she wanted to unburden herself. I have often wished she had not. Thure Lejongård was my father, despite what she said. The other man was nothing to me but a picture on a cameo, a figure with whom I could never have any relationship. The shock of that revelation is probably why I hesitated and finally did not tell you of your true father. With my sons, my shame had silenced me; with you, I wanted to spare you the agony I had suffered."

I understood at last: Agneta's reticence, but even more, Stella's motivation in revealing the truth. "She wanted me to find out, exactly as you had."

Agneta gave me a bewildered look.

"Stella," I clarified. "Your mother wanted to avoid having me on her conscience as well."

"I cannot deny that," Agneta admitted. "And I would be lying if I said I did not regret her action. Even though I admit that you had every right to know."

Trembling, I took a deep breath. I studied Agneta's expression, the lines of concern on her face, and the misery evident in her eyes.

"Your sons had the same right. Maybe you should have told them on their twenty-first birthdays. If they'd heard it directly from you, perhaps they wouldn't have gotten so angry."

"Who can say? Maybe it would have turned out the same. Maybe not. But they despise me now. They surely believe that their mother was a creature of easy virtue."

"Ingmar, at least, certainly doesn't think that," I assured her. "Nor did he consider my mother a fallen woman. I cannot speak for Magnus, but Ingmar is a compassionate soul, and I know he loves you fiercely."

46

I felt terribly heavy when I opened my eyes. For a moment I thought I had merely dreamed everything from the previous night. But then I realized it was almost noon, and Agneta hadn't sent the maids to check on me. Perhaps she herself wasn't awake yet.

I pushed away the comforter, opened the curtains, and looked out at a chilly gray morning.

What other secrets are you hiding, Lion Hall? I tore my gaze away from the park and went into the bathroom. After I'd finished there, I went downstairs, where everything seemed more still than usual. The grandfather clock chimed noon. The dining room was deserted, so I went to the kitchen. I was starting to worry. Was something wrong? Surely Agneta would have awakened me if something had happened to Lennard.

The kitchen was just as empty. A big pot of pea soup slowly simmering on the stove filled the air with its fragrance. Then I remembered. It was Thursday, the staff's afternoon off!

But it was strange that Agneta wasn't up. Had she simply overslept? And Lennard—had he decided not to wake her?

I went upstairs and knocked on their bedroom door.

"Come in," called Lennard, so I opened the door, steeling myself to find them both in their nightclothes, but Lennard was already dressed. Agneta, however, was still in bed—staring at the ceiling.

"Good morning," I said. "May I bring you your breakfast?"

"That is sweet of you, Matilda," Lennard replied, "but I think I should step out with you for a moment. We need to have a word."

I nodded and withdrew to the hall. Lennard followed.

"I do not believe Agneta will get out of bed today," he said carefully. "She is in a state of shock, as some might call it. She is not speaking, and she is incapable of getting up. This sort of affliction comes over her from time to time."

This worried me. Usually when women stayed in bed, it was because of migraine headaches. I'd seen that with some of the hotel customers. Agneta's behavior was different.

"Is there anything we can do?" I whispered. "Fetch the doctor?"

Lennard shook his head. "No. It is best to leave her alone. This comes over her sometimes; the worst time was shortly after you left. The doctor diagnosed it as a reaction to extreme stress and said she would eventually get over it."

"But she seemed completely normal last night! We sat in the kitchen and talked for a long time."

Lennard put an arm around my shoulders. "Agneta has had to face a great deal in recent weeks and months. One disaster after another. Ingmar and Magnus quarreled with her, the estate has money problems—now there's war and she doesn't know where Ingmar is."

"What I told her about Magnus seems to have just made things worse."

"Do not blame yourself. I believe things will come together for her. We just need to afford her a little peace and quiet."

I nodded but was far from satisfied. It seemed to me that if she was suffering from shock caused by stress, she needed help. Who knew what might happen if she didn't receive proper attention?

By Saturday Agneta's condition had changed hardly at all. Lennard finally gave in and allowed me to call Dr. Bengtsen for a consultation. Our village physician spent nearly half an hour examining her before he came out and spoke to us.

"There is nothing physically wrong with your wife," he said, "though she probably needs to drink more water. Has she had anything to eat?"

Lennard glanced at me. "Yes. Not a great deal, but something at least. I have the impression that she has lost contact with us."

"Your wife is suffering from depression. She would probably like to speak with you, but she cannot summon the energy. Have there been stressful events in her life recently?"

"Our son is missing in Norway. You have probably heard the news from there."

The physician nodded. "I am very sorry to learn that. It could well be part of the explanation. Your wife has to assimilate this trauma. I can provide her with medication, if you agree."

"What sort of medication?"

"Well, something to help her sleep, and something to distract her from obsessive thoughts."

"You intend to anesthetize my wife?"

"I would not characterize it that way, but sleep could help her come to terms with whatever is weighing upon her spirit."

I was skeptical. Sleep had never particularly helped me through my times of difficulty. It had been an escape, no more. When I awoke, nothing had changed.

"Very well," Lennard said at last. "Do whatever you can to help her."

The doctor nodded and scrutinized Lennard. "Count Ekberg, since I am here, I would very much like to examine you as well. You have not been to my office in a long time, even though we agreed to see one another more often."

"Is that necessary?" Lennard groaned. "I feel fine most of the time. And if not, I grit my teeth, wait for a moment or two, and it passes."

"Nevertheless, I would like to check your liver. Just to be sure."

Lennard sighed, but then disappeared into the guest bedroom with the doctor.

I remained outside Agneta's door.

Depression. I'd never thought Agneta might be prey to such an affliction. We'd occasionally had hotel customers who claimed to be depressive, but everyone assumed they were playing a game to call attention to themselves. Depression was very much in vogue in certain artistic circles.

I'd learned to tell the difference. Tilda had told me a story of real depression; after Tilda's brother died in a construction accident, their mother hadn't been able to get out of bed for weeks. She'd lain staring at the window, completely inert. She had frequent long crying jags Tilda could do nothing about. Her mother had finally tried to slit her own wrists, which led them to confine her in a psychiatric asylum.

What would happen with Agneta? Would Lennard have to stand guard to make sure she didn't turn suicidal? Was this a milder form of depression that would lift after a period of staring and weeping? I wished I knew more about such things.

The door opened. I was surprised. Had Dr. Bengtsen completed the examination already?

"Miss Wallin?"

His tone alarmed me. "Yes, Doctor?"

"May I have a moment? In private?"

"Of course. Please come this way."

I accompanied the physician to the smoking room. I had no desire to discuss health matters in the office. Words leave shadows that can haunt a person.

I offered him a seat.

"Count Lennard tells me you are his niece."

I nodded. "I am."

"He also says that there is no way to get in touch with his sons. Therefore you are the closest responsible relative available to him."

I began to tense up.

"Your uncle's condition concerns me very much. I do not know how well acquainted you are with the details."

"Not very well, I'm afraid."

"Count Lennard had long suffered from diabetes, which eventually caused cirrhosis of the liver."

"My uncle has diabetes?" I echoed, astonished. "But he's thin as a rail!"

"That may be. Not every case of diabetes is caused by excess weight. In his case it remained undetected for a long time. It came to light only when we found his liver was in poor condition. I regret to inform you he has taken a turn for the worse. His blood pressure has reached a dangerous level. That, also, is a secondary symptom of his illness."

"Is there nothing that can be done? There are so many different medications these days."

"Not for cirrhosis, unfortunately. The only relief might be through a special diet, but it will not cure him. He needs to go to the hospital for an X-ray of his liver. Unfortunately, he categorically refuses. But in the current situation—with your aunt suffering from severe depression, and your uncle—"

"You want me to convince him to have the X-ray."

"Yes. And it would also be good if you could relieve him of the responsibilities of administering the estate."

My lips tightened to a thin line. *I can't possibly!* I almost exclaimed. But what alternative was there? Magnus, who intended to return to the estate only once it was his by right of inheritance? And Ingmar was missing.

"I beg you, Miss Wallin. I understand you are eminently qualified to handle their affairs. Your uncle refuses to go to the hospital for fear the estate will collapse. But if you were to take the helm and agree to take care of both your aunt and the estate? It would of course be temporary." The doctor looked at me, his expression almost pleading. "We will have a much better idea of Count Ekberg's condition in a couple of weeks. And your aunt will gradually revive from her depression, I am sure. She went through this once before, and after a time she recovered."

I remembered Agneta's words. *"Can you stay longer?"*

I could, but I didn't want to. After everything I'd learned here, I yearned for the tranquility of my own house after the usual busy day at the hotel. I needed to see Tilda and Mr. Clausen. I even missed the stern personnel director and the hotel owner. But I was cornered. Someone had to take responsibility here, and I was not hard-hearted like Magnus; I couldn't refuse.

"I will think it over."

"Please do not delay. The count needs to be admitted quite soon, before his maladies get out of control."

"Why didn't you get him to the hospital earlier?"

"We did, but his illness has developed with alarming speed. The count's last X-ray was six months ago. His condition was serious then, but not life-threatening. But now . . ."

I nodded. The doctor wasn't promising me Lennard would improve if he went to the hospital, but at least we'd receive a prognosis. I felt a heavy weight on my shoulders and a cold hand about my heart.

"I will inform you tomorrow," I said. "Give me that much time to think about it. The fact is that I have a very good position in Stockholm that I am reluctant simply to give up."

"I understand." Dr. Bengtsen got to his feet. "You can contact me at any time. And do not hesitate to call if your aunt's condition gets worse. I will come immediately. I will make sure a messenger delivers her medications no later than tomorrow morning."

I accompanied him, and he took his leave at the front door. I stood in the front hall, where the stillness was oppressive and inescapable.

Lennard was probably seeing to Agneta. She would be lying in bed, her eyes open but focused on shadowy preoccupations in her mind—her own prospects, her past, her failures. When would she awaken from that horrifying dream state?

What should I do? My heart would break if I left Lion Hall, but I didn't want to give up the Grand Hôtel either.

Staying here would mean throwing away everything I'd achieved.

47

On Monday, I drove Lennard to the hospital in Kristianstad. I'd charged Lena with keeping a close watch over her mistress and instantly fulfilling any desire she might express. The countess's illness had interrupted all routines, but the maids seemed to know what had to be done.

As I steered around potholes, I remembered my telephone call with the hotel owner. My boss had been anything but pleased to hear I wanted to resign, especially on such short notice. He relented somewhat when I described the conditions of my uncle and aunt, my closest living relatives.

"I release you with a heavy heart, Miss Wallin. You have been a boon to our hotel."

"If I had my choice, I would happily continue working for you. The impulse that drove me to alarm our poor personnel director five years ago turned out well for all of us."

My employer laughed. "Heaven knows that is true! We will be telling that story for years to come." He paused. "Take good care of yourself. I will not replace you for six months. If your family situation resolves itself before then, you are welcome back. I will engage you instantly."

"You are very kind," I said, even though I foresaw no possibility of a return. "I will gladly take your offer if I have the chance."

"I hope so, my dear, I really hope so."

I hung up and bawled like a baby. I hated disappointing the people who'd become colleagues and friends. I hated the fact that Lennard was gravely ill, and I hated Agneta's depression. Would these burdens never cease?

I drove directly to the hospital's front entrance, for Lennard couldn't walk very far. "No need for you to accompany me," he said.

I shook my head. "I must make sure they take proper care of you." I took his bag from the back seat and deposited it on the steps. A nurse picked it up and guided us to the right section of the hospital.

A chill went down my spine. It seemed just yesterday that we'd rushed Ingmar here. He had recovered and left, but what were Lennard's chances?

The physician on duty had instructions from Dr. Bengtsen. Lennard would have to stay for two days at most as they analyzed his condition.

"Take good care of Agneta," Lennard said as we gave each other a final hug.

"I will. And you take care of yourself too. Don't hesitate to call; I'll be in the office most of the time."

Lennard gave me an encouraging nod. "Thanks. I will remember that."

My heart ached as I drove back. What awaited me at the manor? Would Agneta have eaten? Would she have managed to get out of bed? Should I talk to her about Lennard? My stomach knotted with dread.

I ran upstairs as soon as I arrived. Lena was in a rocking chair, mending on her lap and a sewing basket beside her as she watched over Agneta.

"Miss Matilda!" She started to get up, but I signaled not to bother.

I went around the bed. Agneta was staring at the window, one hand clutching the comforter. She looked up when I bent over her. Her eyelids fell and then opened again, ever so slowly. Was that a sign she was coming back to us?

"Lennard arrived at the hospital, safe and sound," I told her. "The doctors are going to take a good look at his liver and see what they can do. There is no reason for you to worry."

Had she heard me? I got no reaction. Her eyes closed.

I straightened up and turned to Lena. "Did the gracious lady have anything to eat?"

I found it upsetting to speak as if Agneta weren't present, but I was not going to get any information from my aunt.

"Yes. And she sipped some coffee."

"Good. Let me know when you want me to relieve you. I will be in the office."

Lena nodded. I looked back at Agneta and then left.

I took my seat at the office desk before the pile of papers but found it hard to make much progress. The anxiety was too great. I wondered if the doctors had finished their first examination of my uncle.

I relieved Lena at noon and sat and watched Agneta consume a light meal as if she were in a trance—very little, but enough to keep her going. After that she sank into herself once more.

I was restless and jumpy the next day. The telephone rang, and I anticipated a report from the hospital, but instead a grain merchant wanted to speak with Agneta. I told him she and Lennard were both in bed with the flu and took down his information about deliveries. I didn't know the man; he was probably a new supplier. Once Agneta was up again, she could telephone him.

That evening I took the initiative of telephoning Lennard, but his news wasn't encouraging. "The physicians want to hold me for two more days. For blood tests."

"How did the X-rays turn out?"

"Well, to judge from the looks on their faces . . ."

I shut my eyes. How foolish I'd been to hope his condition might improve!

"They want to put me on a diet now. Entirely liquid. Like an infant."

"But there is no need to stay in the hospital just for that, is there?"

"No. Perhaps they are trying to get me accustomed to the place. I should probably ask them for beer in their liquid diet."

"Not such a good idea in your present condition."

Lennard laughed heartily. "You know, sometimes I wish I had been more of a drinker. Then at least I would have something to blame." He asked after Agneta.

"She eats and drinks, sits up, stares out the window. She tires quickly and goes back to sleep. She still hasn't said a word."

"That is how she was last time."

"And how long did it last?"

"A week, perhaps a bit more. Then one day she got up and resumed what she had been doing. It was eerie."

I sighed. "Well, that is promising. After all, this began nearly a week ago."

I sat up in bed for a long time that evening, trying to distract myself with a book, but I couldn't read more than a couple of lines before my thoughts wandered away. I wondered whether I was obliged to inform Magnus. His words had been horrid, but maybe he'd been trying to get at his mother through me.

I heard a gentle knock and looked up. "Matilda?" The faint voice came from the hall.

Agneta? Had my ears deceived me? I rushed to the door.

And in fact, the countess was outside my room. She looked miserable, but she'd put a wool throw around her shoulders and was on her feet!

"What is it, Agneta? Why did you get up?"

"I think—I need a little company," she said. "It is so lonely here without Lennard. Would you, just this once, come sleep next to me?"

A surprising request, but I deemed it a good sign. Certainly better than groping around for a razor blade.

"Of course," I said. "Just a moment, I'll get my robe and book. Perhaps I could read to you?"

"That would be lovely," she told me with an exhausted, almost childlike smile.

I ducked back into the room, threw on my robe, and grabbed the book from my bedside table. We went to her room together.

"You can go to bed now, Lena," I told the weary chambermaid. "I will take over from here."

Another good sign: Agneta hadn't sent Lena; she'd gotten up and come to see me herself.

Lena curtsied. "Thank you! Good night!"

The door clicked shut behind her, and Agneta climbed back into bed. I got in on the other side, where the pillows hadn't been touched.

The situation was almost comical. At school I'd often heard that other children would wiggle into bed with their parents on Sunday mornings. I'd never been tempted, and my parents hadn't invited me. My mother's routine always began at six o'clock in the morning.

And now here I was on Lennard's side of the bed. What would he say when he heard his wife's depression had lifted?

"How are you, Agneta?" I put the book down on my lap.

"Those tablets made me so frightfully tired. But the gray veil over everything is gone now. If that is the right way to describe it."

"The gray veil?"

"Yes. I just do not know . . . Every morning, when I woke up, it was as if all the colors were gone. I looked out the window and I could have sworn that the curtains were gray. There was this sad weight pressing me down. I simply could not get up, and it was terribly difficult even to move my arms and legs. Ingmar was all I could think of, and the fact that he might already be dead."

"He is not dead!" I told her. "We would have heard if that were the case." I waited a moment and then asked, "The day that this veil fell over you, did you know we were in the room?"

"Yes, but I could not speak. I did not care to. I was lost in darkness."

"Lennard said this happened to you once before."

"It did. Not long after you left. It took me by surprise back then, but this time—this time I knew what it was."

Her speech was slurred. Maybe it was time to put a stop to the drugs. I would call the doctor the first thing in the morning.

"Lennard is going to die," she said suddenly. "I feel it in my bones. His illness . . . He does his best to put on a good face for me, because he knows how vulnerable I am. But he will die. This year, most likely."

Her prediction horrified me. Was the gray veil hovering overhead about to fall on Agneta again?

"Dr. Bengtsen wanted them to X-ray him at the hospital. Nothing more. That doesn't mean he's going to die this year."

Agneta took my hand. She had visibly aged. She was suddenly an old woman.

"You and I have known one another for almost nine years now," she said softly. "I am so happy you found your way back to Lion Hall. And that you extended your leave for us."

I bowed my head. "I resigned."

Agneta turned her head slowly and tilted it to study me. "Really? But why? You said—"

"Yes, I said the hotel needed me. But you were having such difficulties and Lennard needed to go to the hospital, so it was clear I had to take care of Lion Hall. Back then, when you were my guardian, you did so much for me. You gave me a home and an education, and you protected me from your own son. I can never repay you. But perhaps the money your mother left me could help save the estate?"

"That money is yours alone, Matilda. And there is no need to repay me in any way. You are my—" She stopped short. Her eyes told me she feared saying something wrong.

"Niece. I am your niece, I know. But I wasn't able to accept that for a long time, was I?" I patted her hand. "Now it's my turn to support you. Whatever fate has in store for Lennard, I am here for you both. I will not abandon you."

Tears glistened in Agneta's eyes. "Thank you, Matilda!"

That was a long, restless night. I'd read only a single page when Agneta's eyes closed, but I couldn't manage to lose myself in sleep. Her mental condition had improved, but the thoughts tormenting her were far from rosy.

Lennard's time on earth was nearing its end. I was still trying not to accept that reality. He was alive, and I didn't consider him a dying man. The physicians were conducting tests, I told myself, that was all. They were putting him on a diet. I wanted him to get through this, especially because Agneta would fall apart without him.

Eventually, I drowsed off, only to shudder awake, thinking I'd heard a noise. For a moment I thought Agneta had left the room, but I found her sleeping peacefully on her side of the bed. I'd never seen her like this; in fact, during all the time I'd lived at Lion Hall I'd never seen her sleep. She'd never shown any sign of fatigue. But the afflictions of these days had robbed us all of our vitality.

48

Two weeks passed without news of Ingmar. May came but brought none of the grace and lightheartedness we all desired. Everyone feared the future. The German invasion of Norway rolled swiftly onward, and that peaceful country fell entirely into the hands of the Nazis.

Sweden clung to its neutrality. The government instituted mandatory blackouts and stricter rationing of basic goods.

All exterior lighting and interior illumination of the barns had to be extinguished. For the manor we received so-called air raid lamps to use inside, and the windows had to be masked with blackout curtains. Our automobile had to be equipped with special headlamps so approaching German pilots couldn't use it to track targets.

These measures caused great consternation at first, but they soon became routine.

Lennard was discharged after more than a week in the hospital. He came home with a long list of instructions to our cook for his special diet. He was quite disgusted with the doctors' orders.

"I am being treated like an infant," he grumbled as he glared at the contents of his glass, which resembled watery oatmeal porridge. "This is nothing more than baby's gruel."

"A gruel designed to keep your liver working," our newly invigorated Agneta replied. Looking at her now, one could scarcely believe that depression had laid her so low. Sometimes she was emotional, but it was obvious she'd found the wherewithal to oppose her world of troubles.

The government had called all eligible Swedish men to military service in late April. Many of our stable lads had to report. Only Lasse Broderson, too old to be conscripted, and our very youngest boys, new to employment, were left.

Agneta was appalled. "And how are we supposed to get our work done?"

"I will help," I told her. "I'm perfectly capable of mucking out the stalls and feeding horses. Maybe it's time to assign the maids some of the easier tasks. And after all, we still have five men to do the work."

"These youngsters can hardly be characterized as 'men.'"

"They are between fourteen and sixteen, and all are strong. And Mr. Broderson is still with us. They will take on the heavy work, and we women can do the rest. I have no problem getting my hands dirty. And the administrative work will go on regardless." I glanced up to see Agneta looking anguished. "We can do this! And maybe it will even do you some good to trundle feed to the barns and curry the horses. They're usually out to pasture in summertime. And who knows how things will be a few months from now? Maybe our lads will be back here before winter."

Agneta sighed. "And we all thought that war would never return to Sweden. But now . . ."

"The country is not at war. Our king is smart enough to stay out of it. Believe me, Gustav will not allow the Germans to set foot on Swedish soil. And if they do, we will send them packing. We were the terror of Europe once upon a time. The fact that we are peaceable now has never meant we're incapable of defending ourselves." I took her hand. "Please remember the Agneta you used to be. The one who sat with me in the principal's office. The one who took charge of Lion Hall after her father died, even though she had planned a different life."

Her eyes glistened with tears. "I am old, Matilda, and getting older. I fear my memory is not as good as it once was." A twitch of a smile manifested itself. "But I will do my best."

That afternoon I summoned the maids and explained the situation.

"You all know that our men have been called up for the military, to prepare for the possibility of a German invasion. There is no confirmation that such a thing is likely, but times like these require extraordinary measures. The most important concerns of Lion Hall are the horses and their barns. They take precedence over housekeeping at the manor. An unmade bed or cold coffee is unfortunate; starving or neglected horses would mean catastrophe. For that reason, I ask you to think about what tasks you can take on. Feeding, rubbing the horses down, watering them, helping out in the fields, anything of that sort. The gracious lady and I will also be pitching in with the work in the barns and out in the fields."

The maids exchanged astonished glances, but they all agreed.

"My father's a farmer," Silja volunteered. "I know how to curry horses."

"I can help all sorts of ways," Rika said. "After my father died, my mother had to take care of the farm by herself. She's married again now, but I help them out on Thursdays. It's no hardship to cart a bit of hay to the horses!"

We quickly agreed that because of the challenges of wartime we would work double shifts.

Agneta was grinning when we returned to the office.

"What is it?" I asked. "Did I say something funny?"

"No, it is just—I was imagining your job at the hotel. I assume you led meetings with the staff?"

"The housekeeper did that, but yes, I substituted for her from time to time."

"I suspect your hotel has the country's most capable employees. At least, it did, as long as you were there—true?"

"Well, it is not up to me to judge . . ."

"No false modesty! I really believe they were the best by far, and they must have been very sad to see you go."

"They were. In fact, the owner is leaving the position open for six months in case I want to go back."

Agneta gave me a bleak look. "Are you going to?"

I shook my head. "No, not as long as the war continues. Or Ingmar stays away. I promised I would not leave you without assistance."

"I am deeply grateful. I want this war to end as soon as possible, but I do hope that you will not abandon us again."

"I will never abandon my Lion Hall family, not even if Ingmar comes back to take over the management. One way or another, I will always be here for you."

Agneta was delighted. "Well, in that case, we should look to see if we have clothing appropriate for our service on the front lines."

Lasse Broderson couldn't believe his eyes when I walked into the horse barn clad in farm clothes and rubber boots.

"Gracious miss, I cannot permit you to work here," he said after I'd explained that thenceforth the estate's female employees would be helping in the barns and pastures.

"Listen to me, Lasse. The war is raging. You have lost half of your people. Women might be less muscular than men, but we are capable. Just tell us what needs doing."

"The young lads can do double shifts."

I shook my head. "No talking back, Mr. Broderson! We are helping. And that includes the countess herself. She has not located rubber boots in her size yet, but she will walk through that door at any moment."

"You sweet thing!" exclaimed Broderson, astounded. "Well, since you asked: the pregnant mares must be fed. And hay has to be carted out to the pasture. The first horses have already gathered out there."

I grabbed a bucket. "I know what to do!"

Feeding the mares was a very pleasant duty. They were kept in a large interior space where they could move around. The pasture was still wet and slippery; we wanted to avoid the risk that one might fall.

Intrigued, the horses came to me as I walked up with the feed pail and then filled the mangers with hay. This work was much more invigorating than trying to reconcile impossible numbers in the sticky closeness of the office.

Later, Agneta sat beside me as I drove the wagon out to the meadow. I hadn't guided a team for a long time. I remembered well how Lennard had undertaken to teach me the skills, and how clumsy I'd been at first. I eventually caught on, and I was pleased to see I hadn't forgotten.

"You are entirely right," she said as she looked around. "This has been missing in my life. It is lovely to go back to doing something immediately useful."

I distributed feed and water to the mangers and troughs in the meadow. Agneta helped, and then she stood at the fence patting a horse that had thrust its head across.

"I should come outside much more often," she commented. I offered the horse a couple of sugar cubes I'd filched from the kitchen. "I never imagined I was going to turn into my mother."

"She didn't go outside?" I asked cautiously. We hadn't spoken of Stella Lejongård in a very long time.

"She did not care to. Her world was the salon, the manor house, social occasions, and clothes. She learned practically nothing about the business of the estate. She avoided it, and she was completely at a loss when my father died." She sighed. "Unlike her, I knew every nook and cranny of the estate. I often helped out. It is a shame I forgot what good it does me to be here. To pat the horses."

"Well, that is a pleasure you can allow yourself every day from now on, and not only in wartime. I will happily accompany you. And when summer comes, we can move our ledgers outside to the pavilion or work under a willow tree. We are not obliged to work in that stuffy office. Everything seems more difficult there."

"I certainly concur." She looked at me. "The times are changing, so we should do the same!"

We stayed out in the pasture for quite a while and returned only as the sun was sinking below the horizon.

We were having coffee in the office, pleasantly fatigued, when Agneta raised a new subject. "Now we must consider the problem of the Ekberg estate. Who can we get to harvest the grain?"

I hadn't thought of that. Lennard's sister, Elisabeth, and her husband were running the place, and they'd been harder hit by the conscription of able-bodied men.

I mused for a while. "We have threshing machines there, don't we? And a tractor. How about lending them to the neighbors? The peasant farmers don't have the means to buy machinery. Not all Swedish men have been called up, since the population still has to be fed. Our breeding business is less important to official eyes, but the Ekberg fields, a secure source of food, certainly must be vital. So let us draw up a contract with the local farmers: they can use our machines, if in return they provide the manpower necessary to harvest our fields."

"An excellent idea!" declared Lennard, who'd entered without our noticing. "I will talk with the people. I am sure they will agree to such an arrangement."

Agneta gave him an astonished look. "How long have you been listening out there?"

Lennard smiled. "The door is open. I heard everything."

"I had not realized that you were such a sneaky fellow."

"Well, I suppose we all have our secrets." He winked at me. "True?"

Not long after we'd made our arrangements to keep the estates running, a conscription notice for Ingmar came fluttering into the house, summoning him to report to the nearest processing depot.

That threw us into a panic.

"What should we do?" Agneta cried. "Ingmar is not here!"

"We could tell the police he is in Norway."

"Then they will assume he is a traitor to Sweden."

I shook my head. "How does visiting friends in Norway make him a traitor? The only real problem is that we cannot give them an address." I thought for a moment. "Suppose we report him missing? Really, we could have done so long ago."

"But I knew where he wanted to go. It is not as if he vanished in a midnight fog."

"True, but it has been almost three months now. No one knows what has become of him. Maybe this is a way to locate him."

Agneta wrestled with that idea. There was a real possibility that Ingmar might be accused of cowardice or even treason if he failed to report. Then he'd be subject to arrest and punishment when he returned.

"Please, let us go to the Kristianstad police and file a missing person report," I suggested. "Perhaps they can trace him and let us know."

"Are you sure that will help?" she asked fretfully.

"Sure? No, but at least then the authorities will know he cannot be conscripted."

"Will they assume he ran away to avoid the army?"

"We will see that they take down the facts just as they are. What do you think? Shall we leave right away?"

An hour later we were on the road to Kristianstad. Agneta was too upset to drive, so I was at the wheel. An open military truck came the other way as we entered the city. In the back sat a band of frightened young men in civilian clothes who didn't seem to understand what was happening.

"Magnus is likely to be called up as well," I commented as the truck roared past. "Do you think he will let us know?"

"I have no idea," Agneta muttered.

The police station was calm. The clatter of a typewriter came to us through the open windows. The day promised to be warm.

"The last time I was here, the inspector in charge thought he had located the arsonist," Agneta volunteered as we walked up the steps. "He was mistaken, but it was a very stressful experience. Fortunately, we have had no contact with the police since that time."

I opened the door for her. "And for that very reason they will believe what we have to say."

We walked up to the front desk. The duty officer was a squat policeman with sparse reddish-blond hair and a mustache. His uniform was fairly rumpled.

"We want to report a missing person," Agneta told him. "It concerns my son."

The policeman grinned. "Aha—fellow made himself scarce when he got his draft notice?"

Agneta turned to me for help.

"Not at all," I intervened. "My cousin disappeared in late February. He told us he was going to Norway, but we have received no news since. So naturally we are concerned."

The officer gave us a skeptical look. "You're telling me it's not because he was called up? You know, if it was, the military police will go after him."

"My son has committed no crime," Agneta asserted firmly. "And to prevent the military police from being called in unnecessarily, I am reporting him missing. Despite my sincere desire to cooperate, I cannot tell you where he is."

I saw we hadn't convinced the officer. He probably suspected we were hiding Ingmar somewhere. But why would we turn to the police if that was so? My heart hammered against my ribs. I was furious. How dare he assume such a thing?

"Listen to me, Officer," I said. "The Lejongård family has never feared combat. Maybe you're not familiar with Lion Hall history, but the king awarded our family the estate in recognition of our support in the wars. The Lejongårds never shirk from supporting king and country."

The officer's jaw dropped, and he looked as if he'd just been struck by lightning.

"Countess Lejongård?" a voice interrupted us. We looked around to see a tall, mustached man with gray hair crossing the reception area. The desk officer stiffened to attention.

"Inspector Hermannsson?" marveled Agneta. "What are you doing here? I thought you had retired."

"Ah, well, I suppose I'm not quite that elderly yet," he replied and offered her his hand. "I was reassigned a couple of years ago from the criminal investigation division. I'm the chief of the Kristianstad force." He turned to me. "And who is this charming young lady?"

"This is my niece, Matilda," Agneta replied. "We are here because of my son, Ingmar. Your colleague seems to assume he is hiding out to avoid conscription. In fact, he disappeared in Norway some months ago."

"That is terribly unfortunate!" the inspector said. "Especially now, in these difficult times. You must be worrying yourselves sick."

"I certainly am," she said, with a dark glance at me. "And now we've received his conscription notice from the military authorities. I have no wish for my son to be written down as a deserter."

"That, I believe, we can take care of. Would you ladies be so kind as to step this way?"

He accompanied us to his office and offered us coffee. It was a thin brew—for which he apologized, commenting that rationing had also affected the police.

He took down the details of Ingmar's disappearance and promised the force would do its best to locate him. "You might have come to us earlier."

"We thought he would contact us any day," I replied. "My cousin is anything but thoughtless, and it is quite unlike him to cause his parents to worry."

The inspector studied me. Was he trying to decide if I was being honest? He looked down at his notes.

Agneta was smiling as we stepped out of the station. She stopped and turned to me. "Thank you."

"Why?"

"Because you said *we* when you told that officer who we are. You stood up for your family, even though we treated you so badly."

Her words took my breath away for a moment, then I returned her smile. "Sometimes it's only the present that counts, isn't it?"

Agneta nodded, and we went back to the car.

"Why was the inspector giving me such a strange look?"

"I am sure he was surprised to hear my son had a cousin. He may well have been wondering whose child you are."

"Lennard has a sister, though, and she has children my age. It shouldn't be so surprising."

"No, but I suspect that he noticed the resemblance to your father. Hendrik was well known in the region. And even if Hermannsson never met him personally, there is no doubt you are a Lejongård. No one could deny it."

I looked into the rearview mirror, pretending to adjust it while studying my own face. All I could see were the features I shared with my mother. I wasn't familiar with the appearance of the man who'd engendered me. I hadn't been interested, for Sigurd Wallin was my father.

Perhaps I should ask Agneta for a photo of Hendrik.

49

May wore on and June would be upon us soon. We hadn't had time to plan for midsummer because of all the work in the barns and elsewhere.

"Oh, my dear, how could we have neglected preparations?" exclaimed Agneta.

"Well, these are times of war, despite the fact that they've lifted some of the blackout restrictions." I was vexed with myself. Not because of the celebration, but because I'd naïvely supposed that within a couple of weeks or months the war would no longer be a concern.

"I would cancel it if I could," said Agneta. "The year when my father and Hendrik died, I wanted to do that, but my mother would not hear of it. She said it was our duty to show our faces to society."

"Why not?"

"What do you mean?"

"Why not skip the festivities this year? You know the effects rationing has had. We are allotted more than an ordinary household, but not enough for a gala ball. And the king won't be coming."

Agneta's lips tightened. It still greatly upset her that the royal family had distanced itself from us.

I had an idea. "We could still invite him," I offered. "That would be a way to maintain contact with the royal family."

"He will not come in any case," Agneta said unhappily.

"You can't be sure of that!" I pointed out. "Besides, as one of Sweden's leading families, we can decline to be affronted. It would be only polite to send an invitation. If he turns it down, we'll know where we stand. But if we don't try, we'll still be in the dark."

Agneta looked doubtful, but at last she nodded. "Very well. We will send His Majesty an invitation."

"As if nothing has changed," I added. "Who knows? Perhaps a shot or two of aquavit will clear things up."

"The king is not particularly fond of alcohol," Agneta objected, but there was a trace of hope in her expression.

Agneta prepared the invitation herself. She took her finest stationery, and I was amazed by her beautiful calligraphy. But her hands were trembling when she slid the letter into its envelope.

I gave her an encouraging nod. "This is the right thing to do. We are not begging; we are simply showing the palace that our relations with the royal family are not affected by commercial matters."

"And when he does not accept?"

"Then we will have lost nothing while showing how magnanimous we are." I took the envelope from her, for I didn't want to give her time to reconsider. "Now we should turn our attention to the rest of the invitations." It was a tactic to distract her. I pointed to the address book. "We should cut the guest list a bit, since otherwise it will be too much for Svea to handle. We should probably omit those whose estates are very distant from here."

"But they will notice they have not been included."

"What does that matter? They are facing the same difficulties in sustaining their operations. Now that the Germans have taken control of both the Netherlands and Belgium, no one is likely to blame us for our political stance." I paused. "We will invite our business partners, of course, close neighbors, and people from the village. A simple buffet is appropriate for times of austerity, and we will hire the fiddler instead of a band of musicians. We can suggest a long promenade to tour the estate and pass the time. That will tire our guests, and they will not need as many jiggers of aquavit."

"I am afraid that the aquavit is the principal reason they come. A bit of inebriation does wonders in these dreadful times." Agneta pondered, then nodded. "All right. We will have a midsummer celebration but keep it as small as possible, essentially us and the villagers. My so-called friends have not rallied around Lennard in his deteriorating condition, so I see no need to invite them."

"I will ride to the village and make arrangements with the innkeeper."

The weeks passed. Response after response dropped into our mailbox. Many RSVPs were positive; a few begged off, citing business difficulties or problems at their estates. None mentioned royal disfavor, but Agneta was convinced it was a factor. She was deeply upset.

There was no word from the palace.

"You see?" she cried after we'd sorted through the responses and turned our attention to seating charts. "He is not coming. He is ignoring us. And so is his family!"

"Perhaps the letter wasn't given to him."

"Perhaps he has banned us from all contact!" Agneta was terribly frustrated. "If only I could speak to him! I should have gone to the palace immediately."

"And risked being turned away at the gate?" I shook my head. "No, you handled it exactly right. I know—from my time at the hotel—that business partners can change their minds. The Grand was not at all pleased when they were told that the Nobel Prize banquet wouldn't be held there anymore. Nothing could be done. But there were other related events, and many participants booked rooms with us."

"Our situation is completely different!"

A knock at the door interrupted us.

"Come in!" called Agneta.

"Gracious lady, you wished to be informed as soon as the mail arrived," Lena explained as she entered with letters on a silver tray. One was in a particularly elegant envelope. Agneta picked that one up with a shiver of apprehension.

"Thank you, Lena," she said. The maid curtsied and went out.

Agneta grabbed the letter opener and slit open the envelope. Her hands shook as she extracted the contents. She turned pale.

"What is it?" I asked and got to my feet.

Agneta said nothing. She shook her head, more and more vehemently.

"Agneta?" I went to her. Before I could lean over her shoulder to read, she thrust it at me. The letterhead displayed the royal coat of arms.

"Here! Read it for yourself!"

"*Heartfelt thanks for your invitation,*" I read aloud. "*'Unfortunately, the royal family is unable, because of other commitments—*" I broke off. "He's not coming."

"What did I tell you?" Agneta cried. "The Bernadottes have banished us."

I looked down at the letter. Its neutral phrasing gave no hint of an underlying reason.

"At least they answered." I was just as disappointed, but it was better to know than to founder in uncertainty. "They are not ignoring us entirely."

"They are completely indifferent to us!" Agneta raged. "But what do I care? Let them be that way! We will get through all this!"

I stepped forward and took her into my arms. She fought against it for a moment but then gave in.

"Don't worry about this, Agneta! All right, the king is not coming. We will try again later. We will try every year, and eventually he will accept. And besides, we have far more important things to do than worry about the royals. And with all the changes you and I have made, the estates are no longer in immediate danger."

Agneta seemed about to dispute that, but stopped, considered, and then nodded. "You are right. And, to tell the truth, I would have much preferred to receive a letter from Ingmar."

"I feel the same," I assured her and felt a stirring of grief and worry. Ingmar needed no invitation, after all; he knew very well when the celebration would take place. Would he ever appear and relieve us of at least part of our burden?

Despite the regrets from the palace, that year's midsummer celebration was one of the loveliest ever. The sun had long passed its zenith when we set out en masse on our promenade. There were about a hundred of us, and we filled the meadows with song. Agneta and I walked on either side of Lennard, for he'd insisted on coming. The sunlight's benevolent glow bestowed so much energy upon him that he had no problem completing the circuit.

Women from the village brought cakes and roast chickens, and the fishmonger provided pickled herring. I'd joined the maids in decorating the maypole, and instead of renting a bandstand and folding chairs from Kristianstad, we set out furniture from the manor. And there we sat with the villagers, maids alongside peasant farmers, farmwives at our sides, all toasting one another and enjoying the wonderful sunny summer evening. For this extraordinary occasion, Lennard was permitted to have a regular meal, which clearly pleased him. The European war seemed very far away.

Ingmar's absence was the only thing that cast a shadow on the celebration. Agneta and I had hoped he would surprise us, but there was no sign of him, no matter how often we peered down the drive. But the aquavit dulled our senses, and the meal left us feeling sated.

After the festivities ended and the guests set out for home, I sat quietly with Agneta in the pavilion for a while in the glow of the blackout lamp.

"I have something for you," she said suddenly. She handed me a small object that turned out to be a locket.

I snapped it open and saw a photograph of a young man who closely resembled Agneta. It took a moment for me to realize who it was. "This must be your brother!"

"Your father. Yes. He gave me that locket. I found it when I was cleaning out a drawer."

"Thank you." I peered at the photo. He was very good-looking. "Why did you never paint a portrait of your brother? You enshrined your parents in portraits after their deaths, but not your brother."

"I never painted him because I could not bear to do so." She picked up her little glass and tossed back the remaining aquavit. "The last sight I had of him was when he was in the hospital, wrapped in bandages. And I had not seen him for months before that. It was almost as if I was afraid to remember him as he had been before that terrible accident. Anyway, I do not think I could bear seeing his portrait in the hall every time I take the stairs. On the other hand, I have no trouble meeting my parents' eyes."

I ran my thumb lightly over the likeness. "It is a terrible shame I never had the chance to know him."

"Yes, a great shame. He would have loved you very much. You and your mother. He would have faced scorn and harsh criticism, but Hendrik would certainly have had his own way. And look how the world has changed. The day will come when no one worries about who marries whom. Perhaps someday a Swedish king will wed a commoner. Who knows?"

"Thank you," I said again. "Thank you for the portrait. I'm grateful for a glimpse of my real father."

Agneta nodded. Her eyes glistened, but she wasn't weeping; she was smiling.

I felt a little tipsy when I went to my room later, though still clear-headed enough to go to my desk. I pulled the drawer open and placed the locket next to the lighter. Those sacred souvenirs of my fathers shimmered golden in the lamplight. Both had belonged to men whose lives had ended too soon.

I would honor them both for the rest of my life.

50

Since there was no prospect of a royal visit, shortly after midsummer Lennard suggested over dinner that we take a few days at our vacation house in Åhus. I was looking forward to fresh sea breezes after the nearly three months I'd been cooped up at Lion Hall.

Agneta wasn't enthusiastic. "Are you sure you are strong enough for the trip?"

"I feel better than ever! And I would so much like to contemplate the sea again. I have not been there since this illness struck, and by now our beach home is probably beginning to fall apart. We should use and enjoy the place where our love really began."

Tears filled Agneta's eyes. She reached out and took his hand. The two had never been reluctant to show their affection, but his declaration and her gesture moved me so much that I had to fight back tears too.

"Let's do it!" I said. "Preparation will not take long. I can drive us to Åhus, and we will not take much luggage. No need for formal wear or servants. I can take care of whatever needs doing at the beach house."

Agneta turned to me. I read deep concern for her husband in her expression.

"Listen to Matilda!" Lennard said. "We will enjoy it, just the three of us. She has earned a bit of vacation and so have we. Let us take advantage of the summer . . ."

Agneta nodded and bowed her head. She must have noticed, as I had, that he hadn't completed his sentence. *Let us take advantage of the summer* . . . while we still have the chance. Beauty was still out there, and no one could predict what the rest of the year would bring.

"All right then," she said. "We will spend a week at Åhus. But you must promise me to tell me if you are unwell."

Lennard raised her hand to his lips and kissed it. "I promise."

He beamed at me, looking happier than he had in a long time.

Agneta had been determined to take no staff, but she had doubts once we began packing.

"Perhaps Lena should come," she said as she went down the packing list. "You will not be able to do everything alone."

"What is there to do? The housekeeping doesn't have to be perfect, since we won't be receiving guests. And besides, the maids are needed here on the estate. Mr. Broderson has a higher opinion of them than he does of his lads. We will not be on public view; we can stroll on the beach and enjoy the water. Times have changed."

Agneta nodded. "Indeed, they have. If I had ever told my mother we would be traveling without servants, she would have hit the ceiling."

"It will be lovely at the seaside. You and I can care for Lennard. And considering the Stockholm tales you told me, you know quite well how to get along without servants."

"That is true. When I think of my wretched little box of an apartment in Stockholm . . ." She took on a dreamy look. "I did not care, back in those days. The cracked ceiling, a broken window—none of it bothered me. I cooked my own simple meals, painted, and joined the women for demonstrations. My life was almost ordinary."

"Well, then we will have no trouble at the beach house. It's only for a week. The estate can do without us for that long. And we will be reinvigorated when we return."

Despite my brave words, I felt a pang as we said goodbye to Lena and the others. I was sure they'd continue their good work and wouldn't begrudge us the time away, for we'd been toiling just as hard as they had, but I had a queasy feeling that something unpredictable might happen during our week away. How would we cope if it did? Åhus wasn't so far away, but even so . . .

I couldn't put my finger on what was bothering me. That vague premonition made me profoundly uneasy.

The drive to Åhus lifted my spirits. Maybe my misgivings had arisen simply because we'd be out of direct touch with the estate. How strange it was that I'd fled from Lion Hall twice, and now I was afraid to leave!

The beach house was built of wood and stone. Its whitewash hadn't stood up particularly well to the weather, but the timbers still looked sound. The rear veranda looked out over the small stone jetty to the sea. The rush of the Baltic waves enchanted me. I closed my eyes, savoring the shrill calls of seagulls alarmed by our presence.

"I believe I will take a short nap," Lennard announced. He hadn't fared as well on the drive as he'd expected.

"I will join you," Agneta said as she untied the bow that secured her hat. "Once our finances improve a bit more, we should purchase a new automobile. This one's springs have given up. Every bone in my body seems to have rattled loose." She looked at me. "You, on the other hand, do not appear fatigued at all."

I shook my head. I felt wonderful. The crash of waves and the salty sea air infused me with new energy and a pleasant exhilaration I'd sorely missed. "I think I will take a stroll," I said. "Then I will unpack and see if there is anything usable in the pantry." Svea had packed an enormous picnic basket for us, but it wasn't enough for the whole week.

"Go ahead, but be careful!" Agneta admonished, as if I were a little girl. What could possibly happen to me here? I nodded anyway as I left the house.

My afternoon walks during our time in Åhus became a regular habit. So did Lennard and Agneta's afternoon naps.

The estate was perpetually on my mind, but I enjoyed our time away. Everything here was peaceful. Blackout regulations were in force, but our beach house had good, stout shutters.

The days were long and full of light. I wandered the beach in the sunshine, and the waves surged at my feet. It would be simple for German pilots to spot us, given the many hours of daylight. Why did the authorities assume they would come by night? To elude antiaircraft fire?

I skirted a cove where driftwood had piled up. A clump of trees stood nearby. This had become my own special place. I doubted any other vacationers were in the area. If so, they'd mostly be women. The war seemed very far away.

But today the sound of a snapping twig brought me out of my reverie. I looked around and saw a man emerge from the wood and walk directly toward me. I sprang to my feet. Had he been lurking in the bushes? What did he want?

Then I recognized his hair color and gait.

"Ingmar!" I gasped. "Whatever are you doing here?"

"Shh!" he said, putting a finger to his lips. "Matilda, listen, I need your help."

"Help? With what? How long have you been back in Sweden? Are you in trouble?"

"Well, in point of fact, yes, I am, but not the way you probably think." He looked about as if he was afraid of being spotted. "I joined the Norwegian resistance movement. My friends and a lot of others are organizing to fight the Germans."

I shook my head. This couldn't be true!

"How did you get to Åhus?" was the first thing that came out of my mouth. My other thoughts were too confused to put into words.

"Your friend spoke to me. That Paul fellow."

"He found you!"

"No, we met by pure chance. He contacted one of my friends because he wanted to evacuate his wife to someplace safe. When we saw each other . . . well, you can imagine my surprise. He was terrifically excited and showed me the letter you wrote. He hadn't been able to locate me, but there really was no way he could have."

This was too much to take in. Paul's wife was in danger. Was Ingmar here because of her? And what in hell was he doing in the Norwegian resistance?

He grabbed my hand, his expression terribly earnest. "We need help. A safe place to shelter refugees in Sweden. Jews, Norwegians, people being persecuted by the fascists. Conditions in Norway are atrocious. We need somewhere to lodge them, and I suggested Lion Hall. I thought you could help transport people there. Especially since Paul and his wife are with them. Surely you'll help us?"

I stared at him, shocked. "You want to send us refugees?"

"Yes, if no one objects. We would put them on boats and then transfer them out at sea. We have already recruited a number of fishermen."

"But—that's dangerous!" I didn't know what else to say. "Not for us, but for you and your friends and the refugees. The Germans are certain to be monitoring ship movements."

"Of course, but we're careful. All I need is agreement we can land in Sweden and turn the people over to you."

I didn't know what Agneta would say. "Why don't you ask your mother directly?" I exclaimed. "She's over there in the beach house. I have no authority in estate matters."

Ingmar shook his head. "Not possible. She wouldn't let me leave. But I have to, Matilda, I simply must. I cannot sit idly by and watch what is going on there. The same thing might happen here, quicker than you think."

My head spun. "That's admirable of you, but what about your mother? What about Lion Hall and the Ekberg estate? You're putting yourself in danger!"

"I know, but this is more important than me. Or any of us. Anyway, my brother is still in Sweden."

"Your brother doesn't give a damn about the estate! I went to see him, and you can imagine his reaction. I have the impression he despises even you!"

My voice had gotten shrill. I told myself to calm down. I had to convince Ingmar to give up this insane project, no matter how noble his goals were.

His face contorted. He looked down, and when he finally raised his head, his eyes were suspiciously red. "He is angry because of what we learned. It turns out that Lennard is not our true father."

"I know," I replied. "Agneta told me. And she said you quarreled."

"Did we ever!" snorted Ingmar bitterly. "First the two of us quarreled with Mother, then I fell out with Magnus. That fool was so incredibly stupid that he went out to find that brute—and then claimed we'd have been much better off if we'd grown up with the cad. It was more than I could take."

"Why didn't you write me?"

"I didn't want to upset you, after all you'd gone through with us."

"There was no reason for you to hold back. I could have helped. I know exactly how it feels." I heaved a sigh. "Agneta has a special talent for keeping deep secrets."

"Yes. There is no doubt about that." Ingmar rubbed a tear from the corner of his eye. "It looks like you've forgiven her."

I shook my head. "No, not really. But I finally realized that I love Lion Hall more than I used to think. And I cannot leave Agneta to take care of Lennard all alone. You have no idea how we have suffered. His health has been failing—" I stopped and seized his hand. "But won't you stop long enough to see them? Your mother is still your mother, no matter what happened, and Lennard has been a good father, hasn't he? That's all that really counts."

I recalled how I'd stood at the bridge railing, clutching my father's lighter, and I remembered the woman who'd thought I was about to throw myself into the water.

"You're right, but I can't," he replied. "I have to focus on my duties. I can't allow either love or sympathy to distract me. Can you understand that?"

"Honestly, I find it difficult. But it seems I have no choice."

He stood looking at me for a moment. "I have to go. The ship in Gothenburg won't wait. Here." He pulled an envelope from his pocket and gave it to me.

"I hope this is a letter to Agneta."

"It is. I try to explain things as best I can. And there is an address inside that you can write to after you talk to Mother about the refugees. Our contact there will pass everything along immediately. Please reply as soon as possible, all right?"

"I will." I hugged him. "Ingmar, promise me you'll be careful. And promise you'll contact us from time to time. It's not only your mother who wants to know how you are. I need to know as well."

Ingmar nodded, then leaned over and planted a kiss on my cheek. "You take care as well, cousin!"

"And you too! You, especially!"

I was tempted to follow him but held back. He disappeared through the trees, a motorcycle engine roared to life, and the sound quickly faded into the distance. God only knew when I would see him again.

I needed a while to get myself together to return to the house. The envelope in my hand was as heavy as a stone, and Ingmar's words blazed in my mind. He'd joined the resistance; Paul and his wife had to flee the fascists; they all needed our help; and Ingmar wanted Lion Hall to house refugees.

I tucked the envelope inside my blouse and stared out at the sea. Then I returned to the beach house.

The bedroom was still quiet. I could have awakened Agneta and Lennard, but why? Ingmar was gone.

I went into the kitchen, which smelled of the fish I cooked there daily. I put Ingmar's letter on the table and stared at it. The first sign of life in such a long time! I should have insisted. I should have told him how much grief he'd already caused. Next time—if there was a next time—I'd do exactly that.

Time passed and at last I heard steps behind me. "Matilda?" Agneta asked. "I thought you were going to take a long walk."

"I did," I told her. "However, this time I met someone out there."

Agneta's eyes widened. "Someone accosted you?"

"No, I'm perfectly all right. It was Ingmar. He came out of the woods."

"Ingmar—" She clapped a hand over her mouth.

"He's fine. He didn't have much time, but he gave me this letter."

"And you did not stop him from leaving?" she asked, suppressing a sob and going to the table.

"He could not stay. I tried to convince him to come speak to you, but he was in a terrible hurry."

Her lips quivered. "He is still furious with me."

"No, it's not that. He has joined the Norwegian resistance."

Agneta's eyes opened wide. "That cannot be! He—he must have been joking."

I shook my head. "No, he was deadly serious. And he asked for help. But shouldn't we read the letter? I can get Lennard . . ."

"No, let him sleep. Who knows what is in that envelope? I do not want to disturb him any more than necessary."

"All right, then; I suggest you have a seat and I will read it out loud."

We took our places at the kitchen table. I fumbled with the envelope and got it open. Ingmar's handwriting suggested he'd been rushed; perhaps he'd written it at sea.

Dear Mother, dear Father,

I can well imagine how worried you are at this time. The news you have received must be very alarming. And I cannot deny that conditions in Norway are frightful. The Germans swept into control of the country, and it is shocking how many sympathizers they found here. Soldiers patrol the streets day and night.

I went to Oslo to help my friends, both Norwegian, who have been active in the underground. What shocked the whole world was for us only one more link in the chain of events my comrades had been monitoring for some time. They were not at all surprised by the German attack. Norway's National Unity Party had already met secretly with the Germans in December to coordinate plans for the takeover.

Many people in Norway are now threatened by the same despicable policies the Nazis instituted in Germany. Members of opposition parties, communists, reporters, Jews, and many opposed to the regime are being rounded up. The aim is to break the back of the opposition. It is only a question of time before they resort to wholesale murder.

But do not worry—there are many of us and we are extremely careful. We are currently improving our organization. I am part of Civorg, the civilian branch of our alliance. Over the past months I qualified as a pilot—not in fighter planes but in civilian transport aircraft. There are various resistance groups in the far north of Norway that need to be supplied.

We are also setting up escape routes to Sweden.

That is why I am appealing to you. We are sure we can transport refugees to the Swedish coast, but they need some place to shelter. We have obtained the consent of some towns and estates, and I want to ask if you too are willing to take in people who are in danger in Norway.

I know this request will shock you, but assistance is absolutely vital. We cannot stand by and abandon these people. The Jews, in particular, are being persecuted by the new rulers. You certainly recall Miss Grün, who worked for us; her people desperately need your help.

I beg you to take them in. I enclose a forwarding address you can use.

I promise I will get back in contact as soon as I can. Until then, please stay as healthy as possible and do not worry about me. I have many friends here; we are like family. If all goes well, we will soon drive the Germans out, and then I will come back to you.

With love,

Your son Ingmar

I was glad we hadn't immediately shared the letter with Lennard. Ingmar's news was terrifying. Even worse for them was the revelation he'd decided to collaborate with the resistance. I knew him; his temperament was anything but violent. If the Nazis captured him, they'd probably execute him on the spot.

Agneta was as rigid as a pillar of salt. She sat silent for minutes on end, as if needing that time to digest Ingmar's words.

"We will tell Lennard none of this," she finally decided.

"But, Agneta, we must. At least that he was here and has joined the resistance. The details are not important, but Lennard must understand the big picture."

I took a deep breath. Agneta's instinctive response to bad news was to conceal it, that was clear, but she must be aware by now how much damage that reaction had caused in the past.

She nodded at last. "Very well. You may tell him. But be gentle. I want to upset him as little as possible."

"Ingmar will be careful. And after all, shouldn't we be proud of him? Just imagine, in a couple of months, when the war is over, he'll be able to tell us about his adventures."

Agneta looked at me unhappily. For a moment I glimpsed in her face the listlessness that had afflicted her when she couldn't get out of bed. *Not again!* I prayed.

But her voice was firm. "Let us go to Lennard. Perhaps he will share your opinion. You two have been considerably more optimistic than I recently, and perhaps I should follow your example."

Lennard was just as surprised and shaken as we'd been. He wished Ingmar had come in to see them, but he was clearly relieved to have an address by which to reach his son.

"We cannot write to him all the time, but they will certainly deliver personal letters," I said. "At least, as long as we avoid overburdening them."

"Then we should write as soon as possible," Lennard replied. To Agneta, he said, "Surely you will not object to taking in refugees. The old place could do with a bit of livening up."

Agneta hesitated. She was probably trying to decide how we could explain the new arrivals. "No," she said at last, "I have no objections. Let us write and tell them to come."

I did exactly that as soon as we got back to Lion Hall that weekend. I wrote to the contact to say we were very pleased by Ingmar's suggestion—carefully leaving out what that was—and included a long letter from Agneta and Lennard. I took the correspondence to the post office, silently praying that someday Ingmar would return safe and sound.

The news that we'd heard from Ingmar reassured everyone. Though there was no expectation he would return soon, a new light shone on the manor. Hope had returned.

But the opposite seemed to be the case with Agneta and Lennard. They were relieved, but now they had immense new worries. Helping refugees was a risky undertaking. If the Germans caught Ingmar at it, the fact that he was Swedish would mean nothing. Maybe Ingmar wouldn't even declare his nationality, out of fear for his native land. But his parents stuck to their promise to help.

One afternoon in September I accompanied Agneta on an inspection of the manor to decide where refugees could be housed. We did not know when they might arrive, but it was best to be prepared well in advance.

"This is quite odd," Agneta commented as we visited the guest rooms. Since we'd had so many fewer guests, the servants had covered the furniture. The mattresses were folded up and shrouded with sheets, just as in my parents' house. Maybe I should go to Stockholm and tidy up there as well? Surely dust lay thick over everything in the house on Brännkyrka Street.

"What is odd?" I prompted.

"All these rooms. They seem so superfluous now. Where did noble families get the notion of constructing their houses with so many rooms?"

"Well, because of the balls and other formal events, I assume."

Agneta shook her head. "No, it could not have been for that alone. Even in my parents' time, these rooms were never all needed. I assume it was a question of maintaining a huge mansion, so as to impress the neighbors. A question of prestige."

"The manors may have functioned as fortified castles," I speculated. "Our history teacher told us that in wartime they provided refuge for the local people. Feudal lords couldn't afford to lose the very people who supported them through food production and taxes. That was why the lords built those thick walls. The Vikings did the same, when they hid their women and children away in their great communal halls."

Agneta smiled. "At least your explanation is more democratic. Perhaps the spirits of knights and Vikings lived on in our family."

"And now we have the opportunity to shelter people in this huge residence once more. I'm very glad you two agreed to do so."

"Well, I fear it was not entirely unselfish," Agneta said. "A mansion like this is simply too big for three persons. It must be lived in, or it begins to fall apart. And besides, I am hoping Ingmar will accompany the refugees. I hope we can finally have a heart-to-heart."

I gently laid a hand on her arm. "I am sure you will have the opportunity."

We sat looking at one another in silence for a while, then she nodded and put a hand to a bedpost. "Fine, well, we can lodge two, perhaps three, persons in this room if we bring in another bed, right?"

"Yes, we can put up a small family here. And the larger rooms can accommodate four."

"We should draw up a chart. When we receive news of their arrival date, we will uncover the furniture and give the rooms a scrubbing. Perhaps we could use old sheets to manufacture bandages."

"That's a very good idea." I made a mental note to ask the hospital for medical supplies, since no one knew in what condition the refugees might be upon their arrival.

51

We continued preparing into November, collecting beds and mattresses as well as clothing and other supplies.

We hoped every day for news, but Ingmar's network didn't contact us. Agneta began to fret that plans had changed, but I urged her to be patient. Now that the damp and cold of winter were encroaching, transport would be that much more difficult. And the radio brought more disturbing news almost every day.

Christmas was a time of tension. Agneta grumbled about Ingmar's failure to write, and I had my hands full distracting her and trying to fend off depression. Lennard's condition worsened, but he did his best to hide it. The two of us orbited around Agneta like planets around a sun that threatened to go out at any moment.

In January 1941, Ingmar wrote us an encrypted letter that I decoded with the help of a key the contact person had provided. We felt like characters out of a detective novel in the Lion Hall library.

Everything is set. I have fifty travelers for you, sailing to Gothenburg. Estimated arrival February 17.

Gothenburg. But that was on the far northwest coast! Why couldn't they simply sail down the west coast, past Denmark, and around the south? They could offload at Åhus, which was much closer to Lion Hall.

The answer was simple, of course: Sweden had mined its Baltic coast. That had been in the news quite a while earlier. The Germans would pay dearly if they got any stupid notions about a naval attack.

But the question remained—how could I transport the travelers, fifty refugees of all ages, the 170 miles to Lion Hall? Putting them up on the estate would be simple; we'd made all the necessary arrangements. But transportation from Gothenburg posed a huge problem. Our car could accommodate five persons at most. I didn't dare ask the Swedish military for help.

I remembered the encounter with my old classmate. Birgitta had two delivery trucks. Maybe she would loan them to us. I knew what a kind heart she had. Certainly she couldn't refuse!

I set out for Kristianstad that same day. Her employees were quite surprised to see our venerable roadster chug into the yard behind their buildings. They gathered at the windows as if witnessing a royal procession.

I pretended not to notice as I got out and went to the office. News of my arrival had spread fast, so Birgitta herself was already at the back door.

"Tell me, dear, why are you getting my employees so excited?" she exclaimed with a smile and embraced me.

I'd considered telephoning to let her know I was coming, but I'd decided it would be better to broach the subject face-to-face.

"I didn't think an automobile would cause such excitement. Your people must not be used to seeing a woman driver."

"That's not it. It's the car! It's a museum piece."

"It's still quite reliable!" I protested. "In times like this we have to use whatever resources we have, you know." I paused for a second. "That's why I'm here."

Birgitta's finely plucked eyebrows rose. With her beautifully waved hair, she had the air of a film star. "This sounds like business."

"Not at all. But I need your help. Desperately."

"Let's go to the office. Would you like a coffee? Martha can prepare one for us. I don't have much left because of rationing, but we can treat ourselves in honor of your visit."

"Thanks, that would be lovely."

I'd thought chaos reigned in the Lion Hall office, but that paled in comparison with my former classmate's workspace.

"The end-of-year inventory," she said apologetically, as she quickly removed tall piles of folders from the armchairs. "We should have finished it long ago, but my husband was called up. Running the business alone is a terrible burden; I hope the war will end soon. I almost don't care who wins, just so long as we're left in peace."

I settled into one of the high-backed chairs. Birgitta's assistant appeared right away with a tray, a porcelain coffeepot, and matching cups. The unfamiliar smell of pure coffee did me good.

"Thank you, Martha." Birgitta dismissed her and took the seat opposite me. "So—what brings you to me?"

"I wanted to ask you to loan me your delivery trucks for a couple of days."

Her astonishment was obvious. "My trucks?"

I nodded. "I promised to help Ingmar, and you're the only person I know who still possesses the vehicles to make it possible."

"Ingmar, the one who didn't want to go out with me?" she commented with a hint of sarcasm.

"He's helping evacuate refugees from Norway. We need to transport them from the port to our estate, but we don't have the means. We cannot ask them to walk in winter weather; besides, there will probably be children among them."

"How long will you need the trucks?"

"Four days," I answered. "Maybe five."

"That's a long time." Birgitta frowned.

"Yes. But you will be helping these people enormously. I don't have anywhere else to turn. Most firms have had to give up their vehicles to the military."

Birgitta studied me for a moment. She took a lighter and cigarette case from her skirt pocket.

"I use the trucks only when we have no other choice," she said. "Fuel is rationed, probably so the soldiers can go gallivanting who knows where."

"Birgitta," I said, "you know they're defending Sweden."

"It's a total waste of money, if you ask me," she said, lighting a cigarette with some difficulty. "Even these things are rationed. I can't even find enough to feed my habit."

"Then you'd better give up smoking," I suggested lightly, but then got serious again. "Please, Birgitta, help us! Nothing will happen to your vehicles, I swear. All I need is two drivers. We'll pay them and bring the vehicles back with full tanks. I'll pay to lease them, if necessary."

Birgitta blew smoke into the air and thought it over. "Well, I can't make the decision on my own. I have to consult my husband. And he'll probably be able to tell me whether the Germans might get wind of this."

"He will?"

"Karl does business with them."

"With the Germans?" I stared, astounded. Had I endangered Ingmar by coming to Birgitta? "I really doubt they'll hear of it. And these people are in terrible danger in Norway."

"Communists and Jews, I assume."

"Perhaps. But we're in Sweden. Why would the Germans care if we take them in? They haven't declared war on the United States over the Jews who emigrated there."

"Not yet. But if the Germans take over here, Karl's prospects will be compromised if we've helped Jews."

I shook my head. "You cannot be serious!" I cried. "Jews are human beings just like the rest of us. They have a different faith, but their blood is just as red as ours. If they ask for asylum, it's our Christian duty to help them."

"Since when have you been religious?"

That did it; I was tempted to storm out of her office. Not only because they were doing business with the Germans; she and her husband were positioning themselves to profit from a German occupation. "Are you going to help me?"

She gave me a long look. "I'd be happy to, if it was up to me. But if conditions change . . ."

"It seems to me your husband is in the army to make sure they don't," I pointed out. "I'm talking about only five days. Five days, during which you probably won't need to make any deliveries anyhow. It's not up to me to comment on any business you may have with Germany, but please don't forget your humanity. Wouldn't you want someone to pick you up in a vehicle if you were stranded somewhere, penniless? Wouldn't you pray for help? And don't imagine business connections would keep you safe. These Norwegians have lost everything! Their acquaintances were no use at all. Who knows what the Germans will do to us if they invade? We'll need help then too."

A deep silence settled over the office. Birgitta took another nervous pull on her cigarette. "Like I said, I have to consult Karl." Bitter disappointment sank into my soul. "But I will talk to him about it. That's a promise."

"Thank you."

The ensuing silence was uncomfortable for both of us. *Coming here was a mistake. And I need to leave now.* I could only hope that Birgitta's husband wouldn't betray the refugees to the Germans.

"Wait," Birgitta said, as if this discussion hadn't just taken place. "Stay with me for a while."

But I shook my head. "I cannot. I have to go back and try to work out our options if your husband doesn't agree. Take care!"

I left but had to pause for a moment outside to calm myself. I shut my eyes and breathed deep. How could I have been so wrong about my classmate?

Feeling the employees' eyes on me, I pulled myself together and walked as casually as possible to my car. I would have plenty of time to curse and accuse myself aloud once I was back on the road.

I spent the following two days terribly worried, obsessed by the fear that Birgitta's husband would inform the Germans of our plans.

On the third day, as Agneta, Lennard, and I were listening to the evening news, there was a loud knock downstairs. I looked up in alarm. Who could possibly be calling at that late hour?

A few moments later Rika brought up a letter on a silver tray. "A messenger boy delivered this for you, Miss Matilda."

A messenger? From the telegraph office?

"Thank you, Rika," I said as I turned the envelope over. My name and Lion Hall were the only words written there. Was this another encrypted message from Ingmar's people? Or something more threatening?

My fingers trembled as I ripped it open.

The sheet of stationery was stiff. My heart pounded as I unfolded it. I held my breath.

> *Dear Matilda,*
> *You will have your vehicles. Karl agreed. I will provide the drivers and cover the costs. Perhaps it is time now to show a little patriotism. Simply let us know what date you need them and everything will be ready.*
> *Best wishes,*
> *Birgitta*

I heaved a sigh of relief.

"What is it?" Lennard asked. "Good news?"

"Yes," I told him. "Birgitta is loaning us her trucks. I still cannot be certain the Germans will not learn of it, but this is a huge step forward."

"How can someone possibly do business with the enemy?" Agneta exclaimed, shaking her head.

"Technically, the Germans are not our enemies. Not yet."

"They are enemies of the whole world, it seems to me. But you seem to have persuaded Birgitta at least."

"Let's hope so," I said and shoved the letter back into the envelope.

52

We got underway very early in the morning. I drove ahead in the old automobile and Birgitta's two trucks followed. We'd spent the whole night making the cargo areas as comfortable for passengers as possible. It had been a difficult task, but blankets from Birgitta's warehouse would warm any travelers suffering from the chill of sea air.

We drove with few interruptions and stopped at a small inn for the night. I bought dinner and rented rooms for all. We got back on the road early the following morning.

I wondered if Ingmar would be with them. The letter hadn't mentioned him, probably because they wanted to avoid revealing too much. I was hopeful, nevertheless. And I hoped Paul and Ingrid had made it aboard. That would reduce my worries considerably, even though I would feel guilty seeing Ingrid. I was sure Paul hadn't confessed he'd gone to bed with me. I hoped she suspected nothing.

Anyhow, the manor was vast, and it would be easy to avoid them. I'd made the firm decision not to speak to Paul any more than absolutely necessary to avoid tempting him. Or giving in to temptation myself.

We had no trouble locating the ship in Gothenburg harbor. When we rolled up in our trucks, a crowd wrapped in coarse, warm clothing huddled on the dock, flanked by several men in uniforms.

A very handsome man with Norwegian military insignia approached us. His hair was as flaxen as a young boy's, and his eyes gleamed silver gray.

He saluted me as I got out of the car. "Countess Lejongård?"

I was startled. "No, I am not the countess. My name is Matilda Wallin. I am her niece."

"Glad to meet you! I am Lieutenant Karsten Solberg, in charge of this operation." His accent was like Ingrid's.

"The pleasure is entirely mine. Did you have a good voyage?"

"In fact, it was somewhat rough," he responded with a glance behind him. "But we are back on land, so we can proclaim it a success."

"Optimism is always appropriate," I commented, which elicited a hearty laugh. "How many are they, then?"

"Sixty-three," Solberg answered. "A few more than we advised, but we wanted to leave no one behind. I hope that is not a problem."

I shook my head. "We can accommodate them all."

"Thank you for your support and the long trip you have taken. The people will be extremely grateful."

"We help where we can. Often it is not enough simply to collect clothing and blankets. We are pleased to have this opportunity."

He smiled. "You speak quite like your cousin!"

"You mean Ingmar? How is he?"

"You can ask him. He is settling business with the captain, but you can speak to him in a moment."

Ingmar was here! I almost squealed with joy.

Solberg waved toward the vehicles. "These are your transports?"

"Yes. The trucks belong to a friend. I hope they will suffice."

He squinted, considering. "Well, it will be crowded, but our passengers are used to that. Shall we begin to move them to the vehicles? Yes?"

I agreed, and the lieutenant walked toward the ship.

I followed him with my eyes and craned my neck, looking for familiar faces in the crowd. I found one at last—but it wasn't Ingmar's.

"Paul!" I called out and ran to greet him.

Paul stood motionless and put down his knapsack. He was exhausted; his eyes were dull. But he recognized me immediately. "Matilda!"

We fell into one another's arms. I didn't care if Ingrid saw. An embrace didn't mean I wanted to steal away her husband. I was shocked at how gaunt he was. His thick coat disguised it, but he was little more than skin and bones. His face was far more lined than I remembered.

"How lovely!" I said. "Where is Ingrid?"

Paul gave me an odd, fixed look, and then his face crumpled.

"What's wrong?" I cried, pulling him to me again. "What happened?"

"They shot her."

Devastated, I shook my head as if to deny it. "Shot? But why?"

"We were trying to reach Ingmar and his people, but they'd already started arresting Jews in Oslo. I was afraid; I didn't want to go out in the street. We heard shots. And then they came for Ingrid. I tried to hide her, but they tore the house apart. One of my workers had denounced her and accused her of terrible things. They dragged her out to force her into a truck. I tried to stop them, but they knocked me down. Ingrid resisted. One of them lost his temper and pulled out a pistol."

An icy chill invaded me.

"I tried to get to her, but the men pulled me away. After he shot her, one of them laughed and told me to go find a real wife. They didn't even let me take her body. *Our job is to collect all the Jews, alive or not,*' one of them said. They tossed her into their vehicle and left."

He broke down. Several of the others were watching us as he sobbed.

"I should never have left her behind!"

"You didn't! She would want you to live. She would want you to escape, no matter what."

Paul nodded.

"Good, then." I stroked his cheek. "We will talk more, but first we need to get you to safety."

I led him to the trucks, then drew my coat closer about me.

They'd shot Ingrid. I was horrified. I couldn't imagine how Paul was feeling.

Desperately I scanned the crowd again. "Ingmar!" I cried.

He turned. He'd gotten thinner but was more muscular. His eyes lit up. "Matilda! It's wonderful to see you again!"

We embraced enthusiastically, and I leaned back to look at him. "You have no idea how much we all miss you," I said. "Are you coming with us to Lion Hall?"

"Matilda . . ."

I grabbed his hand. "Your father is very ill. And your mother has been suffering for months. They were terribly disappointed when you didn't speak to them last time. You can make up for that now. Please, I beg you!"

"But my comrades and I—"

"Ingmar! Please! Visit your parents, show them you're alive and well. Just for a day, no more. We will get to Lion Hall early the day after tomorrow if we drive through the night." I held his arm. "Please! You need to do this."

Ingmar stood looking at me, rubbed his temples, then nodded. "All right. I'll talk to my comrades."

"Excellent!" I released him. "And don't try to sneak away!"

Our convoy got underway an hour later. Ingmar rode in the car with me, along with Lieutenant Solberg and another comrade. Paul had insisted on riding with the others; he refused special treatment. I understood. The refugees—women, children, some elderly folk but also some young men—were almost all Jews, and he shared their fate. He was one of them now.

"How many years have you possessed this automobile?" Solberg's question interrupted my thoughts.

"Unfortunately, I don't know. Ingmar could tell you better than I."

I glanced at my cousin, who seemed a bit embarrassed. Hadn't he told his comrades of his origins? Or that our destination, an aristocratic estate, was his ancestral home?

"Almost twenty-six years," he replied. "It's as old as I am now. It was bought just after we were born. It must have caused a lot of excitement back then. Automobiles were completely out of the ordinary."

"It's still good on the road," I put in. "And it's too old for the army to want to confiscate it."

Solberg laughed heartily.

Our convoy rolled through the Lion Hall gates the following afternoon. There'd been heavy rain, and the roads were in particularly poor condition. But even a thunderstorm couldn't dampen my spirits. We'd done it! Paul was here, and so was Ingmar. The circumstances were different from those I'd expected, but in these times we had to be grateful for every moment of happiness.

Agneta stood at the front door.

I drove up, and the other vehicles stopped on the drive. Agneta came down to meet us.

"Mother!" Ingmar exclaimed, running to her with open arms.

I held back. This was their moment, no one else's. They had a lot to say to one another.

I went to the trucks, where the refugees were starting to emerge. Most of them were staring, astonished at the imposing edifice before them. One child pointed excitedly to the sculpted lions on the facade.

Maybe the young ones would make up stories about our lions, just as Agneta had done. She'd even named two of them: Grumpy and Brother.

We took the Norwegians to their quarters. I put Paul with some younger single men. During my time at the Grand Hôtel, I'd developed a sense for compatible personalities.

As the people settled in, the maids and I got to work distributing coffee and an initial allotment of food. There would be a hot meal for dinner, but our guests were famished and shouldn't be obliged to wait that long.

I was grateful for Paul's help as an interpreter. Grief and exhaustion had taken their toll, but having something to do distracted him from his own miseries.

"Here," I said, handing him his portion, which like all the others was meticulously wrapped in fine, clean paper. "The coffee is mixed with chicory, but you get used to it after a while."

"Thank you," Paul said somewhat uncomfortably. "I'm almost ashamed I once assumed I wouldn't be welcome on this estate."

"You've always been welcome here," I said and touched his arm. "And you still are."

Paul nodded and shuddered. Silent tears shone on his cheeks. I embraced him.

"Ingrid!" he sobbed. "How can I go on living?"

"You will find a way."

"I should have died with her! I should be with her now."

"That's not true," I said and ran a hand over his shoulders. "She'd have been angry if you'd let them kill you too. You're here. And that's what counts."

Ingrid was gone. No sacrifice of his could bring her back to life.

I guided him to his bunk and made him sit. I stayed at his side until he finally calmed down.

"I dream of her every night," he said, rubbing his face. "I see her in front of me, laughing, and she holds out her hand. And there's this black, swirling mass that snatches her away. She disappears into that blackness, and I try to follow her, but I can't."

I didn't know what to say. I'd never had such dreams. He would have to endure, get through them, rise the next morning and devote himself to the day. Anything less would destroy him.

"Lie down and rest," I said gently. "And eat something! You need to regain your strength."

He fumbled for my hand and looked at me through tear-swollen eyes. "Thank you, Matilda! Thank you for everything! I should never have left you. If I'd only stayed . . ."

"Shh," I said. "Don't torment yourself. Nobody can predict what fate has in store. I'm here for you in any case. Talk to me anytime you need to. We'll have lots of time for that in days to come. Right?"

Paul nodded.

Something else occurred to me: the Ringströms could take their son in. "Should I inform your parents?"

"No. I don't want them to know. Mother would cluck around me like a mother hen; I couldn't stand that. And Father—he was against my decision to marry into a Jewish family. He always insisted she convert to our faith. We refused. I don't want to know what he'd have to say now."

I nodded. It was becoming evident that no family was as happy as it appeared.

"All right. When you feel ready, you can write to them."

"If I ever do feel ready," he echoed. That thought twisted his face in a miserable little smile.

That evening I was finally able to spend a little time with Ingmar. His friends had gone to their quarters to rest, but Ingmar wasn't ready to retire yet.

"It's fine to be home again," he said as we strolled through the dark garden. The bushes were bare except for a few evergreens; everything was decked with frost. Our breath swirled before us and drifted as spiraling mist in the dim gas lamps along the path. If the Germans happened to fly over that night, they might mistake our way for a curious little glowworm.

"Come back to stay, and it'll be like this every day."

Ingmar shook his head. "I cannot. My work in Norway is too important. I can't let my fellows down."

"But your family needs you too," I said. "Now more than ever. You saw Lennard, didn't you?"

"Yes," he said, his expression grave. "His illness seems not to have gotten any better."

"He's restricted to an almost entirely liquid diet. He has his good days, but on others he really suffers. He feels nauseated and ill, and he can't keep his porridge down. And your mother—" I weighed whether to tell him the truth.

"What's wrong with her?"

"She's subject to severe attacks of depression. We couldn't reach her at all after she heard war had broken out in Norway. The doctor gave her medication, but there's no guarantee her black mood won't come back. If it does, I'll be the only person running the affairs of both estates."

Ingmar nodded and rubbed his chin, a sign he was perplexed. "Have you heard from Magnus at all since the awful visit you mentioned to me?"

"Not a word."

Ingmar sucked breath noisily between clenched teeth. "It was really brave of you to try. Did you already know then about the incident with the man who—engendered us?"

"No. If I had, I'd never have gone to see Magnus. He says he doesn't intend to set foot on the estate until he inherits it. A lovely prospect, don't you think?"

"Magnus is an idiot."

"And that's why I'm asking you to consider coming back home. Your work in Norway is important, but Lion Hall needs you. Especially now that the refugees are here. Maybe you could set yourself up in some kind of liaison position, relaying telegrams or something . . ."

"I could, but the resistance needs me to keep flying."

I took a deep breath. *Flying!* Could there be any more dangerous duty?

"Right! How's that going?" I asked, trying to sound casual, even though I wanted to grab him by the shoulders and shake him senseless. His brother had no interest in the estate, his father was gravely ill, and Agneta might sink back into her oblivion at any moment. And here was Ingmar, playing the hero!

"Really well. Better all the time, ever since I qualified as a pilot. I fly back and forth to England most of the time." He watched for my reaction. "Taking a safe route, of course. We make a wide detour, to keep out of sight of the Germans. We wouldn't be able to defend ourselves from the machine guns of their Stukas."

I had a momentary recollection of the model airplane he'd constructed as a boy. "Are your planes reliable, at least?"

"Yes, they're very solid." I couldn't tell whether he was telling the truth. "They're not the newest model, but we maintain them well—not so easy when officially you have no planes at all. We laid out a landing strip in the far north, one we can camouflage with brush. Clearing it every time is a hell of a job."

A camouflaged landing strip in the wilderness and the long way around to England—that information was more than enough to give me stomach cramps.

"Ingmar, be honest. How dangerous are these flights really?"

He refused to meet my eye. "Well, the fact is, we've often had sightings of the enemy. But they haven't caught us yet. We vary our routes."

"Please be careful!"

"Everything has been fine so far."

I took a shaky breath. Ingmar put his hands on my shoulders. "Matilda, there is no need to worry! I have it all under control, and I promise to be careful. I know how much depends on me." He leaned over and planted a chaste kiss on my forehead.

On our walk back to the house, he raised a different subject. "How is Paul getting along?"

"Paul?"

"Your friend. The Paul I brought here from Norway."

"He told me his wife was shot by fascists who came to take her away."

Ingmar nodded. "That's how they terrorize the country. Many Norwegians hate them. The Germans use violence every chance they get, to frighten and control the citizens. They torture communists and resistance fighters, and they arrest people who do no more than express dislike for the occupation. Plenty of Norwegians don't recognize their own homeland."

I could well imagine it. What would it be like if Sweden were occupied? The Swedes had never been a people to accept being pushed around. Would the echoes of our war-filled history be enough to deter the Germans?

"I often wished Paul had never gone to Norway. Did you know that one reason his parents sent him away was that they thought I was too stuck-up? And that was back before I knew I was related to you!"

Ingmar shook his head. "There's no lack of stupid people."

"And then finally, when he'd succeeded, married and established his business, he lost it all. All those years of hard work."

"He's still a young man. He can start over." Ingmar regarded me. "Do you still have feelings for him?"

I wanted to deny it but couldn't lie to Ingmar. "I used to think of him from time to time. We saw one another once in Stockholm, when he and his wife stayed at the hotel. I thought I'd managed to forget him, but when I consult my heart—yes, the feelings are still there. Even though I know they're not appropriate."

Ingmar took both my hands and pressed them to his chest. "Maybe there will be a new start for you two. And if not, you can still be friends. But you probably shouldn't wait too long. A beautiful woman like you needs someone, a husband, now more than ever."

I made sure he saw my skeptical expression. "A man to lose again, when war does come?"

"You cannot be sure it will. And that would make no difference anyway. It will be far more tragic if you close your heart to love. I have no idea how things were for you in Stockholm, but I imagine your ambition to shine in the hotel business drove lesser men away."

"I've had my admirers," I replied. "But those relationships never lasted long." I paused. "The truth is that neither my ambition nor the hotel was to blame. I was probably comparing them all with Paul. And apparently they knew it."

"Well, maybe that was fate. This was terrible for Paul and his wife, but it could mean the beginning of something for you."

"I'll have to think about that. If war has taught me anything, it's that one must do things in order. One step at a time. Always."

53

Before Ingmar left with his comrades, he promised to write at least a couple of times a year. Would he keep that promise? I wasn't sure. While at Lion Hall, he understood what a burden of responsibility lay on his shoulders. But would he think of us once he was back in Norway?

We had little time to worry about that. The refugees settled in over the following weeks. We'd assigned them to rooms in groups of four, making sure that families were kept together. We put single men and single women in different wings, to avoid causing them embarrassment as they went about their daily routines.

I regularly got choked up when I saw how delighted the people were to have a bed or enjoy a fire in the hearth. The children ran everywhere in the house, using it as an immense playground. We let them enjoy themselves. The only rooms we locked were those that had expensive, fragile objects. If more refugees arrived, we would clear those and open them as well.

With every passing day, I became more aware of how lavish and excessive our lives had been. Rationing had made us unhappy, but that was nothing compared to the suffering these people had endured.

I made a point of visiting Paul every day. His wife's murder had left him a broken man. I eventually managed to persuade him to write to his sister. Daga must have been worrying terribly. I told him to give her my best wishes and to convey my personal invitation to Lion Hall. She'd never visited me here; her work hadn't allowed her to get away. And maybe her mother had told her not to.

No response came. I wasn't particularly surprised. A letter would probably take a while, and maybe she needed some time to assimilate the fact that her sister-in-law was dead and her brother had narrowly escaped death himself.

"If only I had something to do," Paul moaned one afternoon as we ambled about the grounds. Spring had announced itself with pale lilac-colored crocuses and bright snowbells. "I miss work. It would keep me from brooding all the time."

I didn't want to burden the refugees with tasks on the estate. I had no means to pay, and I refused to exploit them. They'd suffered too much already, and they deserved to be treated with respect.

But I knew what Paul meant. He'd always been defined by his work. The question was, simply, what sort of task should I suggest?

"I was taking a long walk on your land and I noticed a kind of cabin," he continued. "It seemed fairly run-down, but the structure looked solid. Do you know the place I mean?"

"Well, yes," I said, a little surprised. "That's where the estate's managers used to live. It hasn't been used for quite a while."

Not to mention the fact that it was Magnus's longtime hideout. The interior might well be covered with gruesome sketches or obscure texts.

"I could renovate it. And then, if you'll let me, I could live there."

I didn't know if that was such a good idea, but for the first time since he'd arrived, Paul was expressing enthusiasm for an idea. I couldn't bring myself to deny him.

I said I'd speak to Agneta. "If she doesn't mind, why not?" I hesitated for a moment, wondering whether to mention Magnus. If Magnus ever returned, he'd be anything but happy to find someone in his lair. But Paul had never met him, and I was pretty sure Magnus wasn't going to show up. After all, his mother was still alive.

I sat down with Lennard and Agneta after we distributed the day's rations. We'd moved the dining room table into the former smoking room, which we used as a private space. The Lion Hall menu had been considerably reduced. There were plenty of *pyttipanna* one-dish meals, for there was no lack of potatoes and eggs from our farm. Svea added to the pan whatever she could find—herbs, bits of sausage, even canned vegetables. We never knew what to expect.

Lennard reluctantly stuck to his liquid diet. He lost weight steadily, but his liver did not pain him as much as before. Agneta and I both hoped that this regimen would grant him at least another couple of years of life. We reminded him of that whenever he began to complain again about his gruel.

"I spoke to Paul this afternoon," I began, once we'd staved off the worst of our hunger. It was incredible how delicious eggs and potatoes could taste. "He asked me for permission to renovate the old hut where the manager used to live. He needs something to do, and it seemed like a pretty good idea to me."

I saw Agneta go rigid. "Why the hut, exactly?"

"Well, it's pretty ramshackle. Paul asked if perhaps he might move in. In return, he'll undertake to repair it. He could serve as a caretaker."

Agneta poked her fork around her plate. "That damned hut," she muttered. "I should have had it torn down."

"Because of Magnus?" I asked. But then I remembered: Magnus and Ingmar were conceived there.

"Why not allow it, really?" Lennard finally spoke up. "It would be a fine idea. That way we could finally chase away the ghosts on this estate."

Yes, I thought, *we especially need to exorcise Magnus.*

Agneta wasn't convinced. "If he wanted to tear it down . . ."

"Agneta, please," I exclaimed. "Let him do it! If we receive more refugees, we'll need more space immediately. The manager's house would be an asset. And besides, that would give Paul a little more space."

"To turn that shack into a pleasure palace for young men?" Agneta took a deep breath. "Oh, fine. I do not care. But he needs to understand that our tools are not particularly good. As for construction material, he will have to make do with whatever he can scrape up."

"Paul is an expert carpenter," I said. "He can do it. And the work will do him good."

She just nodded.

"It is horrible about his wife," Lennard commented with great feeling. "I shudder to think what he is going through."

"It's hard for him. And even harder is the fact that he cannot turn to his parents. He fears his mother would stifle him, and that his father would gloat over the daughter-in-law's death."

"I am glad none of this madness has directly affected us," Lennard commented. He took Agneta's hand and kissed it. "It would kill me if anything should happen to you."

"It will not come to that," she replied, fighting back tears.

I brought the news to Paul that same day and we set out.

"Tell me, when are you going to learn to ride?" I asked him as I helped him climb up on the horse behind me. Luckily, the stable boys were busy elsewhere, or they would have doubled up with laughter.

"I don't know," he replied, as he tried to find a comfortable position. "I've gotten along without a horse up to now."

"Well, since you'll be staying here for a while, it'll be better for you to get comfortable riding than for us to break poor Linus's back with your extra weight. You should start riding lessons right away. I'll let Lasse know he should set up times with you."

"I'll have plenty to do in the next few days. And thanks again for asking your aunt."

"Don't mention it." I urged the horse onward. "First take a look and see if there's actually anything you can do. My uncle said the place has been haunted for a long time. I hope you're not scared of ghosts."

Paul's chest pressed against my back as we rode out to the shack, and it was all I could do to push away the memories of our night together. His body heat sent delicious waves of longing through me.

I had to resist; I couldn't give in, after everything that had happened. I didn't believe in heaven, but even so, Ingrid might somehow be aware of us. That unpleasant thought shamed me.

The sight of the old hut brought me back to earth. The structure really did look haunted. I'd had good reasons for avoiding the place for so long.

Paul literally slid off the back of the horse. "I think next time I'll use my own two feet," he said. "Or maybe you could lend me a bicycle?"

"When you have horses, you don't need bicycles." I dismounted and waved at the hut. "What do you think?"

"It looks pretty weather-beaten. Can we take a look inside?"

"Of course." I didn't want to go in, but I didn't want him to make fun of me either. I took out the key and stepped forward.

The porch steps creaked under our weight, as if threatening to cave in.

Paul stamped on the boards. "The planks and stringers seem pretty solid."

"Are you out of your mind?" I cried. "Don't do that! What if they collapse under us?"

"Worst case, we'd land in a termite nest," he laughed. "Or on a molehill!"

"Or break our necks!"

I unlocked the door and opened it. Musty air struck us, and the floorboards inside were even creakier. We could see almost nothing, because the electricity was off and the shutters were bolted. I threw them open.

I'd prepared myself for the worst—perhaps Magnus had hung up weird trophies or gruesome specters would appear. The place looked quite harmless when light flooded the room. Magnus had left no sign of whatever he'd been up to. There were one or two water stains on the ceiling, and the few pieces of furniture were covered with a thick layer of dust. But that was it.

"Looks to be in good shape," Paul declared. "Of course, it'll require some fixing up. I assume most of the roof will have to be replaced." He stood on tiptoes so he could reach up to probe a spot on the ceiling. Paint peeled off and wood dust fell.

"As I said, Agneta gives you free rein with it. She said she'd prefer it to be torn down, but maybe you can return it to its former glory."

"I'll try, in any case. And when it's done, we can have a little christening ceremony for my snug little cottage."

I gaped at him. Not because of his suggestion, but because of his faint smile. "That's the first time I've seen you smile since you arrived, Paul."

That made him blush. "I have a good feeling about this place."

54

On the morning of the midsummer celebration, I made an early round of the quarters with the maids, distributing breakfast. Most of the refugees were up already; only a couple of the oldest were still in bed.

Paul had already moved to the hut. His expert hands had begun to transform it, and it would look entirely new before too long. He'd even managed to find a bicycle, probably somewhere in the village. I had no idea what he'd traded for it, but he was quite proud to have his own transportation, especially as it allowed him to duck our offer of riding lessons.

I preferred a horse, more than ever. The movement did me good, and I was pleased not to be perpetually on my own two feet. I found myself walking and standing enough inside the mansion.

"I wonder if you might have a couple of cigarettes for me too," he said that morning when I resupplied him with rationed goods. "I know you don't much care for smoking."

"It's not good for you. And the black market prices are highway robbery."

"I guess I'll have to switch to smoking lawn grass. There's plenty of that around here."

"I suppose you didn't hear what happened to Ole Hansen?"

Paul's eyebrows rose. "Who is Ole Hansen?"

"A boy from our street in Stockholm. He and his parents moved away before I got to know them. He tried to smoke dandelion stalks one time."

"And? Did he succeed?"

"He took a tremendous crap in his pants. Which was probably why his parents moved out of the neighborhood."

Paul gave me a funny look. "You're just making that up."

"Maybe," I said with a sweet smile. "Are you coming to our party?"

"Sure."

"And will you dance with me?" I asked. The work had allowed Paul to relax. I had no idea what went on in his mind as he slept alone in the hut or whether nightmares still hounded him, but he seemed less bottled up than before. I even glimpsed a slow smile on his face from time to time.

"I'm afraid I'm not a very good dancer," he replied.

"I've gotten out of practice lately, myself," I said. "It should be all right, though, and it won't be a disaster if we step on each other's feet." I took his hand. Maybe the memory of Ingrid made him hesitate. "And if you don't feel like it, that's all right. We'll enjoy the beautiful evening. And we'll all take a stroll, so there won't be much time left for dancing."

That seemed to reassure him.

"Well, then, I won't take up any more of your time," I said and squeezed his shoulder. "Let me know if you need anything." I went to my horse.

I turned to look back as I mounted, and Paul's eyes were fixed on me. I gave him a little wave, settled into the saddle, and rode away.

Scant hours later our gardens were transformed into a festival park. Everyone pitched in. The men carried out tables and chairs and hung crepe paper streamers. The women helped in the kitchen. I'd worried that Svea might not be pleased to have so many cooks, but she got along famously with the Norwegian women. By this time, they'd picked up some Swedish. Our cook avidly collected their recipes and jotted them down in her notebook.

"Mrs. Bloomquist would never have put up with such a thing," Agneta chortled. "She was always very territorial about her kitchen. Even after she retired, she was reluctant to stay away. We are fortunate our Svea sees things differently."

"She's happily taking advantage of it, as far as I can see," I commented. "This way she doesn't have to do all the work for the buffet. And it'll be a lovely change for us to enjoy the Norwegian version of a midsummer meal."

"It's true this is the first time we have had a bonfire," Agneta said, a little uneasily.

"Don't worry. The logs have been laid far from the barns."

Talking to the Norwegians, we'd learned that people didn't celebrate midsummer there, but Saint Hans's Day instead, with a huge bonfire to drive away evil spirits. The men had gathered dead wood, and we'd contributed straw from the barns.

Hans, one of the older men, had promised to perform the fest's traditional song in honor of his namesake. We were all looking forward to it.

"And besides, the bonfire will help keep the bad spirits away from Lion Hall," I added. "We're in need of that, aren't we?"

"Yes. We are in sore need of blessing and protection."

We gathered in the garden that evening. Agneta and I wore light summer dresses; Lennard's brown suit hung somewhat loose. Still, he looked happier and more vigorous than he had for a long time.

Many of the Norwegians sported garlands they'd woven from wild-flowers collected in our meadows. The smaller girls wore crowns of poppies and cornflowers. I was terribly pleased to see that they'd found joy after their frightful ordeals.

Crowds of villagers showed up for the celebration. In earlier years expensive automobiles had rolled around the circular drive to discharge women in glamorous dresses and men wearing tails. I missed that sparkle a bit, but I had to admit there was far more laughter this year.

"It looks to me as if the celebration will be no larger than last year," I told Agneta, who had just picked up a glass of lemonade. I sipped mine as well.

"Yes, the numbers are almost the same, but the composition is certainly different."

"These are good people, Agneta. People who really need something to celebrate."

"I was not suggesting otherwise." She smiled. "When I think what my mother would have said—" Her face suddenly stiffened, as if she'd seen a ghost. I turned around and almost choked on my lemonade. Magnus? For a moment I wondered if it could be Ingmar instead, but their mother would have reacted differently.

"It appears that Saint Hans has not exorcised all of the wicked spirits," she muttered and put down her glass.

They greeted one another with icy politeness. I kept my distance. Agneta, ever the proper hostess, invited him into the garden, but she excused herself immediately afterward and withdrew into the mansion.

I wondered if I should follow to check on her, but before I could, Magnus headed directly toward me. I took a deep breath.

"Cousin!" he exclaimed with that mocking tone. He held out his hand.

What do you want here? was what I really wanted to ask, but this was not the evening for a quarrel.

"Good evening, Magnus," I responded, ignoring his extended hand. "You are just in time to see them light the bonfire."

"I must say, the guest list has changed greatly over the years." He glanced around. "I had no idea that you had hunted up hobos."

His sneer incensed me.

"These people are from Norway. Some were business owners before the war, and the Nazis robbed them of everything. I advise you not to be so smug. The same thing could happen to us if the brownshirts take over."

Magnus leered. "A lovely speech. I knew that you had an affinity for rhetoric. Like likes like; you and they are birds of a feather."

"Very well, if all you want is to anger me, you might as well leave. I'd rather be associated with these people than with the likes of you." I turned my back and walked away.

I looked around for Paul. Hadn't he arrived yet?

I finally discovered him in a group of men sharing a cigarette. He passed the butt to the next man as soon as he saw me.

"You can't kick the habit, can you?" I challenged him with a grin.

"Markus earned half a pack, working for a farmer," Paul explained. "And, of course, now all the smokers are his best friends."

"You really should quit." I took his arm.

"Well, I'm trying, but I can't promise anything." We strolled toward the buffet, where the women were already setting out the food.

"Do you think things will ever be the way they were before?"

"You mean will we be able to buy cigarettes again?" Paul joked.

"You know very well what I mean! Even if Sweden's spared by the war, it looks like the world will never again be the same."

"It's probably always like that. My parents always claimed that everything was better before the Great War. They probably couldn't imagine another one would happen so soon."

"That's how Agneta sees it too. Let's just hope that this frightful menace passes Sweden by. It's terrifying, having to wonder what every new day's going to bring—who'll attack, who'll surrender."

"The fighting in Oslo was over in a matter of hours. It was a nightmare. The Germans came marching in and we saw Quisling waiting for them with open arms. We'd all hoped to wake up the next day and find everything unchanged, but within a matter of weeks, nothing was left of our former lives. Naturally some people weren't affected—those who hadn't put up any resistance; people who hadn't held unacceptable political views. But for the rest . . ." He made a gesture as if flinging something to the ground.

"That's the fear that haunts me. We're terrifically fortunate. But fortune's wheel can turn with alarming speed."

"Yes, it can," Paul said soberly. He looked over my shoulder, hesitated, and gave me a confused look. "Is that Ingmar?"

I looked around and saw Magnus looming behind us. Had he followed me?

"No," I said. "That's Magnus, twin brother to Ingmar. You two haven't met."

Paul approached him and held out a hand. "Pleased to meet you. Your brother is a really upstanding man. I was fortunate to get to know him on the boat to Sweden."

"You're not Norwegian, judging by your speech," Magnus said. "What sent you over there?"

I wanted Paul to avoid being lured into conversation, but he didn't notice my sharp glance.

"I had a furniture business I couldn't hold on to when the Nazis arrived. After they shot my wife, I saw no reason to stay."

"How unfortunate," Magnus said without the slightest trace of sympathy. "Well, I am sure you will find plenty of new friends here. The estate has certainly undergone some changes during my absence."

"As for you," I snapped, "you could also come and be part of Lion Hall."

"I could, but would I want to?" Magnus pretended to consider the proposition, then he grinned and shook his head. "No, I think I am comfortably settled where I am." He lifted his glass in a mock toast and walked away.

"A sterling fellow, your cousin," Paul commented once Magnus was out of earshot.

"He's from the dark side of the world," I said. "Some land where the sun never shines. His looks are the only thing he has in common with his brother."

"Well, I seem to recall Ingmar didn't like me years ago either."

"Ingmar was a little jealous. He's changed entirely since then, as you know."

"You're right about that. Ingmar has grown up to be a fine man. But that one, there . . ."

"Magnus has always been difficult. You remember, maybe, that he was sent to boarding school for bullying me?"

"Oh, right, I do remember that. And how you turned up at my front door and begged me to marry you."

"That was so long ago! I can hardly believe I was so terribly stupid."

"It's water under the bridge. We were so young then."

"And we still are. Even if I feel like an old woman sometimes."

"You? Old?" He smiled. "In my eyes you're as young and beautiful as ever."

A laugh bubbled up inside me. Not because of his compliment, but because of the smile on his lips. For a moment I really did feel lighter in spirit. Just then the fiddler began to play. I took Paul's hand and pulled him along with me.

"Surely you're not going to insist on dancing?"

"Don't worry! I just want to listen to the music."

Somewhat later I saw Agneta standing at one side of the festive crowd, looking worried. She was staring into the flickering bonfire commemorating Saint Hans.

"Is everything all right?" I asked.

She jumped, obviously startled.

"Yes, thank you," she said. "But it bothers me to see Magnus here. What does he want?"

"Didn't you ask him?"

"Of course. But you know how my son is. He never gives a straight answer."

"Maybe he's here to honor family tradition."

"Just like that? Out of the blue? He has not shown his face here since our quarrel. And now he turns up?"

"Does he need money?"

"He said nothing about that, but perhaps he is waiting until the celebration is over."

"Maybe he wants to move into the hut."

Agneta shook her head. "I am sure he does not. It was good enough for him once upon a time, but he would never go back there now." She turned to me. "Anyway, the hut now has a new inhabitant. True?"

I nodded. "Paul wouldn't be pleased to leave, now that he's almost finished the repairs and renovations."

"So there, you see. I will not allow Magnus to use it." Her voice hardened the way a hand suddenly clenches into a fist. "This is my estate, and I am in charge. And that goes for the money as well. I have none to give to a son who is not concerned about the estate. I wish—" She held herself back.

"—that he was the one who'd joined the resistance?"

Her refusal to comment confirmed that I'd guessed right.

"Magnus would never do such a thing," I said. "I've never seen him help anyone. It's not in his nature."

"He is like his father," Agneta replied darkly. "Well, perhaps not entirely, since there was a good side to Hans. The man who called himself Max and with whom I fell in love. But there is no doubt Ingmar was the one to inherit his good qualities. Not Magnus."

So many thoughts filled my mind! I didn't say a thing. Her words were bitter, but I had no right to judge.

"Well, then," she said at last, "there is nothing to be done, is there?" She tried to smile. "I have you here, at least. I hope you will keep me from making any huge mistakes."

I put my arm around her shoulders. "I hope I can."

Fortunately, I saw little of Magnus over the course of the evening, because I did my best to steer clear of him. I made a point of socializing with the Norwegians, and then I pulled Paul out into the dance area. He hadn't exaggerated; he was awkward and clumsy. But the spectators had enjoyed enough aquavit not to notice.

Later I walked some distance toward the hut with Paul. Most of the villagers had left by then. Some of the Norwegians were still sitting together by the fire, but Paul wasn't tempted to join them. He was probably planning more work on the hut the next day.

"A fine celebration," he said after we'd left the manor behind.

"Yes, it really was! And you didn't do such a bad job with the dancing."

"Well, Saint Peter sure won't let me into heaven for my dancing abilities," he joked. "I enjoyed having you close."

We looked at one another. I ached for a kiss, but what would he think of me if I made a move?

"I think it's time for you to go back," he said after a moment. "I can find the rest of the way myself."

"Yes, sir!" I said with a mock salute, but I couldn't hide the disappointment in my voice. "Will I see you tomorrow?"

Paul nodded. "Of course. I promised to help tidy up. Oh, and one of the farmers asked me to cobble together a door for his pantry."

"Jörgens?"

"Yes, he's the one. How did you know?"

"I saw you talking with him." I smiled, then reached out and adjusted his lapel. "Well, then, good night, Paul."

"Good night, Matilda," he responded, smiled, and left me.

A heavy longing settled in my breast as I watched him walk away. I'd tried to believe that things between us had ended long before, and he was only a friend—but the past couple of months had reawakened my feelings.

I turned back at last. The moon was so bright I didn't need a lamp. *This shouldn't be happening,* I told myself. *I need to stop wanting him to be more than a childhood friend. He's a man, and he has to make his own way. Fate sent him here, but that means nothing. One day, when the war is over, he'll go back to Norway.*

"Well, well, Matilda, out for a midnight stroll?"

Why was Magnus lurking around? Did it amuse him to startle me?

"What do you want now?" I snapped.

"Just a little chat," he said. "Surely you cannot object to that."

"I certainly can," I retorted and tried to step past him. He blocked me.

"My uncle's careless mistake seems to have made quite a career for herself. I gather you are running the estate, for all practical purposes."

I crossed my arms. "You want to talk about careless mistakes, Magnus? All right then, let's do that. Agneta told me a very interesting story."

Magnus was taken aback by my attack, but he quickly regained control. "Aha, our dear father," he said. "I knew she would not be able to keep her mouth shut."

"I don't see that you have any reason to sit on your high horse, considering that your father was a ne'er-do-well in disgrace with his own family."

"My father is an aristocrat, whatever else he may be. Your mother will always be a housemaid."

"And that's no reason for you to act high and mighty. We're both illegitimate. I advise you not to get in my way."

"Do you really think that will make any difference to my mother? I am the rightful heir to Lion Hall. It's destined to me alone."

"You never tire of reminding people of that, but you do nothing to deserve it. You refuse to lift a finger for the estate. What can you expect if you keep this up? You can't count on me to work for you, and we've already seen what happens when I'm not here."

He had no reply to that, but I didn't stop there. "You know, Magnus, when I heard the truth, for just a fraction of a second I pitied you. Your mother deceived you just as she did me. But you've become more and more like your father: sneaky, dishonorable, and arrogant. All the traits Lennard never had."

"You know nothing at all about my father," he snarled, and took a menacing step toward me. "After he turned up here, I went to take a closer look. I thought, *Could such a raggedy fellow be my father?* I interrogated him the very next day. He said he was wounded and in a coma for a long time. He had total amnesia. Some memories came back to him years later and made him recall Agneta. She had forgotten him and found herself a husband. He wanted to see her again, and when he discovered he had two sons—"

"You claim you found this person likable?" I deliberately provoked him. "No wonder you turned out the way you have!"

Magnus grabbed my arm roughly. His anger made me fear for my safety.

"My mother should never have fallen for that cad. He dishonored her and he dishonored our family. Likable? No, he was not likable, not at all. He is a filthy bastard. He came looking for my mother with the intention of blackmailing her. For a moment I was tempted to leave with him to live on his brother's estate in Germany, where they had taken him in. To punish her. But I remembered who I am. I said I would wring his neck if he ever showed his face here again. He would not take that from Lennard, but he did from me. He really got the message later when a couple of my friends roughed him up in Stockholm."

I stared at Magnus, aghast. He'd sent Stockholm thugs to assault his own father?

"You're making that up!" I said as I tried to pull out of his grip. He held me fast for a moment but then let go.

"I am not inventing anything. If there is one thing for which I can thank boarding school, it is the network I established. Friends who will pitch in, no matter what you need. I would watch out if I were you."

"Now you're threatening me?" I tried not to rub my arm, even though the place he'd grabbed was aching.

"Not at all. I am advising you to be careful. Especially in what you say about Lion Hall and the choice of people you invite here. I could have gotten rid of you a long time ago, but I could not be bothered. You are not worth the effort."

"You really are your father's son!" I hissed. My heart thundered. "You should have gone with him."

"What for, when someday I will be one of Sweden's richest and most influential estate owners? Just make sure you do your job well until then, so the place is not a pile of smoking ruins by the time my mother dies. I will take that into consideration when I decide whether to keep you on."

He gave me a sour grin and disappeared into the depths of the garden. I was deprived of the chance to scream that I'd rather chop off my right hand than lift a finger for him.

I stared into the night. My knees almost buckled. Had I dreamed this awful scene? I couldn't believe it. Magnus had always seemed like a monster, and it was clear I'd been right from the very start.

And now what should I do? Tell his mother? I had no proof. That would be useless.

I heard a rustling behind me and spun around, thinking Magnus was creeping up on me again. I looked all around but saw nothing but darkness.

55

I had something of a hangover when I awoke the morning after the festival. I hadn't drunk much, but my head felt stuffed with cotton wool. Was it because of the furious confrontation with Magnus?

I hadn't wanted to tell Agneta about it the previous evening. Now I was wondering if in fact I should. What he'd said was monstrous. But wouldn't it upset Agneta unnecessarily? And perhaps it wasn't even true. Maybe Magnus had been trying to intimidate me by bragging he'd sent thugs to beat up the man who'd fathered him.

I got up, washed, and pulled on my clothes. I had little hope that any of the breakfast breads would be left, but I headed for the kitchen anyway.

A loud, desperate cry froze me in my tracks.

Where had it come from? The refugee quarters?

A prolonged shriek came from the master bedroom. Of that there was no doubt.

I ran down the hall and hammered on the door, but no one answered. I heard Agneta sobbing, and the sound squeezed my heart.

I threw the door open and found her stretched across Lennard. He was motionless. Her back heaved as she wailed and sobbed.

Tears filled my eyes. I didn't have to see his face; it was obvious what had happened.

I went to them. Agneta clung to her husband, desperately rubbing his cheeks, but the life had gone out of his eyes. The room whirled around me. I pressed my hand to my face and felt it instantly drenched with my tears.

Lennard was dead. How was that possible?

I remembered the unpleasant exchange with Magnus and the grim feeling his presence had spread over the festivities.

No, I told myself. *He didn't do this. He's not capable of it.*

But doubt tormented me.

Lena came running. "What is it?"

"Call Dr. Bengtsen," I said, although I knew that nothing could help Lennard now. A death certificate would be required, and only the doctor could make it out.

Lena stared, shocked, at the count's lifeless face, then fled the room.

Agneta was still hysterical, and I didn't know how much longer I'd be able to maintain my composure. Just as with my mother, Death had taken Lennard in his sleep. Even as Agneta slept beside him.

"Agneta?" I touched her shoulder. Her hair had fallen into her face and lay tangled about her shoulders.

She looked up. The blue of her eyes glimmered wet in her swollen, red face.

"He cannot leave me," she said. "He cannot!"

"He had no choice. I'm sorry." I couldn't bear to look at Lennard. His eyes were wide open, as if Death had taken him by surprise and not given him a chance to cry for help.

I wanted to pull her away, but I knew she wouldn't go. "The doctor will be here soon," I said. "Won't you put something on? He shouldn't see you like this, should he?"

Agneta sagged. Fear took hold of me. Was she about to lose her mind again? Was dark depression overwhelming her? Less harrowing experiences had sidelined her before.

At last she rose. "I woke up this morning and spoke to him. I thought he wanted to sleep some more, but when I rolled over and saw him staring at the ceiling—"

Her face twisted up, and she broke into sobs again. I rocked her in my arms. Her body quivered and shook, and her tears wet my shoulder. She felt so fragile in her thin nightgown.

I wept too, but without a sound. Grief bit deep into my soul and left it raw.

It took time, but finally our crying subsided. Agneta dressed. We left the bedroom together but didn't go downstairs. Like sentinels, we settled on upholstered stools just outside the door. Neither of us wanted to see Lennard as he was at that moment.

Dr. Bengtsen appeared at last.

"Countess Lejongård." He gave her his hand. "I am so terribly sorry."

Agneta nodded. The doctor gave me his condolences as well.

"Shall we go in?" he asked.

Agneta accompanied Dr. Bengtsen inside. I remained in the hall and overheard scraps of conversation, even though I wasn't listening for them.

The words "suddenly" and "stroke" were part of it, and he said, somewhat louder, that it must have been caused by high blood pressure brought on by cirrhosis of the liver. Lennard's illness had cost him his life after all, although indirectly.

Agneta and Dr. Bengtsen came out again after a while. They seemed calm, although the doctor was visibly moved. He turned to me.

"Your uncle was surprised by a sudden stroke. It appears to have happened very quickly, and he wouldn't have suffered. No doubt that is feeble comfort to you, but it spared him from the long, suffering decline that typically afflicts people with his chronic illness."

I remembered Lennard's complaints about the liquid diet. And the way at the previous evening's midsummer celebration he'd taken the liberty to enjoy a normal meal and had even had some aquavit.

I was glad he'd done so. He'd granted himself a memorable evening. The liquor and the meal hadn't caused his death.

The doctor finally took his leave, and I went to the office to telephone the undertaker. Lennard had to be embalmed before the funeral; that was the family tradition. We also needed to define procedures with the funeral director, since a family crypt was involved.

I found Agneta sitting at the bare dining room table and accompanied her back to their bedroom. Lennard lay under the blanket with his arms crossed over his chest. The doctor had closed his eyes.

"I vividly remember my own father's death," Agneta told me. "The undertaker had smeared his face with a disgusting white paste to hide the burns. He looked like a grotesque circus clown. At least Lennard does not have to suffer that humiliation."

I contemplated my uncle a while, then turned to Agneta. "He is very dignified. Almost as if he's sleeping. And surely his spirit is still with us."

Agneta went to the window and opened it. The stifling air—I hadn't noticed it before—stirred as fresh air poured in.

"He would hate being locked up in this house." She came back and stood silent beside me.

That afternoon the Kristianstad undertaker arrived with embalming equipment that sent a shiver up my spine. I had an idea of the procedure: he would drain Lennard's blood and replace it with a special fluid preservative. The thought made me so ill that I left the manor and hurried aimlessly across the grounds—until a familiar figure appeared.

"Matilda," Paul said. "I just heard. I'm so sorry."

I nodded and managed to keep my composure for a fraction of a second, but then I cast myself into his arms. "Oh, Paul!" I wailed.

He held me tight, and I gave free rein to my grief. My cries probably stopped the birds from singing. Tears burned my eyes and cheeks. For the first time since my mother died, I felt free to surrender to sorrow.

Paul guided me to a small park bench and held me. He knew what it was to grieve, though Lennard's end was far different from Ingrid's.

"Your uncle was a good man," I heard him say finally, as he caressed my hair. "He is at peace."

Late that day, after the staff had paid their respects, the hearse transported Lennard's body to Kristianstad. The funeral would be held at Trinity Church; until then his body would lie in the nave.

The joy that had filled our rooms the previous day was gone. Agneta and I put on black and sat together in the salon. Svea had used our last reserves to brew some fairly strong coffee. I rarely drank it black, but that day the strong, bitter aroma did me good. I was tired, my spirit was shattered, and I was prey to a terrible unease. The problem was how to reach Ingmar. I was at my wit's end.

"Have you called Elisabeth?" I asked. Lennard's sister hadn't been to Lion Hall in a very long time, not since she'd become a grandmother. I could hardly remember her face.

"Yes," Agneta answered unhappily. "She was shocked. She will be here tomorrow. I have already let Lena know to have a room ready. We do not have many to choose from, but I think it will be all right."

"She can have mine," I said. "I'll spend the night with you, if you don't mind."

I wasn't particularly happy about sleeping in Lennard's deathbed, but I didn't want Agneta to be alone.

"Would you?"

I nodded. "I want to keep you from sinking into that black depression again, Agneta. I will do anything at all to prevent that."

A sad little smile pulled at the corners of her mouth. "You are a good girl, Matilda," she said. "The darkness comes when it will. I cannot defend myself."

"I will stay with you anyway, unless you prefer to be alone."

She shook her head. "No, I do not. I am afraid of tonight and the nights to come. I will be very happy to have your company."

I nodded. "I'll tell Lena to prepare my room for Elisabeth and her husband. It's not as spacious as some, but in times like these there aren't many options."

"She knows that, and she will be grateful."

There was a pause, and I sensed that she wanted to raise a subject uncomfortable to both of us.

"You should telephone Magnus."

She gave me a weary look. "Can we send him a telegram? I doubt he will be happy to hear his mother on the line."

"It will be no pleasure for you either," I replied. "But I will call, if you want. And I'll drive to the city and try to get in contact with Ingmar."

I took a deep breath, but the oppressive weight on my chest persisted. Calling Magnus would be about as agreeable as stepping barefoot on a rusty nail. But if he wasn't informed, he would hold our silence against us.

"Perhaps you should wait until tomorrow," she said. "You need rest. This day's troubles have been more than enough."

I declined that suggestion. "The telegraph office is open until late. I can rest after I get back."

On the way to Kristianstad, I was glad I'd decided to go. I'd rolled down the window on the passenger side, so I had plenty of fresh air. I let my thoughts roam.

The call to Magnus had gone exactly as expected. It would be an understatement to say he'd taken Lennard's death calmly.

His response: "So what?"

I gave him the date and time of the funeral and asked him to come to Lion Hall to support his mother. His reaction to that: "What good would that do? It will not bring him back. And besides, the army has called me up." That, in his opinion, was that.

I had to fight back my anger for a long time. Now, though, I felt it cooling slowly in the afternoon breeze. I just hoped that Ingmar's allies could get the news to him, so at least one of Lennard's sons would show up to honor him.

I parked near the telegraph office, which was located in the Kristianstad train station. There were few civilian vehicles on the streets. Occasionally a truck carrying military personnel rolled past. What were they doing all the time? Of course, the Germans kept making demands on us, so danger was still clear and present. The king was very tempered in his responses. He'd already succeeded in keeping us out of the war for nearly two years.

The telegraph office was deserted, and the chief was sweeping up. He saw me and stopped. "Good evening, miss! What brings you to me?"

I told him I had to send an urgent telegram, and he immediately went to his desk. I scribbled out the message.

I could have tried to spare Ingmar with ambiguity, saying there had been an incident affecting the family, but wasn't it better to tell him the truth? An incident, an accident, or an urgent plea to contact us—those were no more than coded signals for a death.

Lennard died suddenly. Funeral June 25. Please come if possible.

The telegrapher took the slip of paper and frowned. He often learned of the fate of his customers; that couldn't be helped.

"This frightful war," he muttered before he opened the telegraph key. "It's not here, but even so, it's doing our people in."

I could have replied that the war had nothing to do with Lennard's death, but instead I nodded and said nothing.

"Did you hear that the Germans are demanding we transport their troops?" he asked as he tapped out the message, obviously able to work and converse at the same time.

I was confused. "German troops in Sweden?"

"Just in transit, according to the Nazis," the man replied. "They want to attack Russia. At the request of the Finns, who've been overrun by the louts. The German troops from Norway are assigned to help the Finns, and they have to cross our territory. Unbelievable, don't you think?"

I was speechless. The Finns were asking for German help? True, they'd suffered at the hands of the Russians and feared yet another attack. But why would someone invite in the wolf for fear of the bear?

"I hope the king thinks about that long and hard," I replied after a moment. "I really do not think the Finns have made the right choice."

"The decision doesn't depend on the king as much as on Parliament. I've heard they're arguing among themselves, so we have every reason to be worried."

I paid for the telegram and wished him a good evening. Perhaps the Norwegians at Lion Hall had already heard the news. They were always clustered around the radio we'd set up in the common room.

Hurrying across the square, I heard a shrill whistle. Huffing and puffing, a freight train rolled into the station. If our trains should transport the Germans to attack, what would become of our neutrality? They wouldn't be crossing Sweden on a holiday jaunt, after all.

"Miss, just a moment!" a voice called behind me. I turned and saw the telegrapher rushing down the steps. Had I forgotten something? I checked for my change purse. It was still in my bag.

The man was panting when he reached me. "My colleague on the other end must have been sitting at the key," he said, handing me a scrap of paper.

WILL FORWARD +STOP+ H +STOP+

I didn't know who "H" was, but I was very grateful to him.

"Thank you," I told the operator and went to the car.

56

I was overwhelmed by the number of people who came to Lennard's funeral. The church was packed, not only with persons lodged or employed on the estate, but with leading citizens from Kristianstad and the Ekberg area as well, all come to pay their last respects. Many men were in uniform. Some had to stand outside, for the church was quickly filled.

I helped Agneta as she stumbled on her way to the front. She'd put on a brave face all day, but I knew that the worst moments were still ahead.

His coffin stood before the altar, covered with elaborate arrangements of summer flowers. Elisabeth and her husband sat in the front pew. The places reserved for Ingmar and Magnus were empty.

I wasn't in the least surprised that Magnus had failed to appear at the funeral of the man who'd raised him. I sensed Agneta's disappointment. As for Ingmar, I kept hoping for a miracle. He'd probably been impossible to reach; otherwise, he'd be with us. The frightful uncertainty about his welfare was taking its toll on Agneta.

We took our places and waited for the organ prelude. Agneta clasped my hand and gave me a grateful glance through the delicate black mesh of her mourning veil.

Organ music preceded the priest's words; the hymns were sung by all. I thought of how good it would have been to hold this sort of funeral for Sigurd Wallin. I'd never come to terms with his death. I hadn't visited my mother's grave for a very long time either. Would she be angry with me? Surely not, after all that had happened.

After the service, we joined the procession to the family mausoleum, and I surveyed the faces in the crowd. My heart leaped when I thought I saw Ingmar, but it was only a young soldier who resembled him.

Dear God, I prayed quietly, even though I wasn't very religious, *keep Ingmar safe. Protect him if he is on his way back home.*

The funeral reception was a somber gathering of only a few. The villagers had offered their condolences at the cemetery. At Lion Hall we sat with refugees and staff, drank coffee cut with chicory, and lost ourselves in our thoughts.

I encountered Paul in the early evening.

"The ceremony was beautiful," he commented.

"I suppose it was, if such an occasion can ever be beautiful." The priest had done a good job, but grief-stricken family members were hardly capable of judging.

"All right, then, let's say instead that it was very dignified." He walked beside me. The gravel crunched underfoot, and a blackbird somewhere in the distance trilled its sad evening song. Neither of us spoke for a long time.

Paul broke the silence. "Did you hear we're permitting the Germans to cross Sweden on the way to Finland? The trains are already moving."

"No, I hadn't heard."

I'd spent what little private time I had staring at the clouds and sky.

"It's awful. Who knows how much longer we'll be able to stay out of the war?"

Did he really think this was a fit subject of conversation after a funeral? I welcomed distraction, but war talk reminded me again of Ingmar.

"If conflict comes, I will volunteer," he announced.

"You will not!" I cried. "I—*we* need you here. I won't let the Germans blast you to bits!"

"Matilda, I—"

"No!" I halted in my tracks and my voice rose to a shriek. "You are not going to the front! Not unless they force you. I don't want to bury another loved one!"

Paul's eyes widened. "You love me?"

I crossed my arms and glared at him. "What do you think? Do you suppose a woman goes to bed with a man she hasn't seen for ages if she's not in love?"

"That was years ago!"

"That may be, but even so! I was crushed by what happened to Ingrid, but I'm glad they didn't shoot you too. I still have feelings for you, and I'm not going to let you run off to war."

"Matilda," he said a little more gently, a shy smile flickering over his face. "Is this true?"

I nodded vigorously. "I never forgot you. We were so close, and I was devastated when you went away. And then I see you again after all that time, and you're married, but even so, the night with you was better than anything in my life. And now you're here again . . . Maybe it's fate, maybe not, but I won't let you leave again."

We gazed at one another for a moment, and then Paul embraced me and kissed my forehead. "All right, Matilda. I won't leave. Not unless I have no choice. But I'm sure you understand I'll hurt the Germans if I get the chance. They took everything I had. If I get the opportunity, I'll make them pay."

I leaned into his shoulder. "I understand."

I was filled with wild confusion. My heart pounded, and a strange tingling surged through the misery of my mourning. Can a person find love even in the depths of sorrow? "But please remember that I don't want to lose you. I never wanted that. You can rebuild here whatever the Germans confiscated in Norway, but not if you're dead. Ingrid wouldn't want that, would she?"

Paul nodded and held me for a while longer. Finally, tentatively, he made a request. "Would you be offended if I kissed you?"

"No, of course not."

His lips met mine, and it was like that time in my room, inflaming my desire. But this was not the time to act on it. I closed my eyes and sought to prolong the wonderful moment. When Paul released me, I opened them.

For a moment I'd been eighteen again, as before, under the willow tree. Now I looked up and saw a man of almost thirty. Time had marked his face, but it must have changed me too. Could the two of us hope to recover what we'd had?

My conscience rebuked me. Ingrid had died scarcely six months before. Shouldn't we observe a decent mourning period?

We could discuss that later. We turned back to the manor, his arm securely around my shoulders.

"Thank you," I said to Paul, "for our talk. And for everything else."

"It was my great pleasure," he replied. "I thank you for the kiss. I'd happily give you another, but I don't know if that's proper, here at the front door."

I smiled. "A kiss is never improper. Don't you agree?" I leaned toward him.

I lay awake for a long time that night, but not because I felt uncomfortable on Lennard's side of the bed. Agneta slept like a rock and snored quietly; she was completely exhausted. I felt unusually lighthearted. Paul and I had kissed. How long I'd secretly ached for those kisses!

It was odd, of course, that it occurred on the day of Lennard's funeral. Or was that a sign?

I'd never discussed my feelings for Paul with my uncle. Lennard had been immersed in caring for the estates, and it hadn't seemed to interest him whether I had a male friend or not. He'd probably heard all about it from Agneta.

What would she say when she found that we were becoming close again? Years before, even knowing that I was her brother's daughter, she'd had nothing against Paul; she'd only warned me against indulging in physical intimacy at too young an age. But I was a grown woman now, and she knew very well I had no desire to live as chaste as a nun.

Maybe it was too early to think of such things, but Paul's kiss offered a glimmer of hope in a world of uncertainty.

57

Three days passed after Lennard's funeral with no sign of Ingmar. The appointment with the attorney for the reading of the will was fast approaching, and Agneta was almost out of her mind with worry. "What if something has happened to him?"

"Nothing has. His friends have to locate him first. And it is not easy to travel from Norway to Sweden these days."

Agneta sighed. "I do not know where you find your optimism."

"Unfortunately, I don't know either—but I'm happy to share it with you!"

"I fear that there is no container ample enough to supply my needs."

She stared through the window for a moment, focusing on a little spot of blue peeking through the clouds. It had rained all morning long, but the showers were gradually letting up.

"All right, I think we need to go." She got to her feet. The attorney could confirm Ingmar as the new Count Ekberg; the heir's physical presence wasn't required.

"I do not know which is more horribly unpleasant," she said. "The attorney's pontificating bass voice or the obligation to sit in the same room with Magnus."

"I don't think the attorney will be a problem. And maybe Magnus won't show up—just as he stayed away from the funeral. If he does, he'll surely behave with proper decorum for once in his life."

"Magnus is named in Lennard's will, as far as I know. There is money at stake, so he will be there."

The air outside was cool and still damp, so we donned light jackets. We descended the steps and were surprised to see a figure in uniform.

"Ingmar!" I cried and ran to him. "You're here!" I flung myself into his arms. "I'm so terribly sorry."

Ingmar gathered me in. "I came as quickly as I could. But the mail takes so long, and almost none of the telegrams go through. Our captain had a message added to a radio transmission. I flew back."

I almost cried that flying was far too dangerous, but I was too glad to see him. He was our much-needed burst of sunshine after so many devastating storms.

Agneta was overjoyed. I released Ingmar, and she collapsed into his arms, weeping bitterly.

"I am so very sorry, Mother," he murmured into her hair. "I wish I'd been here with all of you."

"You could not have changed anything," she sobbed. "I could not prevent it either."

They clung to each other for a while, and she told him to come to the reading of Lennard's will.

Ingmar looked as if he'd rather take a bath first, but he got into the car.

"What kind of uniform is this?" I asked as I steered the car through the main gate.

"Militia," he answered and glanced down at himself. "Nothing special, just a jacket, knee-length trousers, and a military belt. That's how we recognize each other. You could call us Norway's secret army. We're assigned to different districts and commanded by a council of war. Many in the Norwegian army support us. Some of our units carry out active operations against the enemy; I coordinate with my comrades and the refugees. We're really Civorg, the civilian arm. But we get standard-issue clothing even so. I still fly sometimes, when it's needed. Just last week I was in London. That's why it was so hard for them to notify me."

I wanted to urge him to leave the resistance, but I knew he wouldn't listen. Maybe, though, he could get himself reassigned to coordinate with Sweden. That would put him out of the reach of the Nazis.

Agneta was right; of course, Magnus was already at the lawyer's office when we arrived. He wore an ill-fitting infantry uniform that obviously pleased him. He clearly hadn't reckoned on Ingmar appearing in militia garb.

"Hello, Magnus," his brother said and extended his hand. In the past the two would usually hug, but it appeared the past was dead and gone.

"Greetings to you, brother of mine. How is the weather in Norway?"

I was tempted to slap the sarcastic smile off his face. Agneta was obviously just as offended but said nothing.

"A bit chilly—but you knew that already," Ingmar replied and placed himself at his mother's side.

Magnus pointedly ignored her and turned away. I reached out to seize him, but Agneta signaled not to bother. His rudeness hurt her, but she clearly didn't want to let him know how much.

We took seats in the conference room. Mr. Nickel, the attorney, was of conscription age but explained that he'd been exempted from service because of his limp.

I found myself wadding up my handkerchief and pulling at it. Ingmar's presence was a consolation, but being in the same room with Magnus was almost unbearable. I couldn't shut out the memory of what he'd said about his father. That and his inexplicable decision to appear at midsummer had raised questions to which I still had no answers.

The doctor was certain Lennard had suffered a stroke, but what if he was wrong? If Magnus . . .

The attorney cleared his throat and brought me out of that speculation. After the usual formalities, he read my uncle's will.

Being of a clear mind, I bequeath the Ekberg estate in equal parts to my son Ingmar Gustav Lejongård and to my niece, Matilda Wallin. My wife, Agneta Lejongård . . .

I stared at the man in disbelief. His voice became a distant rushing sound. Half of the Ekberg estate was mine?

I felt Agneta press my hand. I glanced to the side and saw Magnus was amused. He was delighted to hear his brother had to share the estate. I couldn't understand how he could find anything comic on an occasion like this.

Mr. Nickel droned on, but I couldn't focus on his words. I vaguely gathered that Agneta would receive a stipend from the estate's earnings; Elisabeth, Lennard's sister, was named as the estate manager and received a large sum of money; and there was a bequest for Magnus that would allow him to live without financial worries for many years. Having heard that, he was probably in a hurry to leave.

After the formalities were complete, we left the office. Just as I'd expected, Magnus wished us a curt goodbye, as if we were strangers, and disappeared. Agneta went to the automobile. Ingmar held me back. "Do you have a moment?"

I looked toward Agneta and then back at Ingmar. "Yes, of course. What is it?"

"I just wanted to say that Father made the right choice. Knowing you'll be at my side on the estate is the best possible outcome of all these unfortunate circumstances."

"I suggest you wait for my full report about the state of the business." My smile was lopsided, and I was again close to tears. I was touched that Lennard had thought of me, but my heart was heavy. I didn't want to move to the Ekberg estate and leave Agneta alone at Lion Hall.

Perhaps I wouldn't have to. The Ekberg property had been managed from a distance since Lennard and Agneta were married. That wouldn't need to change, at least as long as Ingmar was in Norway and Lennard's sister lived on the estate.

"Of the two of us, you're a more talented businessperson," he said, giving me a hug. "I'll worry about the grain and you can handle the books."

"I'll do that." But I was wondering about my future prospects. Was I going to be the spinster relative who owned a share of the estate? Paul was part of the picture again, but I wasn't sure things between us would be as before.

Maybe it wouldn't be a bad thing to spend my life in Ingmar's company. His engagement with the resistance left him no time to look for a bride. Or did he already have someone? I'd ask him when I got the chance.

We went back to the car arm in arm.

"How long will you stay?"

"Three days. I couldn't get a longer leave. But I promise to use the time well. It's fine being back here again. In Norway I often found myself missing the estate."

"You can come back anytime."

He shook his head. "If the war ends. Or when the Germans pull out of Norway. Our work is important for Sweden too, important for you and Mother. The Germans must not get the idea that they can just snap up Sweden anytime they wish. They claimed Norway had contravened the principles of neutrality, but that was just an excuse. They could allege the same about Sweden—but not if we make things hot and tie them down in Norway."

"I heard the Germans are going to send troops through Sweden to Finland, across the mountains."

"That's true, but no disadvantage for us. It deprives the Germans of one possible pretext to attack Sweden. And gives our militia the opportunity to harass them with sabotage operations. Sweden's king and Parliament have done the resistance a favor."

Ingmar fell silent when we reached the car. It was clear he didn't want to discuss these things in his mother's presence.

Agneta waited in the back seat. I got behind the wheel, while Ingmar took the passenger seat in front.

"Ingmar is going to stay three days, Agneta," I said with an enthusiastic smile. "Isn't that lovely?"

"That is not long enough!" She gave her son a reproachful look.

"Mother, you already know—"

"Yes, I know. You have to do your duty. As you should. But as a mother, I nevertheless have the right to declare that the time is too short, I think?"

"It is not a matter of the length of time, but rather of the quality of the time together," Ingmar insisted. "And we have a lot to talk about."

Agneta nodded, but she didn't look happy. With Lennard gone, she could certainly use her son's help. But we both knew he'd inherited her great heart.

He'll come back, I told myself. *When this deplorable war is over, he'll come home again.*

58

I went looking for Paul as soon as we returned to Lion Hall. Ingmar and Agneta needed some private time, and I was bursting with news.

Lennard's decision was a mystery. Had he wanted to make up for the fact that, if Hendrik had lived, I might have inherited Lion Hall? Would I be able to handle owning part of an estate? I knew how to manage one, but I'd never had to make major decisions concerning my own property . . .

I found Paul in one of the horse barns mending a stall door. A stallion at stud, impatient to mate, had given it a tremendous kick, knocking it clear off its hinges.

"Hello, Paul!"

He lowered the screwdriver he'd been using to install a new hinge. "Matilda! Already back from the lawyer's office?"

I nodded, squatted down next to him, and ran my fingertips along the boards he'd used to repair the door. Their raw color stood out against the weathered wood.

"You won't notice a thing in a couple of years," he assured me.

I regarded him. He'd taken on new life since he'd begun applying his craftsman's skills on the estate.

"Lennard left me half of the Ekberg estate."

Paul's eyebrows shot up. "Good heavens!"

"My thoughts exactly. I hadn't expected any such thing."

"Congratulations. So you're the new Countess Ekberg?"

I shook my head. "The title goes to Ingmar, but I inherit half the property."

"No idea what to do with it?" Paul asked with a cheerful smile. "Give it to me, and I'll think of something!"

I burst out laughing. "You'd probably plan all sorts of repairs. There's lots that needs attention."

He reached out, took my hand, and held it tight. "I'm really pleased for you. Now you don't need to fear that horrible cousin of yours. And I'm not talking about Ingmar."

I nodded. Though I was still in deep mourning, I couldn't repress a smile. Paul affected me that way, especially of late.

"Magnus was so pleased at his brother having to share the estate that he couldn't get the grin off his face."

"What a dolt. The brief introduction at the celebration was enough for me; no need for him to say more than hello."

"Thank your lucky stars for that. It will be a long time before I forget the conversation I had with him later."

Paul lifted a hand and brushed a lock of hair off my forehead. "Don't worry your head about him. The count gifted you with a permanent home. That's what counts. When Magnus eventually takes over Lion Hall, you'll have your own place. You're secure for life."

"You're right about that." I took his hand and raised it to my cheek. "It's so good to have you here, even though the circumstances have been frightful. I'm glad you're with us."

"So am I." He took me in his arms and held me for a long time. He looked down with a grin. "If you have a little beer or some aquavit, we could celebrate. In my cottage. We could talk our hearts out or just sit together and not say a word. What do you think?"

Under Paul's skilled hands, the hut's color had changed, the windows had been reframed, and new furniture had been installed. It was a proper cottage and no longer filled me with dread. Agneta had recently said how pleased she was with Paul's renovations.

"Agreed! Tonight, at nine?"

He nodded, and my heart thrilled in anticipation.

Back at the manor, I heard Ingmar and Agneta talking in the salon. I weighed whether to join them and decided to take a nap instead. My head ached, and I wanted to shed the clothing I'd worn to the attorney's office. A cozy, soft linen dress was laid out in my bedroom—black, of course, and it actually resembled a maid's dress, right down to the apron across the front. But I was glad I had it, for the getup I'd squeezed myself into had all but stifled me.

I changed and lay down. Elisabeth, Lennard's sister, had forgotten a book on my desk. I would mail it back the next time I went to the post office. She hadn't been able to stay for the reading of the will, for her daughter was ill and Elisabeth had to care for the grandchildren.

I closed my eyes to listen to the rushing of the wind in the trees. A blackbird's plaint, heavy and mournful, floated on the breeze. There was buzzing as a bee flew through the open window, but it quickly realized its error and whirred outside again. My pulse slowed to a calm, steady rhythm. In a matter of moments everything faded away.

I awoke to a knock at my door. "Yes?" I responded, thick tongued. How long had I slept? I looked over at the window and saw that the sun had transited to the other side of the house. Small clouds had gathered.

"May I come in?" It was Ingmar.

"Of course!" I sat up.

He closed the door behind him. "Are you feeling ill?"

"I'm well, considering the circumstances." The ache in my temples had vanished, but I still felt slightly numb. I patted the edge of the bed. "Did you have a good talk with Agneta?"

Ingmar crossed the room and sat. "Yes, it was really good, even though naturally she tried to persuade me to stay. Because of the Ekberg estate, where I'm the new owner. Along with you."

"You are the newest Count Ekberg. Your father's title passes to you."

"I really wish he'd been given more time. That would have made everything much easier."

"Life doesn't care what's easy. If so, I'd have wished for my mother not to die, all those years ago. And for the man I'd thought was my father not to disappear. But fate pays no heed to our desires."

"Doesn't it seem that fate returned you to exactly the place where you were supposed to be?"

I sighed. "Perhaps. But I'd have asked fate to make up its mind much earlier. And I'd have had other wishes too."

"You just said that fate doesn't care what's easy. Here you are—nothing else matters."

"Ingmar?"

"Yes?" he responded.

"You belong here as well."

"I know, and I promise to take my place. But not yet; right now my place is elsewhere."

"Very well," I said with a sigh. "I won't try to insist; your mother is doing enough of that already."

"My mother understands very well what it's like to have different life goals. And she knows I inherited her stubborn nature."

I again recalled what Agneta had said about Ingmar and Magnus at the midsummer fest. I was glad that the good qualities had ended up with this twin.

I changed the subject. "Just between the two of us, is there a woman in your life?"

"What do you mean?"

"You're a man in his midtwenties. You're not going to tell me you're not interested in women, are you?"

I detected a blush. "Well, of course I am," he admitted. "Do you remember what I said in the café that time?"

"That I was your soul mate?"

"That too, but—as far as falling in love goes, I probably made a mistake. I'm still a bit in love with you."

I shook my head. "You're teasing me."

"No, it's true. My heart was always yours, right up until we lost contact. The fact that you're my cousin—makes it seem improper. I know that offspring of nobility often marry within their own families, but I find that unthinkable. So I did my best to force you out of my head and see you as a sister instead."

My heart was touched with sadness. Paul had always been the one for me, perhaps because I'd never had any other real relationship with a man.

"But don't worry," Ingmar said and took my hand. "I have every intention of choosing the right bride and bringing her home."

"One of your resistance fighters?"

"Aren't you the curious one!"

"More concerned than curious," I explained. "They say that a man with a beloved is more cautious in battle. A sweetheart could be a life insurance policy for you."

"No need for that. And yes, in our movement, from time to time, there may have been some woman or other I fancied. But we can't permit ourselves strong attachments, because our mission is dangerous."

I nodded. Was he still waiting for me, even if he wasn't aware of it?

"How are things with Paul?" he asked finally. "Have you gotten over your differences and become friends?"

"More than that, I think. He was devastated by Ingrid's death. She's still in his heart, and I'm a bit afraid of having to live up to her. I don't know if I can compete with a ghost."

"The ghost is not as strong as you think. Paul thought you were out of his sphere, so he looked for someone else. Surely his heart is the same as before. I just hope he's learned to be a bit more patient."

"I hope so too." I ran a hand through Ingmar's hair. "You're going to watch out for yourself, you hear me?"

"I'm still here."

"But you're headed right back. Three days is nothing at all. And now only two are left. That isn't enough for you to tell me everything."

"Well," he said, "compared to the way things have been, two days is a lot of time. Would you like to take a ride with me tomorrow?"

"That would make me very happy. And it'll give you a chance to see Paul's cottage. It looks like new."

Ingmar raised an eyebrow. "Paul's cottage?"

"The cabin that used to be the managers' residence. And we can visit Lennard's grave. He wants to know how life is treating you."

"You think the dead can understand such things?"

I smiled. "Maybe they do. And you don't want your father to feel neglected."

There was so much we could say to one another, but I had an intuition those things would have to wait. I'd need to tell him about the run-in with Magnus, but I didn't know if I should yet. He mustn't go off to Norway with anger in his heart, for that would only distract him.

I took the path to Paul's cottage that evening, aware of my heart racing. Crickets chirped all around, and insects flittered through the air, often so close I had the impression my face had been brushed by their wings. This had really been a full day.

I'd talked with Ingmar for a very long time about Norway and his plans for when he came back. Then, at dinner, the conversation had turned to romance, and Agneta was surprisingly reticent.

All she said was, "Keep in mind that your heart is free to seek out anyone you wish. I have experienced the pressure society and the family can exert to oblige one to accept a given partner. That must not happen with you, Ingmar." She gave me a pointed look. "Or with you."

Paul was waiting on the porch bench and rose as soon as he saw me.

"There you are! I was thinking you might not come."

"I sat awhile with Ingmar and Agneta. We needed to discuss estate business. When I think of all the work ahead . . ."

"Never mind all that now," Paul said as he embraced me. "This is an evening for celebration."

"If you can call it celebration. I'd have been happier if there'd been no need to read the will."

"Then let's just sit beside one another. How would that be?"

"Much better." I took a place at his side on the bench.

A couple of bugs buzzed around us for a moment and then went away. This was the time of day when the bats came out to hunt, so insects soon made themselves scarce.

Wrapped in Paul's arms, I felt safe. His warmth gradually melted us into a single entity and awakened my desire. I remembered how hungrily we'd made love in Stockholm—and how furious I'd been afterward.

That was less than two years before. Yet everything had changed since then.

"What will become of us?" I asked the nighttime stillness.

"In what respect?"

"Well, you and me . . . Will we ever be able to retrieve what we once had?"

"Frankly, I wouldn't want to," Paul replied.

I sat up in alarm.

"What did we have, after all?" he continued. "We weren't able to be together. Something always stood in the way. No, I don't want those times back. I want a new, different time, one in which we can stay together. Forever, just like this. And maybe even more." He looked at me. "What do you think of that?"

"I think it's grand," I said. Our lips sought each other for a tender kiss. His warmth invaded my body, sank into my breast, and gathered in my lap. There it was again, the desire I'd felt back then.

Maybe it was selfish to think it, but he wasn't a married man any longer; he had no wife for whose sake I had to hold myself back. We were alone together.

Aflame with desire, I put a hand to his chest and slid it downward as our lips and tongues met. I was expecting him to do the same. But he didn't.

I looked at him, surprised. *Don't you want to?* was the unspoken question in my eyes.

"We need to take our time," he said. "I don't want us to surrender to a wild passion. This time I will not leave you, I promise."

I nodded, disappointed, and took my hand back.

He seized it and kissed it. "Let's just stargaze, all right? I have a feeling you need that calm. And I need to have you close."

I leaned my head against his shoulder. *Ingrid,* I thought, *she's still there.* I'd have to respect that.

I returned to the manor shortly before midnight. I paused for a moment at the place where I'd clashed with Magnus, then hurried past.

When I got back, I noticed the salon was lit. I peeped in and found Agneta on the sofa, her eyes closed. She must have dozed off.

I didn't want her to have a stiff neck in the morning. I stepped forward and touched her arm.

She opened her eyes, not startled in the least. "Matilda," she said and sat up. "What are you doing here so late at night?"

"I was with Paul."

Her eyebrows twitched.

"Not the way you think," I assured her. "We sat together on the cottage porch, gazing at the stars."

"That place seems to invite such activity," she said with a sad little smile. "But you are a grown woman. You can do as you like."

I sat next to her. "Were you serious about what you told us at dinner? That we could choose whomever we wanted?"

"Of course," Agneta said. "It is important to find someone to whom you can give your heart wholly and without reservation. It makes no difference where the man comes from or what he does for a living. The question is whether he truly loves you."

I nodded, reflected, and gathered my courage. "I think Paul is the one."

Agneta smiled. "So, nothing has changed."

"To tell the truth, I never seriously considered anyone else. Not even after he married and was unattainable."

"Well, some loves endure forever. I truly believe that Lennard always loved me. My love for him took hold later, but he was sure from the very start." She looked at me. "Finding a love like that is beyond all price. Provided he is serious as well."

"I believe he is. And so am I. All the years, and everything that came between us . . ."

"It appears nothing could drive you apart."

"That's my hope," I said. "I hope and pray, so much."

"Well, you have my blessing," Agneta replied. "But, in any case, he must refrain from dishonoring you or breaking your heart. Otherwise, he will have me to deal with."

I laughed aloud, imagining her chasing him with a rolling pin. "He won't do either of those things. But he needs to mourn Ingrid for now. It's too soon."

"Yes, probably. But even so, be careful! I told you that before, back then."

"I will."

Agneta nodded and put her arm around me. If not for the weight of Lennard's death, this would have been one of my most treasured days.

Ingmar said goodbye two days later. Agneta hugged him at the bottom of the steps and admonished him to stay safe. I drove him to the station so he could take a northbound train.

"Will you be sending us more refugees?" I asked as the car jolted along the road.

"Probably. But things have gotten much more difficult. The Nazis and Quisling's people are forever on our heels. And many of those we wanted to smuggle out of the country are already in concentration camps. It's not easy to move people to freedom."

"I hope that soon it won't be necessary."

"Yes, so do I." He fell silent, reflecting.

"Do you want to see Magnus again before you leave? We have enough time to drop by."

"No." His gaze remained fixed on the passing scenery. "I saw enough of him at the attorney's office."

"You don't write to one another?"

"No. And that's for the best, believe me. He is one person, at least, about whom I have no need to be concerned."

"You don't like him anymore?" I asked.

"Correct. He's my brother, and there's nothing I can do about that, but I'm not obliged to like him. And I haven't, not since the day we learned about our real father. It's just as well you did not have to hear the names he called Mother."

"I can imagine."

"Stay far away from him, if you can. He's a bird of ill omen. I really do not understand how anyone can bear to talk to him anymore."

"Is there no hope of you two reconciling?"

Ingmar shook his head. "No; Magnus is Magnus. Drive to the station and keep me company until the train leaves. That will please me far more."

We made our way through the Kristianstad station to the platform. "This place never seems to change," I commented, gesturing to where an advertising poster hung, exactly as when I'd first arrived. The message was different, of course; this one was for washing powder. Some bright day the mouthwash ads would appear again.

"It's not a bad thing that some things never change. Don't you think?"

We made small talk until the black locomotive hauled its carriages up to the platform.

"Keep in touch, all right?" I said as the smoke swirled about us. "Don't make us wait so long to hear from you!"

He grinned. "I will write—no later than your birthday!" With that pledge, he gave me a hug. "Take care of yourself, Matilda, and watch after Mother!"

"You're the one who should watch out," I scolded him. "My feet are on the ground; yours are up in the air!"

"The air is my friend; she won't hurt me."

He pressed a kiss to my forehead, then shouldered his knapsack and climbed aboard.

I caught another brief glimpse of him through the smoke as the train pulled out, and then he was gone.

How desperately I wished for the war to end!

59

Three months passed. September gradually painted the forests many colors, and occasional cold snaps reminded us winter was coming.

The autumn hunt was canceled again that year, which didn't bother me at all. At least the wild animals in our forests would escape persecution.

I often enjoyed the last rays of sunshine while strolling through the woods to the little lake. While gathering fall flowers I was able to forget, just for a moment, that war was raging ever more cruelly across the world. Sweden was still out of it. Would that be true the following year?

Black depression had stayed away from Agneta so far, but often she seemed a wraith, lost in thought and staring into the distance. She came back to the present only when I spoke to her.

Still, she ran the business side of things with grim determination. She helped me understand how the Ekberg estate was organized.

Aunt Elisabeth managed it still, but one day Ingmar and I would accept the baton from her.

Paul and I grew closer, but only slowly, with covert glances and occasional caresses. He turned up as if by chance more and more often.

When I spotted him, he favored me with a dazzling smile. We enjoyed stolen kisses.

He brought me little presents—a sprig of flowers or something he'd made. I kept a posy of roses on my bedside table along with a tiny church he'd carved.

One morning, I inspected the barns. Soon we'd be bringing the horses inside overnight, for the weather was increasingly damp and chilly. Our buildings were in good shape, and some of the Norwegians had turned out to be knowledgeable about horses. Broderson had mentioned that he'd be happy to hire several if they wanted to stay with us after the war. Perhaps I would discuss the matter with them.

"Here you are!" Paul exclaimed. "I've been looking everywhere for you."

"Where would I have run off to?" I looked around, and since no one else was there, I put my arms around his neck and stole a kiss.

"I have something for you." He reached into his front pocket and took out something in a linen bag.

I had an intuition what it might be. "Today's not my birthday!"

"I wouldn't presume to give you something like this as a birthday present. But it's our three-month anniversary . . . That's worth a gift."

"That's what you say every month," I replied. "And I never have anything to give you."

"You're my present, and that's plenty." He pressed the little package into my hand. "Open it!"

I unknotted the drawstrings, and out came a tiny horse. "Oh, it's so beautiful! Even though you claim you can't stand horses."

"I never said I don't like them. I just don't want to sit on them, that's all."

I rewarded him with a kiss. "Thank you!"

"Will we be getting together this evening?"

I nodded. But just then one of the housemaids came running. She'd gathered her skirts as if wolves were chasing her. "Miss Matilda, come quick! The gracious mistress—"

I gave Paul a shocked look and then raced after the maid. What was wrong with Agneta? Had she fainted?

I heard loud wailing as I entered the manor. A cold hand clutched my heart. What had happened?

I raced madly to the salon, following the sounds. I ripped open the door and found Agneta in a heap on the floor, shrieking and clutching a piece of paper.

I felt a momentary surge of relief that she hadn't been struck ill. But why was she on the floor?

"Agneta, what's wrong?"

"Here!" She thrust the sheet of paper at me. The ink was so smeared by her tears that I had trouble making out the text.

> *Most honored Countess Lejongård,*
>
> *We are extraordinarily sad to inform you that yesterday your son Ingmar's airplane crashed. It fell into the sea just off the Norwegian coast. A fishing boat in the vicinity undertook a rescue attempt. Your son had made his way out of the aircraft and was clinging to a broken wing. Unfortunately, the water temperature was extremely low, and he died from hypothermia before he could be rescued.*
>
> *In Ingmar Lejongård we lost a faithful comrade and a valuable member of our organization. The deeds he performed for the Norwegian people and all of Europe will forever be remembered and honored.*
>
> *We will transport your son's body to Kristianstad this coming Thursday. We are making all necessary arrangements.*

With deep sympathy and great grief,
Lieutenant Karsten Solberg
Milorg

My knees gave way, and I landed on the floor next to Agneta. The letter fluttered out of my numbed hand.

This can't be! It mustn't be happening! Our worst fears had come to pass. Ingmar was dead, frozen to death in the North Sea.

As we carried Agneta to her bedroom, her cries were inaudible under the deafening roar of my heartbeat. Something deep in my breast throbbed in pain. Can a heart actually break?

I ran. I didn't know where the energy came from, and I paid no attention to where my feet were taking me. I fled from the pain, wanting only to be far from the manor. But I knew there was no way of escaping it.

I'd left the letter on the salon carpet. Lena had probably picked it up. I was haunted by the image of my aunt crumpled on the floor. First her husband, then her son, the good son with the sunny disposition. How could she ever recover from that blow? How could I?

I was running blind. My lungs burned and thorns raked my legs, but I didn't care.

Suddenly the cottage appeared before me, visible even through the watery blur of tears. The wind pulled at my hair and goose bumps covered my chilled skin. The cottage—Paul was there. Maybe he could help me batter my way through this agony. And if not, at least he would hold me for a while, for as long as I needed in order to face my responsibilities.

I tottered up the steps and practically threw myself against the door. *Please be home,* I pleaded silently. *Please be there!*

But no one opened the door. Paul was probably still at the barns. I collapsed in tears onto the porch.

I don't know how long I huddled there.

A hand touched my shoulder.

"Matilda?" At first my name seemed to come from far away. I heard it again.

"Matilda?" he whispered. "I heard. I am so terribly sorry."

I nodded and tried to speak, but my throat was too raw.

"Come, I'll help you up," he said, putting his hands under my arms. He pulled me up as if I were weightless, even though I felt as heavy as a toppled tree trunk.

Somehow Paul managed to move me into his cottage. Not long afterward I found myself sitting on the bed, an enamel cup in my hand. The pungent liquid in it burned my tongue. I wondered for a distracted moment how Paul had managed to procure home brew. From some farmer he'd worked for?

That thought held away my grief only for an instant. Then it overwhelmed me.

I babbled, feeling an urgent need to tell Paul about Ingmar. "When we first got to know one another, I went to his room, and there was this airplane. A model. He'd been working on it and told me he wanted to fly someday. And later, when he was in the hospital, I brought him a book about a trip in a hot-air balloon. Flying was his passion."

I took a swallow. This time the burning felt good.

"And then I forgot about it. He went to the university, got his degree, and we didn't see one another for a long time. I hadn't realized he was still interested in flying. And then he came back, and he was gone again, and later, when I saw him, he told me he'd learned to fly in Norway. He'd fulfilled his dream. And he used it to help others. Agneta—" My voice broke, and her wails again echoed in my mind, even more heartrending than when we'd found Lennard. "Agneta was so terribly afraid for him." I looked up into Paul's eyes. "Do you think something comes true only because you fear it so much?"

He shook his head. "No. I don't believe that. Things simply happen, whether you fear them or not. I hadn't been afraid of losing Ingrid, but I lost her all the same."

I nodded, and the pain came back in full force. "We've lost so many people!"

I sank into Paul's arms, and the world around me disappeared into a fog of dark and pain.

60

You have to face it, I told myself, reluctant to open my eyes. *Get up and do what has to be done.*

I couldn't, as much as I tried. My arms and legs were too heavy to move, and my eyes were swollen shut.

For a moment, I'd tried to convince myself it had been a bad dream, one of those nightmares I had when my time of the month came.

But I hadn't been dreaming. Ingmar's funeral was today. I couldn't refuse to go to the ceremony—but how could I possibly endure it?

My best friend was gone forever! And we hadn't seen one another again. As with my father, but even worse.

A knock interrupted my unhappy thoughts. *Go away!* I wanted to cry. I took a deep breath. "Come in."

Lena appeared in a plain black dress. Her hair was in a severe bun. Her face was pale and sad.

"The gracious mistress sent me, Miss Matilda. I'm supposed to give you a hand with your hair."

She'd done the same thing not long before. We and the staff hadn't even put away our mourning clothes.

I was grief-stricken when Lennard died, but Ingmar's death paralyzed me. Was it because we'd seen Lennard's end coming? Because Ingmar was my closest friend?

Lena's presence made me face the day. I'd learned to be stoic in the presence of others. I pushed away my misery and finally, with great effort, got out of bed.

"Just a moment, Lena. I will have a quick wash and then we can get started." I disappeared into the bathroom.

"Shall I bring warm water?" she called, but I declined the offer.

The water in the basin was nearly frozen, but I hardly noticed. My grief overrode every other sensation.

Lena was waiting with the curling iron when I came back. My braids were a thing of the past; my hair now cascaded and curled.

"How is the gracious mistress this morning?"

"I fear I'm not the one to judge," she replied. "She is strong, physically, and she is no longer weeping. But no one can see into her soul."

"Let us hope she will be able to get through this day."

"I hope the same for you," Lena said with a wan smile.

"Do not worry; I will survive," I said, feigning courage I didn't feel.

Looking into the mirror, I saw the unmade bed behind me. I'd sat in this room with Ingmar just months before, and we'd spoken about courting. I'd begged him again to come back home.

What had he thought as his plane went out of control? Did he have time to think at all? Thomas, one of the Norwegians and a fisherman, had told me a man could survive for only a few minutes in freezing water before his heart failed.

I shut my eyes, feeling tears again. Lena stopped her work with the iron. "Did I burn you?"

"No, it's just—the remembering. It doesn't stop."

I opened them again and stared at my reflection. The shadows on my face were as distinct as strokes from a painter's brush. Would I ever again be as happy as when I was young and heedless of the cruel tricks life could play?

The staff and the Norwegians were waiting outside when we left the house. They'd all known Ingmar, and they shared our grief.

"Is it all right if Paul rides with us?" I asked.

Agneta seemed to miss a step, but recovered. She nodded. "Certainly. If it is important to you."

"It is."

Paul's proximity gave me unexpected strength. I murmured a couple of words to persuade him to join us.

He did. "Thank you very much for allowing me to accompany you."

Agneta inclined her head and studied him for a moment. "You are a dear friend of my niece. For that reason, you are welcome."

The funeral was quiet and dignified. I was astonished to see Magnus there, actually looking somewhat downcast. We didn't speak, but he gave his mother his hand. That was something, at least.

I heard almost nothing of the sermon; glimpses of Ingmar filled my mind. How he'd ridden to the cottage with me that first time; how he'd tutored me in dancing; how he'd looked in the hospital. How we'd sat together in the Stockholm café as I revealed the secret of my parentage. How he'd turned up on the beach at Åhus.

I refused to believe the loving, generous-hearted person I'd known was now in the coffin before us.

The priest described Agneta, Lennard, and their son. He spoke of Ingmar's involvement with the Norwegian struggle against war and injustice. He made it painfully clear to me that the coffin covered by lavish displays of autumn flowers enclosed our Ingmar's body. Never again would I speak with him. Never again would I hear him laugh.

The organ postlude began at last, and we all rose. I tried to stand as tall as possible, as did Agneta next to me. She might still be in shock, but she never betrayed emotion in public. She tapped my arm to get me moving. We left the church at the forefront of the procession to the cemetery.

The whole village waited for us there.

Stray leaves littered the path to the crypt. I thought of Lennard. If the stroke hadn't killed him, news of Ingmar's death certainly would have.

The priest said more and pronounced a blessing. I stared up into the trees swaying quietly above us. Ingmar and I had wondered whether the dead could see or hear. I hoped that they could. I wanted Ingmar to see us at just that moment.

Take care, I thought. *And when you see my mother and father, say hello for me.*

Agneta and I lingered inside the mausoleum, giving the invited guests time to make their way to the reception at Lion Hall.

My body was one mass of pain. I hadn't expected to come back here again so soon.

We'd anticipated Lennard's death, even though we'd hoped he'd have a few more good years. But Ingmar was so young. The fact that he'd died while doing something that brought him joy was a cruel twist of fate.

"Matilda," Agneta said as we exited the Lejongård mausoleum, her eyes fixed on the heavens.

"Yes?"

"I have something to discuss with you."

"Now?" I was surprised. "Shouldn't we go receive the guests?"

"This is much more important. It has been on my mind for a long time, and I finally have the courage to ask."

I looked closer. Grief had consumed her; dark shadows lay beneath her eyes. I'd feared with each passing day that she would sink again into depression. But at that moment, she looked stronger than she had in a very long time.

"Please, whatever it is, don't hesitate." Was she going to make another revelation? What was left to reveal?

"I want to adopt you," Agneta said to the clouds. After a long moment she slowly turned to look for a reaction.

"You want—" I repeated with some difficulty. My stomach cramped.

"I want you to be my daughter. At least as far as the law is concerned."

"But I'm already an adult."

"I know that. Adults have parents too. Parents who confer responsibilities upon them and name them in their wills."

I felt like the wind had been knocked out of me. What should I say?

"Not long after you received Stella's letter and left Lion Hall, the idea occurred to me. She wrote that there was no way to make you legitimately a Lejongård, but she was wrong. There is a way. Once I make you my daughter, you are a Lejongård in the eyes of the law."

Her gaze bored into me, not begging or pleading, but full of determination. "Lennard is not here to watch over me. Ingmar is gone as well. My welfare, when I grow old or infirm, would be in the hands of my only remaining son."

She watched me. I remembered vividly the afternoon I'd visited Magnus and tried to persuade him to face up to his responsibilities.

"You can imagine what that would mean."

I nodded. I could.

"I have no desire to waste away or to die before my time," she went on. "I love life. I want to live and manage the fortunes of the estates for as long as possible. You already have much to do as the sole heiress of the Ekberg estate. It is very selfish of me to want to burden you with my own care, but there are no hands more capable than yours into which I can place myself. As my adopted daughter, you will have full authority over matters of my health. And in that capacity you can manage the estate without me."

She was warning me of tremendous responsibility. Would I be up to it?

But of course, it was true. Magnus couldn't be counted upon. The people living and working at Lion Hall would discover that, much to their detriment.

"As you wish," I said. I'd accepted so many other responsibilities, why stop now?

Agneta was surprised. "You do not wish to think about it? In your place, I would have taken my time."

"I don't need time to think," I said. "This is where I belong. It took me a long time to see that. Lion Hall is my home, and I will not let its people down. I will not let you down either."

Agneta nodded. There was no pleasure in her expression, but there was a glint in her eye. "Good. Then let us go home and do our best to get through this day."

The black-clad people in our ballroom dissolved before my eyes into a swirling, undifferentiated mass of faces and fabric. My breast still burned with unbearable grief.

Agneta's words echoed loudly in my head. *"I want to adopt you."* That had sounded so absurd as to be laughable. Only now did I begin to grasp the significance of it.

And of the fact that I'd agreed.

I caught a movement in the corner of my eye. Someone was headed my way. Damn it, couldn't people just leave me alone?

I realized it was Magnus. This was the last straw!

"How capricious fate is!" he remarked. "True? First Lennard dies, then my brother. Congratulations, you have done it, achieved your goal! And I cannot even accuse you of helping them out of the world."

I tightened my lips and balled my fists. How I wanted to throttle him!

"You know who is really to blame?" I said hotly. "At least for Lennard?" I was surprised to hear myself saying it right out loud.

Incredibly, I'd jolted Magnus out of his complacency. "Are you accusing me of somehow being responsible for the count's death?"

"I make no accusations," I snapped. "At the most, I'm saying you know better than I do."

"What could I have done?" he protested, affronted. Or was he merely pretending? "And why would I have bothered? Ekberg was willed to Ingmar alone. It is a mystery to me why Lennard brought you into it. But maybe you two were involved in some dirty dealings of which I was unaware."

"You think so? Lennard had decided who would be willing to support his wife." I heard my voice rising, but Ingmar's funeral wasn't the appropriate place for an all-out quarrel.

"There you two are!" a voice said. Agneta came toward us. I hadn't seen her for some time. She'd taken off her black veil and exchanged her formal mourning for a dark tailored suit. Had she retired to her room to settle her spirit?

"Magnus, Matilda, please come with me." Agneta's voice was controlled, but her hands were clenched. Something had upset her. Or, rather, angered her. The woman before us was not prostrate with grief; she was flaming with rage.

We followed, and I made sure that Magnus went first. I didn't want him behind me.

We went into the office, a room unfamiliar to him. Had he been in this room even once since he was a child?

I was struck by the musty smell of documents and the smoky fire in the hearth. Why had someone bothered to light it? We were not working in here today.

Agneta went to the center of the room, exhaled deeply to expel her tension, and joined her hands before her. She loomed stern before us like a threatening sentinel.

"Our attorney has just spoken to me," she began. "It seems that, shortly before he left for Norway the last time, Ingmar made out a will. I've now taken the opportunity to make a change in my own."

I gave her a questioning look. Was this about adopting me? Had the man told her it was impossible? If so, I didn't know whether to be disappointed or relieved.

Perhaps she was about to fling her decision to adopt me into his face?

"I am disinheriting you, Magnus," Agneta said coolly. "Not once in all these years have you been here for me or for your father. Never did you show you cared about the estate. And do not think I am unaware of your opinion concerning my character."

"But, Mother, I—" Magnus turned toward me, looking as if he wanted to wring my neck. "This comes from her, I know it! The little bastard wants to claw away this estate too."

"I see no bastard here," Agneta declared, "only you and your cousin. She is about to become your sister, for I am going to adopt her."

Magnus choked and fought for breath. "You cannot!"

"On the contrary, I most certainly can. Our attorney has already prepared the requisite documents." She paused, and an expression of righteous satisfaction appeared on her face. "I have long had my eye on you, the way you treat people and your indifference to the estate. How little you did when hard times came, and how little you are doing now. Matilda is here. She has always devoted herself to Lion Hall, and she is my niece! She has no other family, so why should she not become my daughter?"

I felt the heat of Magnus's glare. "Did you talk her into this?"

"I am a grown woman and fully responsible for myself, Magnus!" Agneta raged. "I have eyes in my head, and I have a heart! Matilda had nothing to do with this, and she was shocked to learn about it. You alone are the reason for my decisions." Her eyes flashed and her voice was bitter. "You once declared you would take an interest in the estate only on the day I close my eyes forever. Well, I do not intend to do so for a very long time. The doctor has given me an exemplary bill of health. And I advise you to leave your so-called 'friends' out of the picture, as far as my life and the estate are concerned."

Magnus scowled. "What are you talking about?"

"You are not the only one who knows the hidden paths of this estate," Agneta replied. "At the midsummer fest, just before Lennard died, I heard that little exchange between you and Matilda."

I stared at her in disbelief. She'd overheard us? I suddenly remembered that noise in the darkness. It hadn't been Magnus trying to scare me, after all.

"You claimed you had your biological father beaten."

"That is a lie you heard from her!" he shouted.

"She told me nothing at all!" Her voice was low and vicious, a tone I'd never heard from her. "I also have ears, and my hearing is excellent! And I must admit that you disappointed me greatly. Not only because you had so little respect for your mother that you were looking forward to her last breath, but also because you did not hesitate to send a bunch of thugs to beat up the man who engendered you."

"But I thought that he—I thought he was nothing to you."

"He *is* something to me. Every person with whom I have come into contact in my life is of concern to me. Some have treated me badly; most have treated me very well. But nothing that has happened justifies ambushing a person and doing him bodily harm." She took a moment to catch her breath, then peered at her son, bristling. "I have no idea where these evil traits of yours come from. Maybe you really did inherit them from that man. You were like this as a child, and now you are worse. I should report your despicable behavior to the police. Hans should have done so, but I am sure he was intimidated and confused. Was that your aim?"

Magnus clamped his lips shut, as if trying to hold back an ill-considered outburst. The tension in the room was electric. I found myself wishing I didn't have to hear this. Or if so, that I could have hidden behind a door and eavesdropped. But Agneta had wanted me here. It was important to her. And maybe she was afraid to be alone with her own son.

"You are fortunate I was too concerned about Lennard's health to inform him of your actions. He would have been disgusted. And he would have insisted that you be cut entirely out of our wills. But you are my son, so I will see that your welfare is assured. You will receive a monthly allowance. My father made the same arrangement for me when I left Lion Hall." She gave herself a moment and then continued. "But you will not inherit Lion Hall. My ancestors would be ashamed to hear they had a descendant who threatens people and has them beaten. The simple truth is that you are not worthy of bearing the title of the count of Lion Hall."

Magnus stared at her, not understanding.

"I will not stand in your way if you decide to go to your natural father. But after what happened, you would not care to do that, would you? Especially as conditions in Germany are so uncertain. And you will doubtless revise your desire for my hasty death when it is made clear that your allowance will be paid only during my lifetime. When I die, the well runs dry."

Magnus clenched his fists so hard that his knuckles cracked. "Is that everything you have to say?" he demanded. He tried not to show he was incensed, but he failed.

Agneta preserved her icy demeanor, but I saw she was boiling inside. "That is all. You need not show your face here again. I release you. You can do or not do whatever you please. Goodbye!"

Magnus made no reply. His jaw muscles clenched spasmodically. I couldn't tell which of us he hated more. He whirled around and stalked to the door. He ripped it open and slammed it behind him. The sound echoed throughout the manor.

Absolute quiet followed. Neither Agneta nor I said a word. My heart was in my throat. This incredible sequence of events seemed a hallucination from which I would awaken at any moment.

Then I felt Agneta's hand on mine.

I looked at her, my heart filled with fear, especially of what Magnus might do.

"He's going to try to make our lives difficult," I told her.

"He will not be the first. But we will stand fast. Agreed? We are Lejongårds and will not let anyone get the better of us."

She pressed my hand firmly. Her eyes were sad but determined. Just the two of us were left. We would support one another.

That evening I sat with Paul on the cottage porch. We'd wrapped a wool blanket around us, for the nights had gotten quite chilly.

I'd recounted the aftermath of the funeral to Paul. He hadn't appeared particularly surprised.

"Your aunt made the right decision. Or perhaps I should call her your 'future mother'?"

"Just call her Agneta," I answered. "She doesn't much like being referred to as 'aunt,' and she knows that Mother is my mother, no one else. This is something she's doing for legal reasons. You should have seen Magnus!"

"I wish I'd had the pleasure. Are you really not afraid of him?"

"On the contrary, I am. And I have been for a long time. But I don't believe a person should give in to fear. Whatever is to be, will be. Agneta is in good health. Maybe she will manage the estate for another ten years—longer, probably. It is hers as long as she lives. I very much hope that will be a long time yet."

"I share that hope."

A pause settled in. Paul reached for my hand. "Once you do become the new Countess Lejongård, will you have a corner in your heart for a humble cabinetmaker?"

"Oh no," I murmured, "here we go again! Wasn't it enough that your mother convinced you I wasn't the one because of my exalted social standing?"

Paul had gotten back into contact with his parents, but their relationship was still cold. Unfortunately, even Daga, who now had three children, was upset with him. He hadn't told me why, but maybe someday he would.

"To be honest," he said, "it worries me."

I lifted his hand to my lips and kissed it. "When we were sitting together after Lennard died, Agneta assured me I would always be free to choose whichever husband I wished. I think you can guess my choice."

He pretended not to understand. "Who's that?"

I gave him a poke. "You know who! I've been waiting my whole life to marry you. All right, I gave up that hope a few years ago, but you were always in my thoughts. And now that I have you here, I won't let you go—unless you no longer want me."

"You're asking if I want you?" He pulled me close and kissed me. "I do. Though we'll have to wait until after my year of mourning. I owe Ingrid that much."

"I know. And I would never wish to disrespect her. Besides, the war is still raging, so it will be a while before it's possible to arrange a proper wedding. I may need to convince Agneta to rip up a couple of her beautiful curtains for my wedding veil."

"With veil or without, I don't care," he said, then got up. "But we should do this according to tradition."

"What?"

He vanished into the cottage and reappeared with something in his hand.

"Actually, my grandmother stipulated that, when I married, my wife should receive her wedding ring. Ingrid had that ring, and unfortunately, it's gone forever." He stood there for a moment, then went to one knee. "So I carved a new one."

He opened his hand and held out a wooden ring with an intricate pattern. The wood had a crimson sheen.

"When did you make this?"

"Oh, a while ago. I'd been thinking I'd give it to you for your birthday. But this is a more appropriate occasion." He cleared his throat and fixed his gaze upon me. "Matilda Wallin, soon to be Lejongård, will you marry me?" He grinned and added, "This time I want to be the one to ask."

"We live in modern times," I said. "Why shouldn't women propose to men?"

"Women need to let us do something, since they're already voting and driving cars," he responded. "So what do you say?"

"Yes," I said. "Yes, I will be your wife, Paul Ringström. But we'll have to discuss what our married name will be."

"Any name at all will do. The main thing is to make sure I'm allowed to stay at your side."

"You may." I put my hands around his face and kissed him more passionately than ever before.

Paul leaned back with a deeply moved expression, but then he grabbed me tight and kissed me even longer. I took his hand and drew him into the cottage. We shed our clothes and sank onto the bed where, according to Agneta, her own sons were conceived. That was of no importance to me just then; I wanted to feel Paul's body against mine while we lost ourselves in one another without regret.

61

I looked out the window. The beautiful May morning in 1945 was lit by gorgeous sunshine. A brilliant blue sky fit for a postcard was framed by the hospital window. Birds twittered in trees that had just begun to sprout leaves. What a shame I had no one to write to!

A cooing sound distracted me from the view.

She was awake.

My little daughter had arrived the night before. Fresh and pink, tucked in her diaper and clad in rompers, she lay in the cradle under a soft white blanket. The doctor had confirmed she was healthy and allowed the nurses to place her at my side for the night. The sight of my child next to me was wonderful. I almost melted with joy just looking at her. My arms and breasts ached to hold her, but I had to wait for the nurse.

Giving birth had been both the most difficult and the most beautiful experience of my life. Paul had been terribly nervous, even more than I. His obsessive pacing during my labor nearly drove me mad, so much so that I was glad to be carted off to the delivery room.

But that was all past. Our daughter was healthy, and Paul had cuddled her yesterday before returning to Lion Hall for the night.

The nurse appeared. "Good morning, gracious lady, how are we feeling?"

"Couldn't be better," I told her. I wasn't used to being addressed as "gracious lady," but the Lejongårds were still the hospital's principal benefactors. Certain usages had to be respected.

She gave me my daughter to feed. How incredibly beautiful the child was! Her hair was a light caramel color. I knew much would change, but today she looked like the happy baby in the talcum powder advertisement.

I hoped that the world into which she'd been born would be a happy one.

The war news had changed. The Allies had coordinated their forces and attacked on two fronts. The Germans had been forced to retreat, and the battles were now on German soil. Before we left for the hospital, we'd heard radio reports that Hitler was dead. All this gave us hope as we listened with bated breath.

Could we make a better world for my daughter?

Agneta came to visit that afternoon. She was already in tears when she entered the hospital room. I was holding my daughter, her face hardly visible under the knitted cap, and she'd taken it into her head to sleep through her grandmother's visit. That didn't matter; the two would have plenty of time to get to know one another.

"What a beautiful child." A happy tear ran down her cheek. "She looks just like you."

"Well, yes, but I see a bit of Paul there too. Maybe she'll get his green eyes."

"Let us hope she inherits his eyes and not his manly chin."

"We can afford to wait and be surprised."

"In fact, where is your husband? He has not headed for the hills, has he?"

"No, why would he? After all, I told him not to accompany me into the delivery room. There are some things reserved only for us women."

"I believe that custom will not long persist. After all, we need someone to blame for our pain!" Agneta laughed. The wrinkles in her face had deepened, but otherwise she looked still fairly youthful, despite her nearly sixty years.

She brushed a finger across the little one's forehead. "Have you chosen a name?"

"Yes," I told her. "Solveig." *Path of the sun* in Norwegian, according to one of the women still staying with us. If the war was really ending, they'd soon be able to return to their homeland.

Agneta lifted an eyebrow. "Quite unusual!"

"But it has a lovely meaning," I said. "Solveig is the hope of our estate; she's our sunshine. I'm sure she will be a fine mistress of Lion Hall when the time comes."

"I hope so." Agneta smiled lovingly at her. "We are in dire need of both hope and sunshine."

She ran a hand through my hair. It felt frightfully greasy to me, but that didn't seem to bother her.

"By the way, I got a letter." She pulled it from her purse. "Do you remember Miss Grün? Your governess in Stockholm?"

"Of course I do!"

"She wrote to us from the United States. She and her family managed to emigrate. Is that not marvelous?"

It was wonderful news. I'd thought of her often over the years but had essentially given up hope. And now she'd written! I could scarcely believe it.

Paul erupted into the room. He hesitated an instant at the sight of Agneta but then exclaimed, "Germany has surrendered! The war is over!"

"What?" I exclaimed.

Paul was beside himself. "It's over! The Russians have raised their flag over the Reichstag. We have peace at last!"

With those words he gave Agneta a bear hug and planted a resounding kiss on her cheek. He came to me and Solveig and kissed me.

Our three years of marriage hadn't turned him into a count; he was still a cabinetmaker. And very happy.

"The sun is rising for Sweden, I think," Agneta said. She went to the door. "I will give you two some time alone while I have a word with the administrator."

I nodded, and she left the room.

Paul kissed me again, then gently touched Solveig's tiny head. I knew he was doubly happy. Not only that our lives would finally return to normal, but also because of the revenge he'd longed for.

"Ingrid can rest in peace now," I said.

He nodded. "Yes, she can. But, even more important, the two of you can live in peace. We have nothing more to fear."

"It's too early to be certain of that, but things are bound to improve." It occurred to me that at last we could renew our contacts with the palace. Surely van Rosen's influence had diminished now that fascists and nationalist demagogues had been defeated.

But all that could wait.

I put my arm around Paul and looked down. Solveig, between us, opened her eyes and cooed quietly. My heart overflowed.

About the Author

Photo © Hans Scherhaufer

Corina Bomann is the bestselling author of *The Inheritance of Lion Hall*, *Butterfly Island*, and *The Moonlit Garden* as well as a number of successful young adult novels. Her books have been translated into many languages and have been on bestseller lists in Germany, Italy, and the Netherlands. All the books in her Lion Hall trilogy went straight to the top of the bestseller list in Germany upon release. Bomann was born in Parchim, in northeastern Germany, and now lives with her family in Berlin.

About the Translator

Photo © 2016 Steve Rogers Photography

Michael Meigs reviews theatre and translates literature from French, German, Spanish, and Swedish. He was awarded the 2011 Translation Prize of the American-Scandinavian Foundation and the American Translators Association's 2020 Lewis Galantière Award for distinguished translation of a book-length literary work. Since 2008 he has published the online journal *CTX Live Theatre*, which is dedicated to live narrative theatre in Austin, San Antonio, and the rest of Central Texas. He served for more than thirty years as a diplomat with the US Department of State and was assigned abroad in Africa, Europe, South America, and the Caribbean. He has graduate degrees in comparative literature, business, economics, and national security studies, and he is on the boards of Gilbert & Sullivan Austin and the Austin Area Translators & Interpreters Association. He is a member of the American Literary Translators Association, the American Translators Association, and Swedish Translators in North America.